DOT LA SALLE

Book One

Secrets, Lies &

Cornish Spies

LEIGH
MAYNARD

www.blkdogpublishing.com

Thank you to my gorgeous wife Claire for every step we have taken together. To quote Andy Grammar 'You saved my life.'

To George, Harry, Sinead and Katie for being inspirational every day.

To Lynn and Paula for being wonderful guinea pigs.

To my Editor, Carol. Without your honesty and guidance, this journey would have been so much harder.

And finally, thank you to Oran. A brilliant bundle of heartwarming joy who makes the world a better place.

CHAPTER ONE.

February 1944 – Cherbourg, France.
It was a clear and bitter winter's night when the small fishing boat *Faulcon de Mer* slipped through the eerie darkness of Cherbourg harbour. Its rounded wooden bow created a jet-black undulating swell with white luminescence on the tips of the waves, reflecting the few shimmering lights glowing from the French port's harbour.

Aboard the vessel was Captain Erich Schmid of the German Army intelligence unit, Abwehr. Schmid stood tall on *Faulcon's* port side as they glided in alongside the old concrete dock, the skipper cutting the diesel engine and throwing two ropes over the quay bollards as they did so. Being part of Army Intelligence gave Schmid privileges, the most notable of which was the ability to slip in and out of restricted areas without too many questions being asked by over-curious officials. These privileges also helped Schmid ease the nerves of soldiers, along with their very jittery trigger fingers, usually with liberal donations of cigarettes and wine when needed.

The war in Europe was progressing quickly giving rise to the inevitable rumours of invading Allied forces planning to storm across the Channel at any time. Even with the heightened tensions of the ever-advancing war, today should have been no different from the previous crossings Schmid had made over the last two years. A select few had meticulously planned every aspect of the operation. Attention to detail was always Schmid's forte. But today was about to become anything but the day that had been planned. Today, something had changed.

Caught in one of the headlamps of a Mercedes staff car parked at the top of the agreed landing point at steps No. 7, Schmid could just make out the uniform of an SS Storm Command Leader. This was not expected. It should have been Schmid's trusted corporal standing where the Command Leader now stood. A corporal who was handpicked by Schmid himself, not just because he trusted him, but because he was also trusted by the other superiors he worked with. This was crucial to Schmid. Deception was an art, and his corporal was certainly a first-class artist. He had to be able to outwit any potential threats posed throughout this complex and dangerous operation.

Instead, it was the Command Leader who gave a brief nod in the direction of the boat's skipper standing in the wooden wheelhouse. The skipper acknowledged with a gentle nod of his head in return and then left the wheelhouse. With a single leap, the skipper landed ashore, allowing for no recognition of Schmid's current situation.

The Command Leader stepped aside to let two of his soldiers descend the steps to where the boat had been docked.

Schmid took a deep breath of the chilled air and stood tall as the boat gently rocked following the skipper's departure. It was clear to Schmid that he had not been meticulous enough. From this point on, he knew it was all over. He knew that he had somehow been betrayed, and, for that, he also knew he was about to die.

As the soldiers approached the bottom of the steps, Schmid turned quickly and jumped out of sight behind the wheelhouse. Without any hesitation, he took two running steps, dived headfirst over the side of the vessel, and disappeared into the jet-black waters of Cherbourg harbour. By the time the soldiers had discharged their weapons into the wake he left behind, he had vanished.

CHAPTER TWO.

March. Two Thousand & Three – Cornwall, England.
Dorothea LaSalle entered the Cape Bay café, relieved to find a single empty table with one chair in the furthest corner of the room. She liked to be in a position where she could keep an eye on what was happening around her, a habit from a previous life.

Spring had not yet sprung properly in Cornwall, even though it was late March, and the rain was proving to be completely unpredictable. Trying to understand the changes in weather in this part of the country was proving impossible.

Dorothea, known to those who knew her as Dot, was dripping wet. Her recently cut, blondish, greyish hair thankfully wasn't looking too bad. It would have been a different story if it were still long and uncontrollable, though. Dot always played down her beauty. Most of her life was spent without using makeup. In her opinion, face paint was only reserved for dates, christenings, weddings, and funerals. Mind you, given her fast-approaching retirement and previous job roles, she was of that age where there were certainly more funerals than anything else these days. Dot's face carried a radiant light tan from her recent days of unexpected Cornish winter sun, which gave her a glow that belied the current spate of crappy weather. She had a face that both men and women took a second look at, and she knew it. She also hated it.

Having not obeyed her own mantra, of there's no such thing as bad weather, just the wrong clothes, Dot was now paying the price, standing in a self-created ever-increasing puddle of rainwater. Having guessed the outside temperature from the inside of her house, she had got it wrong. Not that there was much difference between the two, as her house currently had no heating other than ancient woodburning stoves. It was certainly not the first time she had guessed wrong in this beautiful granite stone harbour village, which she was now trying to call home.

Dot, recognising most of the other customers as village locals who had got the weather right, now became the focus of the café clientele. They all stared at her with a mixture of curiosity and a sense of the absurd. Dot took off her sodden, inappropriately thin, and summery coat, hung it on the back of the small chair, and sat down with a squelch. The deliberate silence she had been met with as she walked into the café had been overtaken by a chit-chatty hubbub. This was something that she was becoming used to. She was, after all, deemed to be a stranger in these parts.

Jean, the owner of the Cape Bay Cafe, approached with an indignant look on her face, the whole time shaking her head in clear bewilderment. Dot guessed that Jean's age was somewhere in her late fifties to early sixties and observed that she was dressed in the same style of blue jumpsuit that Dot had seen her wear every time she had been in the café. With her tousled bleached blonde hair and weathered perma-tan skin, Jean looked every part the old school surfer type. Dot had no idea whether Jean had ever surfed in her life; she knew very little about her, other than she was supposedly Cornish and made damned sure that every customer knew this. Mind you, there was a not-so-Cornish twang in her accent, which made Dot certainly have doubts about Jean's provenance.

Dot had also found out that Jean's brother, Charles, had died quite a few years previously, apparently trying to rescue a sheep that had fallen down a disused mineshaft. They littered this part of the land, a legacy of Cornwall, for centuries, being the biggest producer of tin in the world. You would therefore think that it was not the brightest idea to keep sheep in the area, but again, who was Dot to question this? She had been given an abridged version of the tragedy by Jean after she had spoken about the house where she was now living. It would seem that the accident had taken place in an area that just happened to be in its grounds. She had to admit that this gave her the shivers.

"Morning," said Jean, without any type of smiley accompaniment, "I assume it's the usual for you today again, then?"

Dot was daydreaming and wondered which generation you had to have come from to finally call yourself Cornish. "Nice to see I'm slowly being accepted into the community, then, Jean. The others in the café were only quiet for about twenty seconds when I walked in this time. That's got to be at least thirty seconds shorter than when I first came in here. In my book, that's progress. And yes, please, the usual again if you don't mind."

"One pot of tea, an extra pot of hot water, one extra tea bag, and four hours of my internet for free, it is, then. Oh, and just to let you know, if you ask me for a towel, that will cost you extra. As soon as I start giving away things like towels and internet, people take liberties, and then everyone will expect the same from me. And that is not going to happen. And by the way, just so you know, progress in these parts is measured in years. Hundreds of them. So, you have a long way to go yet." Jean let out a gruff humph, spun around, and walked back behind the serving counter, shaking her head and grumbling in Cornish under her breath as she did so. No doubt this was to ensure that Dot had no idea whatsoever of the nature of the curse that was being bestowed upon her.

Deciding to move to Cornwall had been an easy decision for Dot. Who doesn't want to live in Cornwall? Circumstances, though, meant she had little choice in the matter, but that certainly didn't mean it hadn't been an emotional and exhausting journey to get here. In reality, a darned sight harder than she ever thought possible. A journey that had taken its toll on her, and one that she was now trying her hardest not to regret.

The locals in the village were making it very clear to Dot that just because she lived here for a few nanoseconds of a generation, it didn't give her the right to call it home. Apparently, it also gave the locals no right to accept Dot. Why would they? They had seen their world under attack for many years by wealthy out-of-towners gobbling up every available scenic property, then either renting them out to vexatious tourists or just leaving them empty for most of the year as second homes.

Perched on just about every beautifully scenic hill and cliff overlooking the sandy bays and beaches sat ostentatious architectural monstrosities that wealthy out-of-towners called home for two weeks of the year.

As always, though, there were two sides to every story. Very little had ever been spoken of the fact that, in most cases, it was the locals and their families selling their properties and land at vastly overinflated prices to the very out-of-towners that kept the locals' pursuit of righteousness very much alive. These locals were now enjoying the financial spoils of their clearly brilliant property transactions, which, in a lot of circumstances, showed them buying up properties to rent out to the same holidaymakers that the wealthy townies were making their money from in the first place. Pretty shrewd to be fair, yet here was Dot, being rebuked by the same locals for having the audacity to move into their village. In Dot's view, her money being spent here was just as good as anyone else's money, and for that reason alone, despite the challenges, this was now where she lived, like it or not, and quite frankly, screw anyone who happens to think differently.

Jean returned carrying a large tray. She placed the teapot, spare teapot, milk, and spare teabag onto the table. "So, what is it you do on that computer of yours all day? I hope you aren't watching movies. My internet isn't unlimited, you know. Cost comes out of my profits, so it does," she grizzled.

Not wanting to fully enlighten Jean of her own current employment status, Dot replied, "Jean, I'm still waiting for the electrical engineers to finish putting all of the cabling in for the power at the house. And don't worry, when that happens, I'm sure I'll get my internet sorted out, so I can watch my own movies to my heart's content. As to what I do, well, in a nutshell, I help elderly people who have been financially abused to get their money back. Simple as that, really."

Jean had no idea what that meant.

"Must be good money in it," she said, not wanting to show her ignorance. "Especially if you can afford to do up that bleddy great big mansion you have bought." Jean used the Cornish equivalent of bloody to emphasise that this was her rightful place to live.

"Well, here's the thing, Jean. I didn't buy the house; I inherited it." ''Chew on that one for a while,' thought Dot, inwardly chuckling to herself.

Jean stared intently at Dot before speaking. "Well, you kept that one quiet, didn't you. Inherited, you say? That mean you actually *are* Cornish, then?"

"Wow, you've never asked me that before; that must have hurt." Dot was desperately trying to remain poker-faced. Her stomach, though, was having other ideas. The chuckling wasn't abating, even more so, given the expressions of some of the other customers who had been earwigging. They were priceless. Now, this was *real* village gossip. "In all honesty, Jean, I'm really not sure if I have any Cornish heritage in me or not. I'm still trying to figure that bit out, but no doubt, given the old mansion has been there in some form for quite a few generations, who knows? You and I might even be related. Wouldn't that be peachy?"

Jean looked perturbed. Her face had the appearance of someone who had just poured ice-cold water onto a tooth that required root canal treatment. "Well, anyway," she said, "helping old un's get their money back seems like a good thing to do. No doubt you charge an extortionate fee for what you do, but fair play to you anyway. Now I best be getting on, some of us have real work to be doing."

But Jean didn't get on. She was staring into space. She obviously had more that she wanted to say on this matter. "Inherited, you say. But why? God only knows why anyone in their right mind would want to live in Bay View House. It's nothing but a rambling pile of old rocks. It should have been pulled down years ago, if you ask me. That place is cursed. You know that don't you? My Charlie found that out when he fell down that god-forsaken shaft chasing bloody sheep. That mine should have been sealed off properly. Just letting the place go to rack and ruin like that after the fire destroyed the main house. Criminal. People say stuff happened up there that they didn't want anyone finding out about. Using the house as a hospital for soldiers in the war, all the way down here in Cornwall, as well. More like trying to hide people away from everyone else, if you ask me. There's still folk roundabouts that worked up there. They say that soldiers lost their minds. Left their souls behind in the war. I reckon it was one of them who decided to burn it down. Full of ghosts. Makes my skin crawl."

Jean paused and took a deep breath in. "No one from the village has ever seen hide nor hair of anyone up there for years until you turned up with your posh bloody accent with men in fancy cars and suits. Plenty of out-of-towners sniffed around it over the years, but not a single one of them ever wanted to buy the house. Why was that? Says something that does. Even the property developer types didn't want anything to do with the place."

"Well," Dot said, feeling suitably chastised for having the audacity to move into a house that was rightfully hers, "the good news for you, Jean, is that I'm not asking you for your opinion about my house, although the history lesson is very much appreciated. And it's also good news that I'm not afraid of ghosts. Let's face it, if I had listened to all of your like-minded nay-sayers, I would never have had the opportunity to allow such wonderfully cheery people like you into my murky and mistrustful life. And where would have been the fun in that, hey?"

Jean was now staring out of the café window, which was covered by a continual stream of condensation. Two seagulls sat on top of a bench across the cobbled road, staring back, seemingly oblivious of the rain, most probably plotting their next sortie on any unsuspecting individual exiting the café with a pasty.

Jean's eyes had welled up. A small tear was rolling down her tanned cheeks, mimicking the condensation in the window. Dot assumed that the thought of Charlie dying in an abandoned mineshaft on her cursed estate was the reason for the tears. Couldn't really blame her for that; it must have been a horrible way to go.

Jean's silence allowed Dot the opportunity to change the direction of the conversation. It was all pretty grim, and it seemed to be Dot's fault. The entire café had been listening to what they had been talking about, and the watching eyes now falling upon Dot were palpable.

"Jean," said Dot, looking over at the cake counter, "Is that almond croissant up there one that's been left over from yesterday, or is it fresh today?" Dot knew full well it was at least 24 hours old.

"It's fresh today, thank you very much indeed," Jean snorted, wiping her eyes with the back of her hand "I assume, as you have enquired about the almond croissant that you're going to buy it?"

"No," Dot replied. "I just like winding you up. Of course, I would like to buy it. I'm starving, and let's face it, I need to make sure that I keep your profit margins as high as I can for you. Can't have people complaining that I'm not contributing to the local economy, can we now?"

Dot was a bit flushed and annoyed by the verbal encounter. She shouldn't have been. It seemed to be a constant in this place. At least here, though, people did talk to each other, unlike in London, where Dot used to live. In London, ignorance always appeared to be bliss, and real conversation between strangers was non-existent. If dialogue was indeed entered into, then it was deemed as downright suspicious.

London seemed forever ago to Dot. In reality, it was just a few months ago that she was living a life that was light years away from the one she now found herself living in Cornwall. She felt as if she had aged twenty years over the last couple of years. Carving out a new life for herself in Cornwall with the sea air and quiet surroundings was certainly helping with her own mental health. Not that mental health was something she had ever given a second thought to previously. She didn't have time to. Until that was, she met her now-exish, husband.

Jean came over and put the plated croissant on the table in front of her.

"Thanks, Jean," Dot said, now staring at the screen of her laptop. "London," she thought aloud. "Bloody London."

CHAPTER 3.

London – One year ago.
"Mum, look, I'm sorry, but I told you I've got to go into a meeting, and I'm running late. I'll call you back as soon as I'm done, I promise. Yes, yes, I promise, I won't be long." Dot was on the phone with her mother, Anna LaSalle, for the third time that day, and it was not even lunchtime yet. "Mum, seriously, no one is trying to murder you. They all love you there and want to make sure you're happy, that's all. Now, I do have to go. Mum, no, this isn't the police, it's your daughter, Dot. Yes, I'll call you later. Love you, Mum, bye."

She ended the call, as always, with a wave of guilt sweeping over her, knowing it was she who had chosen to put her mother into the care of others. Half the time her mother called, she didn't even know she was talking to her own daughter. There was just a single number programmed into her mother's mobile phone, and that number belonged to Dot. Originally to be used for emergencies only, it had now become the bane of her life. Trying to wean her mother off the obsession of continually calling her number was proving increasingly difficult. So much so that Dot had even contemplated changing her own phone number, but had never actually dared to do it. The staff at the care home had tried to curb the time that Anna spent on the phone, but this just made her mad beyond anything that Dot had ever witnessed.

Anna had succumbed to the progression of what was to be eventually diagnosed as Alzheimer's disease. She had probably had the disease for six or seven years; it was always difficult to tell at first. Everyone loses keys, everyone loses phones, everyone forgets birthdays, and everyone gets a bit cranky with life as they get older. Then again, people also make excuses about things that they see but don't necessarily want to believe. Dot always knew there was something wrong with her mother, but struggled to believe it or to try to come to terms with it. In hindsight, it had been a pretty gradual decline at first, but now, well, it was full on, and, boy, was Anna creating merry hell.

The care home had called Dot last night about increasing Anna's medication following her latest incident. Anna had been insisting that a woman in a room near to hers in the Chelsea Garden Care Home was a German spy. It would appear that the sole purpose of the German spy was to interrogate Anna and extract information from her by any means necessary. Said German spy had allegedly accused Anna of sleeping with German soldiers during the Second World War, and for that, she was going to pay a deadly price. A price that included, amongst other tortuous experiences, the poisoning of Anna's food. But of course, no one was listening to a word that Anna was saying or, for that matter, understanding the threat to life that Anna was now apparently being subjected to by this foreign infiltrator. However, what it did mean was that Anna was now refusing to eat any food put in front of her without first summoning the chef to taste and check for arsenic, cyanide, or any other such undesirable toxic contagions. So, Anna, in retaliation and as was mostly the case with her, had decided that she was going to take things into her own hands at some point and sort out the nefarious bitch, once and for all. The care home staff were fantastic at trying to help her deviate from these types of conversations, but Anna seemed relentless in her accusations and threats.

It was for this kind of reason that Dot had finally made the decision to put her mother into a care home. It had become impossible, in so many ways, to look after her. First at her mother's own house, but even leaving her alone for short periods of time was proving too dangerous. Dot had no choice but to move her mother into the house that she shared with her husband, Jack Andries, in Chiswick. Every day and night that her mother spent at the house felt like an absolute eternity to Dot.

Jack, very conveniently, had decided to increase the amount of time he spent in his office and had also managed to find a whole abundance of new overnight conferences to attend. Dot, meanwhile, had to juggle work life and home life, whilst trying to be a full-time carer for her mother.

No one could predict what kind of episode would happen next with Anna. Temper tantrums, tears, screaming fits, hallucinations, and violence were almost an everyday occurrence. This, alongside her occasionally being the mother that Dot remembered, was simply agonising to watch. Dot had to install alarms alongside additional deadbolts with padlocks on all the doors and windows to make sure that Anna didn't wander off. This was probably the final roll of the dice for Dot. It just made the entire house feel like a prison. And not just for her mother.

Dot emerged from her meeting a couple of hours later and turned on her mobile phone. With her usual trepidation, she waited for the phone beeps to tell her there were messages. The phone beeped five times. Five new voicemails on her phone. Three were from her mother, thinking she was calling 999 and demanding armed officers turn up immediately, one message was from Jack, saying that he might be late home from work, again, and one message was from Vanessa, the regional director at her mother's care home, asking Dot to call her back as soon as she could.

Ignoring her mother's messages for now and not bothering to ring Jack back as he never picked up anyway, Dot hit Vanessa's direct dial number at the care home.

The phone was answered almost immediately. "Thanks for calling back, Dot." Vanessa used her usual 'I'm busy, what do you want' kind of voice.

"No problem, how's things? Not good, I take it?"

Vanessa let out an audible sigh. "I think we need to sit down and work out the next steps for your mother's care. The staff effort needed throughout your mother's current decline needs to be evaluated again, and I think you need to decide if we keep her in her current room or think about moving her to the memory care wing. She really needs somewhere with more security. Somewhere we can keep a closer eye on her".

"I see," Dot said. "You make memory care sound more like a prison than a care home. Though prison would be a darned sight cheaper. Look, as far as I'm concerned, I just want to do whatever we can to give Mum the best treatment and care, that's all. I know we have to keep her safe. I have to rely on your expertise and what you think is best, as always."

Vanessa had been in charge at the care home ever since her mother had moved there, and she possessed an expert ability to make Dot feel inferior. It felt like Vanessa was castigating Dot for not understanding the situation that her mother was in. Dot had never really forgiven herself for allowing Jack to make the decision about the choice of care home for her mother. She had been away at a conference, and Jack had made the decision without her. His justification was that he could no longer cope with her at the house and had gone to see the care home. Apparently, it was the best in the area. When Dot first visited, she had to agree with Jack. Ever since, though, Vanessa's attitude was really grinding Dot's gears, and every encounter was a battle of wills between the two of them. Maybe Dot was jealous of Vanessa, maybe she just didn't like her. Whatever it was, she felt belittled by every conversation she had with her.

"So," Dot said. "I assume you think that moving Mum into memory care is the best thing for her, then. I guess that this is the only option left for her now. Do I need to speak to Mum's doctor again, or will you do that? Just want to make sure they know she is moving rooms, that's all."

"Well, you're of course right, Dot. This is the only option we have left for her. In my experience, moving your mother into memory care is the best way forward. There will inevitably be an increase in the cost for your mother, but, quite frankly, any choice that you make now isn't going to be cheap. I need to be absolutely sure that you're comfortable with this. Do you and Jack want to come over later so we can go through the plan in more detail? I can then work out the exact cost, and we can look at what this means for your mother. I'm also happy to consult with Dr Lloyd on your behalf."

Dot exhaled loudly. "Okay, I don't have any more meetings today, so I'll swing by in a couple of hours, and we can work through the plan if that's ok with you. Not sure if Jack is going to be there, though. He said he was working late. Not that that matters anyway. I'll see you shortly, Vanessa."

Vanessa cut the call without a reply.

Rude bitch thought Dot.

The cost of Anna's care at Chelsea Garden was around £11,000 a month. Ever since her mother had been receiving care, Dot had spent somewhere around £650,000. Not that it bothered her much. As far as she was concerned, it was her mother's money, and it was there to be spent on her.

Acting as her power of attorney, Dot had sold her mother's house in London for just over £2 million, leaving £1.5 million in the bank after debts and costs were paid. Along with her mother's decent pension from her old job in London, there was still plenty of money in the pot to pay for quite a few more years at the care home. Dot didn't need to be a mathematician; Anna didn't have a few more years left. Anna had done well when it came to money. Certainly, no thanks to her husband, who died just after she was born, or so Anna had told Dot. That or he buggered off at the thought of bringing up a child. Maybe her mother didn't know of the circumstances surrounding his death, or more than likely, she just didn't want to tell her. Either way, although her mother had spoken about her father, she never provided any real substance as to their brief time together. There were half a dozen old black and white photos taken at their wedding, which Dot now had in her possession, one of which she had copied and was in a photo frame in her mother's room.

Not that Dot had ever really felt the urge to do much digging into her past, that job was probably one for her days in retirement. Other than her mother, the closest that Dot had had to family was her grandmother. Dot had been sent packing to stay with her on many occasions during holidays when her mother couldn't get time off work. Or at least, that's what she told Dot. Her maternal grandmother used to live close to the centre of Paris. She had never met her grandfather; by all accounts, he was one of the oldest members of the French resistance during the Second World War. Ironically, given the unquestionable bravery of her grandfather's actions whilst fighting the Germans in France through two world wars, Dot had been told by her grandmother that he had actually died from blood poisoning sustained from a rusty nail that he stepped on in a piggery.

Dot's grandmother was always a pillar of enormous strength and resilience. She had also fought within the resistance, losing nearly all of her siblings in the war, but never giving up the cause for freedom. Dot remembered many fantastic times staying with her grandmother. She used to accompany her to the art gallery she owned and ran in Montmartre in Paris. Looking back on those times, Dot had no doubts that her grandmother was also one hell of a party animal. But more than anything, Dot had felt loved. She felt part of a family, something that she had never felt at home.

One of the best things about going to the gallery was the chocolates and champagne. There were always chocolates and champagne. There were never problems in her grandmother's world, just opportunities. No doubt she had passed this dogged determination on to Dot's mother. Dot wasn't sure that it had ever reached her own set of genes just yet, though.

Away from the wonderful days spent living with her grandmother in France, it had been up to Dot's mother to raise her and build a life for them both, as best as she could. Dot often thought it would have been much more fun growing up in Paris, but her mother lived in London, where Dot was born, and this was home. To be fair to her mother, she did a decent job at it. And now it was time for Dot to repay the love, devotion and commitment that her mother had given to her.

One of the regular bumps in the journey for Dot's mother was Jack. While she tolerated him for the sake of Dot, it was clear there was no love lost between them. Whenever it came to talking to her husband about spending £11,000 a month on her mother's care, it was never a collectively harmonious conversation. Even though Jack had effectively chosen the care home, as far as he was concerned, he was watching what he presumed to be his and Dot's inheritance being flushed down the proverbial toilet.

Dot and Jack had argued countless times over the rising cost of care for Anna and where the money should be invested, but Dot held firm on what she wanted every time. Jack was always insistent on trying to capitalise on some new scheme or other, saying that Anna's funds were losing money where they were currently. Dot, though, was having none of it. The money was there to pay for her mother's care. That's what Dot had promised her mother. And, as she kept on reminding Jack, her mother had worked bloody hard for that money, so it was right that it was all spent on her. And as far as Dot was concerned, that was the end of it. Given the news Vanessa had just bestowed upon Dot about the increase in the cost of care for her mother meant only one thing. Yet another argument to look forward to with Jack.

Dot pulled into Chelsea Garden Care Home in West London, just before 5 pm. The car park at the front was busy as usual, so she drove her mini around to the back of the main building and parked it in one of the empty staff spaces. As she got out of her car, Dot spotted Jack's silver Mercedes convertible parked at the far side of the car park. It appeared that Vanessa had managed to get in contact with Jack as well as phoning Dot. Of course she had spoken to Jack. And that infuriated the hell out of her. It was fine for Jack to be at Vanessa's beck and call. But try getting home on time for dinner, or anything else for that matter. Well, that was always seemingly impossible.

"Funny how when I need to think about spending more of my mother's money, your incredibly hectic schedule miraculously becomes clear," announced Dot as she walked into the care home reception, where Jack and Vanessa stood talking.

"Well," said Jack, "as your husband and, importantly, your mother's solicitor, I just want to make sure that you're making sensible decisions on her behalf. It's not easy watching someone decline as quickly as your mother, so I figured it's good to have a rational voice around, that's all. It was good of Vanessa to call me, to be honest."

"Oh, for fuck's sake, Jack," snapped Dot. "You think for one minute I'm going to make inappropriate financial decisions for my mother? I've been the one making the decisions ever since Mum was diagnosed with dementia, and, quite frankly, I think I'm doing a bloody good job of it. Why can't you just stop thinking about the shrinking inheritance for one minute and bloody well support me by making sure my mother lives as comfortably as she can for the time she has left? Christ knows, if you had your way, you would have her shipped off to Switzerland to be put down like a sick animal."

"Well, maybe that's not such a bad idea, in fact, it's one of your better suggestions," Jack snapped back at her.

"Vanessa," hissed Dot, ignoring Jack completely. "Next time, just call me, please, and I'll decide if it's appropriate for my husband to be here. I alone act as my mother's power of attorney, not him."

"Well, I thought it best if you were both here, given the importance of events regarding your mother," Vanessa replied, very matter-of-factly. "So, my apologies. Now, shall we move on and preferably continue the conversation in my office? We don't need to disturb the residents any more than they already have been. I'll get some water for us; caffeine might be a tad too much for you both right now."

Dot was fuming. Yet again, she felt like she was being reprimanded by some stuck-up boarding school headmistress who knew best.

They sat down in Vanessa's rather nice and very modern office. The wallpaper looked like it had been purchased from a London gallery, and certainly not from a DIY store. Dot, not for the first time, wondered if any of the dead residents' legacies had found their way into paying for the expensive furnishings she now found herself surrounded by.

"So", Vanessa began. "It is obviously important for us to make the right decisions for Anna so that we can continue to keep her as comfortable as we can here at Chelsea Gardens. I believe she is now at a stage where we need to move her into a more supported memory care environment. This means she will have around-the-clock care, where she will also have the support of the medical care team. This would mean more one-to-one counselling along with therapy, and I also think that now is the time that we need to take the phone away from her. It's proving far too much of a distraction for her and quite possibly for you as well, Dot."

Vanessa was very clinical in her delivery of the situation and the potential outcome.

Dot was staring straight ahead. She said, "When we spoke to the doctor a couple of months ago, he said that my mother had around maybe one year left, possibly eighteen months at best. I need to be sure that what you are suggesting is the best thing that I can do for her, Vanessa."

Vanessa cupped her hands together in front of her and took a deep breath in. "I can't see any other way to make sure that your mother remains as comfortable as we can possibly make her. We need to ensure she is not in harm's way, either to herself or other residents and the staff here. In my opinion, I believe this will be the best way forward for your mother. Now, in terms of what this is going to cost, I anticipate around an additional £6,000 per month."

Dot was still staring straight ahead. She sighed. Her phone started to vibrate. The incoming call showed number withheld. She left it. If it was anything important, whoever it was would leave her a message.

Jack put his hand on Dot's arm and said, "Dot, it's a lot of money, but it's the best thing for your mother. As you keep telling me, the money is there for her. It's the safest option for her as well. It makes perfect sense to do this."

"Thanks for your concern, Jack, it's noted," Dot replied with the biggest air of sarcasm she could muster. Her phone vibrated yet again. Again, number withheld. Again, she left it. Both Jack and Vanessa were glaring at her. "I am perfectly capable of how I spend my own mother's money, thank you very much. Vanessa, if this is the best thing, then let's just get it done. It seems to be the only option given that my mother is getting a lot worse now, particularly with her hallucinations. They scare the life out of me, let alone what Mum thinks. God only knows what ludicrous story she'll come out with next. Good luck with trying to get the phone off her, though; she is going to go ballistic, you know that. I, for one, wouldn't want to be in the same room as her when that happens. Can you work out some kind of way that she can contact me, even if it's just once a day, please?"

Vanessa merely nodded in agreement.

So that was it. Just like that. Another £6,000 a month was on its way to Chelsea Garden care home, and no doubt a nice little knick-knack would appear in Vanessa's office in the not-too-distant future as a result.

Dot stood up, opened the door, and left the office without saying another word. She could feel Jack's eyes boring into the back of her head as he followed. Walking back to her car, she felt bruised and ganged up on by Vanessa and Jack. Right at that moment, Dot felt alone and vulnerable. Not that Jack gave a crap. As he headed straight back to his car, he reiterated that he would be late home, possibly not at all. Even more so now he had taken time out of his incredibly busy schedule to visit Dot and Vanessa at the care home. It was always Dot's fault.

"Don't wait up." Jack's parting words sounded like something out of a bad movie where Dot was the star as well as the only person watching. But, hey, she should be used to it by now.

She checked her phone for any messages. There were none.

CHAPTER 4.

Jack.

Dot sat in her car and began thinking about how, when and where the spiralling demise of her marriage to Jack had begun. She had thought about it a lot. Probably too much, to be fair, particularly as both she and Jack didn't seem to have the balls to sit down together and figure out what should happen next. Despite the increase in arguments between them, there was still an air of convenience in their lives right now. They were both headed in their own directions, and both had busy careers, but Dot knew they would have to sort this out at some point. And sooner rather than later. That's what should happen, and they both knew it. Life with Jack was suffocating her body and mind. And it had to stop.

It hadn't always been this way. Dot's journey with Jack had been the archetypal whirlwind romance in every way possible. When they first met, everything was exciting and new. There were lots of weekends away. There was ridiculously good sex along with the impromptu date nights in wonderful restaurants and hotels. Life was racing at 100 miles an hour, and, at the time, Dot loved it. In Jack, Dot had someone who didn't worry about how many hours she spent at work. He never went over the top if she was working on a case or chasing some whacko suspect across the country. He always seemed to trust that she would do her job as safely as she could.

He used to text her out of the blue, umpteen times a day, with sometimes nothing more than a couple of X's. It was exactly what she needed at that time in her life. Jack was a qualified solicitor who owned an expanding law firm specialising in estate planning and family inheritance disputes. Jack started out as one of those no-win no-fee businesses that you saw advertised all over daytime TV. Very tacky but very lucrative, and it seemed that Jack was good at what he did.

His five-bed detached house in Chiswick with all the trimmings was a testament to that. And as if to prove the point, Jack was flash. Flash car, flash clothes, flash holidays, and, to be fair, flash presents for Dot. It was attention that Dot had never experienced before. And it was intoxicating.

They had first met when they attended the same conference six years earlier in London. The conference was about the financial abuse of elderly people and how this so-called market appeared to be growing at a considerable rate of knots. Jack was there primarily for the credibility factor. He wanted to ensure his clients understood that his business cared deeply about them and held the highest possible ethical standards and values. It also meant that he could add some more letters alongside the other credentials that were plastered all over his advertisements. In Jack's world, influence meant affluence. The more influence Jack had with his clients, the more affluent he became. Gaining more credentials gave Jack more credibility.

Dot was at the conference in her role as a serving police officer within the fraud and financial crimes unit. She hadn't been at the department for long. She transferred out of her previous job in CID, where she spent 15 or so years. Her various roles within CID had, on more than one occasion, led her into the world of financial fraud, and it was a world that she thought she enjoyed. Well, maybe enjoyed was not quite the right word. She tolerated it. So far, no one had tried to blow her head off with a shotgun, which seemed to happen with ever-increasing frequency in her old job. Importantly, it was a world she seemed to understand, and given the growing number of newly defrauded Londoners, it looked like she was going to be kept busy.

Dot's life and career, like many police officers' lives
and careers, had been darkened by horrific cases, death, and
situations that questioned the very purpose of humanity.
Cases like these stuck to you like stinking tarmac. No matter
how hard you washed and scrubbed, it was impossible to get
rid of the smell. Dot needed a change, and the Fraud Squad
provided that change for her. She closed her eyes and
recollected the day she had met Jack.

She was eating her lunch.

"Hi, mind if I join you? I'm Jack. You might have seen
me on TV."

Dot looked up from her standard conference buffet of
a salad and a curly edged sandwich. Standing in front of her,
she saw a man with a ridiculously good-looking smile staring
down at her. His cerulean, blue eyes were beginning to melt
into hers, and the way he held his head on a slight slant made
her shuffle uncomfortably on her chair. Something was very
definitely happening down there. Dot felt a flood of hot flush
rise from her stomach and into her face. She was blushing.
Very brightly. There was only one thought in her mind.
"Calm down, girl."

The last time Dot had blushed like this was during one
of those fact is stranger than fiction moments in her early
career as a police officer. She had been called to a domestic
argument late at night between a husband and his wife. It
happened to be the husband's birthday, and he had made a
self-assessed judgement that, given the day, he would be
entitled to his mandatory annual shag. His wife had other
plans, and the mandatory annual shag was not part of them.
The row was caused by the fact that the husband had seen
his doctor and received a double dose penile injection with
the expectation that birthday sex was imminent. As a result
of the wife's refusal to participate, the husband had attempted
to lock her in their bedroom. The wife immediately called
the police, and Dot, along with a police constable, duly
arrived to be met by the naked husband opening the front
door sporting a huge erection. Dot was blushing red as she

arrested the husband, who was insisting on staying naked so that his wife could see what she was missing, apparently. The police constable tried, without fail, to use his helmet to cover the husband's modesty. The helmet wasn't big enough. The man and his erection were taken back to the police station and charged with causing a breach of the peace. Rumour had it that the erection lasted for two days, and he was in agony. His wife dropped the charges on the absolute assurance that her husband would never see his doctor for an erection injection again.

"Er, yes, of course, please, feel free to sit where you like, er, nice to meet you, Jack, I'm Dot, er, short for Dorothea. And no, I don't recognise you from the TV. To be fair, I would have to watch TV in the first place." Dot was staring at Jack with the image of a huge phallus in her head. This could not have looked good!

"Wow," said Jack as he pulled the chair back and sat next to Dot. The table was circular, which made Dot feel like she was now sitting very close to him. "The last time I made someone blush like that was at school. I gave a girl a Love Heart sweet, and she turned bright red. From memory, I think it said, I Love You, on it."

Dot was desperate to make light of the situation. "Do you always carry sweets in your pocket ready for when you meet someone, then?"

Jack was smiling his ridiculously good-looking smile at Dot again. Her stomach was buzzing. And it wasn't the substandard excuse for a salad that she had now left on her plate that was causing it. "A little too old for that, I fear. Shame though, would have been a much better opening line for you." Jack's eyes were still holding Dot to ransom.

"So, did you?" continued Dot.

"Sorry, did I what?" replied Jack.

"Love her, you know, the girl you gave the sweet to," quizzed Dot.

"Oh, good God no, I thought I was just being nice. I loved the taste of those sweets and happened to have a packet on me, that's all."

Ironically, Dot would later find out that the story was indeed true. The not-loving bit, well, that was not so true. The girl actually turned out to be Jack's future wife.

By 6 o'clock that evening, Dot and Jack were having dinner together in Kensington. By midnight, they had already had sex three times in an expensive hotel in Park Lane. ·

If this was Jack's modus operandi, then, for now, Dot liked it.

Dot and Jack married at the end of their whirlwind first year together. It was a pure fairytale wedding held in an old English castle with no expense spared. The entire castle had been hired out for the occasion, and every guest bedroom had been paid for by Jack. Ironically, given the extortionate cost of the honeymoon suite, the marriage was consummated in a broom cupboard behind the ballroom. Neither Dot nor Jack could wait until after the main festivities concluded, when they could get to their four-poster bed. In essence, and over time, the whole wedding would ultimately highlight the main difference between Dot and Jack. Dot wouldn't have cared less if the wedding was held in their back garden. She just wanted to be happy. Jack, though, wanted everyone else to see how happy he and, equally importantly, his money, had made Dot. And everyone else, for that matter.

To start with, married life was good. The only thorn in Jack's backside was that Dot had always insisted on continuing to use her maiden name. She said it was a police thing and made life a heck of a lot easier all round. It was standard practice within the job. Jack got annoyed as hell with this and initially did all he could to change her mind, but after a while, he gave up trying to reason with her. In her mind, maybe deep down, she was keeping a piece of her old life close to hand. Just in case. As usual, she was proven right.

A couple of years after the wedding, Dot and Jack began to grow apart from each other. The sex had slowed down. The weekends away stopped as Jack became busier and busier at work, and the little presents he used to buy her disappeared altogether. Ironically, Dot discovered that the castle they were married in was a prime weekend wooing spot for Jack and his previous prospective wives to be. Bet they didn't screw in the broom cupboard though.

Dot, by now, had also become a lot busier at work. The seminar presenters at the conference where they first met had been correct. The world of financial fraud was indeed booming. Dot was also convinced that Jack was screwing one or even both of his secretaries at work, quite possibly at the same time, knowing Jack. In all honesty, Dot didn't feel bad about it. He had an incredibly high sex drive and clearly needed to let off steam somewhere. Just not with her. Rightly or wrongly, Dot, being the most pragmatic person she knew, tended to find excuses for Jack's behaviour. It seemed to be her way of moving on, but in reality, it was just easier that way. Trouble was, she was also the most insecure person that she knew. She probably deserved it, and anyway, trying to keep up with Jack was exhausting. Well, that was her reasoning, and she was sticking to it.

Jack was now being the Jack that Dot had eventually found him to be. She wasn't close to him anymore, but she would have drawn the line if he had used their home for his alternative sexual exploits. The fact that she didn't feel a lot of jealousy about what Jack was or wasn't doing proved to Dot that life had to move on and move on quickly.

Dot worked in a job where she spent her time trying to figure out if people were lying to her or not. Although she was rather good at figuring out who was and who wasn't lying, the last thing she now wanted was to bring it home with her. Maybe she was just scared of knowing the truth. She didn't want to know, to be honest, although if her pragmatism was having a day off, burying her head in the sand seemed to work quite well. What she was sure of was that Jack was lying to her about most things. As a result, she felt the need to watch her back. Having been a police officer for so long, she had developed a sixth sense about people. And Jack was one of those people. You never knew with Jack what he would do next. Not in a physical, nasty or even criminal sense, just the unexpected emotional sense.

More recently, Jack had started to have problems at work. Apparently, there were far more competitors in his market now, meaning that, as Jack always put it, he had to diversify his portfolio. And it would appear that diversifying portfolios always came at a cost. Speculate to accumulate, that sort of thing, is what he always said. In Dot's world, speculating generally got you into trouble. It was facts you needed. Not that Dot ever imagined for one moment that Jack's business would get into any real trouble, but her own instinct meant that she was keeping the control of her mother's money very close to her chest, and no other bugger was getting near. And by no other bugger, Dot meant Jack, which, as she knew, infuriated the life out of him.

Before Dot met Jack, she had never been married. She had had a couple of long-termish partners, but her love for policing always seemed to create barriers between her, the job, and any personal life that her partners thought there was an entitlement to. There were, of course, the one, two, and three-night stands, but as always, the inevitable casualty of full-time policing was any potential relationship. Throw in the fact that no one wanted to take on a seemingly scatty, emotionally buggered-up policewoman, and Dot spent far more time as a single woman than not.

Mind you, Dot also knew she tended not to attract the kind or sympathetic type, or perhaps, deep down, it was always her intention not to attract that kind or sympathetic type. She felt protected within her own lifestyle bubble. It might not have been an ideal world for the average woman of her age, but she made the rules. And that, she did like.

This didn't, though, put a stop to the one thing that kept nagging at her. Her maternal clock was ticking. And it was ticking very loudly. Although she had never really felt that maternal in her head, her body was screaming something different to her. The problem was that working with some of life's nastiest and most repulsive characters, individuals that most people in society wouldn't believe existed unless they saw them on the Ten O'clock News, meant that Dot had a very different view of life than most. A hardened, cynical, sometimes angry view of life. A life where Dot felt it was her duty to help transfer the worst of society off the streets and into a life of incarceration.

Given her choice of men that she had encountered so far, none of them had felt right. Whatever right meant. Maybe that was the problem. Mr Right was still a mystery, but also a dilemma to her. She knew a lot of police officers who had married within the force. She also knew a lot of police officers who were divorced. To Dot, everything was about trust. This dilemma was what was holding her back in the marriage stakes. It probably pissed her off more than actually not having children. She was a difficult woman to be with. Looking at the evidence throughout her life, she had always known this to be the case. But when she met Jack, things were somehow different. It was unlike any of the other relationships that she had failed in. This was something exciting. Jack seemed to care about her and made sure they spent time together. Moving schedules at work, picking her up at 1 am after a long shift. Booking last-minute trips away. Not being annoyed if Dot had to cut them short and head back to work. All the little things that she had pushed herself away from previously. She had never made it easy for anyone; she knew that. Except with Jack. He was trying to make her life easier. But that didn't mean that she trusted him. And that was the problem. As usual, Dot was right.

As time went by in their relationship, Dot found herself going back to her original habits again and again. As she began immersing herself in the long hours of work, the arguments between her and Jack increased. Dot's sixth sense, trust, was kicking in, and her way of dealing with any conflict was always to get herself back into the world she knew – the world of policing. She blamed herself at the time for not being the person Jack had married, but if the truth be told, the reality was that Jack was simply getting bored with her. He always needed to move on to the next bright shiny thing, whatever the next bright shiny thing happened to be. Dot was obviously no longer shiny enough. As usual, she was scarily right about who she did or didn't trust.

It had also become clear to Dot early on that children would never be on Jack's agenda with her. She had played it right down. She was having fun, but her trust issues were always pecking away at her. Her mother wasn't happy about the situation. She would have given anything for a grandchild, especially as Dot was an only child. Her mother was as supportive as she could have been, and to be fair, was always quipping with Dot that it was just taking time to find the right man to start a family with. The irony of this was that Dot really didn't understand the direction their lives were going to take but trust always told her to keep an eye on the rearview mirror. Most times, she was right. Most times, trust had proven her right. But sometimes, she should concentrate on the road ahead. Preferably, a road that didn't have potholes. And that was tough for Dot.

Unlike her, Jack had been married before. Apparently, to someone who had a penchant for love heart sweets. Who knew? He had always said that it was a comfortable wife, a comfortable life-type arrangement, although his ex-wife might not have agreed with his marital analogy.

Jack had known his ex-wife for many years previously and said that they just kind of fell into marriage. It seemed the right thing to do, apparently, almost out of habit, he had said. Despite the perceived tedium of the conjugal arrangement, one positive to come out of their doomed marriage was Jack's son, now Dot's stepson, Jamie.

In her mind, he was the real reason that Jack had always avoided those awkward child conversations with her. Dot always suspected that Jack was terrified of his ex-wife going into meltdown if there was ever any competition for Jamie. The Karma for Dot, surely, had to be that whatever guiding light Jamie followed, it sure as hell wasn't his father's. Jamie was a kind, caring, and intelligent young man. He was also currently at the tail end of his two-year probationary period as a rookie police officer in the Met. Dot would always take at least some of the credit for Jamie's career path, although Jack saw it as an abject failure that his one and only son and heir wasn't going to follow him into the family business.

Jamie had excelled at Police Training School, passing out as the top recruit. Despite Dot's protestations, he had already been tipped to go into CID, and he seemed to relish every challenge that he was given. He had already been singled out by senior officers in the force as one to watch. And this pleased her. Very much indeed.

CHAPTER 5.

Chelsea Garden Care Home. The first incident.

Dot jumped as her phone vibrated. Without realising it, she had been sitting in her car for the best part of forty-five minutes. The number that flashed up on the screen showed as her mother's. She answered. "Hi Mum," trying hard to be as cheery as she could. "Are you ok?"

Anna, sounding very out of breath, replied, "Is that the police?"

"No, Mum, it's me, Dot, your daughter."

"Who?" spluttered Anna. "Put me through to the police, my daughter is a police officer, you know, and I have to talk to her right now."

Dot let out a long sigh. "How can I help, Anna? It's the police here."

"Oh, good, good," Anna said, "and about blasted time too. If you argue with everyone who calls you on the telephone, how on earth can the police be expected to catch any criminals? Now, you listen to me and write down exactly what I tell you, it's jolly important and a matter of national security." Anna's tone had changed. Her enunciation of words had become almost aristocratic, not really befitting her relatively unentitled upbringing. The sad thing about this for Dot was that her mother did not sound like someone in the final throes of dementia. She sounded like, well, her mother again. "Are you listening to me, girl?" Anna's voice had real grit.

"Yes, I am, Anna, and I have a pen and paper right here, so fire away." Dot's resigned tone was almost defeatist in her reply.

"Good. Now then, I have a German spy locked in my cupboard. It was a bit of a struggle, but I managed to restrain her using some plastic strap type of things. You know the ones. The same ones I use to tie my roses against the trellis. Anyway, I've managed to silence the scheming nazi infiltrator using one of my nappies. The brevity of this situation meant that I had to use a dirty one. I saved it, especially for the occasion. Pure genius on my part, I'm sure you will agree. Mind you, have you ever worn an infernal nappy? No, I guess you haven't. Why would you? Dreadful things. Immoral." Anna gave a small triumphant chuckle.

"Mum, those plastic straps are for gardening. Not for tying up people, for God's sake. And who, who is this woman that you say you have in your cupboard? And where's the nurse? Have you missed taking your medicine this morning?"

Given Dot's years of police interview experience and hearing just about every excuse or duplicitous crap used by every lowlife she had ever arrested, she was genuinely thrown by the conversation she was having with her mother. Was this another hallucination that her mother was having? It couldn't possibly be real, could it? In the background, Dot could hear muffled screams followed by a loud banging sound. This certainly sounded very real.

"Mum, stop whatever it is you're doing and listen to me very carefully. You need to let whoever it is you have there go and then call for the nurse. What was that banging I could hear in the background? Mum! Mum!"

After a few seconds of quiet, the banging started up again, only this time it was louder.

Anna, speaking very calmly, said, "It's the bloody Gestapo trying to break down my door. You need to get here quickly, Inspector LaSalle; I can only hold them off for so long." With that, the phone went dead. Dot hit the redial button, and it went straight through to voicemail. She tried again with the same result. How the hell can this happen in a care home?

Dot jumped out of the car and did a kind of walk-run-walk as fast as she could towards the front of the building, where the main entrance was situated. She was fearful that if she sprinted through the doors, the residents would assume one of their own had died and cause geriatric pandemonium. Mind you, after her mother's call just now, anything seemed possible.

As she arrived at the front of the building, the high-pitched sound of an alarm started going off inside. This was not the fire alarm. This was the security, batten down the hatches, someone is trying to escape, alarm. She hoped that the noise didn't affect any of the hearing aids of the residents, because it was certainly doing its level best to burst the drums inside of her own ears. The dogs in the area must have been going apoplectic. She could make out the heavy frame of Gerald, the resident security guard cum general dogsbody, frantically waving his arms in the main reception area and shouting what Dot could only assume were orders at the residents inside.

Arriving at the automatic doors that should have automatically opened but on this occasion failed to automatically open, Dot realised that as the main alarm had been activated inside, the security protocol meant that the main doors had automatically locked!! This was not good news. She pressed the security buzzer at the side of the door and kept her finger firmly placed on it. She could see the reception desk where the buzzer was connected, but the desk was vacant. She knew from previous evening visits that the buzzer made a noise, but not a very loud one. Given how loud the screaming alarm was, it was clear that the buzzer had no real bearing on the situation. Dot could also see through the open door into Vanessa's empty office.

Gerald seemed oblivious to his surroundings and was still frantically waving to some of the residents seated in the front foyer to move back to their rooms, but who, by the look on their faces, were not going to miss any opportunity to watch whatever theatre was about to happen right in front of them.

Dot was now simultaneously pressing the buzzer and smacking the palm of her hand against the window at the side of the door as hard as she could. Gerald looked over in her direction and seemed to panic even more. He was struggling to deal with the situation at hand, let alone with a mad-looking resident's daughter trying everything within her power to break down the front door. After what seemed like an eternity, he eventually ran over to the reception desk, leaned underneath, and pressed the activation buzzer to open the front entrance doors.

Dot pulled the doors open quickly and firmly, not giving the doors time to open automatically. Once in, she ran straight through the foyer and headed for the wing where her mother's room was located, glancing over at the residents now firmly rooted in their seats. She swore they were actually enjoying the interruption to their day. Dot arrived at the door to her mother's care wing and went to push it open. The door didn't budge.

"Damn it," Dot shouted.

The door was locked.

She let it be known via a further stream of expletives that she was not impressed, again to the amusement of those now watching her. Lockdown mode for all doors. She looked through the small glass centre panel in the door, which was set at eye height, and saw several people, including Vanessa, standing outside the closed door to her mother's room. Vanessa looked over towards Dot, turned back and continued talking to her mother's door, clearly with no intention of opening the door that Dot stood on the other side of. Too many bloody doors.

Dot ran back to the desk, where Gerald stood, looking defeated but still trying in vain to negotiate with the residents to return amicably and calmly to their rooms. The residents, though, were having none of it.

"Gerald", shouted Dot. "Have you got the key code to the door over there?" pointing over to the other side of reception, "I need to talk to my mother urgently."

Gerald stared straight through Dot. In his mind, he was trying to comprehend if what he had just heard was even allowed to happen without Vanessa's authority.

She stepped closer. "Gerald, open the door before I seriously lose my temper. I'm a serving police officer, and there's a situation happening less than fifty feet away that you obviously do not have the ability to handle yourself. Now, please open the door." Dot's voice was calm and measured.

Gerald did not move. Frozen to the spot where he stood and not having a good day, his brain was trying to compute the worst of two possible outcomes. Dot or Vanessa.

Dot moved within one foot of him, placed her finger firmly in the middle of his chest, and screamed at the top of her voice, "NOW. Open that bloody door!"

Dot won. Gerald caved in and ran over to the door in question. He punched in four numbers on the keypad, and the door unlocked with a firm click.

At this point, the residents, now fully entrenched in their foyer chairs, all applauded. Not since two residents had been caught in a compromising position on the piano in the foyer had they had such a good day. Apparently, said couple was trying to recreate a scene from *Pretty Woman*. As far as the residents were now concerned, this was a damn good sequel with the only thing missing being popcorn and hot dogs!

Dot couldn't help but allow herself a wry smile as she pushed her way through the door and headed straight towards Vanessa.

Gerald just stared at the residents in bewilderment.

Once Dot had thrown open the door, she almost sprinted down the corridor towards her mother's room. "Christ, Vanessa, what the hell is going on? My mother was fine when I left her earlier." She found herself shouting, trying to be heard above the alarm.

"Well," Vanessa shouted back. "It would appear we have a bit of a tricky hostage situation on our hands. Your mother, though God knows how, has managed to barricade herself inside her room, whilst entertaining her neighbour, Ingrid. She is now refusing to open the door to anyone until she has spoken to Inspector LaSalle. That's who she asked for, not you, per se, as her daughter. We've just been trying to encourage her to open the door so that we can make sure that Ingrid is all right. Particularly as we've heard nothing from Ingrid at all yet, but she is definitely missing from her room."

"And all of this for a mere £17,000 a month. One hell of an entertainment package if you ask me," mocked Dot. "I spoke to Mum briefly earlier, and she was saying something about a German spy of all things. These hallucinations seem to be getting much worse now. Let me talk to her".

Vanessa moved aside and asked Anna's other neighbours to go back into their rooms and shut their doors. There would of course be an enjoyable nightcap for them later to accompany their dinner for complying with her request. The two neighbours didn't need to be asked a second time and left Dot and Vanessa at the locked door, wondering exactly what tipple they could look forward to later. They looked incredibly pleased with themselves.

"Mum, can you hear me?" Dot shouted through the door. "Vanessa, for crying out loud, can you get someone to shut off that infernal bloody alarm? And quickly. Nobody can hear themselves think around here. Mum, can you hear me?" she repeated, this time louder than the last.

"I'm waiting for Inspector Dorothea LaSalle to arrive, nobody else," Anna fired back from the other side of the door. "Until she is here, this door shall remain firmly closed."

Dot, not for the first time that day, let out a huge sigh. "Anna, it's Inspector LaSalle here. Please listen to me. I need you to open this door so that I can speak to you face-to-face. Is there anyone else inside the room with you?"

"At last. It's taken you long enough to get here. I will allow you, but only you, inside this room, Inspector LaSalle. Anyone else tries to enter, I garotte the poor unfortunate bitch I have locked in my cupboard. Is that understood?"

Vanessa looked at Dot. She was clearly horrified.

"Is that understood!" barked Anna forcefully, sounding frighteningly authoritarian.

"You do know that it is my duty to inform the police of the situation happening here, don't you?" Vanessa said. "And I have a duty of care to keep all of the other residents and staff safe."

Dot, totally infuriated by Vanessa's holier-than-thou manner, barked out, "Well, who the bloody hell do you think I am, Vanessa, Miss Marple or something? And," she continued, "your duty of care with my mother appears to have failed catastrophically, given the current situation we now find ourselves in. You have allowed my mother, a woman who is nearly 90 years old, to kidnap another resident and barricade herself in her own bloody room. Nearly 90 years old, who the hell could she possibly hurt other than herself? Now, I need to get inside and assess the situation. Then, and only then, will you make a call as to who else, if anybody, needs to be contacted. Do you understand me?"

Vanessa's face was a picture of continuing horror. Her eyes were wide, and she was still desperately trying to assess the situation herself. "Ok, you have ten minutes. If you haven't sorted out this mess by then, I will call the police." She stood back from the door.

"Fine, do whatever you think you need to do," said Dot. "Now, have you tried the master key in the door to check it's actually locked?"

"It was the first thing we tried," said Vanessa," but the door wouldn't move. I think Anna has pushed something behind it."

Dot stood tall, took a deep breath, and shouted calmly but firmly towards the door. "Anna LaSalle, it's the police here. I need you to open the door in front of you. When you have done that, you need to take three steps back. Can you do that for me now, please, Anna? Do you understand me?" Dot was standing with her feet slightly apart, one hand on the door handle and the other placed firmly in the middle of the door.

"Anna LaSalle, did you hear my request? I am Police Inspector Dorothea LaSalle, and you must do as I say and do it now. Open the ..."

Dot was interrupted before she finished her request. "No need to be so bloody officious, Inspector", responded Anna. "I am, after all, the innocent party here. Stand back, I'm about to action your request. I apologise in advance for the stench in the room. This bloody prison insists on serving pulverised cabbage and Brussels sprouts with every meal so that we don't all choke on the food. The end result is not a pleasant one, I'm afraid to say. Now, I need a minute to remove my barricade, and I will then unlock the door."

The alarm thankfully stopped its incessant shrill. Despite this, Dot's ears continued to ring. There was the sound of something being moved on the other side of the door. After quite a few attempts, the object was cleared out of the way, and the door was unlocked.

Dot pushed the door open and was met by her mother. The large over-shirt she wore was soaked in sweat and covered in light brown patches. Dot's immediate response was to put her hand in front of her mouth to stop herself from throwing up. The room smelled like it had fallen victim to a malodorous muck-spreading accident. It was unquestionably one of the worst smells that she had ever experienced. Given some of the situations that she had found herself in as a police officer, the smell that now met her would give even a decomposing body a run for its money.

Anna took a small bottle from her over-shirt pocket and sprayed some liquid onto Dot's cheeks. "Chanel No5, darling. There's no smell that Chanel can't conceal. Wonderful stuff, you know."

"Mum, what on earth have you been up to?"

Dot was trying to look beyond her mother to see if she could spot anyone else in the room. Anna's apartment was a small one-bedroom studio with a shower room and a kitchenette. A metal Zimmer frame, presumably the barricade, propped at an angle under the handle to stop the door from opening, was to one side of the door. Dot couldn't see anyone else. The smell in the room was nauseating and affecting her train of thought. It was continuing to make her gag. "Mum, you said earlier that you had someone locked in a cupboard. Is that true?" She knew that there was a large built-in wardrobe out of view in the bedroom area. She also knew there was a cupboard behind the front door.

Anna stood her ground, staring with steel in her eyes. Something that Dot hadn't seen for many years. It was quite unnerving. "The bitch is in the cupboard behind the door". Anna virtually spat the words out. Gone was the cheery demeanour that had greeted Dot moments earlier. "And I hope she stinks of crap for the rest of her miserable life." She turned around and walked over to a small two-seater sofa, collapsed down into it, held her head in her hands and started to cry.

If Dot was going to safely remove whoever it was from the cupboard, then she needed her mother out of the room. "Mum, I need to go and look in the cupboard. Before I do that, I need you to go and sit in the medical room until I can come back to get you. Is that ok, do you understand me?"

Anna looked at Dot, defeated. She nodded as she got up slowly from the sofa and moved towards the front door. As she was about to open the door, she stopped and turned towards Dot.

"Be careful of the woman in the cupboard, Dot." Anna's voice was hushed, but steady. "She is very dangerous indeed. It's taken her a lifetime to find me, and she'll never give up trying to find out what she wants. And I, for one, will never give her that."

"Mum, I don't even know if what you are saying makes any sense at all. What is it this woman wants? What are you hiding?"

Before there was time to answer the question, there was a soft knock at the door. Anna turned and pulled it open. One of the care assistants stood there, covering her mouth with her hand, eyes wide, staring at Anna, trying to look inside the room. Dot stood behind her mother and gave her a squeezy hug of her shoulders.

"Mum, this lovely young lady is going to take you for a cup of tea. You need to go with her. Now. And please. Be nice to her."

Anna didn't say a word; she just took the arm of the care assistant and walked off down the corridor. She looked shattered.

Dot entered her mother's room again and moved quickly around to the back of the front door. She slowly opened the door to the cupboard, unsure as to what she was going to find. The smell that greeted her was utterly disgusting. Far worse than the smell already permeating through the room itself. It made Dot immediately gag again, and she covered her mouth with her hand. There, sat on the floor facing her, with her knees pushed up under her chin and her hands behind her back, was the frame of an elderly woman. Only her body was visible. Her head and the top of her face were covered by what Dot assumed to be an adult nappy. A nappy that appeared to be full of faeces. The whole top half of the woman was covered in the stuff. Only her nose and mouth were visible.

"Vanessa," Dot shouted. "I need a hand in here, please. Now."

Vanessa was already standing behind Dot. Her face was horror-struck.

Judging by the wet stains covering the front of Vanessa's expensive silk blouse, she had already attempted to hold back some vomit.

"Thought you would be used to this kind of smell by now, Vanessa," said Dot as she grabbed a towel from one of the shelves in the cupboard. Holding the towel at either end and using it like an oven glove, Dot gently removed the nappy from the woman. Her mother hadn't done anything by halves, that was for sure. The woman's entire head was covered in excrement. Dot could make out a few grey hairs poking through the filth.

"What's your name, sweetheart?" asked Dot in a soft voice. She was looking at the woman in the cupboard, whilst at the same time trying her hardest not to retch. Clarification of the name was required. Dot had only been told the name by other people. It was a police thing.

"Her name is Ingrid, I told you that," said Vanessa, who was now bending over Dot.

"Ingrid, is it okay if I call you Ingrid?" Dot almost whispered. "We're here to help you. We need to get you out of this cupboard and cleaned up. Are you hurt anywhere at all? Do you have any pain?"

Ingrid didn't reply to any of the questions. She simply responded by shaking her head very slightly.

Dot got another towel and asked Vanessa to dampen it with water.

"Let's get your face cleaned up for you, shall we? Then we can see if there's any damage, eh?" Dot was endeavouring to be as calm and as matter of fact as possible to get the job at hand done quickly. She really couldn't help but feel sorry for Ingrid.

Vanessa was retching at the sink, trying her hardest not to throw up the last of her lunch whilst she poured water onto the towel.

Dot almost grinned as she watched her.

"I know what you're thinking," Vanessa said. "Let's just say that these kinds of things don't tend to happen every day, and if they do, I have other people here to deal with them. Unsurprisingly, this just happens to be the first time I have had to deal with a hostage situation where excrement has been used as a weapon of choice." She was looking a distinct shade of pale grey as she spoke through pursed lips. It was as though she didn't want to open her mouth again, for fear of what else might come out of it, or, for that matter, what went in it. The smell wasn't abating. She handed Dot the wet towel.

Dot very gently began to clean away the excrement from Ingrid's face, wiping her eyes first, then her nose, and then her mouth. Another towel was thrown at Vanessa, who went over to the sink to wet it. Dot managed to get most of the muck off with the first towel and moved closer to Ingrid to look behind her. Anna had been as good as her word. Ingrid had her hands locked together behind her back by a long black cable tie. It was also clear that the cable tie had not been forgiving in any way. It had been pulled tight, and Dot could see that both wrists were chafed to the point that the skin was broken and bleeding.

"Vanessa, could you see if you could find a pair of scissors or a sharp knife for me, please?"

As Dot asked this, Vanessa was already passing the request along to someone in the corridor. A few moments later, one of the nurses retrieved a small pair of nail scissors from a medical bag and handed them to Dot. She cut through the cable tie as gently as she could and pulled it away carefully from Ingrid. Throughout the ordeal, Ingrid had not spoken a single word. She simply sat there, obeying every instruction given to her. Vanessa moved away from the door as one of the care assistants reversed a wheelchair into the room, left it there, then backed out of the room again.

Dot motioned for Vanessa to move to her right-hand side. They both slid their arms under Ingrid's armpits and gently pulled her up into a standing position. Once standing, they both held her still until they were sure she wasn't going to collapse back down onto the floor again. At this point,

Ingrid stiffened her back, pushed both arms out in front of her, and flicked them up and down. She cleared her throat and said sternly, "Get your filthy hands off me. Right now. Both of you. I can assure you that I'm perfectly capable of walking on my own two feet. Now, move out of my way. I would like to return to my room so that I can have a shower and get this stinking mess off me. That lunatic bitch should be in a secure unit, not in here, where she is free to assault whoever wants to. She is a menace to society. Broadmoor would be more befitting for that psychopathic, demented geriatric. Now, I'll not ask again, get the hell out of my way, so that I can go and have a shower."

Dot moved out of the way. It didn't seem the appropriate time to offer any sort of apology at that moment in time, given the vitriolic abuse Ingrid had just spewed out regarding her mother.

"Ingrid," said Vanessa, intervening. "We really do need to get you checked out by the nurse first. And we must ensure that your wrists are looked at as well. We don't want you to catch anything. We have a wheelchair here to take you to the medical room, or you can walk if you like." Vanessa's tone was a little bit shaky but very matter-of-fact. It was clear to Dot that Ingrid was a force to be reckoned with, and her reply provided adequate corroboration of the fact.

"I'm going to have a shower in my own room. Once I'm done, and only when I'm done, you can carry out whatever checks you see fit. Until then, you can quite frankly clear off and leave me alone. If you wish to challenge me at any point, then I'll ensure my lawyers will sue you and your incompetent prison staff for every penny you have. This god-forsaken place is not fit for purpose. It's that bitch Anna that should have been tied up. If I were living back in my wonderful homeland, this would have never happened. Now, good day to you all."

With that, Ingrid walked gingerly up to the wheelchair and pushed it as hard as she could out of the room. She then turned around to face Vanessa, pushed her fingers through her hair, and theatrically flicked her hands, discarding the last remnants of Anna's nappy in the direction of Vanessa. Moving two steps forward, Ingrid then proceeded to wipe both her hands on the front of Vanessa's blouse. She then turned and left the room.

Vanessa, looking disgusted, turned towards Dot. "You might want to give Jack a call, Dorothea. I suspect you are going to need a good solicitor to represent your mother after this little episode," hissed Vanessa.

Dot nearly broke out into laughter. "I can assure you that Jack is the last person I would call if I needed a good solicitor, Vanessa. If you looked after your residents properly, this would never have happened. Now, I need to go and make sure that my mother is alright. And you might want to change your blouse."

CHAPTER 6.

West London.

Jack had just finished a meeting with his company accountants and was driving back towards his office in Ealing, West London.

Andries Legal was currently not having a particularly good time of things. Jack had taken his eye off the proverbial ball and now found himself having to deal with issues that he had never had to deal with before. Business was down nearly 40 per cent over the last twelve months. More competitors had entered into his market, meaning that prices were becoming cutthroat. The new competition was operating, in most cases, from cheap out-of-town industrial estates. Competition that also knew their way around all of the fancy new tech that was now available, not to mention having the ability to operate call centres in India.

The world appeared to be changing rapidly. Too rapidly for Jack. He had even hired a consultant to look at the potential threats in his business areas. The conclusion of this was that clients would always want face-to-face meetings and generally in an office that best represented the standing of that particular business. In other words, his business should have been fine going forward. The cost of the report? Twenty-five thousand pounds! Twenty-five bloody grand to tell Jack that everything should have been fine.

Now here he was. The accountant had been making things very clear to him indeed. Reducing costs was of the utmost importance, and the quickest way to do this was to shrink headcount. In most other companies, there was a specific way to deal with redundancy. HR departments earned their money through these processes and should have made this Managing Director's job a little bit easier as well. Well, in his business, Jack was the HR department and out of the twelve staff that he employed within the business, two of the three that had been identified for the chop just happened to be women that Jack had had extramarital sex with. Well, not that sex had been a part of his marriage for some time now, so he didn't see it as extramarital, just sex with people who liked to have sex with him. The bottom line for Jack now, though, was that this was likely to get very messy. Neither employee would be expected to go quietly. And no doubt, it was also going to prove very expensive. It would be best to get this over and done with. And he had to do it quickly. His business needed to be in decent shape for his other plans to succeed. Going bankrupt was not an option. He needed cover. And his business was his cover.

Jack's phone rang. The screen flashed up with Vanessa's mobile number.

"Hey," said Jack. "Everything ok?"

"No, everything is not ok, Jack. The situation we have here right now is anything but ok."

Jack had never heard Vanessa speak to him like this. She was pissed off about something, that was for sure.

"Okay, ok, calm down, V, tell me what's happened."

Whatever this was going to be, Jack was sure it wasn't going to make his day any better.

"It's your mother-in-law, Jack. She dragged Ingrid into her room, cable-tied her arms behind her back, covered her entire head in shit, actual human shit, and then gagged her with a filthy, disgusting nappy. Anna has been calling Ingrid a German spy all morning, and then she just turned psycho. Your wife went all Cagney and Lacey on me. She took over the entire situation. This has not been a good day. Half of the residents were watching the entire thing. I have had to bribe them all just to keep them quiet."

"Wow," said Jack, stunned. "After the meeting I have just had, I didn't for the life of me think anything would make me smile today, but that just did."

Vanessa could hear the humour in Jack's voice, which did nothing to calm the situation.

"Jack, for Christ's sake, didn't you hear me? Your mother-in-law has been calling Ingrid a German spy. That means she must know something, and she wasn't hallucinating; I hadn't given her any of the tablets. There's no way she would just pluck something like that from thin air. I swear, Anna may well have dementia, but she sounded sharp as a tack today. She knew exactly what she was doing with Ingrid." Vanessa came up for air.

Jack was right, his day wasn't getting any better at all. "Where's Dot now?" Jack asked.

"She's in with Anna, making sure she is okay and quite frankly, probably trying to figure out why she did what she did to Ingrid. I need to put a report through to Head Office to try and explain what happened today without getting sacked and figure out exactly what I'm going to do before any lawyers decide to pitch their oars in."

Jack could hear a quiver in Vanessa's voice. "Right," Jack said, attempting to take control. "The first thing we need to do is to move Anna into the memory care wing ahead of what was agreed at the meeting earlier. This is the perfect excuse to do it quickly. At least this way, we can keep her locked up and away from causing Ingrid any more trouble. She needs to be loaded up to the eyeballs with meds as well. Try mixing diazepam with a double dose of melatonin. Get her on that, and it will keep her quiet while we sort this mess out. Given what she did today should make this easy enough to sort out with the pharmacist as well as Dot. This is not going to change our plans, V, so you need to stay strong and focused. You need to go and see Ingrid to find out what she got from Anna. Hopefully, there will be enough to move forward with. Let me know what Ingrid says, and I'll see you back in the room later."

Vanessa's head was spinning. Gerald had managed to speak to the alarm company and told them everything was fine at the care home, so there was no need for any emergency service intervention. From a bystander's point of view, she should be able to convince anyone who asked that it was just one of the residents having a cognitive brain fart. Hid their meds; this was the consequence. That kind of thing. All sorted now, though and nothing to see. It was time for Vanessa to go and see Ingrid. For Anna to react the way she did, Ingrid must surely have found out something. Vanessa hoped this was the case. She couldn't take too much more.

"See you later, Jack."

CHAPTER 7.

Back at the Care Home.
Dot had waited patiently for her mother to finish in the shower.

The nurse had checked her over in the medical room earlier and diagnosed her with a stubborn attitude intermingled with totally sarcastic behaviours. In other words, all good. One of the care home cleaners had done a brilliant job of bleaching and mopping out the cupboard, along with the remnants of excrement in the room. It would take a while for the smell to fully go, but the bleach and air freshener had at least taken the edge off it.

The nurse was due to come and see her again in the next few minutes. Dot wanted to talk to her mother before she was prescribed lord knows what kind of medications to calm her down.

Anna appeared out of the shower room in her dressing gown with a towel wrapped tightly around her hair. She walked across the room and sat down on the sofa by the large, partially open window, locked partially open so that the residents couldn't perform their own version of the great escape.

"I know you think that I'm completely doolally, Dot," she said, "but I still have a few brain cells that haven't been obliterated by this bloody awful disease, you know. Everything comes and goes, and I have no control over when or where things happen. Quite frankly, I can't even remember what the hell happened most days, but I do know one thing. That bitch Ingrid is after me. By the way, is the honeysuckle out yet? I do love this time of year. The smell in my garden is simply divine. I do love honeysuckle. That reminds me, I must call the mower man; I'm sure that the grass needs cutting again. She is a German spy, you know. Been chasing me ever since the war. They're all in cahoots together here at this damn place. Particularly that Vanessa woman. What an absolutely devious cow she is. Always having to check over my shoulder. Whatever possessed you to put me in a care home like this in the first place? It's not easy for me, you know. When you pop in next time, could you give the car a start for me? Don't want it not starting when I need to drive to the NAAFI on Saturday."

Dot was used to these types of conversations with her mother. They moved in all sorts of different directions, and she knew that it was best to just listen and agree with her until she stopped. She had given up arguing with her mother a long time ago. Doing so just made her mother upset, become argumentative, or even worse, violent. It's always best to just go with the flow, for both her and her mother's sake. Mind you, she was spot-on about Vanessa. She was a right cow.

"I started the car last time I was here, Mum, and it was fine," she lied. "All ready for you next time you want to use it. So, what makes you think that this Ingrid woman is a spy? What has she done to give you that impression?" She was now using her mother's habit of switching and swapping conversation topics.

"Impression! Impression! Fact, young lady. Bloody woman has been snooping around me for years," Anna murmured. "Trying to be my friend when all she wants is information from me. Asking me the same thing all the time, driving me insane. I kept on telling her that it was none of her business, and then she turned up in my room and tried to tie my hands up with those plastic things. Said she was going to interrogate me. Tying up my hands of all things. Can you imagine? Just as well I had used them before to tie up my creepers. Remembered how they worked and then gave the bitch a dose of her own medicine. Sweep of her leading leg, and she was in a pile on the floor in no time. She didn't like that very much; I can tell you. She was calling me all sorts of names. Saying I had slept with German soldiers and that I had a duty to her country to hand over the information that I had. How dare she? Shut her up pretty well, though, thought it was pure genius. She refused to stop spouting utter hogwash, so I gave as good as I got, all over her head. Nappy had been in the room since last night. Funny, something told me she might be after me today. Left quite a mess, mind. The woman is smart, let me tell you. But not smart enough for me. Have you got a tape recorder hidden in your clothes or something? I can't see you writing down anything that I'm telling you. It's all very important, you know. Are you going to arrest her? I've told you everything I know about her. You probably need to speak to my solicitor as well. He needs to know that the Germans have found me." She stopped talking and stared straight ahead, looking at something deep somewhere in another world that Dot could never see.

"Mum, Jack is your solicitor, you know, my husband Jack, I can tell him what you have told me if you like." Dot was exhausted.

"No, no, *NO!*" her mother screamed. "Not your Jack. Your Jack is in on all of this as well. Can't trust the man. Quite frankly can't bear him either; nasty piece of work if you ask me. God only knows what you ever saw in that ghastly man. Big bank account, little willy, no doubt. No, my solicitor is Stephen, you know Stephen. You should do; you have met the man. You were younger then. I think he is somewhere in London, yes, London, er, Bell Yard, something like that anyway. You know, the one who did my will for me. No, of course, you don't know, why would you, why would a police officer know who my solicitor is? Now, it must be time for you to go. I'm sure I'm out for dinner tonight. Go on, off you go. You must have a million things to do. So many murders these days, I've no idea why you want to sit here talking to me. Now, please excuse me, I need to get changed for dinner." And with that, Anna stood up from her chair and went back into the shower room.

There was a knock on the door to the room. Dot opened it. The care home nurse greeted her, holding a cardboard container with tablets and a small bottle of liquid.

"How is she?" the nurse asked.

Dot replied. "Pretty confused to be honest, I'm not sure what is fact and what is fiction these days. Are you going to sedate her?"

The nurse nodded, "Just looking to make her comfortable for now and to make sure that there are no physical injuries that we couldn't find earlier. Once she is relaxed enough, we'll move her over to the memory care unit, where we can keep a closer eye on her."

"Ok, thanks. Don't envy the next occupant of this room, though." Dot then turned, left the room, and walked into the corridor. She stood still for a moment, trying to understand what she had just listened to. Her mother was getting worse. Was there a solicitor she had never heard of? Dot could have sworn Jack had sorted her will out. Then there was the talk of the war, sleeping with German soldiers, secrets, and Ingrid. She was almost right about Jack. Certainly, couldn't trust him. Definitely a shit. But she was wrong about the willy thing.

CHAPTER 8.

Still in the Care Home. Ingrid's room.

Vanessa walked into the medical room looking for Ingrid but instead found one of the nurses.

"Have you seen Ingrid yet? Do you know how she is doing?"

The nurse shrugged. "Stubborn lady that one. Refused to take Diazepam or anything else, for that matter. As soon as I cleaned up her wrists she was gone. Straight back to her room. Given what she went through today, she looked in rather good shape to me."

"OK, thanks," replied Vanessa. "I'll pop down and see her. Sign out four diazepam for me, will you, and I'll take them down to her now." She took the tablets from the nurse and headed down to Ingrid's room.

She knocked quietly and let herself in using her master key. Ingrid stood at the window staring at the space that was the outside world. "That was one hell of a show earlier, Ingrid." Vanessa's voice was hushed.

"She knows. She knows everything. Dementia, my arse. Verdammte Frau. Bloody woman." Ingrid spoke in a very disciplined tone tinged with a Germanic edge.

Vanessa thought carefully. "When you say she knows everything, Ingrid, what exactly do you mean by everything?" She leaned in closer. She needed to clearly understand what was about to be said.

Ingrid coughed. "Anna won't give me any information. She knows what we're looking for. And she damn well knows where it is as well. She knows where I come from, and she knows that you must be involved in all of this. The bitch was getting extra food from Krystina in the kitchen. She had a pretty good idea that someone was trying to drug her, so she did not eat the normal food. She thought someone was going to kill her once they got her to tell the truth. I was trying to get her to drink tea with scopolamine in it, but she was having none of it. It was just a truth drug, not cyanide. She flipped. She threw the tea at me and kicked my legs away. You saw what happened next. As I said, dementia meinen Arsch."

Vanessa was thinking hard. "Do you think Anna said anything to Krystina?" Her voice was ice cold.

"I can't be sure, but as we know, Anna is smart. Perhaps too smart for us." Ingrid was shaking her head as she replied to Vanessa. "Do you mind if I have a lie down, Vanessa? I'm exhausted. I'll talk more later. And please, keep that woman away from me."

"Yes, yes, of course. We'll find a way to get what is rightfully yours, Ingrid, I promise." Vanessa went to the window, closed the curtains, and left Ingrid in her room alone.

CHAPTER 9.

And still in the Care Home.

It felt to Dot that what happened earlier with her mother was just another step closer to the inevitable ending. What on earth was going through her mother's head right now? Dot felt shattered, confused, emotional and sad all at the same time. Not a good mix for a serving police officer. She walked through the door into the main reception area, where Vanessa stood in quiet conversation with Gerald, the so-called security chap. Vanessa stopped talking and moved across to head off Dot. "How is your mother doing, Dot?" she asked. She looked as tired as Dot felt.

Dot grinned inwardly. Vanessa was still wearing the same blouse as earlier, which was still speckled with vomit and poo.

"Given the day she has had, not too bad to be honest," she replied. "The nurse is with her now, getting her ready to move into the full concierge service wing with a naked butler serving champagne as we speak. How is Ingrid doing?"

Vanessa's reply was terse. "Ingrid is doing remarkably well, given the hideous treatment she received earlier from your mother. I think I've managed to persuade her not to pursue legal action against her for now." She looked vaguely triumphant.

"More likely not suing you or this bloody care home," Dot replied sarcastically.

"Well, at least Gerald had the presence of mind to set off the main alarm when he heard Ingrid scream," Vanessa fired back. "God only knows what could have happened if Ingrid were stuck in your mother's room for any length of time, given what she managed to do to her in the few minutes her door was locked. All the care home security protocols within the home worked exactly as they should. As soon as he sounded the alarm, Gerald locked down the area, ensured residents stayed where they were until told where to go, and alerted the appropriate individuals. All's well that ends well." Vanessa was now the one who had a look of smugness on her face. "And" she continued, "at least with your mother moving into the memory care wing, we can keep a much closer eye on her to ensure that nothing like this can ever happen again. Now, please forgive me; as you can imagine, I have several reports that I need to complete before the day is out. Have a nice evening, Dorothea." And with that, she turned and headed for her office.

No wonder the bitch didn't have a wedding ring on her finger, thought Dot as she walked toward the front door. She looked over at Gerald, who quickly moved in the opposite direction, as he tried his hardest to look busy. Nothing was fooling Dot. Seventeen grand a month for this! Seventeen bloody grand! And how dare that woman call her Dorothea? Not even her mother called her that anymore. Mind you, she was called all sorts of other things by her mother these days. Dorothea, indeed, who the hell did Vanessa think she was? She needed a huge glass of Chablis. And a hot shower. She smelt like she had been swimming in a slurry pit.

CHAPTER 10.

Still in the Care Home. The not-so-secret apartment.

Vanessa watched as Dot left the building through the front entrance. She made one telephone call to impart some of the information she had managed to glean from Ingrid. She then made some notes from the day, in preparation for any reports that the lawyers at head office might need. Finally, she stood up from behind her desk, walked out of her office, closed the door and locked it behind her. She spun around and headed towards the corridor opposite the entrance. It was past nine in the evening, and she felt exhausted. She punched in the 4-digit code into the door lock. Once through, she headed up the fire escape stairs to the first floor. She turned left and, when she got to the very end of the corridor, used a key card to enter a private one-bedroom apartment.

This particular apartment was very occasionally used by the families of wealthier residents who had tripped in to see their loved ones and wanted to stay close in their final hours. Vanessa, however, used it more than most, and not for the reason for which it was intended. As a result, it was completely off-limits to all the other staff members, unless specifically invited. Those who did get invited were generally one of the three chefs, hand delivering dinner, lunch, or breakfast.

Vanessa lived less than ten minutes away from the care home; however, the apartment was very convenient for her covert activities, particularly as the fire door led directly outside to the rear car park, where the CCTV and alarm were not working. Well, actually, deliberately made inoperable.

Just one of the reasons Vanessa had taken on Gerald over a year ago as the so-called security man. The closest he had come to working in security previously was as a part-time store detective-cum-cleaner at a local convenience store. Not being the smartest person in the world meant that he didn't tend to ask any awkward questions. Vanessa told Gerald, during his first-ever walkaround, that as the CCTV was managed by an external company, he didn't need to worry about it. She had, however, told him that the alarm was indeed working, so that would be sufficient for security and insurance purposes. The fact that Vanessa paid Gerald an extra £5 an hour on top of what he was earning previously meant that he generally tended to do what he was told. "Christ," thought Vanessa, "I wish all men did as they were told." Gerald was cheap, cheerful, and loyal. Just as Vanessa liked her staff.

She pushed the door shut behind her but left it unlocked. The suite was larger than all of the others in the care home. It contained a lounge, a separate dining area with a kitchen, a large double bedroom and a bathroom with a bath and separate shower. She walked over to the dining area, took a large wine glass from one of the cabinets and opened the fridge. She then took out a bottle of Dom Perignon, popped off the cork like an expert and filled the glass to the brim. She put the bottle back in the fridge alongside the six others. Taking a long, slow mouthful of the pale gold fizzing liquid, she slipped off her shoes.

Entering the bathroom, she put the glass on the side of the bath, turned on the hot and cold taps, and then poured in a huge amount of lavender and geranium bath oil. Right now, she smelt just like the residents out there in the rest of the building. And it made her shudder. The faster this whole disaster with Ingrid and Anna was sorted out, and she got the hell out of this godforsaken place, the better.

She pulled off her clothes and threw them onto the floor. She then walked naked to the bath and slowly lowered herself in. The warm steam and smell were divine. A million miles away from that bloody awful Anna and her shitty smell. "The quicker she chokes on her food, the sooner this will all be sorted out."

Vanessa allowed herself a wry smile as she sipped her chilled champagne and closed her eyes.

CHAPTER 11.

The Care Home Security Office.
Gerald Compton sat down in his very compact office. Otherwise known as the cleaning and storage room, it barely had enough room for a small desk and chair and was situated next to the main kitchen at the Chelsea Garden Care Home.

Gerald's shifts at the home were from 4 pm to 4 am, starting on a Wednesday and finishing on a Sunday. This was a much easier and far better job than the one he had had previously. Spending most of his working days arguing with shoplifters was not something he had enjoyed, and not something he was very good at either. Although he was well over 6 feet tall and weighed nearly 16 stone, Gerald's idea of confrontation was immersing himself in *Call of Duty* on his PlayStation 4. Once the local reprobates at the convenience store had worked out that Gerald was a total pushover, pilfering goods on his watch became a daily occurrence. This was made much worse as they also provoked the life out of him on practically every shift.

It was a huge stroke of luck when Vanessa Foxx offered him the job as head of security at the care home. She had bumped into Gerald in the shop and stopped to talk to him. Something generally no one did, unless it was to hurl vitriolic commands at him or complain that a certain item was out of stock. Vanessa told him that he was an exceptionally good security guard, particularly as he refused to resort to violence when dealing with shoplifters. That was very professional indeed. How would he like to become head of security at the prestigious Chelsea Garden Care Home? No cleaning involved. He would even get his own office.

Since accepting the new job, Gerald had never been happier. And because of the shifts that he was doing, he got free food in the evening as well. He didn't get that at his last job. To be fair, if he had worked at the convenience store for much longer, the odds were that he would have been sacked anyway. In Gerald's eyes, Vanessa was his saviour.

There was a knock on the door, followed by the sound of a booming Italian voice. "Spaghetti bolognese whenever you're ready, Big G."

"Thanks, Tony, you're the best," he replied. Gerald knew that spaghetti bolognese was on the menu. This whole end of the care home carried the aroma of it, and to Gerald, it was as good as being in a Michelin-star restaurant. Not that he had ever been in a Michelin-star restaurant, but he had heard Tony talk about them. Gerald liked Tony; he was the nicest of the chefs there. There were two other chefs at the home, one who Gerald didn't really know, as their shifts didn't overlap, and then there was Krystina. She was nice. And very pretty. But she had a boyfriend.

Just as Gerald was about to open the door and retrieve his delicious smelling dinner, a high, shrilling beep reverberated from a panel on the wall behind him and stopped him in his tracks. Some time ago, whilst doing his rounds at the care home, Gerald noticed that one of the doors leading out to the rear car park was secured by an alarm that didn't appear to be working. He knew this because the alarm box on the outside wall above the door didn't have the two little blue lights flashing back and forth like the rest of the alarms on the building. It would have been remiss of Gerald if he hadn't arranged for this to be fixed. He was, after all, Head of Security. So he got an electrician to have a look at the alarm, and apparently, it was really easy to fix. The wire had just been disconnected, the fuse was removed, and the two flashing LEDs were missing. The electrician had said that this was very strange, but at least it was fixed now. Well, almost. The two little blue LEDs hadn't been replaced, and the maintenance man didn't have any spares, but that was fine. Gerald had tested the door after the repair and knew that the alarm was working properly. The fact that the alarm now sounded in his office absolutely confirmed that it was working properly. Gerald felt thoroughly chuffed at this achievement.

The problem now was that this posed a question. Why had the alarm been activated? Who was coming in or going out of the fire door? Gerald felt a mild sweat starting to emerge in his armpits. He didn't like confrontation. Anyway, right now, the most important thing was not to upset Big Tony. Gerald opened the door to his office, picked up his dinner, took it back inside, and closed the door. He was famished. It had been a ridiculously crazy day, which, quite frankly, had taken its toll on him. That crazy woman Dorothea whatshername had no right to scream at him the way she did. Just because she was a stuck-up police officer didn't make her better than anyone else.

And anyway, the door being opened was probably just Vanessa going out the quick way from her office to where she parked her car. Gerald had seen her do it before. Yes, that was what it was. He would go and have a check whilst he was on his rounds after his dinner. He had earned his dinner. And besides, Tony's spaghetti bolognese was his absolute favourite. He reached up to the panel and disarmed the alarm. Smiling to himself, he sat down and started eating.

CHAPTER 12.

Still in the care home – The not-so-secret apartment again.
Vanessa lay back in the bath, enjoying the warmth and peace that flowed over her now, relaxed body. Finally, the smell of excrement had all but evaporated from her nostrils and had been replaced by the scent of lavender and geranium. For the first time in days, she was starting to feel a bit calmer.

Whilst there was bedlam at the care home earlier, clearly Ingrid had got to Anna. The question now was, how to get the information out of that wily old weasel Anna. She was certainly very smart indeed and appeared to be brilliant at playing people. Vanessa had spoken at length to Anna's doctor about her Alzheimer's, and it was clear that death, although not imminent, was just around the corner. But one thing was undeniable. Anna had the resolve and strength of someone much fitter and younger. Moving her to the memory care wing was an inspired move. Vanessa could control the drugs that were given out to her, so she would at least keep her mouth shut when other people were around. The job now was to get the information out of her as quickly as possible. They were closer than they had ever been, but time was running out. When Anna died, the information would die with her.

The click of the handle opening the door to the suite made Vanessa jump and brought her quickly back from her thoughts. A few seconds later, a creak directly outside the bathroom door made Vanessa unconsciously cover up her exposed cleavage as she sat up in the bath. Vanessa moved her steam-dampened hair to one side of her face so that she could see properly. Only one other person held a key card to the room, and Vanessa's excitement prickled through her body at the anticipation of that person entering the bathroom.

CHAPTER 13.

The care home car park.

Dot left the care home and walked back to her car. She unlocked the door and, totally exhausted, almost fell into the seat. Checking her phone, she saw two new messages that were waiting to be answered. She hoped the care team had managed to take possession of her mother's phone; she couldn't handle another call from her right now.

Her mother's dementia had two distinct periodic fundamentals. BD and AD. Before dark and after dark. Generally, before dark, her mother was much less demonstrative and seemed far more peaceful, much calmer, cognisant, and, as Dot had often witnessed, even downright sharp. After dark, well, that was a whole different matter. It was as though sleeping demons had awakened within her body and decided to create merry hell with every part of her brain. Given it was now well after dark, Dot hit play with some trepidation and listened.

"Hi, Dot, it's Jamie. Just wanted to see if you're around later, I wouldn't mind picking your brains on a case study I'm working on for CID. Skip is giving me a bit of grief on it, and I'm not sure what I'm missing. Pizza for payment as usual if you fancy. Let me know, thanks. Oh, yeah, hope Grandma is ok, Dad just rang and said something about her throwing nappies around at other people. Top woman."

Dot couldn't help but chuckle. "Bugger," she thought. The last few hours had been a total blur. Day had turned to evening. In all honesty, she didn't think she had the capacity to problem solve for Jamie at the moment. She would give him a call in the morning. She cut the call and sent off a quick text to Jamie to apologise. Dot knew the Skip, the Police Sergeant that Jamie mentioned. He was fair, but he was also very firm. A bit intimidating, but perfect for mentoring rising stars like him.

Dot hit play again.

"Dot, it's Jim here. Jim McKenzie. I need you to come into the office for 8 am tomorrow. I've got something I have to run past you in person. No ifs, no buts—just be there, please. Thanks."

Dot cut the call. Double bugger. This was not good. The Jim in question was Chief Superintendent James MacKenzie. Her boss's boss. Praise or punishment? She wasn't sure which it was to be. She knew that she was pretty much up to date on her current cases, and her team, consisting of one sergeant and one detective constable, had not been in contact with her since first thing this morning. If anything had happened, there would have been a message alluding to any problems. She thought about texting her direct boss, but given that the message was from Jim, it was inevitable that her boss had been told to say nothing about the meeting. Otherwise, he would have called her himself. She started the Mini with every intention of driving home. It felt a bit chilly. Or was it that she was just dog tired? Either way, she turned the heater up in the car.

Her mind returned to the events earlier with her mother. Something that she had said was bugging her. In fact, a lot of what her mother had said today was bugging her. She had seemed remarkably lucid for much of the time whilst holding Ingrid hostage. She was certainly the most coherent she had been in a while, yet here she was making up the most absurd allegations about Ingrid. Who even thinks up that sort of stuff?

Dot plugged her phone into the car charger, unlocked the screen, and searched for *Steven, Solicitor, Bell Yard, London.* After a few seconds, the search results started to come through. It would seem that Steven appeared to be one of the most popular names in the whole of London's legal profession. She touched the image icon on her phone. One by one, images of Stevens appeared. Nobody looked familiar to her, not even vaguely. She changed her search from Steven with a V to Stephen with a PH. Yet again, an overabundance of Stephens appeared. Nothing that she read was familiar to her, so once again, she changed the search to images. She scrolled through a few pages of different versions of Stephens until one seemed to stand out from the rest. There was something vaguely recognisable with Sir Stephen Rupert Tarquin Hargreaves, retired, of Trereen House in Cornwall.

The problem with being a police officer for as long as she had was the sheer scale of images and people you have to look at throughout the course of an average day. Trying to figure out friend from foe becomes an everyday challenge. There had been previous occasions where Dot found herself nodding or smiling to people that she recognised in the street, only for her to remember later that she had sent them down years before for some crime or another.

But just how her mother would know a London solicitor, now apparently retired and living in Cornwall, let alone a Sir, was something she couldn't fathom. Her mother had clearly told her that she had met the man. And he did seem familiar. Subsequent searches revealed that Sir Stephen had sold his legal practice several years ago to a much larger firm. No doubt for a not-so-insignificant amount of money, given the size of his substantial country pile in the West Country that he now quite possibly lived in.

Sir Stephen's business did indeed used to be based in Bell Yard, London. Dot knew where it was but couldn't think of a single time she had been there. Mind you, given its close proximity to the Law Courts and the Old Bailey, where she had been on numerous occasions, there may have been a possibility that she had proverbially bumped into Sir Stephen at some point. Sir Stephen also appeared to have a propensity towards philanthropic activities, given the large amounts of money he had personally donated to various dementia charities.

A further search showed that Sir Stephen Rupert Tarquin Hargreaves's wife, Lady Karenza, had succumbed to the effects of vascular dementia several years previously, which, no doubt, would account for the generous charitable donations. It certainly looked like she was a popular lady, given the amount of gushing obituary content written about her. All Dot had to figure out now was why this man seemed recognisable to her. There were no contact details available for him other than the house he potentially lived in.

Dot continued reading about Lady Kerenza. Wow. Had Dot been wrong! The house had, in fact, belonged to her and not to her husband. It had been in her family for over five generations and had passed to Sir Stephen upon her death. "Nice one," thought Dot, "the old boy landed on his feet with this one, that was for sure."

Dot opened another page on her phone and clicked on an Ancestry site that she had used previously in the course of her work. It sometimes helped her track down people who otherwise didn't exist on any other database. Dot entered Kerenza Hargreaves into the search box. The page took a while to load, and when it eventually filled the screen, Dot let out an exasperated gasp. She couldn't quite comprehend what she was looking at.

There, right in front of her, the page was headed, 'Karenza Hargreaves Nee LaSalle'. LaSalle. This had to be a coincidence, didn't it, thought Dot. Alongside the narrative was a black and white photograph of what looked like Karenza as a young girl. In the same photograph, taken at, presumably, a summer ball or a birthday party within the grounds of a grand house, Dot found herself staring at another young girl who was standing in a light-coloured, floral-patterned dress. The girl was looking directly at Karenza and smiling. Dot stared at the photograph for quite a few seconds. She realised that her phone was shaking in her hand. There was no doubt about who she was now looking at.

The woman smiling at Karenza in the photograph was her own mother, Anna.

Dot decided she would put an urgent call through to one of her colleagues at Devon and Cornwall Police to see if they held any details or could find a number that she could call Sir Stephen on. Not strictly legal, given there was no official investigation assigned to her enquiries, but this was a massive itch that now needed to be scratched.

Her mind was racing. One old black and white photograph had unleashed a lot of questions. Questions that she needed to find the answers to. She took a screenshot of the photograph on her phone and continued her search for any other potential Stephens but found nothing new or familiar. She contemplated going back into the care home to see her mother, but she knew that would be hopeless. Her mother would have succumbed to her nightly cocktail of drugs by now.

Dot looked at the red LED clock. It was almost 8 pm. She had been in the car for nearly an hour. Her eyes felt heavy, the warmth of the car having enveloped her exhausted body and mind. She sent a quick text to Jack to see if he would be at home or not. She called it text roulette with Jack. She never knew what she was likely to receive in response, if indeed there was a response. Unfortunately, though, the odds of a decent outcome never seemed to be stacked in Dot's favour. A small part of her missed someone opening the front door for her when she got home. But a large part also knew that Jack was happily screwing god knows who, so she had grown used to going home to an empty house. And deep down, she also kind of liked that. Texting Jack was just a habit. And one that she should really stop. She put the car in gear and headed down the gravel drive of the care home. As she approached the exit, an ambulance with blue lights flashing came in past her and pulled up in front of the entrance doors.

She slowed her car to a halt, and her eyes followed its path. She watched as Gerald, the security man, ran out of the entrance doors to greet the ambulance. She continued to watch as the ambulance crew hurriedly loaded up their kit from the rear of the vehicle and then, following Gerald, ran through the main doors. Although seeing ambulances was a regular occurrence at care homes, the main difference this time was the blue lights. Most of the residents had Do Not Resuscitate orders on their files, so generally, there was never a rush for ambulance crews to get to their patients. It would appear, though, that on this occasion, there was no DNR notice in place for whoever it was needing urgent medical attention.

Dot checked her phone. No missed calls or texts. If there was something wrong with her mother, Vanessa would have called. She was sure of it. A stuck-up bitch though Vanessa may be, she was a stickler for the rules, and that meant notifying next of kin of issues very quickly. Dot's phone pinged. She took a breath in before looking, hoping it wasn't Vanessa.

Three words appeared on the screen. *Not home tonight.* Jack had excelled himself. Not only was there a reply, but the text consisted of more than a single word. Dot needed to sort this out once and for all. Her relationship had now become an affiliation by certification only. Nothing else. The main problem with it was that it was exhausting. Irritatingly so. Irritating because Dot was the only one who had given a damn about their marriage. Jack was now just an inconvenient hanger-on, making up his own rules as he lied his way through every day.

Dot was two and a bit years away from her sixtieth birthday, and this was what her life currently consisted of. Failed relationships, part-time carer, and at the moment, part-time bloody police officer. But as usual, her only way of dealing with it all was to compartmentalise her current tempestuous world, have a bloody big slug of cold Chablis, and get some sleep. That's what she needed to do.

She realised that the scent of Chanel No 5 was wearing off and that she still actually stank from the earlier faecal exploits courtesy of her mother. Right now, her head was full to bursting point. Tomorrow was exactly the same. Full.

The boss's boss, her mother, Sir Stephen Rupert Tarquin bloody Hargreaves, Karenza LaSalle, Jamie, and, as always, finally, Jack. She couldn't put off going home to the big empty house in Chiswick any longer. It had three things she desperately needed. A hot shower, a cold glass of Chablis and her bed.

Feeling assured that the care home emergency didn't involve her mother, she started heading back towards the big empty house in Chiswick. Well, at least that's what she thought she was doing.

CHAPTER 14.

Back to the care home.

Dot had turned right out of the care home, off the gravel and onto a tarmac driveway leading down to Chiswick High Road. As she approached the main road, she slammed on her brakes as a BMW 5 Series car hurtled into the lane she had just driven down, very nearly sideswiping her. The BMW was quickly followed by two Metropolitan Police Ford Focus cars with blue lights flashing and doing their damnedest to keep up with the BMW in front.

This blue-light entourage was definitely not for someone who didn't have a Do Not Resuscitate sticker on their file. This was something different.

Dot had managed to stop the mini on the right side of the road. Cursing under her breath at the unknown driver of the BMW, she wondered what the rush was. Mind you, was this really any of her business? She sat for a minute or two and concluded, for whatever reason, that she didn't have a good feeling about what she had just seen. Putting the car into gear, she did a three-point turn and, with wheels screeching, headed back towards the care home car park. She parked the car, threw open the door, jumped out, and headed towards the front of the building where the contents of one of the police cars were already waiting in situ. Two police officers in uniform had positioned themselves prominently at the front of the building. A sergeant and a constable.

As Dot approached the entrance of the care home, the uniformed sergeant held up his hand and stopped her in her tracks. Without saying a word, she reached into her coat pocket, fumbled about, pulled out her warrant card, and handed it to him.

"Made it here pretty quickly, then, ma'am?" the sergeant said as he scrutinised it. "No idea how you heard about this job, we have been radio silent on comms all the way from the nick, and I don't believe your name is on the need-to-know list. I'm under instructions that no one is to be allowed through the doors, doesn't matter who they are or why they are here. No entry is the current order of play."

Unsure as she was about why she was even standing in front of the care home, the sergeant's stubbornly officious manner and lack of respect for her rank helped her decide that, even for the sheer hell of it, she was getting into the building. She changed her stance and held up her hand towards the sergeant in direct response. He had just given one of the best rehearsed versions of bugger off she had heard in a while.

"Look, my mother is a resident in there, and in my book, that gives me a right of access," Dot told him. "Who is the senior investigating officer inside there, the one from the unmarked BMW?" She did her best to stare the sergeant out.

"SIO is DCI Fallon, ma'am," replied the sergeant, doing a very good job of trying not to be intimidated by Dot's rank.

Dot froze. She knew DCI Fallon very well, and her opinion of the man in question was not a virtuous one. The fact that he was there just pushed her even further. She was definitely getting in now.

"Well, if the Serious Crime boys are here, and my mother is also in there, I'm telling you right now I'm going through those doors whether you like it or not. There's currently one single incompetent member of security in charge of this entire care home. If the residents see a bunch of men running around with weapons in there, there won't be enough people trained in the use of defibrillators to deal with the amount of heart attacks that are likely to occur. Now, you either get a lot more officers here right now to hold the fort, or you physically stop me from going in. Your choice."

Both officers looked uncertain. The constable's eyes were firmly fixed on the sergeant, who remained silent for what seemed like minutes and then buckled.

"Apologies, ma'am, just following orders. I hope you understand. In you go, but please do me a favour and say that you entered via an unchecked door if asked. Saves me a right bollocking, ridiculous amounts of paperwork, and months of night shifts south of the river".

"You have my word."

She was already heading towards the entrance doors. Unlike the last time, this time the doors weren't locked and opened in front of her.

The main reception was empty save for the two paramedics who had just returned from wherever it was that Gerald had guided them. They were now packing up the remains of their medical kit into their oversized rucksacks.

Dot looked over at Vanessa's office. The door was closed, and the office was in darkness.

The memory care rooms, where her mother had been moved to, were located on the left side of the building. She had to find out where Fallon was and, more importantly, why he was here.

She walked over to the paramedics and flashed her warrant card as they looked up at her. "You weren't in there for very long at all. What's the situation? Is there a casualty?"

The senior paramedic, a woman who looked in her forties, squatted on the floor. "Been told to keep our mouths shut by the arsehole in charge. One hell of a mess in the room, though. Never seen anything like it in all my years working as a medic." She was clearly disturbed by whatever it was that she had just witnessed.

"Was the casualty male or female? Do you know if they were a resident here?" Dot just needed some bare facts of the situation, and she wanted them quickly.

"Look, we've been told in no uncertain terms to keep our mouths shut." The senior paramedic was now staring down at the floor as she spoke. She was clearly nervous about saying anything at all. "I already told you, the arsehole in charge made it clear that if we didn't, we would be in some very deep trouble. He wouldn't let us stay there. As soon as he arrived, he told us to get out of the room. We've been instructed to go back to base and remain there until the police arrive to take a statement. That's it. And that suits us. Right now, I need a stiff drink."

Dot's mind was racing. What had they seen that had disturbed them so much? She continued to push the medic. "Just tell me if it was male or female. Resident or staff. Please, I need to know. My mother is a resident here, and I can't find her anywhere." She lied to them in the hope they would reveal some details. Any detail. She felt it was necessary to try to find out the truth.

"Female, staff, and looked very bloody deceased to me," said the paramedic.

"Thank you. Which door?"

The paramedic pointed to a corridor next to Vanessa's office. She then turned around, picked up her huge, oversized rucksack, threw it over her shoulder and headed towards the main door with her colleague.

Dot watched them leave, then turned and headed towards the corridor that the woman had indicated. Yet again, she was faced with an infernal security keypad on the door in front of her. Dot hadn't seen the code that Gerald had punched earlier into the keypad on the door leading to her mother's old room.

At that moment, one of the nurses who had helped deal with Ingrid earlier emerged from the memory care corridor, hastily pushing a pharmacy trolley. Hopefully, Anna had been a recipient of some nice, strong sleeping pills after her epic day. Dot pulled out her warrant card once again and held it up in front of the nurse.

"Remember me? You did a brilliant job of looking after my mother earlier. Thank you! Listen, I need to get through this door. A colleague of mine is waiting for me, and I don't have the code. Could you let me through?"

The nurse was about to say something to challenge Dot, but thought better of it. She had seen her performance earlier that day and was in no mood to be on the receiving end of the police officer's anger. She went straight to the door and punched in the key code. Dot watched over the nurse's shoulder to see the digits being entered. The nurse pressed 0000. Gerald, you're a bloody genius, no wonder you're Head of Security. She thanked the nurse once more and pushed the door open.

She walked along the corridor as quietly as she could, having no idea of what to expect ahead. Given the paramedic's description of the scene, she was now on edge. Like the other wings in the building, the room numbers started with 1 or 2, indicating two floors. As far as Dot could see, all of the residents' doors looked shut all along the ground floor where she now stood. There was a uniformed care assistant sitting at a medical station, halfway down the corridor. She was talking quietly on her mobile phone while at the same time being very animated, waving her left arm around in silent explanation of the words she was whispering. There was no police presence that Dot could see on this floor, so she moved quickly back to the beginning of the corridor to the emergency staircase and headed up to the top floor.

Arriving at the fire door, Dot could clearly hear Gerald remonstrating with someone in an incredibly high-pitched voice. She assumed that he was aiming his words at one of the police officers.

"Why have you arrested me? Why have you put me in handcuffs? Please take them off, they're hurting me," cried Gerald. "Why are you doing this to me? I haven't done anything wrong. I'm the one who called you. Why would I call you if I had killed anyone? Please just let me go." He was sobbing uncontrollably.

Dot then heard an unknown voice hiss back at Gerald.

"Sit on the floor and shut your mouth before I fill it with my boot. One more word from you, sunshine, I swear I'll take your eyes out with my pen." The unknown voice clearly lacked the basic skills and manners that should befit any self-respecting police officer.

Dot pushed the fire door open an inch or so and looked left toward the voices. She could see Gerald sitting on the floor, clearly in a position that he had been forced into, as his legs were unnaturally pinned beneath his body. His hands were secured behind his back by handcuffs, and his eyes were very swollen from what Dot hoped was crying and nothing more sinister. She pushed the door open wide and entered the corridor.

Gerald looked up at her. He had pure, unquestionable terror in his eyes. Dot had seen this look in many people over the years. She had learned that the look could have also been mistaken for the wrath of a man who had been caught doing something he shouldn't have been doing. There was a fine line between anger and panic. In Dot's experience, Gerald was in a state of total panic.

The police officer whose voice was unknown turned towards her and stared. He was dressed in a grey suit, white shirt and matching grey tie. He carried the bulk of a man that, no matter what suit he was dressed in, imitated a bag of coal. He looked like he had just stepped out of an episode of *The Sweeney.*

"Strictly off limits, darling. You shouldn't be here; I'm a police officer, and we are currently investigating a crime scene. Now you know who I am, I would suggest that you take your backside from where it came and leave us to do our job. There's a good girl."

Dot, not for the first time that day, put on her best arsey bitch face and started walking toward Gerald and the unknown voice man. "Right now, the only crime I can see being committed is the way you are treating a valued member of staff from this care community. Unless he is actually under arrest, then, for starters, you are committing gross misconduct as far as I'm concerned. And just for your records, this backside has a name and rank. I am Inspector LaSalle. Now, who the hell are you?" Her voice was unwavering, and her stare was ice cold.

Gerald started sobbing even louder than before and was about to say something to Dot.

"Not a word, Gerald, not yet," she said, shaking her head at him. She was now standing at the end of the corridor where the unknown voice stood directly outside the room, displaying a guarded male macho stance with legs wide apart and arms folded across his chest.

"Guv," shouted the unknown voice through the slightly open door of the room that he appeared to be guarding. "You'd better get out here. I think we might have a problem."

"Oh, you have a problem alright," Dot told him.

The door was pulled open, and a man dressed in white coveralls over a dark suit, dark blue shirt and no tie emerged.

"Bloody hell, what's that smell? It stinks like a public convenience out here. So, what's wrong? Has the suspect got the better of you, Charlie? Thought you said you could manage big boys."

The man in the coveralls and suit paused, stared straight at Dot, and sniggered. "Well, well, well. You don't look like much of a problem to me. But you do look very familiar; I know you, don't I? Of course I do. Detective Chief Inspector Fallon, by the way, but I'm sure you remember that."

Dot found herself staring at what ordinarily would have been a very dapper man. A man who she very much remembered. Just a bit older with streaks of grey in his dark hair. Standing at around 6ft 2in tall, he was still in very good shape, given the way the suit fitted under his coveralls.

"Well, I can't say it's good to see you again." Dot's voice was intimidating. "Still sexually assaulting innocent women and getting away with it, are you? At least there doesn't appear to be any lasting damage to your right eye socket."

Fallon narrowed his eyes. "Hello, Dot. Still filling in spreadsheets down at the Fraud Office, are you? Couldn't handle working in CID, from what I remember. Never forget a pretty face, or pretty tits for that matter. Eye is fine, thank you, just a hazard of the job, I guess. So, pray tell, what brings a fraud officer to a residential care home in the dead of night and, more importantly, into my jurisdictional crime scene?"

"My mother happens to be a resident here," she said, not taking her eyes off him. "I was just leaving and saw you lot arrive en masse. Given the state of the security arrangements in this place." She paused and then looked directly at Gerald, "I felt it was my duty, as a daughter and concerned officer of the law, to see what was happening and if there was anything I could do to help."

Fallon glared over at Charlie and hissed, "Missed that one, Sergeant, didn't you?"

So, the unknown voice at least had a name and rank now. Dot didn't recognise Charlie, especially given that he looked like an East End boxer; his face wasn't an easy one to forget.

Fallon continued. "The Inspector is very obviously right. The security here would appear to be dreadfully poor. Oh, and just for the record, Charlie, I want to see those two plods from the entrance in my office when I get back to the station."

The sergeant was just about to open his mouth in reply, but the look on DCI Fallon's face made him think twice. "Get a van up here right away and get this big fella away for a nice cup of tea and chat. Get him a shower as well, I think he shat his pants. I'll deal with the unexpected appearance of my esteemed colleague. When you get back to the nick, let the SOCO boys know the situation and tell them I'll call them when it's clear for them to do their stuff. Shouldn't be too long, I don't want to be here all night."

The DCI's tone left the sergeant in no doubt as to the consequences of any failure in carrying out his instructions. The sergeant kicked Gerald in the leg and motioned for him to stand. Gerald was struggling with his hands behind him to get enough leverage to stand up on his own, so the sergeant grabbed hold of the cuffs and yanked him up. Gerald screamed out in pain. The sergeant pushed the whimpering Gerald down the corridor, away from Dot and DCI Fallon. He stopped and turned towards Fallon. "As soon as I'm done at the nick, I'll head back over here." He turned back around and pulled out his phone. He was soon shouting at whoever was at the other end to get an additional officer with a van to accompany him and Gerald to wherever the cup of tea was going to be served. It certainly wasn't going to be at McDonald's.

"So, what does the exact jurisdictional crime scene you happen to be referring to contain, Sir?" Dot said sarcastically. "Oh, and just for the record, I came in through a ground-floor door on the memory wing that was open, not through the front entrance. Told you. Security in this place is not the best." She was trying to establish what was happening in the room behind the door that Fallon stood protecting, at the same time not forgetting her earlier promise to the officers outside the entrance. She might need their help at some point in the future. She was also now very aware that she was alone with a man who had previously sexually assaulted her. A man who had lied through his teeth at the subsequent inquiry, passing the blame to Dot, and had managed to get away with it scot-free.

Fallon stood firmly between her and the door. "This is my crime scene, Dot, and, as such, nothing to do with you, alright. So, you can cut the bullshit about your mother and tell me why you're really here." Fallon was getting more aggressive as he spoke. "And let's not get caught up in the past, eh? Just a small misunderstanding from what I remember. Let bygones be bygones and all that."

Dot was sure that Fallon was grinning inside as he remembered exactly what he had done to her. Lack of any factual evidence, according to the subsequent sexual assault inquiry. It was all hearsay. That's what they had told her. Inadmissible. That's what the final report said. The same report concluded that it was very noble of Fallon not to press charges of assault against Dot, given the severity of the eye injury she had inflicted upon him.

Fallon stared straight at Dot, waiting for a reply.

"My mother is here. I saw an ambulance with blues on, and then not long after, you and the cavalry nearly took me out in my car. Police officers are curious by nature. That's why I'm here.

"This is none of your business. One of the residents has had a bad day, that's all. This is my case, and in all honesty, the last thing I need right now is to be stuck here in God's bloody waiting room all night with you poking your nose in. And before you ask, everything I've just told you will be all doc'd up and logged, so nothing new for you to find. Now, not to labour the point any more, why don't you pop along like the good Inspector you are and go and see your mother, eh? There are a couple of residents on this floor who will be evacuated to the lounge downstairs, and the staff will no doubt give them tea and garibaldis. And with all due respect, you look like you could do with a drink yourself. Forgive me if I don't do the decent thing and offer to take you out for one; you seem to have a habit of losing your temper from what I remember." His voice was calm but carried a cold, sinister undertone.

Dot didn't bite. "Where is Vanessa, Fallon, the Exec Director of the care home? Why isn't she here, given you appear to have arrested her head of security for murder? Have you called her? Has she any idea of what's happened here?" She was desperate to find out more, but knew that Fallon was extremely pissed off that she was even there in the first place. She also knew that Fallon had a terrifying temper, having been on the receiving end of it. She was also not forgetting the fact that he outranked her.

Fallon looked straight into her eyes. He was calm. "Firstly, never forget LaSalle. It's DCI Fallon. Now. You tell me. When was the last time you actually saw or spoke to Vanessa, Inspector?"

Dot, taken somewhat off guard by the question, replied, "I've done both a number of times today. It's been a particularly busy day here, so I would have imagined that Vanessa would be tucked up at home, no doubt with a bottle of champagne intravenously connected to her arm. You obviously haven't spoken to her then?"

"Well, I'm glad you find this amusing, Inspector.

Clearly, Dot hadn't concealed her own image of Vanessa well enough.

"So, Dot, are you going to tell me? When was the last time you actually saw Vanessa? How was she when you last saw her?" Fallon's voice had lost its calmness, and he had switched into hard interview mode. Dot knew the score very well indeed. She used the same technique herself most days. Her voice, though, was nowhere near as cold as Fallon's.

"It's Vanessa in there, isn't it?" she said. "It's her in that room; it's her that's been murdered. Gerald said that he didn't kill anyone. For him to say that must mean that someone has to be dead. Is it her in that room, is it Vanessa?"

Fallon was silent for a few seconds. You could almost hear the gears grinding in his head about what he was going to say next. "Firstly, I wouldn't believe anything that resident delinquent says. And secondly, I would curb your imagination, Inspector. You, of all people, know that rumours do nothing to help an investigation. Now, go and find your mother, make sure she is ok. This is way out of your league. I have one of my officers briefing the staff to keep things here as normal as possible, and the nick is sending me a couple more plods to help out if needed. We'll cover security until a replacement is found, so that should keep you happy. One of the residents is dead, and we're dealing with it. That's it. That's all you need to know. Now, as the senior officer in charge here, I'm not asking you to go and see your mother, I'm telling you. And when you're done with that, get your nose out of my business and stick to your own patch."

She was about to reply to Fallon but thought better of it and saved her response for another day.

Fallon took a step forward. His face was now within inches of Dot's face. His breath smelled of mints. Exactly the same as it had when he had sexually assaulted her. She shivered. He whispered, "And remember this. One more word from you and I'll make sure you'll be up in front of the Chief Super first thing in the morning. And when that's done, you will be washing traffic cars by lunchtime." He stood firm, waiting for her to respond.

She nearly smiled at the irony of what Fallon had just said to her. As it currently stood, she was up in front of the Chief Super in the morning anyway. She turned and went to walk back down the corridor. A few feet down, she stopped. She turned around and walked back towards Fallon until she could smell his breath again.

"If you think for one minute that this is over, Fallon," she whispered, "think again. You got away once before, you piece of shit. I promise you. It won't happen a second time. Whatever you're trying to cover up here will come back and bite you firmly on your arse. And I, for one, know you are covering something up here." Her stomach was churning nervously. She didn't want to give Fallon the satisfaction of seeing her this way, but she had to say something to him.

"Well," he said. "Given that you haven't appeared to age very well at all since our last chat, you won't have to worry about me shagging you again anytime soon. Unless, of course, you decide to start sticking your nose into something that you shouldn't be. Now, do us both a favour, Dot, and get out of here. Otherwise, I really will lose my rag."

She walked up to the far end of the corridor and headed back down the stairs towards reception. She was raging inside, but she knew that Fallon was lying to her. The paramedics had been clear. The body was female and a member of the care home staff. Fallon had told her it was a resident. She believed the medics. As she entered the reception area, she saw Gerald sitting in an office-style chair. His hands were still cuffed, but this time they were securely locked to the chair that he now sat in. His head was down, and he was sobbing softly to himself.

The sergeant was outside talking to the two officers who were there earlier, undoubtedly delivering the good news that they were to report to Fallon as soon as backup arrived.

"I didn't do anything, Miss LaSalle, honest, I didn't. I went up to check the alarm on the fire door at the end of that corridor, that's all." Gerald was now blubbering. His every word started with a deep intake of breath. "The alarm went off when I was having my dinner. But it was spaghetti bolognese, Miss LaSalle, it's my favourite, so I finished my dinner first. And then I went to check the alarm. It was horrible, Miss LaSalle, horrible. I've never seen blood like that before. It was everywhere. The door to the bedroom at the end was open. Who would do that, Miss LaSalle? Who would do something like that?"

The entrance doors at the care home whooshed open, and the sergeant strode through. Dot quickly knelt on the floor, her face now level with Gerald's. His eyes looked sore. Puffy, red, and welled up in tears. She placed one of her hands directly on Gerald's arm. "Who was in the room, Gerald? Who was it? You can tell me, I'm here to help you. Was it Vanessa, Gerald? Was it Vanessa in that room?"

Dot could see the fear in Gerald's eyes as she spoke to him. His eyes then moved over her shoulder to where the sergeant was fast approaching them both.

"Oy, you," he bellowed. "Say one more thing, and I'll do everything within my power to get you a nice little holiday in Belmarsh Prison. Do you know where that is, Gerald? The other men would love a big boy like you to play with in there."

Gerald immediately shut his mouth and looked down at the floor.

Dot pulled his face back up so that she could look straight at him. "Gerald, just tell them the truth and stick to it no matter what. I'll come and see you as soon as I can, I promise. Tell them exactly what you told me and stick to it. Don't sign anything that says something different to what you have told them."

Dot was trying to get the words out in such a way that she knew he would understand exactly. In other words, don't let this Sergeant or Fallon try to stitch you up.

Gerald looked back at Dot and just said, "I don't read so well, Miss LaSalle. I'm scared."

The sergeant stared at Dot and smiled at Gerald's reply. "Guv says you should have disappeared by now, Inspector. Said it was my job to give you a polite nudge out of the front door if you didn't."

Dot knew that he was serious about what he was saying. She looked up at the CCTV camera above the entrance doors and started walking towards them.

"Don't worry about the cameras, Inspector," smiled Charlie. "We have all the disks in our possession, safe and sound. Now off you go. No hard feelings, eh?"

She watched as he uncuffed Gerald from the chair and led him out of the building. The recipient of Charlie's earlier call was now waiting outside in a police van. Gerald glanced back at Dot as he was pushed unceremoniously into the van and out of sight. He looked even more terrified. The sergeant went to the driver's window and began speaking to the occupant at the wheel.

Dot felt exhausted. She knew that he would be back to deal with her imminently. It was getting late, and she needed to prioritise what the hell was happening around her. And quickly. She took her phone out of her back pocket and checked for any new messages. None at all. She wasn't sure if she was relieved or not.

A number of the care staff and nurses had gathered in the main reception area. They were being spoken to by Evie, the senior nurse at the care home. Some of the staff were crying. Dot walked over to listen to what was being said, but, more importantly, to ask if anyone had seen Vanessa recently.

Evie looked tired. "Look," she said quietly to the other staff. "The police have asked that you all remain here until they have spoken to you. So, I suggest that you all wait in the restaurant. The residents still need to be looked after, and we need to make sure none of them is freaked out if they see the police walking around. With a bit of luck, they'll all be gone by the time we start serving breakfast. If we need to, we'll serve the residents in their rooms on a rota basis."

One of the staff put her hand in the air. "Yes, Sophia," Evie said.

"Evie, how long do we need to wait here? I need to get home to the kids. My boyfriend is on earlies, and I haven't got any other cover."

Evie was about to open her mouth in reply when everyone looked up and over Dot's shoulder.

"We'll get you away from here as soon as we can, Sophia. The police just need to ask you all some questions, and then you can continue with whatever it was you were doing."

Dot spun around and found herself facing Vanessa. Dressed in a full black trouser suit with a white blouse. She clearly had time to clean herself up and get changed after the earlier debacle of the day.

Vanessa continued, "Unfortunately, there was an incident here earlier this evening, which the police are now trying to get to the bottom of. The sooner they speak to everyone, the quicker we can get on with things. Hopefully, we can get everything sorted out by the time breakfast is due to be served. Now, as Evie said, we suggest you use the restaurant as your base and do what we always do. Look after our wonderful residents. I'll be along with you when I've spoken in more detail to the police. Now, off you go." She swivelled on her heels and looked directly at Dot. "You look like you have seen a ghost, Dorothea. I leave the care home for a couple of hours to have a shower and look what happens. Now, you will have to excuse me, I believe there is a Detective Chief Inspector who is waiting to talk to me."

Dot was very rarely lost for words, but this was one of those occasions. "Vanessa, wait." She knew she sounded desperate, and that really infuriated her. How was it that this bloody woman waltzed in looking as though she had just stepped out of a Bond Street fashion house, whilst she herself looked like a sleep-deprived miscreant still stinking of her mother's excrement?

Vanessa, who had already begun to walk away, stopped, turned her head, and with steel in her eyes, hissed back at Dot. "What?"

Dot held her breath for a few seconds to allow herself a moment to think. "DCI Fallon told me that she was murdered. What did he tell you, Vanessa?" Dot went with her gut feelings, based on what the paramedics and Gerald had told her earlier that evening and not what Fallon had said about the victim in the room.

Vanessa's cold expression held firm. "The police are looking for Krystina's boyfriend. They need to either eliminate him or arrest him for this awful crime. Now, I believe there is a police officer over there who wishes to remove you from this building. I'll personally ensure that your mother is looked after by my team, as they always do. And I can assure you that you have nothing to worry about until you are allowed back in." Vanessa's tone had a real chill to it.

"So why have they arrested Gerald, Vanessa? He has just been dragged out of here and into the back of that police van out there. This doesn't make sense."

"I have no idea why Gerald has been arrested, Dot. You're the police officer. You figure it out. Now, if you don't mind, I have things to attend to. And looking at what's heading in your direction, so have you."

Dot looked over to see Sergeant Charlie walking towards her, so she started walking towards him. There was no way she was going to give him the satisfaction of throwing her out. Dot's mind was in overdrive. Why had Fallon lied to her, yet Vanessa had seemingly been told the truth? And who was Krystina, and why was she now dead? Gerald seemed truthful in what he had said and was genuinely scared. If they had arrested Gerald for murder, then why were they after the boyfriend? Was he involved, too? And Fallon. Of all people. Why the hell did it have to be Fallon in charge?

As Dot walked past Sergeant Charlie, he smiled and whispered, "Overstayed your welcome again, I see; now bugger off home and stay there until you hear otherwise."

Dot stopped and stared eye-to-eye with the sergeant. "That's bugger off, *ma'am*, you snivelling little shit. You'd better hope and pray that I don't run into you when your backside isn't being covered by Fallon."

She walked across the car park and got into her car. Immediately pulling out her phone, she went on to the Chelsea Garden care home website and typed in Christina. The name Krystina came up instead. Eastern European was Dot's first thought. Her name was included in one of the positive reviews on the site, left by a family member of a previous resident. *Krystina was amazing. She even specially prepared some of Mum's favourite food for her on her birthday. Nothing was too much trouble. Thank you, Krystina.* So, Krystina was one of the chefs at the care home.

Whilst murder, if that's indeed what this was, is a horrible crime, it should be dealt with on its own merits by Fallon. He had been unmistakably clear in telling Dot that the person in that room was a resident, not a member of staff. Why would Fallon say that to Dot? He must surely know that she would eventually find out it was a member of staff who had perished. Evidently, it was easier to say it was a resident. Maybe this would seemingly be more believable. Fallon clearly wanted to cover something up. But what exactly?

Dot watched as the police van containing Gerald and Charlie headed across the gravel entrance and then down towards the road. Along with a whole load of other priorities, one of the first ones was to find out exactly where Gerald was being taken. And why. Her mental to-do list now sat firmly in the overwhelmingly bursting camp.

Her mother had accused a woman called Ingrid of being a German spy and actually held her hostage. Who is Sir Stephen RT Hargreaves, and what the hell is her mother doing in a photograph with another woman named LaSalle? Her mother had never spoken of any family other than her parents. She had made another will without telling her and had taken serious umbrage over Vanessa and Jack, which, to be fair, Dot could wholeheartedly understand, but this. The way she had said it. Pure venom. Was that the disease talking, or was it her? From what Dot had seen, her mother appeared incredibly lucid when she said it.

Now, an alleged murder had taken place at the care home where her mother just happened to be a resident. The SIO also happened to be a salacious, lying piece of shit who has serious history with her, and a sergeant who needed a damn good beating.

Gerald could be in Belmarsh Prison for all anyone knows.

Add to that, a meeting with her boss's boss – on an unknown topic – in a few hours' time, meant only one thing. That Dot needed sleep. She also needed a hot shower and a bloody great big glass of Chablis. It was time to head back to the empty house in Chiswick.

CHAPTER 15.

Not actually Belmarsh.

Sergeant Charlie Mepham sat in the back of the police van, headed to a predetermined police station in London, whilst observing Gerald Compton closely. Mepham was closing in on his thirty years as a police officer, meaning that, in police parlance, retirement, whatever that really meant, was now just around the corner. He had genuinely felt uncomfortable with the way that he had dealt with Inspector LaSalle, but was left with no choice, thanks to Fallon. It was obvious that Fallon didn't want LaSalle anywhere near this investigation, and Mepham acquiesced with his senior officer as always. This close to retirement, the senior officer was always going to win. Mepham had known Fallon for at least a third of his time as a police officer, and while he didn't always agree with Fallon's tactics, facilitating his wishes meant that Fallon had always ensured that Mepham was looked after. And that will certainly mean a far better retirement than the police service could provide for him.

Gerald let out a continuous, low, muffled sniffling sound, only stopped every few seconds by a big inhale of the runny mucus that threatened to drop onto the floor of the van.

Mepham threw Gerald some blue roll that was kept in the van, generally used to clean up vomit or blood on the weekend shifts.

"For crying out loud, wipe your bloody nose and stop sniffing. Now, when we get to the station, you're going to get asked an awful lot of questions by some important people. If you don't answer them properly, they won't be very nice to you. Do you understand me, Gerald?" Mepham stared directly at Gerald as he spoke to him.

Gerald shook his head at Mepham and simply said, "It wasn't me; I didn't do anything."

"Well," replied Mepham, "obviously someone did it, Gerald. That kind of mess doesn't happen on its own now, does it? You must have been angry with her, Gerald; her face was beaten to a pulp, and she had been stabbed in her neck. What made you do it, Gerald? Did Krystina not like you? Did she not want to have sex with you, Gerald? Was that it? Did you get angry when she told you not to touch her? Answer me, Gerald. I promise it will be much easier to tell me the truth now. The people who will talk to you later won't be anywhere near as nice as I am. I'm trying to help you here, Gerald. You need to answer me; you need to tell me the truth. The more I know, the more I can help you. If you don't help me, then things will get nasty for you, Gerald, and we don't want that now, do we?"

Gerald was shaking his head furiously. "It wasn't me; I'm telling you it wasn't me. I like Krystina, she is really nice, and she used to give me snacks from the kitchen, but she had a boyfriend. I didn't like her that way. I didn't want to have sex with her; she had a boyfriend." Gerald's voice sounded even more desperate. "You can't just make up things about me that I haven't done. I have told you the truth. Miss LaSalle told me to tell you the truth, and that's exactly what I've done. I want to talk to her; I want to speak to Miss LaSalle."

Mepham could see this was going nowhere in the brief time he had with Gerald in the van. It was becoming clear that there wasn't going to be a confession forthcoming anytime soon. "This isn't her case, Gerald, and she is not allowed to be anywhere near you. She won't be able to help you. So, if you know what's best for you, just tell me the truth and confess. We know you were alone in that room with Krystina; we know that you have blood on your clothes. We know that you went into the kitchen earlier, and we know one of the knives is missing from the kitchen in the care home. When we find the knife, we know it's going to have your fingerprints on it, Gerald. If you tell me the truth, I can make things go a lot smoother for you when we get to the station. Do you know what happens to rapists and murderers in prison, Gerald?"

By now, Gerald was openly sobbing. "It wasn't me. I didn't do it. And they can't be my clothes; there was no blood on my clothes. I looked in through the door and saw her lying on the floor in all that blood. I didn't go in. I called for an ambulance straight away, and they told me that the police would come as well. Look. See. My clothes are clean; there's no blood on my clothes."

Mepham took a deep breath and let out a loud exhale. He opened a metal box on the van's floor and took out two pairs of white forensic overalls and a police evidence bag. "Take off your clothes, Gerald and put these on. You need to wear them when you get to the station." He threw the coveralls over. "And do it now, we're nearly there."

Mepham quickly pulled his own coveralls on. Gerald was still hesitating. Mepham stood up and grabbed one of the handrails to steady himself. He reached down to his side and took out his expandable baton from its cover. "You either put the overalls on now, or I'm going to arrest you for resisting arrest and assaulting a police officer. Your choice," he said.

Still, Gerald didn't move. Dammit, thought Mepham. He would have to stay in his clothes. Bad protocol, but he was about to become a violent prisoner. Gerald said, "Miss LaSalle told me to tell you the truth, and that's what I've done, and that's all I'm going to do. She told me she would come and see me, and I believe her, so I'll wait for her to tell me what to do next. You have the truth, and that's it."

Mepham moved quickly and stood over Gerald. The police officer took hold of Gerald's head in both hands and then smashed his own head, face first, down onto the top of the security guard's head. There was an immediate explosion of blood as Mepham's nose split open. He wiped away his own blood, flicked his baton so that it was fully extended, and then swung it as hard as he could at Gerald's head. Mepham repeated the procedure until Gerald collapsed unconscious on the floor of the van.

The police driver's voice came through on the intercom. "All okay in there, Skip?"

Mepham replied, "How long until we get to the nick? The bastard headbutted me, had to gently persuade him to settle back down. All under control now, though."

The voice over the intercom replied, "Shit, ok, Skip. Blues are going on, should be there in six or seven minutes, do we need to stop?"

"No, no, let's just get to the nick. As I said, it's all under control back here." Mepham now had to move quickly. He pulled Gerald flat, no easy task given the man's size. Ensuring that he was still unconscious, Mepham took Gerald's right hand and started thumping it hard against the floor of the van. He continued until the knuckles were clearly broken and blood covered the hand. He then reached into his own jacket pocket and removed a small black-handled knife. He took Gerald's hand and gripped it as tightly as he could around the handle. He then placed the knife into the police evidence bag and put the bag back into the metal box.

His nose was throbbing and hurt like hell. Genuine tears were falling down his face and streaking into his blood that was still dripping from his nose. He pulled Gerald into a more upright position and slapped his face a couple of times to rouse him. Slowly, Gerald came round.

"Gerald Compton, I am arresting you on suspicion of murder, resisting a police officer, and assaulting a police officer. You do not have to say anything unless you wish to do so. Do you understand me?"

Gerald could hear the police officer saying something to him, something about being arrested, something about murder, something about assault. Gerald's head was on fire. He had never felt pain like it. He rubbed the top of his head with both hands and then stared. He was shocked to see them covered in thick blood.

Gerald leaned over and threw up all over the floor of the police van.

CHAPTER 16.

Chiswick. The House.

Dot pulled up across the pea-shingled gravel drive in front of her house. Jack's car, as usual, wasn't there. To anyone passing, the house was a beautiful late Victorian property with symmetrical windows and a stunning tiled pathway leading from the driveway to the front door. Set back on a street with quite a few similar properties all vying to look their best, it gave the impression of a happy family home. All Dot saw now, though, were the remnants of a marriage all but deceased and the torment of living there with her mother through the middle stages of dementia.

Triggered by Dot's car, the security lights switched on automatically and illuminated the driveway and front garden with three 400W halogen lamps. In other words, near enough the same amount of lighting required to guard Buckingham Palace. Jack had insisted on installing them when Anna was living at the house. If she escaped, at least they would know about it and see her running away, something she had attempted on more than half a dozen occasions. Still, it was just like Jack to install a security system that would no doubt make the neighbours downright envious or just bloody annoyed at the intrusive illuminations. Either way, just like Jack, it was always over the top.

Dot emptied herself out of the car and walked down the path. She unlocked the front door and wearily entered the dark house. The alarm box on the wall behind the door started to beep, and a green light flashed. She entered the numbers 0445. Her month and year of birth. The light stopped along with the beeping. She kicked off her shoes in the tiled entrance hall, which felt cold on her feet. Walking down the hall, she entered the kitchen and switched on the light. She opened the fridge, took out an open bottle of her favoured Chablis, and poured the entire contents into a large bowl-shaped wine glass.

She sat down on a metal barstool at the kitchen island and took a big, single swig of the wine. The alcohol ran down her insides, and Dot closed her eyes as it seemed to warm her through. To be honest, Dot wasn't sure if the wine was actually relaxing her, or if, now that she had stopped, her body was just totally and utterly exhausted. Anyway, whatever it was, something was working its temporary magic on her as she started to try to figure out what the hell was going on in her crazy world.

Her mental to-do list was playing pinball in her head, which was causing her to panic over the order of priority. Everything seemed a priority right now, and her head hurt. She looked over at a pile of unopened letters in the middle of the island. Jack must have been at the house at some point and taken in the post. Strange, she thought. As long as he was on his own, she didn't really care. Mind you, it was nice of him to tell her. She leaned over, slid the envelopes across and started separating them into two piles. Hers, and recycling. Jack had obviously been expecting something in the post. Dot knew this, as he never left the post on the table. There was nothing for him other than the usual junk mail.

There were two pieces of post for Dot. One letter was offering her zero per cent on another credit card balance switch. She hadn't used the credit card she had for as long as she could remember. She threw that letter in the junk pile. The other was from the phone company she used for her mother's mobile phone. Intrigued to see exactly how many times her mother had called her in the past month, she opened the envelope. There were five double-sided statement sheets inside. Each sheet must have had at least 60 entries. No wonder she was exhausted. Her mother would have been better employed in a scam call centre in India, banging out numbers like that day and night.

As Dot was looking down the list, she noticed another number that had been dialled and texted at least 20 times. It wasn't a number Dot recognised, and it wasn't on the Orange Telecom family package she used with her mother. In other words, each text had cost twenty pence. Not that the cost mattered, as the bill was paid out of the Power of Attorney account, it's just that, well, her mother had never once sent her a text. In fact, Dot had had several conversations with her mother about getting her to send texts. It would help keep her mind active as well as make it easier for Dot to read messages rather than having to listen to endless voicemails.

She was very tempted to call the mysterious number, but it was far too late at night. She would call it in the morning. Just one more thing to add to her mental to-do list. She finished off her wine, put the empty glass in the sink and headed upstairs for a shower and then to bed. She set her alarm clock for 6 am. That meant about 7 hours sleep.

CHAPTER 17.

Not Actually Belmarsh – Part 2.

Sergeant Charlie Mepham waited inside the police van as it came to a complete stop. The rear door was knocked on twice from the outside. Mepham knocked back twice in response, and the door was opened by the driver. Mepham took a big breath in. The fresh air tasted sweet against the acrid stench of vomit that covered the floor of the van. He pulled Gerald up from the plastic bench and ushered him out of the open door of the vehicle. Gerald's bulky frame, along with the fact that he was still handcuffed behind his back, made this a difficult task.

The driver of the police van pulled at Gerald's right arm while Mepham gave a push from behind. Gerald stumbled, tripped on the metal step attached to the rear of the police van and fell into a heap on the tarmac. He yelled out in pain as the right-hand side of his face connected with the gritty road surface. Mepham jumped out of the van and stepped over Gerald. He was certainly relieved that there was another officer to witness the fall. There was going to be enough paperwork generated on this one as it was.

Gerald was quietly sobbing again, the side of his face covered in blood and tarmac grit, as he was about to be led into the custody suite of the police station to be checked in. He had absolutely no idea what was going to happen to him, but he knew that whatever it was, given what had just happened to him in the back of the police van, it wasn't going to be good. He had to see Inspector LaSalle.

Mepham and the driver picked up Gerald and escorted him, side by side, to the rear door of the police station.

"The van's a crime scene," Mepham said to the police driver. "I need you to secure it for me. You handle that, and I'll deal with big boy from here. Leave your details on the front seat of the van for me and stick the key in the visor. I need to take the van back to the scene for SOCO to do their stuff. If you head round to the front of the nick, they'll get you back to where you need to be. Thanks for your help, I'll let you know when you're needed for witness statements." He pressed the buzzer and watched as the driver nodded and walked back to the van. There was a loud click, click, click noise, and Mepham pulled the heavy door open.

He walked through into a corridor, firmly holding the handcuffs that restrained Gerald as he led him directly to a high counter where the duty custody sergeant stood. He was clearly waiting for them to arrive. The custody sergeant was an enormous man, standing around 6ft 7in and weighing over 17stone. Very few guests at the custody suite ever argued with him. "So, I assume this is DCI Fallon's precious cargo from the care home, Mep. Murder, eh?"

"News travels fast, Terry, but glad to hear you got the right information. Add resisting arrest and assaulting a police officer onto that as well." Mepham replied.

"Yeah, I can see he gave you a bit of a rough ride. Do you need something for that busted nose of yours?"

"Been broken a few times before, Terry. Let's just get this done, eh?"

Terry was in a similar situation to Mepham. He was at the tail end of his career in the police and worldly wise to just about every suspicious human characteristic that there was. Outwardly a wholehearted devotee of the police service, inwardly a man who knew every trick there was to know about how to get away with most things that needed to be buried.

"And Terry," thought Mepham, "had buried a lot of things."

Terry ushered to Gerald to come and stand directly in front of the desk. "Judging by the amount of blood on your clothes and your head, you were quite a handful for my colleague here. We have a bit of paperwork that we need to get together to make your stay here as comfortable as possible. And don't worry, before you ask, I've already requested for a nurse to come down and give you the once over to make sure that you're fit enough to deal with what's going to happen to you here. We don't want to get accused of not following our health and safety procedures for a VIP client like you, now do we? Do you understand me, son?" Despite sounding calm and supportive, Terry's dark eyes were staring directly at Gerald. And they were cold. Ice cold.

Gerald offered no response to Terry's question.

Terry continued. "I'll take that as a yes, then. Do you have anyone that you would like us to contact to let them know you're here, Gerald?"

Gerald lifted his head and nodded. "I want to have Miss LaSalle here. Please tell her where I am. She promised to help me. She is a police officer. An Inspector, I think. Ask him, he knows her."

Terry looked over to Mepham, who shook his head.

"Ok, I'll see what I can do to locate this Miss LaSalle for you. In the meantime, do you know why you are here?"

Gerald just stared down at the ground and muttered very quietly, "I should not be here, I haven't done anything wrong." He looked up and stared at Mepham. "He attacked me in the van for no reason, and I want to complain about him. He is a bully." He stared back down at the ground.

"I understand," said Terry, who had stopped writing notes on the log sheet. "Sergeant Mepham, would you please remind our friend here of the charges of which he has been accused, please."

Mepham nodded. "The man before you, named Gerald Compton, has been accused of murder, as well as resisting arrest and assaulting a police officer. The SIO, DCI Fallon, will be along in due course to assist with the interview process.

"Thank you, Sergeant Mepham. Gerald Compton, as Custody Sergeant, I am authorising your detention until such time as a nurse or doctor can check you out to ensure that you are medically fit, both mentally and physically, to be questioned and, if necessary, further detained here or in an appropriate medical institution. The senior investigating officer, along with Sergeant Mepham here, has confirmed you have been cautioned and arrested for the charge of murder, and I will now let the SIO know that resisting arrest and assaulting a police officer be added to your charge sheet. As such, we need to ensure that you have every opportunity to receive the best possible defence. I'll allocate a duty solicitor to you, who will come to see you after you have been given the all-clear to stay here by the medical staff. At this time, I do not think that you're in any fit state to answer any further questions. Do you understand me, Gerald?"

Gerald had started to sob quietly. He looked up, wiped his eyes, and simply said, "Her, I want her, I want Miss LaSalle."

"Look, Gerald," Terry said. "Finish off my cup of tea here. It's got four sugars in it, and you look like you need a sugar fix it right now. Get it down your neck, son, it will help."

Gerald took the plastic cup and swallowed the warm liquid in one gulp. He was parched, and his mouth tasted of vomit.

Terry looked over to Mepham. "Put him into Cell 6. Bottom on the right. I'll take care of him from there."

Mepham pushed Gerald toward the short corridor that contained the six holding cells. Once outside the open door to cell 6, Mepham undid the handcuffs, gave Gerald a gentle shove into the cell and pushed the heavy metal door shut. Mepham slid the metal plate that obscured the viewing glass to one side. Gerald stood in the middle of the cell with his back to the door. His shoulders were moving along to the rhythm of his sobbing. Mepham stood watching for a couple of minutes and then slid the plate shut, turned, and walked away.

He walked straight past Terry, who was looking down at the paperwork on his desk and continued towards the door that he had entered not ten minutes earlier. As he pulled back the release mechanism of the door and exited the custody suite, Mepham turned his head and looked back to see the huge frame of the custody sergeant, who had now left his paperwork, walking down the short corridor towards Cell Number 6.

Mepham exited through the door, watched it shut and then headed back towards the police van. Although it was late, he still had a number of loose ends to tie up. And tie them up quickly. He reached into the inside pocket of his jacket and took out a mobile phone. He selected the top number on his dialled list and pressed the green button. The phone was answered almost immediately. "Just waiting for the medical assessment to be completed at the station. The evidence bags for forensics will be wrapped up in a couple of hours, guv."

"Good work, Sergeant. SOCO will be here by six am. The scene will be yours to protect until then, which I assume is more than ample time to complete all of your relevant enquiries. See you at our briefing in the morning, then afterwards you can get some sleep." The phone clicked as the line went dead.

Mepham placed the phone back into the inside pocket of his jacket, opened the back door of the van and went over to the metal lock box. The smell inside the van was still repulsive but ridiculously had a tang of Italian herbs to it. He removed the evidence bag that held the knife from the back of the van and closed the rear door. He then walked round to the driver's door, opened it and jumped up into the seat. The call he had just made confirmed that the scene he was about to head to would be clear for him to tie up his loose ends. And once he did, that was it; he was calling it quits. All favours were now repaid. Repaid in full. Mepham was done. He flipped down the sun visor and retrieved the key to the van.

Adjusting the driver's side wing mirror, he then spent the next few minutes deliberately re-tuning the FM radio until he got Capital Radio. He kept checking in the mirror until he saw a red intermittent flash of the internal custody suite alarm being emitted through the small, barred window above the back door that broke through into the darkness.

No doubt, somewhere in the building, a couple of plods were running towards the custody cells. He unconsciously touched his very sore and very broken nose. To be honest, it looked worse than it felt. The nose had been broken several times before, but it would clean up pretty well. He would have a shower and a handful of paracetamol when he was finished, and in a few days, he would be left with just two black eyes for a couple of weeks. Ridiculously, his wife even found it quite sexy. That would indeed be a welcome bonus.

He started up the engine, put the van into gear and drove up to the electronic door through which he had entered earlier. He watched as the gates opened up in front of him. When they were fully open, he pushed his foot hard down on the accelerator. He was headed back to the Chelsea Garden care home for the final time. The sooner he got there and sorted out what was about to become Gerald's mess, the sooner he could walk away for good.

CHAPTER 18.

Chiswick – The House Again.
Dot woke with a start. She shivered as she opened her eyes, which felt as though they had a handful of sand thrown into each one. It was still dark. She had fallen asleep on top of the covers, still wearing the bathrobe she had put on after her shower. The clock radio glowed 4.36 am in a deep red hue. She lay still for a few seconds, allowing her eyes to adjust to the dark, swung her legs off the bed and stood up.

After pulling on a sweatshirt and joggers, she made her way barefoot downstairs into the kitchen and flicked the kettle on. Her head was starting to wake up, but the short sleep had done nothing to dispel the feeling of exhaustion and that sense of jet lag that comes with sleep deprivation. She took a huge cup from an overhead cupboard, filled it with two teaspoons of coffee, the same of sugar, and poured the boiling water in. Stirring the black liquid enhanced the smell of coffee, which seemed to kick her mind into gear. She left the kitchen, entered the hallway and walked to the study. The door was open, and she headed over to the large old Chinese rosewood desk, pulled out the chair and sat down. She bent down and hit the on button for her desktop computer. As she sat waiting for the screen to come alive, something didn't feel right. The only light in the study was coming in from a street light. Enough to see to turn on the computer. She leant across the desk and switched on the tacky brass lamp that Jack had bought from Camden market. She turned around in her seat and froze. Every drawer in the two filing cabinets on the back wall of the study had been pulled open. On the floor in front of them were piles of files that had been taken out. Meticulously taken out. And then placed neatly on the wooden floor. Looking at the tabs on the files, they were all in alphabetical order. This was not Jack. The files. The post placed neatly in the kitchen. This was someone else. Jack was not a neat and tidy person.

Dot got up from the chair and moved back to the hall where she turned on the light. Her senses were now fully alert. She had gone into three rooms when she got back last night. There were nine other rooms in the house to check. She stopped and listened. All she could hear was the ticking of the oversized wall clock in the kitchen.

She headed towards the lounge. If someone had entered the house, it must have been either through the lounge or dining room on the ground floor. The alarm had been set when she got home earlier. She would have noticed if the kitchen windows had been tampered with, and the window in the study was firmly shut. All of the windows had locks on them. Thanks to her mother having lived at the house, Jack had put more locks on windows and doors than Fort Knox.

She checked every unentered room one by one. All were as they should be. No one in them. No broken windows. Nothing. Yet someone had been here looking for something. There was nothing in the filing cabinets that anyone could want. The drawers just contained the usual crap. House stuff. Insurance. Bank statements. Warranties. Her mother's Power of Attorney documents and medical information. She looked again at the files. The one containing her mother's power of attorney documents was empty, along with all of her medical details. Jack had laughingly called the file 'Anna – Boring Stuff'. But who the hell would want to take those? They were useless to anyone but Dot. She was the Power of Attorney. Maybe Jack did take them. She couldn't come up with any other rational explanation. But why take out all the files from the cabinet? She walked back into the kitchen and took her mobile phone off charge. Opening a new text message, she simply said, *Jack. Call me. NOW!*

It had to be Jack. No one else knew the alarm code. Nothing was broken or out of place. But Jack was impossibly untidy. He always had been. He always would be.

"Right," Dot said aloud, as if telling any hidden strangers that she wasn't scared or tolerating any shenanigans. "Let's see if we can make some sense of this bloody mess." She walked back into the study and sat down.

She logged onto her work system and, for now, ignored the sixty-plus emails that sat in her inbox. She started by checking for any information regarding Sir Stephen Rupert Tarquin Hargreaves on the Police National Computer. Nothing came up. That meant, not only was he apparently clean as a whistle, but that his legal work was more than likely civil rather than criminal.

Next, she typed in the name that she was most puzzled about. 'Karenza Hargreaves, nee LaSalle'. For Dot, this was personal. A single entry appeared on the screen in front of her. In 1980, it seemed that Karenza had been involved in a car accident and was subsequently arrested for drunk driving. Annoyingly, there was no file attached, with the copy of a driving licence. Even more annoyingly, though, there was no further information at all on the case involving Karenza. No charge sheet information, no sentencing information, nothing. This was unusual. Or just downright lazy. Dot wasn't sure which, but she was annoyed.

She decided to look up Truro Police Station employees to see if there were any names that she recognised. One name came up. An inspector who had been on the same four-day driving course as her, a few years ago. Dot sent him an email, asking in very roundabout terms for any information they held locally on Sir Stephen and Lady Karenza; in particular, if they could get a phone number for him. She didn't want to raise any suspicions, given that Sir Stephen seemed to be a local philanthropic heavyweight and Lady Karenza was deceased, so she just gave the impression that a colleague in London was trying to find out some details on an old client, and she was doing this individual a favour.

She decided to send two more emails. The first was to the DVLA, requesting any information on Lady Karenza. The second was to the General Register Office, requesting both her birth and death certificates. Her head was spinning even at the thought of this request. What would it mean if she found out that her mother had indeed had a sister? A sister who belonged to the aristocracy. Which meant that her mother also belonged to those very aristocratic circles as well. Circles that her mother had never once spoken to her about, and quite frankly, circles that her mother had always given the impression of despising. This also meant that Dot herself could well be a part of this aristocratic family. If so, this would be beyond crazy.

Next, before cold calling it, she typed in the mobile number that was listed on her mother's telephone bill. Remarkably, it came up as a hit on the system. Even more remarkably, though, it came up as a restricted file. Very restricted. Maybe if there were just one entry of the number on the bill, it might be a total coincidence or a wrong number, but there were multiple listings of the same number. This was no coincidence. Who on earth had her mother been texting, and, more importantly, why?

Dot felt frustrated. She knew that attempting to open the file would raise an alarm somewhere deep in the bowels of the police IT vaults, but then again, she had nothing to lose. It was her mother's phone, after all, and not hers. Her mother had lost mental capacity and would therefore be unable to answer any questions from the IT police, and Dot would just say she was doing her due diligence as Power of Attorney for her mother and trying to find out who she was speaking to. Seemed credible. Sod it.

She clicked on the restricted file, and immediately the screen greyed out. Automatically disabled. Let's see who gets in contact with her now, and equally as important, how quickly. She muttered again under her breath. Why would her mother be texting someone on a restricted list? Dot was wrestling with every angle of the current scenario in her head for a glimmer of a clue. So far, there was nothing.

Her mother had worked for the British government for years, which of course always sounded very James Bondish, but she was a pension specialist. Her job was dealing with insidiously boring things like final salary pensions, state pensions, and mathematical and actuarial equations. She complained about it all the time.

Whenever Dot had asked her about her job, she just waved her hand and gave a big sigh. "Boring, boring, boring, Dorothea," she would say nonchalantly and change the subject. She did say she was exceptionally good at what she did, though, and, given the decent amount of benefit her mother was getting paid from her own government pension, she was clearly quite senior in her department. However, this left her about as far away as you can get from being involved in anything remotely malicious or criminal that would lead to being in contact with a restricted individual. Still, Dot thought, if the number on the restricted list was anything for anyone to be concerned about, her phone would ring. And if they were really concerned, then it would ring pretty soon.

Dot looked at the time at the bottom right-hand corner of her computer. It was now 5.45 am. She had one last thing to cross off the urgent list before she could give herself time to think about why Chief Superintendent McKenzie wanted to see her in just over two hours. She typed Chelsea Garden Care Home into her computer. This was not strictly legal but given the severity of the events of the last few hours, she felt justified in what she was doing.

The list of entries that appeared in front of her was quite long. The majority of these entries were linked to various wanderings by patients from the home where the police were informed or attended. Given the lack of quality of the security arrangements at the home, Dot was hardly surprised. There was one entry that, at first, made Dot chuckle, then as she continued to read the details, her expression changed.

The Regional Director, responsible for fourteen luxury care homes, just happened to be one Vanessa Foxx. Miss Foxx had been formally cautioned on a number of occasions as a result of appalling security arrangements and constant call outs of the police, mostly during the small hours, to search for wandering residents attempting their great escapes. Any further breaches would result in action being taken against her and the care home company. This made Dot chuckle.

What didn't make Dot chuckle was that the senior investigating officer, responsible for signing off the most recent call-out, just happened to be one Detective Chief Inspector Patrick Fallon, the same nasty bastard Dot encountered the previous evening. This made her gasp out loud. What the hell was a senior officer like Fallon doing signing off on what was, in police terms, nothing more than a misdemeanour? Surely, this can't be a coincidence. If it were, that means that the last 24 hours had been one colossal coincidence. Was it just pure coincidence that Fallon happened to be the SIO last night at the care home? Or was there something else at play here that she didn't yet know about?

Vanessa was a total bitch, that much was true, but anything beyond that? Surely Vanessa couldn't be involved in anything other than a bit of lax security. On its own singular merits, this could be a coincidence, but with everything else that had happened, it had to be anything but.

Dot thought back to the previous night and her promise to Gerald that she would help him. She would find out exactly which police station he had been taken to, but right now she needed to concentrate on the next item on her mental to-do list. The meeting with her boss's boss. Why she had been summoned, she had no idea. But given the state of her life and what had happened in the last 24 hours, she harboured a feeling that whatever it was, it wasn't going to make her life any easier.

CHAPTER 19.

London – The posh police station, via the not so posh police station.

Dot drove out of the driveway of her home at 7.00 am. Even in traffic, the drive to the Chief Super's office should only take thirty-five minutes or so, but she wanted to swing by her own office, which was on the way, first.

As she entered the police station car park, it was already mostly full. She found a space, parked up and headed towards the main entrance. She swiped her security pass and entered the building. The desk sergeant looked up.

"Morning, guv. Been busy out there by the sound of things then."

"What makes you say that, Andy? Only been out of the office a couple of days. Morning, by the way."

Andy nodded at the greeting and continued. "Been a bit of coming and going. Asking your whereabouts, that kind of thing. Not really in an official sense, if you get my drift, more in a nosey way. Of course, I directed him straight back to Laney and Tony. You only just missed them, to be fair."

Laney was Detective Constable Elaine Craddock, and Tony was Sergeant Tony Elkins. They were Dot's team.

"Bit of smarminess from said enquirer, if you ask me, but, hey, who am I to know what motives people have nowadays?" Andy was basically saying, I'm watching your backside for you. Policing is as much about internal politics and chest thumping as it is about actual policing. The higher you stick your head above the ranking parapet, the bigger the target you become. For good stuff as well as bad stuff.

"You said he. Anyone I should be concerned about at all, Andy?" Dot asked, thankful for Andy's observational skills and loyalty to her.

"Not sure, guv. A suit called Fallon. DCI according to his security pass. Never seen him before. He started with the 'do you know who I am?' shit. Must have been the reaction to my friendly 'I don't give a damn' face. You know me. Struggle to pass by a little bit of confrontation. He became a right sarky bastard when I told him I didn't know where you were or when you would be here. Just told me to tell you that he was looking for you. Reckon he's been watching too many episodes of *The Sweeney* if you ask me. I asked him for a contact number, and he just said, she knows my number. That was it, he walked out."

"Thanks, Andy, you're a gem," Dot half grimaced, half smiled. "I'll check him out on CCTV. I'm only popping in for some paperwork. I have to get over to SW1 for a meeting."

"You ok, guv? You look a bit pasty. Oh, don't bother with the CCTV. Buggered. Like the rest of us."

"Yeah, yeah, I'm all good, thanks. Just been a busy 48 hours, that's all. Oh, ok, no worries. Best we get it fixed, eh. Thanks again for keeping tabs, Andy."

Andy nodded back at Dot as the desk phone in front of him rang.

Dot's rank and gender meant that junior ranks were supposed to address her as Ma'am. Others that Dot knew well or worked in her team called her guv. And Andy was someone she knew well. She was pleased that she did.

She swiped her security pass again and entered the corridor to her office. She stopped, leaned back against the wall, and exhaled long and loud. What was Fallon doing here, at her nick, on her territory, looking for her? And clearly not in a particularly pleasant frame of mind by the sound of it. And Dot knew exactly what that frame of mind looked and felt like.

She continued along the narrow passageway and entered her office, where Detective Constable Elaine Craddock was already sitting at her desk, peering at a spreadsheet of some sort.

"Morning, Laney, how's things? Much happened yesterday at all? Any update from the Dubai plods yet?"

"Morning, guv. All good here. Nothing back from Dubai yet. Spoke to one of our chaps at the Embassy there yesterday, and he isn't holding out much hope. Our file is currently sat in a very big pile there. Had a few calls for you from SW1, told them you were out on ob's, so best to email you if it was urgent. Sarge is still out, trying to track down the money-washing accountants somewhere in Bromley. Other than that, we only had another four files dumped into our in-tray. All of them important, of course."

"Of course. Thanks, Laney."

Dot hadn't checked her work emails, so she had no idea if there were any in there that were screamingly urgent. SW1, otherwise known as New Scotland Yard, generally phoned when there was a problem. And right now, there seemed to be a few problems building up.

She sat at her desk and logged into her desktop computer. It came back showing an error. She tried again, with the same result. "Laney, is your computer working ok?"

"Yes, guv."

"Must just be mine then. Can you do me a favour? A security guard named Gerald was nicked last night over at the Chelsea Gardens care home. Can you have a dig around to find out which station he was taken to and let me know when you find out? Need it to be a bit hush. The DCI involved is not the friendliest person around."

"Yeah, of course, guv," Laney said. "Isn't that the home where your Mum is?"

"Yes, that's the one."

Laney nodded in acknowledgement. "Will let you know as soon as I find out. What was he nicked for?"

"Not sure yet, but possibly murder," Dot told her.

"Shit. Really? Not in the care home, surely?"

"It would appear so, Laney, hence why I want to keep any enquiries under the table for now. Bit of a personal interest in this one for me. Right, I need to head off to my meeting. Keep in touch and be careful what you ask and how you ask, eh."

"Wow, bloody hell, yeah of course, guv, no worries. I'll let you know when I hear something, soon as, I promise." Laney spluttered her words out. She was used to deciphering spreadsheets and accounts, not being involved in murder cases. This was indeed very exciting.

Dot headed back the way she came and got into her car. She felt like she was living in a surreal world where she was on the outside of a bad dream, looking in, and she was the main character in the dream. First, Fallon comes calling, and now she is locked out of her computer. In her world, there were always one or two things that didn't make sense. It was her job to figure these out. Now, though, there was a whole heap of things that didn't make sense, and she just wasn't getting the time to try to analyse each one. It was becoming very frustrating indeed. As she headed through the morning traffic towards W1, her mobile phone rang. She glanced at the screen. It was Jamie.

"Hey, Jamie, got your message last night. Sorry, I didn't call back; didn't think you would appreciate a late night call. How's the assignment going?" Dot tried to sound cheery.

Jamie's tone wasn't cheery, though. "Have you heard from Dad? I had a really weird message from him last night. I've been trying to call him back, but I just keep getting his voicemail. Do you know where he is? I don't suppose he stayed with you last night, did he?"

"I haven't spoken to your dad since yesterday. I saw him at Grandma's care home, and he seemed in good spirits. What was the message he left?"

There was silence.

"Jamie, what did he say to you?"

There was a long sniff followed by a sustained exhale of breath. "He said he was in a bit of trouble. Nothing to worry about, it would be sorted out, but he needed a few days away. That's not Dad, Dot. He sounded, well, he sounded kind of scared. I've never heard him sound like that. I'm worried. What could he be in trouble with? Has he said anything to you? Anything at all?" Jamie sounded like a scared son, not a police officer. Rationality wasn't present in his tone, and that was unlike him.

"Where are you, Jamie? Are you on shift today?" Dot was registering what Jamie had just told her. Had Dot's world just got even more surreal, or was there a very simple reason? Jack was a wily bastard at the best of times.

"I'm not back on shift until tomorrow. I have to complete the assignment, or Sarge is going to go ape at me. The main reason I need a positive assignment is that I'll be able to go Mondays to Fridays with CID and come off shifts. That is one hell of a motivation. I needed Dad's message like a hole in the head, Dot." Jamie was clearly angry as well as concerned.

"Well," Dot replied, "Your dad has a habit of doing the unexpected. I'm sure that everything is fine with him. He's probably just tied up with stuff at work. I know the business had a few minor blips recently, and he is probably just trying to sort it out. As I said, I saw him yesterday, and he was in good form as usual." Good form, meaning sarcastic as hell. Both Dot and Jamie knew exactly what that meant. "Look, I need to get to a meeting now, Jamie. Let's catch up later and see if there's any news. I'm sure it's all fine; he probably just didn't want you worrying if he didn't pick up his phone, that's all. Chin up, mate, eh? It's all good." Dot had a great way of making people feel better quickly, despite the whirlwind currently spinning in her own head. This latest conversation just added to the turmoil. What the bloody hell was Jack up to now?

"Ok." Jamie was clearly trying to think the situation through. "Good luck with your meeting, speak to you later. Oh, and Dot – thanks."

The call ended with Dot staring straight ahead. She was now minutes away from a meeting where she had no idea what was to be discussed.

CHAPTER 20.

London – The glass room at the posh police station.
Dot entered the main reception area of Police Headquarters at 7.55 am. She was met by a rippling sea of uniformed humanity, all busy within their own departmental domains and hopefully giving justice a helping hand to prevail.

"Good morning, Inspector LaSalle. I'm here to accompany you upstairs for your meeting with Chief Superintendent McKenzie. Please follow me."

Wow, thought Dot. I just got handed an austere greeting at HQ by someone who had clearly completed their homework on her. This wasn't going to be a cosy little one-to-one, that was for sure. The police equivalent of Miss Moneypenny turned on her polished high heels and strutted forward toward the lifts. Dot felt like she had been ambushed by a Sloane Ranger who knew her foe. Given that she had absolutely no idea who the hell this pencil skirted, silken bloused woman was meant one of two things. Either the Chief Super's budget had been increased, or she was in trouble. Dot had a suspicion the latter was true.

The ice-cold temperature in the lift matched that of Dot's chaperone. Dot's line of sight to the control panel was blocked by the pencil skirt. The gut-raising movement meant they were headed towards the top floors of the building. The doors opened on the twentieth floor, and Dot was ushered out of the lift and right, towards a glass conference room at the end of the corridor. She could see four individuals inside the room, including McKenzie, who was standing on the other side of the door to greet her. The last time she had seen him was at a celebratory 'well done for cracking a shitty case' type of do. His face looked older now, and his hair was greyer. Much greyer.

The pencil skirt reached the door. She pulled and held it open. Dot walked straight past and into the conference room with a cursory "Why, thank you." The pencil skirt followed without a response.

"Morning, sir. Good to see you again, I hope." Dot's face conveyed a stern, business-like expression as she spoke.

"Morning, Inspector LaSalle, thanks for being so prompt, especially as I know I asked you here at the last minute. I'll do the introductions of the others as and when I bring them into the meeting, if that's ok. I'm short on time this morning, so forgive me if we crack on straight away." He pointed. "Take a seat, please."

Dot was directed to the opposite side of the long conference room table from the other three. She was facing two women and one man. To be honest, they all looked like they belonged in an old school accountancy practice. One of the women even had a pair of half-moon spectacles perched on her nose as she read some notes on the table in front of her. The spectacled face looked up slightly, catching Dot's gaze on the notes. In response, she slowly turned the notes over and placed her hand on top of them. The other woman completely ignored her.

McKenzie sat himself at the head of the table with his back to a panoramic view over the River Thames. "I expect you're wondering why you're here and who these other people are. Well, I've thought long and hard about how we approach the meeting today and have concluded that, as honesty is generally the best policy in the police service, that's how I intend to proceed this morning." He looked to the bespectacled woman sitting opposite Dot and nodded at her.

Nodding back, the bespectacled woman turned her notes back over, shuffled in her seat and started to speak. "Good morning, Dorothea. Is it okay that I call you Dorothea, or would you prefer Dot? A little more civilised than Inspector, I think, don't you agree?"

"Dot's fine, thanks; otherwise, you will start sounding like my mother."

"As you like. You can call me Angela. I work within the Police Internal Affairs Bureau. I'm sure that you know who we are and what we do. Most people do. As you are aware, when you became a police officer, you swore to abide by the Official Secrets Act, and I must remind you that you are fully bound by the Act at all times. I'm here simply in the capacity of an observer to the proceedings today. That is, to ensure accurate accounts and actions executed in this meeting are placed on record in the correct fashion. Don't be nervous about it, just a formality, really, but it's all for a very important reason, Dot."

"Ok, then," thought Dot. "This is more serious than I thought."

Angela looked beyond Dot and nodded. There was a knock at the door. McKenzie stood up, walked to the door and opened it.

"Good morning, Tony, thank you for coming. Please take a seat." McKenzie extended his hand, which was shaken by the new entrant into the room.

Dot was watching as her own team member, Sergeant Tony Elkins, entered the room and walked around to the opposite end of the table to where McKenzie had sat back down. He took a computer from his bag, placed it on the table and sat down.

Dot squinted her eyes at Tony and calmly said. "Will someone tell me exactly what the bloody hell is going on in here, because I sure as hell haven't got a clue." She felt a rising mix of anger and confusion at the situation playing out in front of her. She hated surprises and being caught unawares. Her mind was racing as to why she was even in this room with these people. And she was getting more annoyed by the second.

Angela was facing Dot, but was actually looking at Tony. "Dot, I would like to introduce you to Detective Sergeant Tony Elkins. Whilst I appreciate that the two of you have in fact worked together for the last couple of years, you will most likely now recognise that it was not in the exact role that you thought he had been retained for." Anticipating that Dot was about to say something, Angela held her hand up to stop her. "I'm sure you have many questions already, but please bear with us, Dot. I'll let Tony take over from here and explain in more detail. Thanks, Tony."

Angela stood up and walked behind where McKenzie sat. She propped herself against the wide plastic window ledge, looking over her shoulder at the world outside.

"Morning, Ma'am. Sorry to surprise you like this." Tony sounded embarrassed. Dot's eyes were drilling into him.

"Since when did you become a Detective? Because that's news to me. And since when did you start calling me Ma'am and not Guv?" Dot needed to say something to emphasise her pissed-off state of mind.

"Er, yes, apologies, Ma'am," Tony stuttered. "Let me explain. No disrespect to you, I, er, think you're a fantastic boss, but my actual boss is CS McKenzie. I've been working with his team for the last five years. The last two years have been spent working on one particular job that involves a DCI you know relatively well, along with a number of other subordinates within his team. Please, could you look over at the screen for me?"

Dot turned her head left and looked up at the large screen on the wall behind where Elkins sat. The screen flickered, and then a clear head and shoulders shot of DCI Patrick Fallon stared right back at her. This was way beyond coincidence now. She hadn't crossed Fallon's path in a long while, and now she couldn't seem to get away from the man. To any innocent bystander, the picture on the screen portrayed a handsome police officer in uniform. To Dot, it portrayed something far more sinister. But what did it portray to the rest of the people she shared the room with? That, she was hoping, was what she was about to find out. She felt the phone in her jacket pocket vibrate. She ignored it.

Tony stood up, moved to one side and turned towards the screen. He pointed his finger at the image of DCI Fallon. "Working with you has been a real pleasure, Ma'am, but my real focus has been operating undercover to expose a number of police officers who we believe to be committing fraud, money laundering, theft and now, potentially murder. It would appear that this one particular individual, DCI Patrick Fallon, is at the heart of the group responsible for the offences. Working undercover as part of your team has been a perfect cover to make the necessary enquiries without suspicion, so thank you. The covert aspect of this operation was vital, Ma'am. As you will see, no disrespect, but we can't trust anyone."

Dot's mind should have been racing. Instead, it seemed like she was trying to run through mud. Everything was moving in slow motion. To be fair, given what Tony had just said, he was bloody good at hiding stuff. She didn't have a clue that he was, in fact, living a second life right under her nose. Even more proof, as if she needed it, that she had been distracted by the chaos wreaking havoc in her own personal life. Quite frankly, she felt more embarrassed about this than anything else. Looking directly up at Tony, she asked. "So, what's the MO for this internal gathering of esteemed colleagues, Tony? Given the presence of Angela over there, I'm sure you know I have history with Fallon. For those with short memories, let me remind you. Man subjects woman to sexual assault. Woman manages to break man's eye socket in self-defence. A panel of middle-aged men decides that said man walks free, and the woman gets reprimanded for occasioning actual bodily harm. Subsequent report gets flushed down the stinking toilet; man gets a hearty pat on the back for not pursuing woman for assault occasioning actual bodily harm, and woman is expected to continue along her own little yellow brick road as if nothing has happened. Sound familiar?" Dot was winding up nicely now. She was getting angry.

McKenzie stood up. "Look, Dot. I said the best course of action for this morning was honesty. And I intend to fulfil that. The gentleman opposite you happens to be the author of the very report you have just been alluding to into your alleged sexual assault. And Dot, he is here to apologise to you personally, so please hear the man out."

Dot was trying to register what had just been said to her. "Alleged assault, sir? Alleged my arse. And what do you mean? Apologise to me? Apologise about what? About the fact that I was fucking right, and I told the truth. About the fact that the report nearly cost me my job, my career and quite honestly, my bloody sanity. So, what exactly are you going to apologise for?" Her hands were trembling.

The man McKenzie had introduced remained seated at the table as he began to speak. "Dorothea, Dot, I'm here to apologise unreservedly about the report that was subsequently submitted to the disciplinary board regarding the events that happened between you and DCI Fallon. I fully understand you are not going to like or even accept the reasons I'm about to give you for the actions at the time, but all the same, you have the absolute right to hear them." The man placed both hands on the table in front of him, pushed himself up, and continued speaking. "Unfortunately, and it is unfortunate, we had a duty to protect Fallon at the time. He was involved in something that was, quite frankly, for us, too big to fail. If we had prosecuted him for the assault on you, Dot, it would have meant a gross misconduct ruling for him, which in turn would have meant his dismissal from the force. For reasons that will become clear, this was not allowed to happen. Because of that, we had to pass judgment that Fallon was innocent of any wrongdoing in the assault case against you. You have to appreciate that it was incredibly difficult for our entire team at the time. We know it goes against everything we stand for in the police service, and for this, I, we, are truly sorry." He sat back down in his seat.

Dot felt a nauseous, warm, stinging sensation rising up through her stomach.

McKenzie stood up. "Dot, look. I know that this all seems like a total mess for you right now, and we aren't exactly covering ourselves in glory, but you will see what we are dealing with and why it's important for you to stay calm and focused. You are about to become an integral part of this ongoing investigation, but we needed to put the dirt on the table first so that you understand exactly what happened and why. You will, of course, be totally exonerated of all accusations within the report, but we need to do our jobs first and sort out Fallon and his team once and for all. Dot, this will give you the best form of karma, I promise you."

Dot's phone vibrated again in her jacket pocket. Again, she ignored it.

Almost as though perfectly stage-managed, the pencil skirt entered the room with two fresh thermos jugs of coffee. Given that Dot hadn't even seen or heard her leave the room in the first place just added to the woman's clear ability in the art of clandestine manoeuvres. Everyone in the room watched as she poured coffee into only two cups. One was placed in front of Dot, and one in front of McKenzie. She then left the room again. This was a very well-orchestrated meeting, that was for sure.

Dot was struggling to figure out what she had been told in the last few minutes. How the hell had she missed all of this? She wanted to cry, but not in front of this lot. She took a gulp of the coffee and straightened her back. It did nothing to stop her from feeling sick. She took a deep breath and spoke.

"So, what's to stop me from walking out of this room right now and suing the entire arse out of the police force. Given what you have just told me, I think I have every right to do so. This is outrageous. Your actions nearly cost me my sanity, for Christ's sake. I hope you're writing THAT in your bloody notes, Angela" Dot was doing everything within herself to remain calm. As usual, it wasn't really working.

McKenzie looked directly at her and spoke in the calmest voice. "Because if you walk out of this room now, we will have no choice but to arrest you as an accessory to murder. Do you understand me?"

Dot was stunned. "Seriously! You expect me to understand what you have just said? No, no, I don't understand that at all, but what I am beginning to understand is that you have lied to me, and now you aren't exactly giving me a whole bunch of choices here. Murder? Where the hell has that even come from?"

Dot was beginning to figure out that until she knew exactly what the hell was going on, she was stuck in a Catch-22 situation. Right now, the only choice she had was to hear how on earth she was allegedly involved in all of this and then take stock. Rationality was needed. "So, what do I need to do to not be arrested as an accessory to murder? Help put this bastard Fallon behind bars? I assume that's the intended outcome for you. You had that chance once before and failed miserably. If so, once that's done, I can work out my compensation package for sexual assault and the cost of all the time I've spent battling through all of this mental shittyness. I assume that's why everyone is in this room right now. To make sure I give you whatever it is you need without screwing up the entire operation because of my post-menopausal mouth. Ok, then. Let's get to it. You said you didn't have much time. Let's find out exactly what it is you want me to do and why you need me. No doubt because I haven't got a dick between my legs. It generally takes a woman to sort a man's shit out." Dot was doing her damnedest not to cry. It was the closest thing to being rational she could do right now.

Tony was still standing in front of the screen. He was looking utterly sheepish. "Ma'am, I need you to look at the screen again for me, please. And I need to remind you at this time that it is a criminal offence to disclose any official information without lawful authority. Do I make myself clear?"

Dot just stared. She preferred the old Tony. That one wasn't such a prat.

He continued, "For the record, I'll take that as understood. So, we have more than enough reason to believe that Fallon is working with one, possibly more, Estate Planning professionals to unlawfully change the outcome of legitimate legal documentation. In other words, redirecting money and property away from the rightful recipients of trusts and wills for his and others' personal benefit. To be clear, this is not loose change. So far, we believe that the amount is in tens of millions of pounds. This money is then being used to purchase cheap Class A drugs from other Organised Crime Groups. Cheap because Fallon and his cronies are putting pressure on the OCGs to fulfil their requirements; otherwise, said OCGs would see, first-hand, the long arm of the law. Totally ironic, don't you think? A senior police officer steals money, launders it, and then uses it to buy drugs via an OCG. Pretty smart on the surface, but let's face it, skipping this close to the law, along with handling huge amounts of money, pretty much meant that something was always going to give. It generally does when people get too greedy. This, Dot, is where you come in. Now, please, look at the screen again for me. Time really is of the essence."

Dot looked up at the screen. There in front of her were several picture-in-picture CCTV images of Fallon talking to another man. The building they were standing in front of looked remarkably familiar. Dot stared closer at the screen, and her body froze. She put her hand over her mouth to contain her words. She couldn't trust what might come out. The other man in the images talking to Fallon was Dot's husband, Jack. Her phone vibrated again in her jacket pocket. This time, she took the phone out and looked at the screen.

It read. *Left a couple of messages for you guv. Found out that Gerald is dead. Hung himself in a custody cell last night by all accounts. Laney xx*

McKenzie intervened. "Dot. Dot. Are you ok?" He sounded genuinely concerned. An entire lorry load of crap had just been proverbially emptied right over Dot's life, and his department was entirely responsible for driving and emptying the lorry.

Dot was still staring at her phone. "I need a minute to respond to an enquiry from the one remaining member of my team. Assuming she, too, hasn't been dragged over by you lot to the dark side." Dot's anger was turning to emptiness. She was trying to digest what she had just seen on the screen as well as what she had just read on her phone. Everyone in the room was infatuated with getting everything done in double-quick time and expecting her to comply. How the hell could she comply when at every turn, she was being subjected to yet another monumental thunderbolt?

The other male in the room, who had so far said nothing, let out a short excuse me kind of cough and then spoke. "No need to respond to any enquiries, Inspector. Your phone is currently under surveillance by our team. As is your desktop at home, which I believe contains some remarkably interesting search histories from the last few hours. The email requests that you made this morning have had a hold put on them to preserve our integrity in this case, and quite frankly, using the Force database for personal use could be construed as gross misconduct. We know that PC Craddock has just given you information regarding Gerald Compton and his unfortunate demise. I'm sure you're already working this out, but Mr Compton's death is also a part of our ongoing investigations. We have a very fluid situation right now, and one which appears to be hastening. And no, PC Craddock has not decided to come over to the dark side as you so eloquently put it."

Dot sat still in her seat. Totally speechless. Numb. Feeling betrayed. This was personal now. Gross misconduct. Seriously! How, on earth, had she not seen any of this happening? Not that she even knew what was happening, but bloody hell, she was a seasoned police officer. Surely, she could not have been so wrapped up in her personal life as to miss what was happening right in front of her eyes. But that's just it. What on earth was happening?

McKenzie walked around the table towards Dot. He then perched himself next to her. "Dot, look," he said, "I know you have just taken on board a huge download of information. I can't even begin to imagine what you're thinking, but we do need to move quickly on this operation. We are aware that Fallon has been asking about your whereabouts, so we know that, at a minimum, he wants to talk to you. That means you are getting too close to something. As of now, you will get protection from us. We have pretty solid intelligence that Fallon and his team are about to move money from Europe. This is not a few thousand pounds. We estimate around fifteen million is being moved. We also know that two of his team are close to retirement and that Fallon has also indicated his intent to pursue an early retirement. All legitimate exit strategies on the face of it. If they get themselves and their money out, they could go anywhere and disappear. That kind of money can buy significant amounts of silence in countries with no extradition treaties with the UK. As far as we know, Fallon and his OCG are unaware that we are closing in, but as I said, we need to move quickly. We didn't see Gerald Compton's death coming. We don't want any more surprises." McKenzie took a breath and wound up. "I need to get going. The rest of the team will debrief you and answer any questions you have, and I'm sure you have quite a few for the team. Not that this means jack shit right now, Dot, but please accept my apologies. And I just hope that there is nothing else to uncover." He stood up straight, walked back around the table, thanked the room and left.

Pencil skirt appeared out of the shadows in the corridor and accompanied the Chief Superintendent to the lift. Of course, she did.

Good cop, bad cop. Accessory to murder, gross misconduct. Don't worry, Dot. Hurry up, Dot. We are sorry,

Dot. We are not sorry, Dot. She needed Chablis. Right now!
Coffee just wasn't doing it for her.

CHAPTER 21.

Another not so posh police station in London.
Detective Inspector Patrick Fallon leaned back in a cheap office chair in one of the police station's pool offices. It was kind of an overflow station. Saved the taxpayer's money on building anything new, which kept the Home Office happy. He drank a big mouthful of coffee and then slowly rubbed his eyes. He was knackered. It had been two days since he had had any real sleep. Two days where his adrenaline had kept his body and brain moving at breakneck speed. Breakneck because a couple of the idiots involved in his illicit empire were being exactly that. Idiots. Which meant that Fallon had to cover up details that had the potential to bring his whole world crashing down. The organised crime group that Fallon headed was about to retire from the business of ill-gotten money and drugs, and he was not about to let anything stand in his way.

There was a knock on the office door.

Fallon looked up from his chair and could make out the huge frame of Sergeant Terry Osman through the pane of frosted glass in the door. "Come on in Terry."

"Morning, guv," growled Terry. "Got you a coffee. Glad I did, looks like you need one." He entered the room and placed the cup on Fallon's desk.

"Grab a seat, Terry. Thanks for the coffee, it's the only thing keeping me going right now. Any sign of Mepham out there?"

"He is just getting himself a coffee from the machine downstairs. After nearly thirty years of drinking that muck, you would think he would have caved in by now and bought himself a decent drink. His veins must be clogged up with that shit." Terry sat down in one of the two chairs in front of the desk that Fallon occupied. Almost immediately, there was another knock on the door.

"Come on in, Charlie," Fallon said, loudly enough to be heard from the other side of the door. Charlie Mepham entered the room, put his small white plastic coffee cup on the desk and sat down.

Looking at the other branded coffee cups on the desk in front of him, Mepham simply said, "Retirement's just around the corner. Need to save the pennies for my plastic surgery."

Fallon grimaced and shook his head. "I've seen you looking worse, Mep. Not much, though. Listen, I just want a quick debrief, and we can be on our way if that's ok, gents. I appreciate it's been a long night. I assume you kept your heads down on the way in."

Both nodded back at him.

"Good. Terry, how are we doing with the reports and post-mortem details on Gerald Compton? Can you see any problems with any of it at all?"

Terry Osman slurped the last dregs of coffee from his cup. "Sweet as a nut, guv. He was out like a light when I got to the cell. Rohypnol in his tea worked a treat. It was a bit of a battle getting the heavy bugger pulled up to the light cover and into the belt, though. To be honest, I wasn't sure if it would hold for long enough, but it did, and it was all over in less than a minute. Got back to the desk and hit the panic button. Suicide assessment will show there was negligible risk. By the time the post-mortem is done, given that we've not asked for a toxicology report, nothing will show in his system. Stated as coherent and no immediate detection of alcohol or drugs. My report gives all positive responses from Compton to his arrest and detention. Given the violence we had him down for, it will fly through. Just got to keep an eye out for any family that comes crawling out of the woodwork. There was nobody marked down as his next of kin on his paperwork at the care home, so hopefully should be ok. It was bloody lucky I was on shift. I wasn't expecting that kind of job last night. Just hope that's the last one we have to do."

Fallon nodded in agreement. "Good, well done. We weren't expecting the job either, but we didn't have a choice. We might have one more to do, but all being well, I'm going to handle that one myself. Is that all, Terry?"

"No, not quite, guv. Forgive me for mentioning it, but what the bloody hell did happen last night? There was no planning, no briefing, nothing. I thought you said we just had to wait for the money to come through, and we were done. Switching off some poor bastard's lights last night wasn't sitting and waiting for the money to come through. Sitting and waiting would have involved a nice, easy night on shift, chatting up the new desk sergeant. Last night was the closest call we've had in years. Getting caught with our pants right down by our bloody ankles was nearly a reality last night. But hey, other than that minor fucking hiccup, that's it, I'm all good."

Fallon sat quietly, looking directly at Terry. "You finished now, Terry? Sometimes you don't see the car heading your way. There you are wandering over the zebra crossing contemplating how good life is and then – bang! Out of nowhere, some dickhead loses their concentration, and before you know it, lives are ruined. Well, last night, I managed to stop us from being involved in an almighty car crash. Just so you know, Krystina Benko did a job on one of our clients a few months back. Well tried to anyway. It wasn't pretty. The client should have fallen asleep and never woken up again. The problem was, she did wake up again after having a heart attack. Luckily for us, though, she ended up a vegetable, so couldn't say a word about what we were doing. But before Krystina could sort out her mess, the nurse moved her to another care home that had better medical care for her. Krystina wasn't the same after that. She said she was ok, but she wasn't. The boyfriend regularly checked her phone and made a note of the numbers she was calling. No problems with them until last night. She made two attempts to call one number. The calls were short, and they connected to voicemail. We've no idea if she left any messages, but there was no way we could take a chance." Fallon picked up his coffee and took a mouthful.

Mepham filled the conversation gap. He sounded as though he had the worst bout of flu going. His broken nose was starting to turn a nice shade of deep blue and purple. "Did you find out who she made the calls to, guv?"

"We did. The number came up on PNC. As police staff. The calls were to Dot LaSalle."

Terry looked pale. "Inspector LaSalle? As in the bitch that tried to take you down, guv?"

"The very one, Terry. That's why we had to take Benko out at the care home last night. I couldn't take any chances, and it just so happened that the stars aligned nicely. The security guard nearly cost us, though. We missed some security detail that he came to check out while we were about to clean up the mess in the room, and he poked his nose in at the wrong time. I heard him coming, headed out the fire door, and waited. As I thought, he called triple nine for the ambulance when he saw Benko in the room, explained what he saw to them, and control insisted on an immediate police presence. I heard the call come through over the radio and placed myself closest to the scene. Mep knows the rest. He grabbed a couple of plods and pegged it over to the scene in my Beemer. Far too close for my liking. But at least it gave us a cast-iron alibi for taking Benko out. Just in case the security guard didn't play ball, we also had an all points out for her boyfriend. Belt and braces, but way too close, gentlemen. Way too close." Fallon finished his coffee.

Mepham picked a small lump of dried blood from his nostril. "Surely, LaSalle would have said something to you last night, guv. You know, if she knew anything. I would say she looked really surprised to see you there. If Benko had got to her, it would have played out differently. And given

LaSalle hasn't come looking for you, I reckon we're in the clear on this one."

Terry let out a big huff. "Sorry, you mean LaSalle was at the bloody care home last night as well. And you didn't think of telling me. Look, I'm not one for superstition or anything, but this, this, is just way too coincidental, guv."

"Terry, I'm not one for superstition or coincidence. That's why we did what we did last night. I don't like this any more than you do, but it's sorted. Just keep your head, stay focused and act like a police officer. That's it, that's all you need to do. And Mep, I hope that you're right about LaSalle. That's why I'm keeping eyes on her. We've done everything we can. We just need to crack on and stick to the plan now. So, Mep, all good with you now? Anything we need to sort out on your side of things at all?"

"No, all good, I reckon, guv. The scene was easy to sort. The knife had Compton's prints all over it, along with Benko's DNA. I took some clothes from his room and covered them in her blood. Report shows he changed straight after murdering her. There were plenty of his hairs from the baton, which are now in the room. I also know that the post-mortem will show Compton's knuckles are nice and bruised. My statement will show that he head-butted me and tried to throttle me. But at no time did he ever punch me. Just her DNA on his hands. It's open and shut, guv. There's absolutely no reason for anyone to look outside of what it actually is. Oh yes, even better, when I spoke to Evie at the care home last night, she told me that Compton definitely had a thing for Benko and that she found it a bit freaky. I made sure the plods got all of that info into the statements. So, I reckon, as long as you keep that bitch LaSalle out of our lives, everything should be ok."

"Excellent, Mep, thanks," Fallon said. "After you have grabbed some kip, can you go round and take a statement from the paramedics for me? The longer you leave it, the better. I gave them a bit of a tough time last night. They were poking their noses in way too quickly for my liking, so I asked them to leave. Told them I had a doctor on the way to confirm time and potential cause of death. Bloody lucky I had the radio with me. Final thing, Mep. Can you sort out the van driver? Make sure he bigs up the violence element in the van in your favour. Other than that, I think we're all good."

Mepham nodded.

Terry looked up from his coffee.

"How much longer before we can walk away, guv? I have my pre-retirement meeting with HR next month. The missus has already got her heart set on three months in Marbella. Not sure how the hell I'm going to handle that. We've never spent three months together in our entire lives. She might be the love of my life, but I can walk out of the house every day. Keeps me sane, that does. No wonder police officers have the highest rate of suicide of any profession after retiring. It's either that or getting nagged to bloody death."

Fallon smiled. "I'm sure we can find something to keep you busy, Terry. As of now, the last packages are due to be delivered within hours. Once the handover is complete, the money gets transferred from Switzerland into the primary offshore account for onward transmission into our own offshore accounts. Once in your account, all previous accounts get shut down. Between now and then, we just need to make sure that we've swept up every outstanding detail we can think of, double check it, triple check it and keep doing our day jobs."

Fallon reached under the desk and picked up a plain black sports bag. He took out two medium sized brown envelopes and handed one to each police officer. "Don't lose these, gents," Fallon said. "They are your retirement plan. You have a new SIM card to use in the Nokia's from today. Lose the old SIM cards. You have also got a little present in there. It's a telephone number on a card with a code word. Use your Nokia's to contact the number on the card. The number is manned twenty-four seven. Give them the twelve-letter code word, and they'll text you the address of your brand-new apartment in Dubai. The properties are listed under a trail of shell companies but are ultimately owned by you. The trail is virtually impossible to follow. If anyone ever asks any questions in the future, you will simply be there as security consultants on behalf of some friends in the Middle East. And good luck if anyone tries to extradite you from Dubai. Given the amount of money invested by the shell companies there, the authorities will be very unlikely to comply with any request from the UK this side of the thirtieth century. Not quite Marbella, Terry, but I'm pretty sure the missus won't complain too much. When you arrive there for the first time, you will receive a US dollar bank card. Each card will be linked to an account that holds three million US dollars in it. You can move the money around to wherever you want from there. The more we spread the money around, the less chance of anyone asking too many questions."

Both sergeants stared at the contents of their envelopes.

"In the meantime, you will have five hundred thousand dollars transferred into your own offshore accounts this morning as the penultimate payment. The money will be cleared straight away. Does that answer your question about how soon we wrap up the group? Yes? Good."

Both men remained silent.

Fallon closed the bag and stood up. "I'll check in with you when you are both back on shift. Not long now until the big payday, gents. Keep smiling."

Fallon left the office without any further conversation. He was leaving the two men alone in the room. Deliberately. Unbeknownst to both of his sergeants, Fallon also left a recording device strapped underneath the desk. He trusted no one. Especially not his own police officers.

He left the police station and walked into a small independent coffee shop diagonally opposite the station and ordered a black Americano. He knew that both Terry and

Charlie frequented either the chain coffee shops or the sludge machine in the station reception; therefore, his vantage point while having yet another coffee should be covert enough. He didn't have long to wait.

Terry walked out of the building first and turned left, heading towards the tube station. Stopping, he looked around, pushed both hands into his trouser pockets, gripping his envelope under his armpit, and started walking.

Two minutes later, Charlie walked out and turned right. Fallon was fairly sure that Charlie had parked in the multi-storey car park at the far end of the street. A corner of the envelope could be seen poking from under his coat.

Neither Terry nor Charlie looked in the direction of the small independent coffee shop.

Fallon finished his coffee over the next few minutes and then headed back into the police station.

He had booked out the room in the station for two hours, so he still had an hour left on the clock before anyone else used it. More than enough time to do what he needed.

Entering the room once again, he sat back at the desk, reached underneath, followed the length of the drawer with his fingers and then untaped the recording device. He rewound the device to the beginning and then fast-forwarded through the conversation they had all had previously. He reached the point where he had vacated the room, and Charlie and Terry were left alone.

"So, what do you reckon, Charlie? Do you think this is finally going to be over now?"

"I don't know Terry. We've racked up a few bodies since we've been doing this. It feels like Fallon is getting ready to run, but it also feels, well, I don't know, something doesn't feel right. Then again, nothing about what we've been doing should feel right. But it's one hell of a lot of money, and that's what we're here for. What do you think?"

"Same. I'll be a darn sight happier when I check that the five hundred grand has gone in. Tell you what, though, didn't see the turnaround with Jack happening. Did you see the way the guv beat him to a pulp? From what I can figure, he still needs him to sort the paperwork out, so he needs him alive. I don't know why he did that. Something must have wound Fallon right up. You don't half kill the person that is responsible for sorting out the entire money part, do you?"

"Fallon wouldn't do that unless the money was already on its way. He's not that stupid. I wouldn't let the Jack thing worry you, though. I reckon he has outlived his usefulness for Fallon. Let's face it, if there was one person who was capable of blowing this whole thing apart, it was always going to be Jack. And quite frankly, Terry, if he couldn't see that, then he's not as smart as we all thought he was. Look, to be honest, I don't like it either, but I, for one, am not surprised if Fallon wants him gone."

"Charlie, can I ask you a question?"

"Yeah, of course, Terry. What's on your mind, mate?"

Terry exhaled loudly. "You and me, we've known each other a long time, right. You've had my back, and I've always had yours. That's the way we work, always have."

There was silence. Fallon could only assume that Charlie had made an affirmative response of some sort, given Terry's slightly delayed reply.

"I took out my own little insurance policy, Charlie. I thought it made sense at the time. Wanted to make sure I had some protection in place for me and the missus. Just in case, you know. Just to cover my arse, that sort of thing. The problem is, though, Jack sorted the paperwork out through his firm. To be honest, I don't think he trusts the guv any more than I do; I think he was scared of him. Anyway, if anything happens to me, then Fallon's cover is going to get blown wide open. Dates, times, places, people, that sort of thing. Problem is, now that Jack has had seven bells kicked out of him, he might use my insurance policy as leverage against the guv. People say desperate things in desperate situations. And Jack's in a pretty desperate situation right now. Worse than that, though, I don't know where Jack's keeping my policy. I can't ask around at his office. Too many people around. I didn't figure on him becoming public enemy number one. I need to keep Jack alive, Charlie. If anything happens to him, well, doesn't look like ending well for any of us. Do you see what I mean, mate? If he says anything to Fallon about it, well, then I am in big, big trouble."

Quite a few seconds of silence followed.

Charlie spoke next.

"I assume that I'm not included within your little insurance policy then."

Again, silence. Fallon had to assume that Terry agreed to Charlie's question as he continued. "Look, we can't guarantee that Jack will be alive by the time we get the hell out of here, but we can try and do our best to stop the guv from killing him. Not sure how yet, but we can think about that one. It sounds to me like you're overthinking this, Terry. Look at what the guv has just given us. He wouldn't do that if he was thinking of offloading us on the final stretch, mate. There's a lot of work gone into the contents of our envelope. He wouldn't do that if he didn't think we weren't all in on this. So, let's see what we can figure out about Jack and then let's just get through the next few weeks. It's what we've both been working for, and it's what we both deserve. We don't want to bust the whole thing open now. We're too close. Now, you better go and tell your missus to start buying guidebooks for Dubai and not Marbella. And, Terry, don't do anything stupid."

The sound of scraping chairs meant the two sergeants were leaving the room.

Fallon pressed stop on the device. Jack had already told Fallon about Terry. Now it was confirmed.

He took out a phone from his bag and sent a text. *Hold 2 X $500k offshore payments. DO NOT PAY. Text Y to confirm.*

A single Y was received back almost immediately. He had been right. Never trust a bent copper. Now let's see if

Charlie Mepham does the right thing and calls him. If he did, another £3.5million would be included in the Fallon retirement fund. If he didn't, the fund would increase to £ 7 million.

CHAPTER 22.

London – The glass room at the posh police station.
"Well, this turned out to be a bit bloody awkward, then, didn't it?" Dot spoke as she watched CS McKenzie and the pencil skirt disappear into the lift. "So, what happens now? I'm sure, given the number of times you have reminded me of what I can and cannot say, you have a nice little to-do list for me. And, no doubt, once I've read it, I'll have to eat it. So come on, who is the most important person in the room right now that McKenzie has gone?"

Dot was still raging. Trying to even process what she had been told about Fallon was in itself enough of a trauma, let alone the rest of the crap that came with it. And what the hell was Jack playing at? He was smart and stupid in equal measure, but surely, not that smart and not that stupid.

The man who had delivered the apology to Dot regarding Fallon's sexual assault on her stood up again.

"Ah, you again," she spat. "Got any more extraordinary pearls of wisdom that you want to drop into what's left of my life right now?"

"I came here to deliver an apology and a sincere one at that." The man spoke softly and eloquently, his voice almost hypnotic. "Let me introduce myself. I'm Commander Nick Truss, head of the Serious Organised Crime Agency, and this is my team on this particular case. A case that, quite frankly, has hit home incredibly hard within the police service, and one that we're prepared to throw whatever resources we need at to conclude quickly. The Home Office are on direct dial with us on this."

Dot's mouth opened, and she let out a long, slow exhale of breath. "Please accept my apologies for my behaviour, sir, but I was, and still am, to be honest, a tad pissed off. It's been one hell of an eye-opening kind of day, and I have a feeling it's not going to get any better. Can I ask you a question, please?"

He nodded. "Of course, whatever you need, within reason."

"I know my husband can be a total pain in the arse and quite frankly I gave up caring about him a long time ago, but do you know if he's ok? I had a call from his son on the way here, ah damn, I forgot, you're listening to my calls, aren't you? Is he ok? Jamie, his son, is really worried, even though Jack is a total arsehole; I certainly wouldn't wish him any harm. Jamie said he was going away for a few days. What can you tell me?"

Truss looked over at Tony Elkins. "DS Elkins, would you mind showing the actual footage from the CCTV stills that you had up there earlier, please? That might help Inspector LaSalle get a better idea of what we're dealing with."

"Of course, sir," Tony clicked something on his laptop. "Ma'am, what you are about to see isn't very nice, I'm afraid. Here goes."

The CCTV started playing on the screen. Dot watched Fallon walking out of Jack's office, followed by Jack himself. It was dark, the recording was slightly out of focus, but Dot could make out the time of 01.23 am in the top left-hand corner. The way Jack was remonstrating as Fallon walked in front of him showed that he was clearly having an argument of some sort. Jack put his hand on Fallon's back. Without any warning, Fallon turned around and punched Jack so hard in the face that he fell back, hitting his head on the tarmac as he landed. He was still conscious. He tried to push himself up from the ground and managed to get into a position where he was putting all of his weight on his right elbow. Fallon then walked over to Jack and kicked him three times in the head.

Each kick looked harder than the last. Jack's head looked exactly like one of those boxing machines in an amusement arcade. It was thrown back further with each kick. Finally, Fallon appeared to spit on Jack as he lay motionless on the tarmac.

The room was silent.

Dot could not take her eyes off Fallon. There, right there, that was the pure evil she had seen in him before. Throughout the entire ordeal, Fallon had been smiling. The same evil, malicious, disgusting smile that Dot had seen when she had been assaulted by him. Now, it was there for everyone to see. Jack looked dead. Not moving. His body crumpled on the tarmac. Whatever it was he had done to provoke Fallon, he didn't deserve this.

Fallon gestured to someone out of the shot of the camera. Moments later, two men ran across to Jack. They picked him up by his legs and arms and carried him out of the camera shot. Dot was sure that one of the men looked familiar.

Tony Elkins continued but did not discuss what they had just witnessed on the screen. "We've got what we think is the vehicle they used to take Jack away in. Trouble is, the same vehicle was found burned out south of the river. The forensics team found a body on the rear seat. They know it's not Jack's. The body on the back seat was that of a female yet to be formally identified, although we've a good idea of who it is. The fact that Jack wasn't in the car hopefully means that he's still alive. Therefore, we have to surmise that he is still needed by Fallon for something. But we don't know where or for how long. We have people working on this right now."

"So, you think that, if it is Fallon who has taken Jack, he still intends to kill him?" Dot was now worrying more about Jamie than anything. Jack was his dad, and Jamie still loved him for who he was. Unlike Dot.

"Let's just say that we can't rule that out from happening. That's one of the reasons we're in a hurry." As Tony spoke, Truss was looking out at the view over London that came from being on the twentieth floor. He walked over to a side table to get himself a coffee. It was certainly a beautiful day out there in the capital, completely defying the mood within the room.

Dot's mind was still whirring, trying to figure out how Fallon and Jack even knew each other. They were total opposites. Chalk and cheese. "So, at the moment, you have no idea where Jack is? Surely if they were going to kill him, he would have been in the burnt-out car along with Jane Doe. Or buried somewhere else if they didn't want anyone finding him."

"Or as DS Elkins said earlier. Jack is needed to perform a function for Fallon. And that's our current line of enquiry." Truss took a long, slow gulp of his drink. "What we do know is that there've been three murders in very quick succession, which either means that civil war has erupted within the OCG, or they are moving towards a conclusion for the group. We believe it's the latter. Shall we get to the reason we've pulled you into the team, Dot?"

"Might be an idea, I suppose, sir. I don't fancy accessory to murder being added to my police record to accompany my assault of DCI Fallon."

Truss finished his coffee and placed the cup back on the sideboard. He walked over to the door. "That much I do understand, Inspector. I need to get going. Everything else you need to know will be explained to you now. I'm leaving you in the competent hands of my team. Just remember, Dot, all of the team in this room has my complete authority to do whatever's necessary to put these bastards behind bars. Give them whatever help they need. And thanks for your understanding. I know how difficult this must be for you right now."

And with that, he headed down the corridor. As he reached the lift, the pencil skirt appeared as if from nowhere. Of course, she did. How the hell did she do that?

Tony Elkins stood up from his chair, picked up the laptop clicker from the table and walked to the side of the screen. "Ok, ma'am. You want to know more details about why you are actually here. Let's get going on that. Before we do, though, I must remind you..."

He was stopped dead in his tracks by Dot. "For crying out loud, Elkins, I was learning the Police and Criminal Evidence Act whilst you were still getting your backside wiped by your mother. I get it, keep my mouth shut, listen, and do what I'm told. Now get on with it. Please."

"Apologies, ma'am, just following standard procedure, that's all. And for the record, I'm an orphan, so I have no idea who wiped my backside."

Touché, thought Dot.

Angela from Internal Affairs stood up and headed towards the coffee pot. "Might be an idea for you to fill up your cup, Dot. I'll get some more coffee and some water. I'm done here for the moment anyway. Please continue, Sergeant Elkins."

He nodded. "Thank you, ma'am."

Angela left the room, leaving a half smile with Dot.

Elkins watched as Dot walked over and poured herself a coffee. She was starting to feel like the star witness of a very important trial.

"Inspector LaSalle, I'm obliged again to tell you again ..." Dot stopped Elkins mid-flow and raised her hand like a child wanting to answer a question.

"Yes, ma'am?" he asked.

"Drop the formalities, will you, Tony, and for crying out loud just call me Dot."

"Umm, as you wish, er ... Dot. Now, as I was about to say, we need to go back quite a while to establish how we got to where we are today. It won't take long, but as you will hear, some of the details are not particularly pleasant."

Dot looked at the woman opposite. The woman who blanked her when she first came into the room was still ignoring her. She looked a similar age to Dot. Her hair hadn't appeared to go grey yet. Either she was just very lucky, or she had a great hairdresser. The clothes she wore, though, were a cut above anything that Dot could afford. Unlike Dot's M&S wardrobe, this woman was clothed by the resident fashionistas in the West End. Her time to introduce herself would no doubt come.

"Dot, sorry, are you ok? You look like you zoned out there for a second." Elkins had resumed with his very credible poker face. "We do need to carry on. As has been previously disclosed, time is of the essence."

"I'm good, thank you. Just a bit tired. Please, continue." Dot rubbed her eyes and immediately wished she hadn't. They felt rough and salty, and she could feel watery liquid welling up in them.

The woman with no name reached into her plain black, but no doubt very expensive, handbag and retrieved a handkerchief. Not tissues that mere mortals would have to hand, a bloody handkerchief. She pushed it across the table towards Dot.

Dot said, "Thank you, I'll get it washed and ironed before returning it." She wiped both her eyes and then, very loudly, blew her nose into the expensive piece of cotton cloth. It was safe to say that the look she received in return was not a friendly one.

"Are we NOW okay to continue?" Elkins' resolve was starting to crack. He continued. "The usual route we've found in previous internal affairs cases where class one drugs are involved usually revolves around confiscated narcotics. Corrupt individuals on the inside try to find ways to move the drugs out of police premises in various guises and replace them with identical packages in both appearance and weight but containing sand or chalk. They know that at some point, the drugs will be disposed of, usually via an incineration process. When that happens, it generally appears that all evidence has been fully eradicated. The stolen drugs are then sold back into the market via contacts of the corrupt officers, and the money that's made is then placed in a series of bank accounts, mostly abroad, and Bob's your uncle, fry-ups for life in the Costa Del Crime. This process, in the main, only happens once or twice. Some are opportunistic, some are calculated. Most are fairly predictable, ending up with perps enjoying internment at one of our esteemed governmental hotels."

Elkins checked that Dot was still listening. She was. Intently.

"What Fallon's been doing is different. It's a far more complex process with multiple layers. It involves a different approach to obtaining the money and drugs, and quite frankly, we were lucky to be able to connect all the dots. And there were a lot of dots to connect. Pardon the pun, ma'am. Don't get me wrong; we knew he was dealing drugs, but we needed to find the source of funds. Fallon has been buying millions of pounds' worth of cocaine and stockpiling it. He obviously wasn't getting that kind of money on a DCI's salary. He was stockpiling so many kilos of drugs that he actually had an effect on the retail price right across London. If you look at when the prices started to increase, you will also find a correlation with our intelligence relating to Fallon being involved in the drugs game. At the same time, very coincidentally and conveniently, other prominent dealers in London started to disappear. Fallon's OCG were in command of the supply and the demand. He is a kingpin. But he is also a kingpin who has made enemies along the way. And some real nasty enemies to boot. Now that the price of drugs is sky high, we believe Fallon is getting ready to flood the market and then run. There's about to be a cocaine tsunami hitting London, and we need to stop it. We have to get Fallon and his people to somewhere the sun won't shine for a long, long time.

"Ok," said Dot. "Fallon appears to be a genius in the drugs business and seems to have found a way to single-handedly determine and control the entire supply and demand of the London narcotics scene. I get that. But, where, and how, exactly, do I fit into all of this? Surely this is all down to you and the drugs boys and girls to sort out. Obviously, I'm very flattered at being in the presence of the great and good of British law enforcement, but can we now get to the crux, please?"

Elkins had clearly been anticipating Dot's lack of patience and looked over to the donor of the handkerchief, who nodded and stood up.

"Thank you for the overview, Sergeant Elkins. Dot, thank you for your time thus far. You're quite right. We need to give you some of the finer detail for why you are here. I'm Commander Joanne Templeton. I'm attached to Military Intelligence, currently seconded on this operation with Commander Truss. The bottom line is that we want to do all we can to keep Fallon's drugs off the street. Causes quite the mess, as I'm sure you can appreciate, and attracts new groups into the market, that, quite frankly, we would rather not have trading on our shores."

Dot's mind was doing somersaults. Just being in the same room as this lot was exhausting.

Templeton continued, "There are three reasons you are currently in this room, Dot. Very simply, the first reason you are here is your husband's infidelity. The second is that the money used to purchase the narcotics is illegally obtained from wealthy widows and their estates and then further defrauded by shell companies set up by your husband's businesses. Finally, the proceeds of drug sales are then funnelled via offshore trust schemes through God knows how many further offshore companies. And yes, you guessed it. All set up by your husband. In other words, Dot, pretty much all your areas of expertise are in play here, along with your husband. Or potentially, from where some people in the police force are sitting, your capability to be an accessory to conspire to commit a whole bunch of very high-profile crimes. And we need to know which it is, Dot."

Dot was silent. She was doing her damnedest to try to process what she had just been told. She walked over to the window and looked down. She saw hundreds of tiny people, all going about their own business. People were streaming into the office building opposite. She envied every single one of them. What they were doing was normal and ordinary. Currently a million miles away from anything happening in her own crazy life.

Templeton had told her there were three reasons she was there. In her head, there were only two. The first was her husband, the second was Fallon. And until a few minutes ago, she had absolutely no idea of what they had been accused of. Her priority right now was to find out about Jack. Was he still alive? If indeed he was, then how exactly was he wrapped up in all of this? She needed to know. She needed to be honest with Jamie. She then thought of Gerald. She hadn't known him long, but she had made a promise to help him. A promise that was never carried out. She needed to ensure that his death was not in vain.

"Appreciate if you need a moment to gather your thoughts, Dot; the toilets are past the lift on your left." Templeton stood right behind Dot as she spoke.

"No, it's fine, thank you. You need to know if I'm in collusion with my husband and Fallon. Well, I can assure you I'm not. I had no idea what they've been involved in. I've been busy at work as well as distracted by my mother's illness. I also know that you believe me; otherwise, you would have arrested me long before today so that whatever I say could be used in evidence. While it may well be difficult for some of your onlookers to believe I'm not involved, you can take this one statement and, for all I care, shove it where the sun doesn't shine. Other than Fallon being a total piece of shit, I had no idea about anything you have told me here this morning."

Templeton held a fantastic poker face. "We know that you have been distracted, Dot. We've been watching you. Much as you recognise the protocols under standard police procedure, what we have in this room is not standard police procedure. This comes under need to know. Which basically means if we say we told you your rights, no one will query it. What we need to establish is just how much you know about the OCG that Fallon and your husband are involved in.

Conveniently or not, as the case may be, your name pops up in situations which, from our point of view, are very questionable. You have been identified as being at the Chelsea Garden Care Home last night, during a serious criminal investigation led by Fallon's team. A young lady in the prime of her life was brutally murdered, and the main suspect conveniently hangs himself in police custody a few hours later. The whole case cut and dried in record time - allegedly. We have witnesses that confirm you were seen speaking to various police officers and paramedics at the scene, yet your name has not been included in any of the witness statements or officers' notebook entries. We also know that Fallon has been looking for you. Maybe the tribunal did actually get the right outcome. Maybe you have been colluding with Fallon the whole time. What do you think? What are you trying to hide, Dot?"

"I'm not hiding anything. Fallon is. And looking back at the tribunal, maybe I should have just broken Fallon's neck. That would have saved us all a whole lot of trouble. For your information, I was actually at the care home because my mother is a resident there. I was just leaving when I saw the medics go in, followed shortly after by Fallon and his goon squad. So don't insult my intelligence by saying that you didn't know that. Now. Where is Jack? Is he safe?" Dot had a duty to find Jamie's father. And she was getting really bloody angry.

Templeton let out a long, slow sigh. "Can you say categorically that you saw Fallon arrive at the care home last night, Inspector?"

Dot was caught off guard. She was thinking hard. Her brain felt like it had been pureed. She remembered the BMW nearly hitting her car. Did she see Fallon? "I can't say for sure I saw Fallon arrive, ma'am. I do know what I assumed to be his car nearly took me out, though. By the time I got back to the care home, two officers had already been stationed outside the entrance. So, what are you saying? Fallon wasn't in the car."

"That's exactly what I'm saying, Inspector. Fallon was already at the care home. And so were you. None of the officers present can place you there, and CCTV tapes are conveniently missing. So, you see my predicament. Your paths cross a little too frequently to be a coincidence."

"You just said witnesses saw me at the care home, but then you say that none of the officers can place me there. You must believe someone, surely. If not, then it would appear that you have me bang to rights. Guilty as charged. In your humble opinion. But only your opinion. Well, let me tell you this much. I've absolutely no bloody idea how or when Fallon got into the care home. I didn't see him. I was sorting out a whole pile of crap, literally, for my mother and then sat in the car on my phone before the care home was besieged by uniform. And that's the best you're going to get, because that, ma'am, is the bloody truth, like it or not."

Dot was starting to doubt her own judgement. What Templeton had told her was enough to make the most sceptical individual believe that there was some truth in it. But there was *no* truth in it. And how the hell did she not see Fallon, if indeed he was already at the care home? Where was he? Who was he with? How did he get in? He had to be with someone inside the care home.

"Well, I'm sure that you agree that's quite a litany of offences that could be interpreted as being associated with you, Inspector. However, thanks to the diligence of your detective sergeant here, your phone does indeed indicate that you were otherwise engaged on it for some while during the time we are investigating. That still does not account for some of the missing hours, but given mitigating circumstances, such as your mother being a resident there, I tend to believe that you are telling the truth."

Dot couldn't believe what she was hearing. "Oh, thank you very much indeed, ma'am. Nothing to do with the fact that I'm a bloody good police officer with some scruples, who does the best she can to uphold the principles of the law, then?"

"Well, I'm sure we'll find out exactly what principles you have over the coming days, Inspector. In the meantime, corrupt police officers are about to flood our streets with vast quantities of drugs whilst trying to disappear with tens of millions of pounds. The drugs and the money, in themselves, are bad enough. The fact that the operation is being facilitated entirely by officers within our force is wholly unacceptable. If you become a discarded by-product of this journey, then so be it, but I hope that we can at least rely on you to help where we need it. That is, after all, your job."

Elkins felt the need to politely intervene. He walked back over towards the TV screen. "We're doing everything we can to track Jack down, Dot. We know he was put into the car before it was burnt out, so we're checking CCTV along the route to see if he was dropped off somewhere or if he was put into another car at the burn site. They picked the burn site well. Closest CCTV is on a main road, 50 yards past the side road where it is located. That means we have to watch all traffic from both directions and cross-check any vehicles we don't see entering or leaving the road. We will *do* it; it's just taking time. Even if we do locate the car, we then have to see if we can track it to its final destination. It's important we find Jack. Without him, we might not establish exactly where the drugs are going to be sold. We're pretty sure that he knows, and we want to catch Fallon and his team in the act before they head off into retirement."

Templeton continued. "For now, I suggest we're going to give you the benefit of the doubt, Inspector. You need to stay with the team for the time being. If Jack escapes, we need to know where he'll go. We also need you to keep in contact with Jamie in case Jack contacts him. And don't worry, we have eyes on Jamie in case he is used by Fallon as leverage. It's clear that Jack has upset Fallon, but at this stage of the proceedings, we don't know why. Right now, we don't want any surprises. We just want to curtail this little internal organised crime group's activities for good, and all go back to our day jobs."

Dot's thought process felt like an old bagatelle ball bouncing around the metal pins. "Commander. Can you tell me how Jack became involved in all of this and how you found out about him? I guess if nothing else, it will help me with the divorce proceedings."

Templeton smirked. "It's not a particularly nice story, Inspector. You sure you want to hear it?"

Dot nodded.

"Ok, long story short, Inspector. I'm sure that you are well aware that Jack's business predominantly targets widows and widowers to establish financial trusts for them. He then helps to pay their legacies to charities when they pass away. You would be amazed at how many people don't have loved ones to leave huge amounts of money to. And Jack knows it. He set up a series of offshore accounts, made to look like holding accounts, for legacies to be paid into, and then set up dozens more, spuriously named after well-known charities. His company was, of course, acting as Power of Attorney for all of these individuals and in order for his clients to do business, they also had to lodge their wills with him. He had total control. So, when these individuals passed away, Jack, acting as the attorney, pays off all remaining debts, sells all available assets and pockets the difference into the offshore accounts. The wills are changed to show, ultimately, there were no assets left after debts had been paid following death, so consequently, there are no issues with probate or any distant relatives who appear on the scene. He is very good at it. And in all honesty, he may well have got away with it for some considerable time."

Dot was dumbfounded. She also had a gut-dropping feeling. She thought back to the emptied filing cabinets at home. What if Jack was trying to do the same with her own mother? "The crafty bastard was working in my area of expertise, right under my nose, and I knew nothing about it. I always thought he was just ambulance chasing elderly people. That's embarrassing. I'm hoping that you deliberately kept this away from Laney and me, then, Tony?"

"To be honest, it was easier than I thought. You had your own cases, and you were preoccupied with your mother. Gave me a clear run to keep this stuff off your desk." Elkins was obviously being very diplomatic.

Dot rubbed her eyes. They were still gritty as hell. "The last few times I saw Jack, he gave the impression that his business wasn't doing very well. He certainly didn't look like someone who was flush with cash."

Elkins cut in. "He was spending so much time ripping off elderly clients for drug money that he had taken his eye off his original legitimate business. And of course, there was no way he could funnel any of his illicit money across to the business without Fallon finding out. Our theory is that Fallon couldn't care less about Jack's real business, as there is going to be a huge payday for everyone when they all walk away. But neither Fallon nor Jack had accounted for one small detail. One of Jack's secretaries was blackmailing him. She had been responsible for setting up some of the offshore accounts, and she knew they were dodgy. Just not how dodgy. She got very close to Jack, and, er, forgive me here, ma'am, ended up sleeping with him. The affair lasted for quite some time, but it would seem Jack got bored with her."

Elkins watched Dot's face for any reaction. He saw just a slight grimace. He continued. "Jack's secretary had been making some financial demands from him for some time. She told him it was to stop her from telling you that he was having an affair. Jack paid her twenty grand to shut her up, which seemed to do the trick for a few months at least. Then she asked him again, and he told her in no uncertain terms where to go. This was the point at which she got in contact with us and tipped us off to what Jack was doing. We financially encouraged her to stay and continue to pass information to us, which she did. She had no idea of the scale of what was happening. We started our enquiries. Fast forward to this week. She overheard Jack talking to his accountant about releasing staff as business had fallen, and that she should be one of the casualties of the downturn. Easy for Jack. Payday was coming anyway, and she wouldn't be needed in the future. She had a row with Jack, and she told us she was being made redundant with immediate effect. That was the last time we heard from her. We can only assume, but believe it to be true, that Jack found out she was informing the police or, at the very least, threatening to inform."

"Christ," Dot said, horrified. "The woman in the burnt-out car, it's her, isn't it?"

"We need to wait for formal identification. Dental records, etc., but yes, we believe the body in the car is hers." Elkins went to pour a coffee.

"This," said Templeton, "is why time is of the essence. People are dropping like flies, and we're currently one or two steps behind everything Fallon and his team are doing. We need to be in front and figure out where the drugs are before they sell."

"One more question, if I may, Commander." Dot was being a police officer. The first time in a while.

"Go ahead," Templeton said. You could hear a pin drop in the room.

"Very simple, really. Do you know how, when and where Jack met Fallon?"

"Elkins, if you wouldn't mind, please. I don't want to get the detail incorrect."

"Of course, Commander." Elkins stood up while Templeton took out her mobile phone and headed for the coffee. He looked straight at Dot. "Ma'am. I have to warn you again. What is said in this office stays in this office. No ifs, buts or maybes. You will not like what you are about to hear, but that must in no way undermine this operation."

Templeton, now with a coffee in a takeaway cup, walked towards the door. "I have some calls to make. Thank you for your time, but we now need to finish this job. Inspector LaSalle, I appreciate your honesty today, especially given the information you have to digest. However, I will say that if you so much as whisper a single word to anyone outside of this room regarding this operation, I'll make sure that your feet will not touch the ground all the way to solitary confinement in Holloway Prison. Do I make myself clear?"

"Crystal clear, ma'am. It's great to see that confidence of police officers within the force is at an all-time high."

"Prove me wrong, Inspector."

As Templeton left the room, the pencil skirt emerged from a closed door and handed over a file. Dot wondered if they had a training school especially for pencil-skirted police officers. Her phone vibrated. It was a message from Jamie.

At the same time, Elkins looked at his own phone.

"You're kidding me, aren't you, Sergeant? You said that you were watching my computer and phone. I didn't think that meant literally!"

"Benefits of working with Military Intelligence, Dot. By the way, tell Jamie not yet, you're still looking into tracking down his father. Well, it's just us now, so hopefully no interruptions from here on in." Elkins spoke too soon.

"Any chance of asking Moneypenny to get some breakfast, Detective Sergeant. I'm starving."

Elkins raised his eyes and shook his head at Dot. "For your information, Moneypenny out there holds the rank of Chief Inspector, so I'll get one of the security chaps to get some pastries from the restaurant. She really is the last person I would want to antagonise; that's for sure. Now, anything else before we continue, ma'am?"

Unless you have access to a time machine that can take me back to my last holiday in Italy? No? Shame. Clearly, Military Intelligence isn't all that then. Let's continue."

Dot's stomach rumbled.

CHAPTER 23.

A Victorian Terrace House in Hoxton, East London.
Police Sergeant Terry Osman shut the door to his small but perfectly formed home in Hoxton. He placed the envelope that he had received earlier that morning from Fallon on the sideboard in the hall. He stared at it for a few moments before walking to the kitchen and pushing down the on switch on his kettle.

Terry had a real affinity for the property he called home. He was born in one of the small upstairs bedrooms nearly fifty-seven years ago. This was the house that his parents had started renting from the local council in the early fifties and subsequently purchased under the right-to-buy scheme. Soon after, Terry's father had moved away to live with another woman in Bolton, and he had not seen him since. Terry, therefore, felt duty-bound to look after his mother after his father left. Now in her old age, she was living in a council-run care home just around the corner in Hackney. She had had the full works of old age perils over the last few years, finally culminating in mixed dementia, but being in a home surrounded by East Enders like herself meant she was happy. And being happy was the most important thing of all to Terry.

There had been a significant increase in property prices over the years in East London, starting with the rise of the Docklands development, meaning that his little house in Hoxton was now worth a small fortune.

Terry's wife was hard at work at a local doctor's surgery. She had worked there as a receptionist for the last fifteen years and had enjoyed every day she was there.

Thirty-four years on from the day that they were married, Terry was still unequivocally in love with his wife and she with him. They had always kept themselves to themselves in their locality, whilst giving back to causes such as the local youth boxing club and helping to run a dementia café. Terry, of course, had been cajoled into joining the area neighbourhood watch scheme. They had never had children. This wasn't through personal choice, but rather the fact that his wife was unable to. She had been diagnosed with cancer of the womb in her early twenties, something that was relatively rare in those days. Subsequent treatment and surgeries meant that she would never be able to bear a child. She took responsibility for never being able to have children personally. To Terry, it was obviously a huge disappointment, but his love for his wife never faltered. If anything, over time, knowing what they had been through made their feelings for each other even stronger. So, aside from not having children, all in all, the Osmans had a pretty decent life together.

For Terry, hindsight was a wonderful thing. However, it was also a curse. If Terry had one piece of hindsight he could overturn, it would be to walk away from the moment he accepted an offer from a young police sergeant named Patrick Fallon. And for Terry, that decision, made many years ago, was now threatening the very existence of both him and his wife.

CHAPTER 24.

A dark, wet, derelict shop. South East London. 1987.
Terry Osman was a budding Detective Constable working undercover in the drug squad. He had been working on a particular Jamaican Yardie gang who, through violence and coercion, now controlled the distribution of cocaine throughout his patch in South East London.

Terry had been immersed in this case for a mind-numbing two years, but was now closer than he had ever been to taking out the hierarchy that had been responsible for upwards of fifty drug and gang territory deaths. And these were the deaths they knew about. This was just the tip of the iceberg. There was an epidemic of narcotic cocktails being sold in London, which showed no real signs of abating. Until now.

Terry found himself kneeling on the first floor of a derelict carpet shop. The ground floor had fallen victim to an arson attack a few months earlier. Allegedly, the owner had refused to pay an increase in protection money from the local street boss and ultimately paid the price. The shop was located at the cheaper end of the high street, but from Terry's perspective, it was a perfect observation post of a side door entrance that led to an upstairs flat diagonally opposite from where he was located.

It was a freezing cold, dark November evening. The rain had abated slightly but still poured in through a broken window, soaking the already rotten floor where he knelt precariously. The light originating from the neon signs opposite meant that Terry had to wear a black balaclava to conceal his head and face. It was itchy, but it was warm. An earpiece linked him through to two response teams, located in vans at either end of the high street. The vans were old and marked up as painters and decorators. In the pocket of his dilapidated donkey jacket, he had a handheld radio. All comms were to be silent until he indicated otherwise. No words, just pressing a button on his radio. One quick click for no change. Three quick clicks for relevant movement of a target and standby. Five quick clicks for go. No two or four clicks. These were left as indications of a mistake made by Terry. As if.

As he sat in the cold and dark, he was very aware of his own bodily smell. He hadn't washed for a few days, avoiding going home, in case he was being followed. He had spent his two years undercover gaining the trust of sellers, then the dealers, and finally the 'area managers'. These were the go-betweens for the street dealers and main suppliers. Quite simply, his modus operandi was playing an ex-police officer who had been convicted of theft and disgracefully dismissed from the force. He had tipped off dealers on numerous occasions, enabling them to outrun the police. Some tip-offs were pre-arranged with the police to make it look real. Some weren't. These were the ones that got him into trouble with the hierarchy, but it brought him more trust with the dealers. Terry had even served twelve weeks in prison to give credibility to his cover. It was the toughest twelve weeks of his life. For both him and his wife.

If tonight went as planned, it was to be the culmination of all his undercover work for these last two years. Tonight, the main dealers were due to exchange over one million pounds of drugs. The dealers had opened up two new territories following a violent turf war, and this was to be the start of their expansion. Taking this amount of drugs out of the market would be a huge disruption and give the police the opportunity to identify and take out the main players.

As Terry adjusted his balaclava, a black Mercedes passed slowly in front of him. He could only make out two occupants through the windscreen, as the rear side windows were blacked out. The vehicle almost came to a stop, but then increased in speed and drove off out of sight.

Terry's heart rate increased. Recognising one of the occupants in the front of the Mercedes as the local area manager, he clicked his radio three times. The driver was doing an observation run. If he were confident, he would drive past again shortly.

Terry heard the three confirmation clicks sent back to him by Sergeant Patrick Fallon. Terry liked Fallon. He was a good officer to have on your side. A right nasty one otherwise.

The Mercedes had turned around out of his sight and was now moving slowly in front of him again. It came to a complete stop opposite the side door that was under observation. The front passenger door opened, and a large frame, covered in a long coat and wearing a baseball cap emerged. He had his back to Terry as he looked up and down the quiet high street. He then turned slightly and banged the palm of his hand three times on the roof of the car. Almost immediately, the two rear doors opened, and two men dressed in hooded tops and long raincoats emerged. Not quite the height of fashion, but impossible to determine identity.

Terry had seconds to establish a go or not. Was this a decoy or was it the dealers they were waiting for? Given he had recognised one of the occupants during the first drive-by and a further two individuals had exited and were now going through the side door entrance, he made his decision. One, two, three, four, five clicks. His involvement was now over. Within seconds, the High Street would be swarming with people. Police and interested local parties. And Terry couldn't be seen with either.

He watched as both vans screeched to a halt, blocking the Mercedes in. The driver got out and started running towards the building where Terry was situated. Shouts of "Stop! Armed police" rang out. Terry could see that the driver was brandishing a handgun. As he lifted the weapon and pointed it towards the police officers in front of him, three gunshots rang out and the driver fell to the ground. Given the side of his head had been blown away, he was clearly dead.

Terry slowly stood from his kneeling position. His kneecaps clicked loudly. He turned away from the window and tiptoed gingerly to the back of the building. He had to watch every step. The floor had been badly damaged in the fire, and what was left was soaked through. Reaching the rear of the building, he opened a blackened window and stepped out onto a rickety metal staircase which stopped about three feet from the ground. Terry climbed down and jumped the short distance. He walked through the dark concrete yard and out through a gap where a gate used to be. Confident that no one had seen him, he disappeared into a labyrinth of passageways.

Terry's earpiece had erupted into life. The driver had been eliminated, four suspects had been detained in the building, along with four holdalls of cash and eight holdalls of what appeared to be cocaine. It had been a very good night.

CHAPTER 25.

A café in London Bridge, the morning after Terry's drug bust.

It was seven-thirty the following morning. Terry Osman walked into a typical greasy spoon café next to London Bridge railway station. It was already busy with a mix of commuters and tradespeople looking to get their fix of strong coffee with bacon and eggs.

Sitting at the very back of the café, Sergeant Fallon looked up at Terry, acknowledged him, and then held up his cup. Terry went to the counter and ordered two large coffees and a bacon bap. He walked through the crowded café, headed over to Fallon's table and sat down.

"You, Terry, are a bloody genius. Last night was epic. Better than anyone ever imagined, mate, but then again, you knew that didn't you?" Fallon could barely contain his excitement.

"Couldn't say anything, Skip. Last I saw, the driver was being taken down. So, what's the score? Was it a good tip-off?"

"Good? Good? The top brass are bloody ecstatic, Terry. Can you believe that one of the targets had flown in from Spain to negotiate a deal for the new territories in London? No one had a clue he was even in the UK. Right result. We recovered 6 million in cash and 70 kilos of cocaine. You, son, have just become a legend."

Terry didn't feel like a legend. He absolutely hated any kind of congratulatory plaudits. As far as he was concerned, he was just doing his job. "I'm pleased we got the right result, Skip. A lot of effort went into getting to last night. I really am pleased but to be honest, I've had enough of doing drug squad. I've had enough of lying to everyone I know and, quite frankly, I'm bloody knackered. I just don't want my missus walking out with the milkman. He sees more of her than I do, and I've chanced my arm with her for long enough. I think I want to go back to uniform. I've thought about it for the last few months, and in my head, it just makes sense to do it now."

"Christ, Terry, you need to think about this. You're one of the best at what you do. I mean that. And that's not just me saying it. You're going to get a commendation for the job last night, mate. That's how much they think of you. Honestly, you just need some R and R, that's all, mate."

They both stopped talking as the coffee and bacon bap were placed on the table.

"Red or brown sauce with that, darling?"

Terry shook his head.

The waitress wasn't looking at him. She only had eyes for Fallon. "Anytime you want to feel my baps, darling, you just let me know." She walked away and disappeared into the kitchen.

Fallon's eyes followed the waitress all the way. Terry shook his head at him.

"Oh, come on, Terry, they were very nice baps from where I'm sitting, you can't say they weren't."

"Wasn't my type, Skip, you know that. Unlike most of you, I still fancy the hell out of my missus. And talking of my wife, I really wouldn't mind taking some time off and getting to know her again. Like I said, she's had a tough time of it since I've been working undercover and quite honestly, I'm knackered after this op. It's been a long two years, so, if it's okay with you, once I've sorted the paperwork out, I figured I could take a few weeks, and you could weave your magic to get me back to uniform. I've been threatened by more scumbags in the last couple of years than most officers get in a lifetime, so I could do with a break.

"Look, fair enough, Terry, I totally get it. Most people wouldn't be able to spend a week in your shoes, let alone two years. Let me go back and talk to the Chief Super and see what I can sort out. How does that sound?"

Terry was busy demolishing his bacon bap. He was starving.

Fallon sat in silence, waiting for Terry to finish.

"Sounds good to me, Skip, thanks, I appreciate it."

Fallon finished his coffee. "Going to get another coffee, want one, Terry?"

"I'm good, Skip, thanks. Going to head off to start sorting out my paperwork. The sooner that's done, the sooner I relax."

"Give me a couple of minutes, Terry, got one more thing I need to go through with you if that's ok."

Terry nodded, a curious look on his face. He sat watching the other people in the café. After two years of working undercover, the mind starts to play tricks on you. Everyone you look at in public either seems to be a suspect or a threat. That's why he needed a change. It hadn't just got him. Undercover life was becoming part of him. And that terrified him. Besides, he always missed being in uniform. That's why he really became a police officer in the first place. He liked helping people. Not watching them being shot.

Fallon returned to the table with two more cups of coffee. "Thought you might change your mind, so I got you a coffee anyway."

"Thanks. So, what's on your mind, Skip?"

"I have been speaking to the Super over the last few weeks. He wanted me to know that if we got the right result on this case, then one of his units would be mine to take over. Permanently. And of course, that would come with an Acting Inspector badge with it. Given the result last night, it's a shoo-in for me. I wouldn't have got this without you and the team, Terry. I'm gutted you want to step back into uniform, but I respect your decision. You could have been a big part of the new team, mate."

"Well, that's great news, Skip. You deserve it. You really do. And besides, you boys always need the help of uniform. Eyes and ears of the street. Can't do without them. You know that."

Fallon reached down to a backpack he had placed on the floor by the table leg and took out a thick envelope. He pushed it across to Terry, but kept his hand placed on the top.

"What's this?" said Terry, his eyes narrowing as he spoke.

"This, Terry, is a little thank you for taking a whole load of shit off the streets and putting some very dangerous criminals behind bars. Sometimes, you get presented with opportunities that can help you get the better things in life. This is one of those times, mate, and you deserve it. All of it." Fallon moved his hand off the envelope but still kept it close.

Terry leaned closer to the table and put his hand on the envelope. He pulled back the flap and opened a tiny gap. He saw Christopher Wren's face looking back at him. Fifty-pound notes. A lot of them. "Skip, seriously. I can't take this, you know that. If I get found out, I'm done for. And I'm never going back inside, not for anyone."

"Terry, I get it. But it's all good, mate. I promise. Hear me out, OK? According to the evidence bags from last night that are now down at the nick, the money in that envelope doesn't even exist. And it's not like the lot we arrested are going to complain about it. Nobody can put you away for taking money that doesn't exist, mate. It's just a way of saying thank you and to help you pay off the mortgage. We both deserve to have our lives made a bit easier. Nothing will make up for your time in the nick, Terry, but this might just help ease that pain, mate."

Fallon took the envelope and placed it back inside the backpack.

"Terry, there's thirty grand in there for you. More than enough there to take care of your mortgage and leave you with some spare as well. Enough to set you up for the rest of your life, but not enough for anyone to come sniffing around. And besides, if they do, I'll always be watching your back."

Terry stared at the table in front of him. He was silent, and Fallon left him that way for a minute or so while he finished his coffee. Fallon went to his backpack and took the envelope out once more. He stood up, and as he walked past Terry, he dropped the envelope onto his lap. "As I said, mate, it's not going to be missed. It's a thank you, and it can make a difference. I'll speak to the Super today about the transfer. He won't like it any more than I do, but I'll make sure he respects your decision."

Fallon left Terry staring at the envelope in his lap as he walked over to the counter and said something to the waitress. The waitress smiled and then laughed. Fallon smiled back at her and left the café.

Terry held the envelope in his hands and took another look at the contents.

He closed the envelope again, placed it inside his coat, stood up and followed Fallon out of the café. In that one moment, Terry's life had changed. His debt to Fallon had just been generated.

And the repayment terms were going to be high. Very high.

CHAPTER 26.

London again. 2002 – Back in the glass room at the posh police station.

Dot decided to make Elkins wait just a little bit longer. Along with a whole bunch of other things, she was trying to figure out how much of what she had been told she could actually trust. The last couple of hours had been a gathering of the who's who of law enforcement hierarchy, accusing her of utterly ridiculous events, incidents, whatever they wanted to call them. Elkins had buzzed down to someone in reception to order pastries to be delivered ASAP. He was clearly still in a hurry to get through things. Dot was stalling to try to find out more about what they had on Jack. Where was he? Did they have any clue at all? Was he still alive? And why was he so important in all of this? Did he really hold the key to when the drugs were hitting the streets? It just didn't make any sense to Dot. Jack? Seriously?

There were other players in this game that Dot would have thought far more important. Fallon, for example. Neither commander had spoken about him other than to brief on his history and current movements, courtesy of some pretty nasty CCTV footage. Dot was doing everything she could in her head to piece this all together. How on earth had she missed this? It must have been on the periphery for quite some time now, and she had no idea. She walked over and filled up her cup to the brim with warmish coffee. Opening three sugar packets, she emptied them into her cup, stirring at the same time.

"You should try water sometime, Dot. Much better for you and helps you think. It's a key superfood, you know."

"Thanks for the advice, but trust me, when you're in the position I'm in right now, water doesn't cut it. Tell me, was it easy for you? You know, hiding all this shit from me for so long. How clueless was I? Be honest. For two years, you reckon. How to make someone look like a complete idiot without them knowing anything at all? Either you're bloody good, or I'm absolutely useless."

Dot could almost hear Elkins' brain whirring, trying to choose the right words so as not to offend her. It didn't really matter now; it was way beyond offensive.

"To be honest, Dot, you made it quite easy for me. It helped that your mother was in the care home. You spending a fair bit of time away from the office made life easier for me. You may also have realised that there was a steady stream of new cases coming in through the door. Well, thanks to my contacts on CS McKenzie's team, they were doing very well at rooting out cases for the team to keep everyone busy. Laney has enough work to keep her going for the next ten years. And she loves what she's doing. Handed over everything to me once the analytics were done, and hey presto. I was busy; Laney was busy, and you were, well, er, hitherto occupied with your own life. Laney was a genius for me, though. Unbeknownst to her, she unscrambled a whole load of offshore companies and bank accounts used by your husband and Fallon. She thought they were part of a corporate tax evasion scheme. She doesn't know it, but we have a lot to be thankful for what she did."

As if being offended wasn't enough, Dot now felt mortified. If attempted murder and accessory to God knows how many drug-related crimes didn't cut it, then dereliction of duty had to be up there somewhere on a list.

"Well, I'm pleased that my department could help you, Detective Sergeant."

There was a knock at the door. The pastries had arrived. And, for once, Dot noted, not accompanied by Chief Inspector pencil skirt. Clearly, the pastries were not important to her. She probably ate air and drank water every day. It was the only way she could fit into the skirt.

Dot grabbed one of the pastries and took two big bites. "So," she said, licking her fingers. "What's the real situation with Jack? You must have some idea of where he is. He may be on the way to being my ex and clearly up to his neck in trouble, but I still worry for Jamie worrying about him, if that makes sense. I need to say something to Jamie soon, otherwise he'll start digging. And I don't want him to find anything out until I've had a chance to talk to him."

Elkins nodded in agreement. "We have eyes on Fallon and some of his associates. Given the activity we've seen in the past few days, we're convinced that the largest shipment of drugs is going to be handed out by Fallon soon. It seems that most of those who were in the know are either now dead or missing. Fallon is clearing out his wardrobe, so to speak. Jack is in the missing category right now. We're sure that one of the chaps on the CCTV putting Jack in the car was a PC from Fallon's unit. Bit of a nasty bastard by all accounts. He is closely linked to Charlie Mepham, another one of Fallon's right-hand people."

"Of course, that's it. I thought I recognised him. Yes, he is," agreed Dot. "He was at the care home last night, along with that Sergeant Mepham. Mepham was the one kicking seven bells out of Gerald, the security guy. Christ, how many officers are involved in this?"

"By all accounts, quite a number of officers are beefing up their retirement accounts. And yes, we know he was at the care home last night. We also know that Gerald Compton was taken to a police station conveniently manned by another of Fallon's chaps, one Terry Osman. He and Fallon go way back. And he makes Mepham look like a cuddly toy. We've been watching them all for quite a while now."

"So why was Gerald murdered, if, in fact, that's what really happened? He seemed an innocent party in all of this. Was it a question of wrong place, wrong time? I made a promise to him that I didn't keep. And I feel terrible about it." Dot was shaking her head as she spoke. As far as she was concerned, she had let Gerald down. Badly.

"Dot, I doubt there was much that could have been done about Gerald. From what we have, we think he was being framed for the murder of Krystina Benko, the girl at the care home. She was one of the chefs there. We're still not one hundred per cent sure of her role in all of this, but we do have eyes, ish, on her boyfriend, Massimo Albricci, who we believe is acting as a runner for a drug gang. We're just not sure if it's one of Fallon's own gangs or a rival gang that could be challenging Fallon. Another reason we think he is moving quickly. It appears that Fallon wants to flood the streets with drugs, take the money, and run to whatever bolthole he has ready and waiting. Elkins was treading carefully with Dot. This was all very personal for her. When things get personal, people can act differently. He needed Dot focussed on the job at hand, but she was thinking about something else.

Dot was thinking about last night and was talking out loud. "At Chelsea Gardens," she murmured. "The paramedics were right. Vanessa was right. But Fallon lied to me. He just wanted her out of the way quickly. What was Krystina's role in all of this?" She gave herself a little shake and spoke louder. "So, am I still a suspect in all of this, this, whatever this is, or am I going to be exonerated?" Dot sighed.

Again, treading carefully, Elkins simply said, "I believe you, Dot. I'm just not that sure if some of the others do."

"So, you lot keeping me here this morning should achieve one of two things, then. If your teams see movement out there amongst the OCG, they'll assume I'm not a party to their, well, er, party, so therefore I'll be in the clear. However, if things come to a grinding halt out there and the OCG go into headless chicken mode, then the assumption is one of their team has gone missing, and I become enemy number one. And in the meantime, Inspector Dot, heartless bitch, isn't in the slightest bit concerned that her stepson is worried stupid that his father has gone missing, possibly presumed murdered."

"Sorry, Dot, but yes, something like that. As I said, I believe you. And that is what I'm working with."

"Well, this is a new one for me. Here I am swimming in a pool full of allegations in one of London's largest ever drug operations, and I genuinely don't know a bloody thing about it. This is one for the training school in the future. Why being distracted is not good for your career." Dot, now feeling the sugar rush from the pastries, had had enough. "Detective Sergeant Elkins, Tony – can we just get to the whatever point you're trying to make to me? What exactly do you want from me? Why were the big guns here today? What are you not telling me? And please, just because I've been a dick for the last two years, doesn't mean I can't figure out that you need my help now. If McKenzie or any of his team wanted me behind bars, they would have made that happen. And I'm not behind bars; I'm here with you. So, come on, you're the one in a bloody rush to get shit done. What do you want me to do?"

CHAPTER 27.

Back at the Victorian terrace house in Hoxton, East London. Terry Osman sat at a small square table in the very simple but beautifully decorated kitchen of his house in Hoxton. Holding a cup of strong tea, he was reflecting heavily on the last twenty years of his life and career. More importantly, though, he was reflecting on the influence of Chief Inspector Fallon during this time. Terry was counting in his head all the number of times that he had repaid his original thirty grand debt, and in his own inimitable way, trying to put a cost against all of the so-called little jobs he had undertaken. How the hell could anyone really put a cost on taking a life? Not in the course of a legitimate police operation, but in cold blood. Murder. With intent. And Gerald Compton wasn't the only one. This, along with accessory to murder, undertaken by both Fallon and Mepham. This was not even considering theft of the original money, extortion, coercion and contributing to just about every type of bodily harm known to man and the law. And for what? Retirement on the run to someplace in the Middle East he had never even been to before. Always looking over your shoulder. Temperatures so bloody hot that you need to sit in an air-conditioned room all day. For what? Taking a lump of drug money to pay off a mortgage. This was the highest interest rate he had ever paid, and the thing was, he would continue to pay it for the rest of his life. Unless he did something about it. Yep, Terry Osman had more than paid off his original debt. Many times, over. And now he had to make up his mind about what to do next. And with whom?

Terry had always known that Jack was no criminal. Agreed, he was outstanding at finding ways to con money out of people who were dying and then making that money disappear into a whole myriad of trusts and other things that Terry didn't really understand. But he was no criminal, not in the sense that Terry was. Terry did the dirty work. The dirty work that had dragged him further into the depths of Fallon's warped dream. A dream that Terry feared was about to shatter. And that was why Terry had entrusted Jack with his insurance policy. Not a policy to protect Terry himself, but one that would mean that, if anything happened to Terry, Fallon's entire history would become common knowledge. Names, dates, amounts of money, amounts of drugs and a very long list of offences. It didn't matter where Fallon chose to hide. Most places were going to give him up once they found out exactly what he had done. He wouldn't have anywhere to go.

But there was a problem with this strategy. A big problem. Jack had also taken out an insurance policy. One that included leaving a legacy for his son, Jamie. A legacy procured from the sale of Fallon's drugs. Without Fallon's knowledge, of course. But Fallon found out everything. Eventually. And now Jack was missing, along with Terry's insurance policy.

Terry took out his mobile phone and scrolled until he found the number he wanted. He held his finger over the call button for quite a few seconds. His tea was untouched, his mouth was dry, but he felt that if he drank it, he would most likely throw it back up again. Terry enjoyed his life, but above all, he loved his wife. He pressed the call button.

The call beeped back at Terry. Number not recognised flashed up on the screen. He tried again. The same result. It was Jack's private mobile phone number. A number that only a select few, including him and Fallon, had access to.

Terry scrolled through his phone again, selected another contact and pressed the call button. It went straight through to an answering machine. *Welcome to the offices of Andries Ltd. We are currently closed. Please leave a message after the tone and we will contact you upon our return. Thank you.*

A chill ran down Terry's body. Jack's offices were never closed. The phones were always diverted to either Jack's or one of his secretaries' phones. He wasn't due to shut up shop for weeks yet. He had either got cold feet or a cold heart. Either one was not good news for Terry. He selected one more contact and pressed the call button. His pulse had increased as he did so, and he could now feel his own heartbeat pumping behind his sternum. The phone was answered almost immediately.

"Terry." The voice on the other end sang out his name. "Told the missus about Dubai yet, mate?"

"Hey, Mep, no, not yet. Need to figure out how to tell her first. It's a bit different to Spain, eh?"

"I hear you with that one, Terry. My wife needs to get new makeup that won't melt in that heat. So, what's up, you still all good with what the Guv said earlier?"

"That's why I've called you, Mep. I think I'm good with it, but I just need to speak to Jack first. Need to smooth a couple of things out and make sure he doesn't screw up my backup plan. You know, the insurance bit I told you about. I want to get it back. Just to be sure that nothing goes wrong. You know what I mean. Have you seen or heard from him? You got any idea where he is?"

"Sounds fair enough to me, Terry, but I can't see Jack snitching to anyone. He, of all people, has got far too much to lose. Are you absolutely sure you want to talk to him? Just don't want you getting into any trouble with Fallon, that's all. You know what he's like when he's pissed off."

"Yeah, I know. I just need to cover my arse, that's all. Maybe I shouldn't have got Jack involved, maybe it was just a stupid mistake, but it is what it is now. I just want to make sure this is kept between the three of us. We've gone through too much for it all to go tits up now."

"Terry, it's your call. Give me half an hour. I'll find out where he is and see if he can talk, given the state we last saw him in. Phone you back in a bit, mate. And Terry. Stop bloody stressing, will you?"

Terry looked at his phone as the call ended. Something just didn't feel right. Decades of policing had a way of teaching someone what a gut feeling really was. And right now, Terry had a gut feeling that something was wrong, even though Fallon seemed to have everything meticulously planned and under control. And Mep sounded as happy as he had ever been. Something felt odd. In theory, the entire plan should be all good to go. But this wasn't theory, this was real life. At the moment, though, he didn't know what that something was. Whatever it was, it didn't feel right. He needed to find Jack, and he needed to find him quickly. He flicked the on switch for the kettle once again. He hoped that his friend, colleague and accomplice would phone him back quickly.

CHAPTER 28.

A small disused lock-up in Shepherds Bush, West London.
Charlie Mepham was sitting on an old, battered plastic chair
in a very small, and very dingy, little lock-up. One of those
that probably still contained asbestos, which was why it was
still standing. It was too expensive to demolish. There was a
single lightbulb hanging from the ceiling at the back of the
room, which gave just about enough light to see the front.
Even though the sun was shining outside, it was cold inside.
The lockup was situated in the shadow of a row of old
Victorian houses, keeping the temperature low. Mepham
had just finished a conversation on his phone. He was angry
now.

He knew that Terry was a bit of a soft touch at times,
but ironically, he had proven himself to be a good police
officer and an even better criminal. For the last God knows
how many years, Mepham's and Terry's paths had crossed
continually. They had worked together on different teams, in
different stations and on different operations, but they had
always remained close. Being close had also helped to
maintain some kind of logic between the two of them when
Fallon was being his absolute nastiest as he climbed to the
top of the drugs game in London. They helped each other
recall what they were doing and why.

But now Mepham was compromised. His friend
Terry had made a mistake. A mistake that he knew Fallon
would not tolerate lightly. If, indeed, Fallon was actually told
of the call that had just taken place. He had to think this
through quickly but carefully. Doing the wrong thing would

be catastrophic, but even doing the right thing might still compromise him.

In the centre of the lock-up sat a large metal trunk with a small vent at either end. Roughly six feet long by three feet wide and three feet high, the metal trunk resembled a macabre coffin from a tacky vampire film. Quite frankly, it gave Mepham the shivers. Inside the box lay Jack. When Fallon had taken him, he had been given enough drugs to knock out a horse, as much to keep him quiet in his surroundings as to stop him from screaming in pain. His body had taken a battering. Fallon's work at his very best; for Jack it was the very worst. Fallon had a real knack for taking someone right to the edge of death before pulling them back. It was like a game to him, and he was the best there was at it.

Mepham knew that Terry would not be having a conversation with Jack anytime soon, given his current predicament. That was going to cause a problem for Terry. He could panic. No, he would panic. If Mepham told Terry that Jack was no longer on the scene and just to crack on with the plans Fallon had put in place, that would similarly cause panic. Terry wanted to know that no one else knew about his stupid bloody insurance policy. If Mepham told Fallon of his conversation with Terry, he had no doubt that Fallon would remove Terry altogether. And if Fallon removed Terry, would that mean that Mepham's loyalty would be called into question, too? There was no telling what Fallon would do, and his violence was beyond question. He was a sadistic bastard when it came to disloyalty. But he was a smart criminal. He checked and double-checked every detail meticulously. As well as having eyes and ears everywhere, he also had some equally nasty bastards working for him. Fallon had protected himself well. Jack hadn't. And Mepham didn't want to end up in the same metal trunk he was now looking at. He had to think about self-preservation. He had no choice. Terry had seen to that. He took his phone out and dialled the second number on a dialled list.

"Nothing wrong, I hope, Mep. Jack still breathing?"

"Jack's still breathing, Guv, but we might have a problem with Terry." He explained the telephone call he had just had with Terry. Fallon remained silent throughout. Once he had finished, Mepham went quiet.

"Is this the first time you have heard about this, Mep? Seems to me that Terry has thought quite hard about how to protect his own arse if you ask me. Hmm?"

"Terry hasn't spoken to me about this before, Guv, I swear. If he had, I would have told you. What do you want me to do? If it helps any, I really don't think that Terry would have used his insurance policy."

"Is that right, Mep?" Fallon's voice was almost down to a whisper. "Well, he took the time to put his little plan into place. He had a thought process, which meant that he might have actually delivered on it. That means he didn't trust me. He didn't trust that I had everything in place to make him and his missus rich beyond anything they could ever imagine. That trust has been broken, gone, and you know how I have to deal with this, don't you, Mep? I have no choice. And right now, neither do you. Shame. Terry and I go back a long way. Why couldn't he just go with it? Laid on a silver bloody platter for him. We're days away from getting this whole bloody deal sorted out, and he goes and does something stupid like this." Fallon was angry. But he was more disappointed than anything. Terry Osman and Charlie Mepham were inner circle. And that circle was now compromised. He had been left with no other choice. Terry was going to have to pay the price.

"Are you going to ask me to deal with Terry, Guv? If you are, I won't like it, but I will do it."

"I know you would, Mep, but don't worry, I'll take care of it. Call Terry back and tell him to sit tight. Tell him Jack is finalising the deal and that he'll call him when he gets back."

"Ok, Guv, no problem. Do you still want me to stay with Jack? I'm back on shift tonight, but I can call in sick. Just blame the busted nose."

"No, don't worry. I've got someone else coming in to babysit. We need to keep things as normal as possible. I need to make the arrangements for Terry. Just a bloody shame, really. We're nearly there with Jack. Just waiting for the last set of paperwork that he put in place to go through once the packages arrive for the Albanians. When that's done, so is he. Seems like no one trusts us these days. First Jack, now Terry. Just hope there's no one else, hey, Mep."

The phone went dead. Fallon was gone, leaving Mepham with only one question. Was Fallon going to make similar arrangements for him as well, or was it just Jack and Terry that he was about to eliminate? Maybe it was time for Mepham to take out his own insurance policy.

CHAPTER 29.

Back at the Victorian terrace house in Hoxton, East London.
Terry had flicked the kettle switch three times in the last ten
minutes. He was pacing around the small kitchen, checking
his phone repeatedly. He had yet to make another cup of tea.
He jumped as the phone started to ring in his hand. "Hey,
Mep, any news on Jack at all?"

"Terry, stop panicking, for Christ's sake. It's all good.
He's sorting out the last of the paperwork for the transfers.
He'll give you a call as soon as he's done, and you two can
sort out this insurance crap together. So, like I said, mate, it's
all good. Jack sounded ok on the phone. Now, I suggest you
just do your day job, and when this is all over, we can have a
lifetime of Pina Coladas or whatever the hell it is they drink
over there in Dubai."

"If you're sure? Thanks for sorting that out, Mep. As
long as this is between the three of us, then I'm fine."

"Take it easy Terry. Speak soon."

Terry flicked the kettle on again and put his phone on
the table. Funny really. Whenever Terry had some issue or
another, his wife would always tell him to put the kettle on
and make a nice cup of tea. Gives you time to think, she said.
Terry must have had a lot of issues. Putting the kettle on had
become a habit. He had told Mepham about his insurance
policy. What he hadn't told him was that he also had a
contingency plan with Jack. And the contingency was very
simple indeed. If Jack didn't answer his phone, or he
couldn't be reached via the office number, then it was game
over. Jack's phone was dead, and the office had been shut
down. The contingency was now in play. Mepham had lied

to Terry. That much was clear. That also meant he had already spoken to Fallon as well.

Terry had made his decision.

CHAPTER 30.

Back in a small disused lock-up in Shepherd's Bush, West London.

Mepham cut the call with Terry Osman as quickly as he could. He was conscious it was probably the last time he would ever speak to his friend. Terry had definitely made his own bed, and not only was he prepared to lie in it, but he was also prepared to die in it. Despite the subtle pushbacks and innocuous warnings Mepham had given Terry not to do anything stupid, no notice had been taken. The one thing they had both learnt throughout their time of working together in the underbelly of the London drugs world was never to cross Fallon. Fallon was the nastiest one of all. He had acquired his knowledge from the very worst of humanity, and the only way he could better them was to be more repugnant, more malicious and more dangerous than all of them. And he had mastered it brilliantly.

Terry was looking for the best of both worlds. He wanted his life in London and Marbella with the money that was due to him. He wanted to live the life of a Sixties criminal, seen through the eyes of an old black-and-white movie. But those romantic days of crime were long gone. Even to the most uneducated eye, what Terry wanted was never going to happen. The money they used to buy drugs was stolen; these drugs were then procured through intimidation at a discounted price, and the violence for anyone who disagreed at any point during these transactions was swift and abhorrent. A lot of people would want revenge against those not one hundred per cent committed.

So, despite Mepham feeling sorry for his accomplice, he didn't want to end up on the wrong end of Fallon's punishment. He wasn't happy with the direction his life had taken over the last few years, but he was pragmatic enough to understand that he had to go with the flow.

It had been easy at first. Fallon just wanted to play on the edges with the dealers. Nothing big. Just some nice extra money that could easily be accounted away if anyone got too close. They weren't driving expensive cars. They weren't living in mansions. They did nothing that would raise eyebrows. What they were doing, though, was purchasing parcels of land abroad through various shell companies and then building properties on them, which were then either sold or rented out. Ridiculously, Mepham owned a small apartment block near Alicante, with the rent going into an account based somewhere in Switzerland. The account held close to £800,000. Was that going to be enough? It sounded like enough. Could he make it enough? If he hadn't been busted by then, he would also have his police pension. And if he did, it wouldn't be a bad retirement. Would it? Should be. As long as Interpol weren't chasing him in the meantime.

And then there was Jack. Well, he was an absolute wizard in the art of making money disappear and then reappear legitimately. Most people would have been happy with that, but not Fallon. He had dangled a huge carrot in front of Jack. One worth millions. And that was when it all started to get a lot worse. Fallon didn't want to just be a player. He wanted to be *the* player. The main man in London. And he was going to do whatever it took to become that man. That meant taking total control of Jack. He was the real mastermind behind making the money for Fallon, and he knew it. When Jack started to say that enough was enough, Fallon made it very clear that one person alone would make that decision, every decision, and that person was him. Mepham had helped with some of those decisions, as well as dealing with the consequences. Consequences he would never be proud of.

And here was Jack. Locked in a trunk three feet away from Mepham, having had most of his living daylights beaten out of him. The same Jack that meant Mepham had eight hundred grand in a Swiss bank. Trouble was, Jack was in the trunk because the end was close. It was almost time to take the money and run. But there would be no money for Jack. Just an unmarked grave somewhere. At least, for now, Fallon still had a modicum of decency. Jack had been given enough bottles of water for a day or so and was wrapped in an old wool blanket to keep him warm. Amazing what could be done when Fallon needed to keep someone alive. He had a nasty habit of taking people to the edge of life, and then, as if to show some humanity, he would bring them back again. Fallon needed Jack. This meant that Mepham had a decision of his own to make. And he needed to make it now.

The cold in the lock-up was seeping into his bones. He needed warmth. Fallon hadn't extended him the same courtesy as he did to Jack. He couldn't think straight. He pulled up a side roller door, bent down and stepped into the daylight. He pulled the door back down again and loosely padlocked it, heading away without looking back. Walking the hundred yards or so to where he had left his car, he looked up and down the West London Victorian Road as he went. He looked at every car he walked past. None of them was occupied. He got in his car and started the engine to get the heater going.

Once the car was warm, Mepham pulled out his mobile phone and made two phone calls. He then removed the SIM card, snapped the little gold and white coloured piece of plastic in half, opened the passenger window and threw both small pieces into the undergrowth of one of the front gardens beyond the pavement. He closed the window, put the car into gear and headed towards East London.

Back in the lock-up, Jack was barely breathing. His jaw hurt like hell where it had been punched, his nose was broken, one of his arms felt dislocated, the fingers on his left hand had been broken and by the feel of it, so were some of his ribs. The drugs he had been injected with had started to wear off. The pain was getting worse. His memory was coming back.

He remembered being in his office. He hadn't been due to transfer the final funds from Fallon's shell companies for two weeks. Fallon had phoned Jack and said there had been a change of plan. The money needed to be moved straight away. Fallon sounded angrier than Jack had ever heard him sound. It was clear that something had happened. Jack, with his usual manner, facetiously mentioned that it wasn't like using a cash machine and that it would take a couple of days to authorise the various stages of the transactions. Fallon had put the phone down without saying anything further. He wasn't happy.

Jack knew something big was happening. His gut told him to move quickly. And that meant not putting the transactions into play as Fallon wanted. Holding the key to the transactions was his ace card. But he needed to put his contingency plan into place. And to do right now.

He went with his own intuition. He had just finished putting the final pieces of his plan into place. The office manager had been briefed that the Solicitors' Regulation Authority were on their way to the office for an unscheduled audit. All the staff had to stay at home until Jack called again with the all-clear. Of course, there was no audit, but he needed everybody away. He had then left a message for Jamie not to call him, but everything was ok. Just a couple of problems to sort out, that's all.

He then reported his mobile phone stolen and told the phone company to cancel it straight away. He had then put a holding message on the office answer machine to say Andries and Co were closed. The first time that any such message had ever been left. Jack had always been open for business. He had then thrown the phone on the floor and crushed it with his foot. Scraping the pieces under a desk, he opened a drawer and took out an old phone. It was a phone he had used when he didn't want Dot finding out about his numerous affairs. It was clunky, it still worked, and it had some charge in it. Just in case of emergencies. Like now. He put it in the inside pocket of his jacket. Thank God for infidelity.

He spent the next hour blocking a whole host of transactions that would have put Fallon on *The Times* top 500 rich list. Not now, though. Jack was the only one capable of putting everything right and giving Fallon access to the money.

He remembered the office phone ringing. Without knowing why, he held his breath. The message played, but no voicemail was left. Then there had been a loud knocking on the office door. Jack looked out of the window. It was Fallon and a couple of his thugs. He then moved slowly to the door and opened it.

"Working into the small hours, eh, Jack? Must be busy? You going to let me know what you have been up to? Sorted out the transactions yet? Rather important we get them done soon as. You understand me?" Fallon's tone was cold and calm.

"As I said on the phone, I can move them forward, but it's still going to take a couple of days. I've requested them as you asked. It wasn't that simple."

"Yes, of course. Not quite like a cashpoint. That's what you said, wasn't it? Yes, cashpoint. Well. Do I look like someone who has spent years getting to this point and then withdraw my money from a cashpoint, Jack? Well? Do I?"

"It was just a comment, Fallon, that's all. I've started the process to get the money through quicker. There's not much more I can do." Jack had moved backwards into the room. Fallon had slowly started walking towards him.

"There aren't enough cash points in the country for the amount of money I'm owed, Jack. You know that, and so do I. Show me the transactions, Jack. Over there. On your computer. You can do that for me, can't you, Jack? Shouldn't be too hard for you. Just want to make sure what you said stacks up, that's all. Reasonable request. Wouldn't you say, boys?" Fallon looked behind him at his two thugs. They both nodded at Fallon in unison.

"I can't do that, Fallon. The transaction codes won't be released until an hour before they are ready. It's standard protocol. You know that."

"Hmm. Yes. Of course. Codes." Fallon snapped his fingers.

Immediately, both thugs stepped forward and grabbed hold of him.

"Dropped your phone, did we. Seems quite a mess on the floor over there. Too much mess for one drop of a phone if you ask me."

Jack started to panic. He should have cleared the phone away, not just scraped some of it under the desk.

Fallon took out his own mobile phone and pressed a button.

"Funny that, Jack. Your phone doesn't appear to be working. Not even a voicemail. So, tell me. How exactly are you going to get the codes for the transactions if your phone doesn't work?

"The codes aren't going to the phone. They are going to email. We have over twenty transactions in progress, Fallon. I can't do all of those on a bloody mobile phone. They need to be done by email. As soon as the bank initiates the codes, we call them, and I will provide a response for each code. You need me for those responses, and you know it. Without me, there's no money. None."

"Think you are so smart don't you? So, why does it feel that you aren't quite telling me everything, Jack?" Fallon pressed a key on his phone for the second time. The main switchboard phone in the office started to ring. It went to voicemail. They all listened to the message. "Sounds to me like you are making plans to go away somewhere, Jack. Wouldn't you say? Tell me. Are you right or left-handed, Jack?"

"Er – right-handed, why?"

Fallon didn't answer. He simply took hold of Jack's left hand and politely asked one of the thugs to break every finger on it. Despite Jack's protestations, this is exactly what he proceeded to do. Finger by finger, each one was pulled back sharply until it cracked and broke. Jack screamed.

"Don't be upset, Jack. Your right hand is perfectly fine. For now. So, I guess we see what happens when the codes are released. I don't like being kept waiting, Jack, so you'd better deliver for me."

The last thing that Jack could remember was being punched hard in the face by Fallon. Then it all went black until he woke up in a trunk. And his body was screaming at him. He had never felt pain like it. He stared into the almost pitch-black trunk. There was a sliver of light at one end where the air vent was. He had to think. He knew that Fallon would be back once the money was due. And that was not something Jack was looking forward to. Then he remembered. The old phone was still in his pocket. The irony of infidelity.

CHAPTER 31.

London – Back at the glass room at the posh police station. Dot brushed the remnants of her pastry from the corner of her mouth, stood up, and headed over to fill up her coffee cup yet again. She had been in the room for nearly two hours now and was still trying to make sense of everything that she had been told. Her now ex-associate DS Elkins had taken an urgent phone call and left the room to answer it. Dot had no idea what was being discussed as Elkins had his back to her and was walking up towards the far end of the corridor. He finished his call and turned to look in Dot's direction to see her staring right back at him. He lifted one finger, indicating one minute, then turned and made another call.

Dot turned to look out of the window. She stared down at the now thinned out populace of London, most of which had disappeared into their places of work or into one of the copious amounts of coffee shops. The door to the conference room opened.

"Apologies for putting you through the grinder, Inspector LaSalle, but you must understand, we needed to ensure that you are indeed on the right side of the law, so to speak."

She turned as Chief Inspector Pencil Skirt entered the room and watched as she pushed the large glass door shut behind her. "It's fine, ma'am, this obviously isn't the first time you've done this sort of thing to me." Her tone was cynical. "Almost a habit, in my book. So, why the sudden change of heart? What makes you so convinced I'm no longer an all-conquering drug lord masquerading as a screwed-up police officer, then?" Dot was pleased with her quick-witted, matter of fact reply. The power of a good pastry and two pints of coffee was unequivocally working.

"Well, given that an apology was issued to you earlier for the necessary albeit unfortunate events concerning you and Fallon, we can now assume that subsequent intelligence has precluded you from at least one line of our many enquiries. That line of enquiry currently being handled outside by DS Elkins would appear to prove your innocence of any involvement in the case being discussed here with you this morning."

Dot was suddenly conscious that she had missed a bit of pastry that was glued to the corner of her top lip. And she was even more conscious that the charmingly spoken Chief Inspector Pencil Skirt was staring straight at said piece of elusive pastry. With a deft flick of her tongue, it swiftly disappeared.

"With all due respect, ma'am, whilst an apology for not pursuing a sexually motivated attack on a serving police officer may be acceptable in your book, it never was in mine. So, forgive me if I still seem a tad pissed off. As for being under investigation for God knows what kind of accessory to a bent copper who now appears to be running the entire London drug market, well, as I said, please forgive me. It would appear that people far more important than I have a darn sight more to be accountable for in allowing this to happen right underneath their noses. So, thank you for informing me that I was found not guilty of something I didn't even know I could be found not guilty of in the first place. I very much appreciate your honesty." Dot took a deep breath of the conditioned air in the room and slowly exhaled. If she was going to be reprimanded for her little speech, then at least it was a speech that felt good.

"Allowing things to happen right under one's nose is exactly why you are here, Inspector LaSalle. Given that your husband is the mastermind behind all of the legal and financial operations that appear to have allowed this particular OCG to evolve and prosper, would give anyone with the smallest amount of intelligence the understanding that you may also potentially be involved. Now, let me introduce myself. I'm Chief Inspector Teresa Clayton. I work directly with Commander Truss. As such, I'm lead liaison between all senior parties working on this case. Please sit down. We need to ask you some questions about your husband."

Just listening to this woman was making Dot exhausted. She moved across to the large table and sat down. "Ask away, ma'am. I'm all ears."

At that point, Elkins walked back into the room. He looked across to the Chief Inspector and simply said, "We've got it."

She nodded her head and said, "Inspector, it's time to move. We need you to come with us right away. You can ask questions in the vehicle."

Elkins opened the door and held it for the Chief Inspector. Dot sat for a moment longer in the chair to try to gather herself. Elkins coughed loudly. "It's very important. We need to go now, ma'am. I have a van waiting downstairs."

Dot's legs felt like lead weights as she stood. The clock above the door said 10.30 am. If it wasn't daylight outside, she would have sworn it was 10.30 pm. She followed Elkins and Clayton towards the lift, still wondering how the hell Clayton could fit into, let alone walk in, her pencil skirt. The lift doors opened, and all three entered. Elkins pressed minus 2 and watched as the doors silently closed.

"So, am I allowed to know where you are taking me?"

Elkins looked at Clayton, who nodded back at him. "We are going to see your husband, ma'am. But please be warned, you might not like what you see. We are hoping that he'll be more receptive with you present, as we have rather a lot of questions that we need answering."

CHAPTER 32.

A different café near London Bridge. 10.05 am.

DCI Patrick Fallon sat alone in the half-empty café near one of the entrances to London Bridge railway station. His morning, so far, had been spent frequenting different cafes. It always seemed to Fallon that most underhanded business was done in establishments like these. Still, the caffeine he was consuming was certainly welcome. He needed his wits about him.

Most of the customers had been and gone for breakfast, and those that remained were either between meetings and appointments or just between nothing at all and making one coffee or tea last as long as possible before having to decide where to go next.

Fallon felt comfortable in these types of places. He was in the mix of regular people, most of whom took no real notice of him. And for those who did take notice of him, it gave him the advantage of opportunity. Opportunity to stay or leave, surrounded by the public, depending on who it was that was taking notice.

The owner of the café knew Fallon. Not personally, not professionally, just as a good customer. She used to run another café not far from where they were now, and Fallon was a regular there. She would have done anything to get really personal with him, but he had always made it very clear that, whilst he appreciated the admiration, he was not interested in anything other than teas, coffees and nice baps. So much so, that, that when she said she was moving cafés, Fallon took his patronage with her. She walked over with a large mug of coffee. Not a cappuccino or a latte, but a stronger, less frothy coffee, specially made the way Fallon liked it.

"You ok, Pat? You look like you've got the whole world on your shoulders this morning. You sure I can't interest you in a little massage to relax you?" The wink of her eye made her suggestion comical; the tone of her voice made the suggestion sexual.

"I'm good, Eileen, thanks. Just a couple of staffing issues, that's all. Really don't like letting people go, but sometimes you have no choice. Thanks for the coffee. And don't take it personally on the massage, hey. Out there somewhere is the perfect man for you, you know that."

"Oh, I know that, Pat, but you can't blame me for trying to nick a sweet out of the sweetie jar now, can you. Especially when you're one of my favourite flavours."

"Haven't you got any work to do? You're making me blush. Don't embarrass me in front of your customers."

Eileen swirled around and walked back to the serving counter, chuckling away to herself.

Fallon poured the equivalent of about four teaspoons of sugar into his coffee from a standard sugar dispenser and started stirring. His facial expression gave nothing away to anyone in the café, but inside, he was apoplectic with rage. Not only had he been let down by individuals close to him, but he was sure he had also been betrayed by them as well. Not content with just taking the money Fallon was giving to them, he was convinced they had given away information. Information that threatened his entire operation. He was within spitting distance of finalising the ultimate deal. The deal that had been years in the making. The deal that would have made those close to him millionaires, multiple times over. He had worked out everything. He had even masterminded a straight handover of his drug territories to the Albanians. They held a few territories in London. Fallon was handing them the rest, along with discounted drugs. They were getting territories without a fight and additional profit from the drugs. They knew it was a win-win for them.

Overnight, they were going to control more of London than anyone else. By then, Fallon would be living under a new identity in Dubai.

Over the last few years, he had put together an elite team of bent police officers and a few nasty outsiders for the real dirty work. But his choice now was very simple. He had to make some of them redundant before they leaked any more information. He had made people disappear before, but they were people that nobody would miss. They weren't long-serving police officers. Officers who, between them, held handfuls of commendations for jobs well done during their tenure. Officers who had families, homes, relatives, friends and colleagues. When a police officer goes down, the entire force feels the pain. And Fallon was about to deliver a tidal wave of that. Before anything could be done, though, he had to wait. He had to wait for financial transactions to go through. Transactions that Jack Andries had initiated at Fallon's request. And he didn't like waiting.

Fallon trusted no one, and because Jack had now begun the process for the financial transfers, he ensured that Jack was in no position to compromise the deal. Which was why Jack was currently in a trunk in a lock-up a couple of miles from where Fallon now sat. As soon as the transactions were complete, Jack Andries would be taken care of. It had to be a clean job to make him disappear; otherwise, his bitch of a wife could be a problem. Despite the fact that he had got away with one crime against her, he knew that he had stirred a hornet's nest. And she was still the angriest hornet of all. Made immeasurably worse by the fact that the woman also happened to have a mother deposited firmly in one of the care homes that Jack was working his magic on. Jack had assumed that with his mother-in-law in situ at a care home, this would give him unconditional access to a whole host of new target widows, without raising suspicion. To be fair, he had managed to procure a lot of new business from the care homes, but he was getting sloppy. Too close to home. Keep crapping on your own doorstep for long enough, and eventually, someone will step right in it. Well, stepping into Jack's pile of crap had cost lives, and quite possibly put Fallon's entire operation at risk. And that was another reason Jack was in a trunk.

The door to the café opened. Fallon had subconsciously been watching the individual who entered. He had been standing fifty yards down on the opposite side of the road, tucked against the window of a charity shop. He was a big, mixed-race man in his early thirties. Massimo Albricci was over six feet four inches, and Fallon guessed his weight at around 230lbs. He sported a short beard and wore a thin beanie pulled down low over his eyebrows. He was wearing a black gilet, and, underneath, the long-sleeved white cotton top did nothing to hide the muscular body. He walked over to the counter and asked Eileen for a double espresso and a glass of water. He paid, turned around, headed directly for Fallon and sat opposite him

"Albi, thanks for coming. You doing ok?" Fallon used the shortened name for ease. Both first name and surname were too much of a mouthful for him.

"I'm good, boss. Was trying to keep my head down until you decided to bring me out in the open. I guess whatever you have is important, then."

Fallon let out a big sigh. "Yeah, you could say that, Albi."

Two women at the table next to Fallon stood up. They then spent what Fallon seemed to think was a wholly interminable amount of time putting on their coats and air kissing, promising not to wait so long to see each other next time and that, if all else failed, they would be invited to each other's works Christmas parties. They slowly walked to the door, and once on the street outside, headed their separate ways.

Fallon realised that his Christmas would be a very different one this year. A long way from here. A long way from those who would no doubt spend their days figuring out ways of getting him back to face justice. He wasn't scared. He had everything worked out. Dead people can't talk. He watched Eileen head over with a small tray carrying the coffee and water for Albi.

"If he's one of the ones you are making redundant, Pat, then tell him I would be happy to take him on. Good pay and extraordinary benefits. Just say the word."

"Christ, don't you ever give up, Eileen?"

"Oh, I think you know the answer to that one, Pat." She smiled and put a deliberate wiggle in her walk back to the counter.

"No disrespect, Boss, but I think she's more your type than mine. So, what's up? Why am I here?"

"We have a couple of problems that I want you to take care of, Albi. One is already contained and will be an easy target; the other will be more difficult. Much higher profile, but the good news is you'll pick up their fee for the job they are trying to pull out of. Oh, and for the fact that they are trying to double-cross me. Double-cross us. Fee is an additional three mill. Plus, another apartment in Dubai."

"Ouch. Double cross. That must hurt. Especially when you're the expert at that. Well, you know me, Boss. Happy to sort out any problems you have, and even happier to take your money. But I reckon this will have to be it after these jobs. Talking of double crosses, there's a lot of heat out there on me at the moment. Bloody police have been chasing me for the Krystina Benko job. The only thing in my favour is that someone gave them a photo of me when I was nineteen years old. Good job, I've been going to the gym since then, but I wonder who gave them that information. Especially as I wasn't the one who took care of Krystina. Wouldn't have been you that passed on the information by any chance, would it, Boss? Needed an alibi, did you?"

"You know it was me, Albi. If we didn't get the chance to implicate that bloody idiot of a security guard, then we needed someone else to implicate. The best person for that was you. We needed to close it down quickly. The more information you give quickly, the more it distracts people until you are ready to move. That's what happened here. It's business, that's all." Fallon sat further into his seat and leaned in towards Albi so that he could speak more quietly. "And if you trusted me, you would also know that I sorted that situation out. I just needed some time to deal with it. Once these last loose ends are taken care of, you're in the clear. We arrested another suspect for the death of Krystina, who confessed, left more DNA than you get at a barrister's toga party, and very handily for us, topped himself in the nick, so to speak. So, you see, I said I would take care of it, and I have. The closing statement for Krystina Benko will go on file later today and will completely exonerate you. Okay?"

Albi leaned back into the chair. He had to be careful not to fall backwards, his frame sitting large in the small seat. "Ha! You are a clever one, Fallon, but a devious bastard as well. So, I get the all-clear once I clean up your mess, yet again. And my incentive, if I behave, is more money, and I get to sail off into the sunset. Yeah, I know your game, Boss. Genius."

"No need to get arsy with me, Albi, I haven't let you down yet, so just have some bloody faith. And remember who it was that picked your sorry backside out of the gutter all those years ago."

Again, Albi laughed. Too loudly for Fallon's liking. "And I thank you for picking my sorry backside out of the gutter, Boss. But to be fair, I wasn't being chased by half of London's police then as I am now. I can't go home because of this, and once again, my sorry backside feels like it's back in the gutter. So, forgive my shitty attitude, but from where I'm sitting, it doesn't matter if it's three quid or three million quid. I can't even get to my fucking bank to get it out."

"Albi, I said you'll be fine, and I meant it. This is completely different to before, and you know it, son. Before, you were in the gutter because you ripped apart the man who robbed and murdered your mother. What you did was wrong in the eyes of the law, but in my eyes, it's exactly what I would have done. Exactly what I would have done, Albi.

That's why I pulled your sorry backside out of the gutter and got you cleared of the charges. I felt sorry for you, but I also knew you deserved another chance. That's why I put everything on the line for you back then, and I'll do the same again if I have to. We are so close to getting this shit sorted. Once and for all. We get away from here. We have more money than we'll know what to do with, and we can start a brand-new life on our own terms.

The two men sat quietly. Neither said anything more.

Fallon had first come across Albi around ten years ago when he got called to a suspected murder robbery in North London. Albi was just a kid then, but Fallon could see, in the terrified, blood-spattered youth, someone who he would be able to use. And use. And use. And then spit out.

Albi took a sip of his water. "I owe you, Boss. Trouble is, trying to figure you out sometimes is tough. Guess I should have trusted you with this, eh? You always know what you are doing. Now, what do you need me to do?"

Fallon's phone let out a quiet ping. He took it out of his shirt pocket and read the text in silence.

"Everything okay, boss?"

"We need to move, Albi. I need to go and collect a package before someone else gets their hands on it first. I need you to go and collect a package as well. Time to go."

CHAPTER 33.

En route.

The lift doors opened into a large, well-lit underground car park. Elkins exited first, followed by Clayton and lastly Dot. Positioned right in front of the lift doors was an idling black police van with its side door open. A plainclothes police officer held onto the door handle. Elkins acknowledged the officer and stepped up into the van.

Clayton walked to the front of the van and spoke to a firearms officer who was dressed in full bulletproof kit. The officer had been waiting for Clayton. The two pips on his shoulder indicated that he was an Inspector, one rank below her. It would seem that, at this moment in time, she was in charge of whatever operation this was.

Elkins called to Dot to get in beside him in the van. Dot was looking into the open door of the van in front. She counted five other firearms officers in the van. This was a decent-sized operation. Jack must certainly be knee-deep in some type of trouble with Fallon or badly wanted by the force. Or both. Dot stepped into the van.

"You don't put this type of firepower together in five minutes, Elkins. You knew something was going down all along, didn't you?"

Elkins said nothing.

Dot sat down and pulled the seatbelt around her. They were cockpit-style seatbelts that wrapped over each shoulder and buckled you in tight. This was certainly the flashiest police van she had ever been in.

Clayton finished her conversation with the firearms inspector and hopped up into the van. Dot was baffled how anyone could make that type of manoeuvre in a pencil skirt. It was difficult enough for an aged Dot in an elasticated trouser suit.

The van door was closed from the outside. Clayton sat down, placed a pair of headphones that had been hanging over her headrest on her head, buckled up and shouted at the driver to go. The headphones had a small microphone boom attached. She then signalled to Elkins and Dot to put on their own headphones.

The van pulled away at speed and left the car park, the traffic making way for the blue lights. There were no sirens on this operation. The sunglasses worn by passersby indicated that the sun was shining outside. The police vans' tinted windows reflected the UV light as well as the stares from the public away from those sitting inside. This painted a very different picture. It created a surreal feeling.

"We should be at our RV in around twenty minutes or so, as long as the traffic plays ball. We're being joined by some of our armed response colleagues from West London as well. Just in case." Clayton's voice came through the headphones loud and clear.

"Just in case of what?" Dot had shouted rather than spoken her reaction to her question from Clayton. Both Clayton and Elkins quickly lifted their respective headphones in frustration.

"Your husband holds the keys to the money, Dot. An awful lot of money. To some, he is valuable beyond belief; to others, he is a huge liability and needs to be taken care of. We are up against both of those, so we're taking no chances with this. Our job is to find Jack alive and get him into protective custody as soon as we can. Given the breaches of intelligence information sustained by the force when dealing with this group, we need to keep everything tight. That's why you are with us."

Elkins was staring straight at Dot.

"Ah, great, I get it now. So, what you said back at the station was bullshit. You don't need me here to comfort and calm poor little Jack when you find him. You need me here, where you can see me. And hear me. And keep tabs on me. Well, take it from me, luv, you have absolutely nothing to worry about, other than my oversized mouth spitting out something that you clearly don't believe. And that's the truth. Until this morning, I had no idea that Jack was involved as the Chief bloody Operating Officer for a crooked OCG. Believe whatever you want to believe about Jack and me. That is, of course, if he is still alive."

Not for the first, second, third or fourth time that morning, Dot had been pushed into an internal apoplectic rage. She was angry because she was being accused of things that she didn't know of. And worse than being angry about it, she was utterly embarrassed by a situation that had been happening right under her nose for some considerable time. Not the best advert for her career as a police officer. Her phone started to vibrate in her jacket pocket.

Looking at Elkins, she asked, "Shall I answer that, Detective Sergeant, or do you recommend I leave it?"

"It's Jamie. Leave it. If it goes to voicemail, ma'am, you can play it, and we can hear what he wants and deal with it then."

"Well, let me give you a clue as to what he wants, shall I? He wants to know where his father is. And, so far, I'm not allowed to tell him anything at all, which in my role as stepmother kind of sucks, but in my role as police inspector is just bloody heartbreaking."

Everything went quiet in the van. Dot noticed that Clayton was speaking into her microphone to someone elsewhere. She had the VIP headset. Clearly.

Dot's phone vibrated yet again. She went to take her phone out of her jacket pocket, but Elkins, holding his own phone in his right hand, scolded her. "Leave it."

"Leave it, *ma'am*," responded Dot in a similar tone. "And no, I'm not leaving it. I have a duty of care to my stepson, and I also need my phone on to keep tabs on my mother. So no, I'm not leaving it." She pulled her phone out and slipped her headphones off. She looked at the screen on her phone. There was one voicemail and two text messages. The first text was telling her there was a voicemail. The second message was from Jamie. It simply said. *Dot, watch your back.* Dot played the voicemail, knowing full well that Elkins couldn't hear what was being said, but had probably heard the original call. Quite frankly, she didn't care if he did hear. So far, amongst all of those she had met in the last few hours, she was the only one who had nothing to hide.

"Dot, I still can't get hold of Dad. There is something weird going on. Just had a call from a training schoolmate of mine based over in West London. Call me when you can. And Dot. Make sure you watch your back."

"So, Mr Eavesdropper, what say you? Call him back or wait. I know I'm intrigued by the message." Dot had played the message on speaker.

The van had slowed. It was now off the main road and negotiating speed bumps. That meant side roads. They must be closer to their destination.

As if reading Dot's mind, Clayton said, "Three minutes out. Elkins, you stay in the van with Inspector LaSalle. I'll be jumping into the response vehicle to run ops from there. Once we have an all-clear from the teams, we'll establish if you are required to attend the scene, return to base, or disappear. You will not move from this vehicle. Do you understand? And please remember, Dot, this isn't just about Jack. There's a whole lot more at stake here. Do I make myself clear?"

Elkins nodded. "Ma'am, understood."

"What the hell do you mean, disappear? Who? Me?"

"Yes, Dot, you. Your husband is currently a highly sought-after prize. That means that potentially you are too. So, as I said. Sit. Wait. Do nothing. Until you are told otherwise by me. Have I made myself clear?"

Dot glared at Clayton. She felt utterly useless.

The van continued over the speed bumps and did a series of right and left turns.

Clayton seemed to be receiving the full story through her headphones. Before the van came to a complete halt, she had already undone her seatbelt and was leaning forward in her seat. The side door of the van was opened from the outside, and she jumped out. The door then slid shut again, and the van reversed into what Dot assumed was a holding position.

Not for the first time, Dot felt as though she was in some way a character in a surreal film or book about a dystopian world where she watched all of those around her command her own life for their pleasure. Never had she felt so out of control of anything in her life. "If I'm in danger, then that means Jamie is as well. Are you taking care of that, Elkins?"

"We're trying to find him, ma'am. Not to alarm you any more than you are already, but he appears to have gone AWOL. We have eyes trying to locate him as we speak."

"What do you mean AWOL? How can he go missing when you are listening to his phone twenty-four-seven? Surely you must have some kind of tracker on it. You have the backing of military intelligence, for crying out loud."

"The backing of military intelligence is all thanks to you, ma'am, no one else. We have eyes looking for Jamie, that's all I can say at this moment in time. We are trying to see if we can triangulate his phone signal, but he keeps turning it off and only has it on for very short periods. We just need to get your husband safe, and then we can concentrate on finding Jamie."

Without any warning, the van lurched forward. The driver had slammed the vehicle into gear and had pulled away fast. He was hitting the speed bumps at pace and was in a hurry. Elkins jumped across into the seat previously occupied by Clayton, put on the headphones and started speaking immediately, presumably to the driver.

Dot was trying to shift in her seat to tighten her seatbelt and to hold on to both of the straps. Elkins was shouting into his microphone. He had his hand wrapped around it so Dot couldn't make out what he was saying. She managed to pivot slightly to get her headphones on properly. They had been displaced while going over one of the speed bumps. She had just managed to pull her microphone back into position when the van struck something. Something metal. There was a high-pitched scraping noise for a few seconds before the van veered violently to the left and came to a crashing but immediate halt. Dot had read statements where people involved in accidents recalled that everything seemed to slow down throughout the whole event. Well, not this event. Dot's world went from sixty miles an hour to zero in the space of a nanosecond. She was sitting facing the rear of the van. Her back felt like it had just been hit by a load of buckshot. Her saving grace was the seat itself. It was high-backed, so there was no real whiplash. Just a solid thud. What wind she had left in her body was forced out by the almighty thump.

Elkins must have known what was coming or was just plain lucky. He was in a position in the seat where his body was braced for an impact. He unclipped the seatbelt and threw it off behind him. One hand was already on the door to open it. With the other, he reached into a compartment down to his right and pulled out a Glock. Ensuring the safety was off, he told Dot to stay where she was. He opened the door and immediately dropped to the ground with the pistol raised. He swept his arms from right to left, surveying the scene before him.

Dot had unclipped her seat belt and was frog-marching herself in small steps towards the open van door. There was smoke coming from somewhere and it smelt acrid, bringing tears to her eyes. Elkins moved towards the front of the van. There didn't appear to be any movement from the driver.

Dot heard the high revving of a vehicle fast approaching. Close and getting closer. The vehicle stopped with a screech of tyres, and milliseconds later, there were loud calls of "Armed Police, DO NOT MOVE. STAY DOWN." This was continually repeated as the police officers were moving closer to where Dot squatted just inside the door of the van.

Elkins had placed his weapon on the ground in front of him and stood up with his hands held high. Dot, for the first time, had seen the object they had struck. A huge old oak tree.

A police officer dressed in black emerged from her left-hand side, shouting at Dot not to move. He was pointing a Taser directly at her. This was confirmed by the small red dot that had appeared on her lower chest. The police officer ushered her out of the van. She complied willingly, not wishing to be electrocuted. He then looked inside the van and shouted a very loud "CLEAR".

Elkins, who had been given the all-clear by the newly arrived armed police, ran to Dot and grabbed hold of her arm. "We need to move to the other van, ma'am. It's not safe here; this van could go up at any point." He pulled her out of the van. Once out, he guided her toward the rear of the van, but she shrugged off his grip and ran back to the front of the vehicle. Her back and lungs hurt like hell as she gasped at what she saw. The driver of the van was unconscious. Given the crumpled condition of the vehicle, she wasn't sure how anyone in the front seats could have survived. Two officers were tending to him, having moved the airbag, which had blown its cartridge full force into his face, out of the way.

Dot turned around and slipped past Elkins' outstretched arm to look at what the van had collided with. She ran 40 yards back down the road to find two other officers in the middle of the road, kneeling beside a crumpled motorbike that lay on its side. It was obvious that this was what the van had struck first, which then caused it to collide with the tree. Strewn all over the road were fifty-pound notes. A lot of them. The rider had lost his right leg in the collision, and it was clear that he was dead. His helmeted head was lying at an angle that no head had the capability of lying at unless the spine had been snapped in two. One of the officers was in the process of removing the helmet. He wasn't being gentle with the task. Undoing the strap, he tugged hard on the helmet, releasing its contents with a thud onto the tarmac. Dot instantly recognised the dead rider. She covered her face with her hands and moved towards him. It was Andy Patterson, her friend and desk sergeant of many years.

Doing her level best to hold back tears and quite frankly failing miserably, she stood up and screamed as loudly as she could, "Will someone PLEASE tell me what the fuck is going on here?" She felt both her arms being gripped simultaneously. She was dragged away from the body and the motorbike and found herself almost levitating towards the open door of the other police van. She was unceremoniously dumped inside by two large police officers. She was further pushed from behind and followed into the vehicle by Elkins. The door shut, and the van started to move.

Elkins leaned across. He was shaking his head at her. "Before you ask, I swear I didn't know that Patterson was involved. Are you ok? I mean physically. Do we need to divert to a medic?"

"No, I'm ok. Just bruised. Given the way the last bloke drove, I suggest you put your seat belt on." Her face was wholly unsmiling. "So, what the hell just happened, Elkins? I assume they didn't find Jack, or if they did, he wasn't alive, otherwise I would be back there talking to him."

"The intel we had on Jack's location was good. We just got there too late. Someone must have tipped them off that we were headed there." Elkins held his head in his hands and rubbed his eyes for a long moment. "I think you can now see why we trust no one. Jack was gone from the location. Given the surroundings he was being held in, at least we can confirm he's being held against his will. We missed him by a few minutes. We have to assume that Patterson was part of the group that was holding Jack, and he was already on the bike when the units arrived. Hence the reason our man in the driving seat took him out. I've been told to get you back into town at double speed and not let you out of my sight. Not until we debrief fully, that's as much as I know."

"So, you have no idea if Jack is dead or alive or where he is, then? They are always one step ahead of you on this. If you had no idea that Patterson was involved, then how the hell do you know who to talk to or not? And how would Patterson know that we were on our way if indeed it was him that told whoever it was that took Jack? Who else knew that we were on our way? Forgive me for saying this, but it seems to me like the tail is wagging the bloody dog here. They know you are onto them, but do they know you know who they are? Who has the better intel here? You or them? Why not just concentrate on Fallon, locate him and take him out? Cut the head off this thing, once and for all. That way, at least, you might locate Jack at the same time. After all, it's got to be easier to track down a serving police officer."

"Because, ma'am, if we take out Fallon, we might never find Jack. If he is still alive, then Fallon needs him. All the time Fallon needs him alive, we still stand a chance of finding him.

"Well, at least you can eliminate me now. Given I've been right under your nose all morning. Just a shame that the rest of your team can't get a handle on all of this. It's not going to look good for the top brass if London is flooded with drugs. And flooded courtesy of police officers. Tell me, if you can't take Fallon out, then what about any of his other associates? Mepham, Osman? What about them? Why can't you bring them in? You must have enough to throw the entire book at them. I just don't get it. You are either bloody stupid, or you are still keeping stuff back. And in your defence, I don't think you are stupid. So, what are you holding back, Elkins?

"Ma'am, you can see how fluid this is. We have to be very careful how we handle the current situation. There's more at stake here than just Jack, drugs and money.

"Oh Christ! That's it, isn't it? Your source. They are from inside Fallon's OCG. It's a police officer, isn't it? Wow, you really can't trust anyone, can you? And I say that in the business sense, Elkins. So, who is it? Who is giving you the information from the inside?"

Elkins slowly rubbed his eyes again. Both he and Dot stank from the acrid smoke from the earlier police van fire.

"It's Mepham. But he has only just turned in our favour. We weren't sure we could trust a word he was saying, but after missing Jack by minutes today, the intel he gave us seemed to be good. We didn't know if we were headed into an ambush or something else. It would seem that both Mepham and Osman have had second thoughts about their involvement. We sent a team over to get Osman, but the house was empty. We don't know if he's gone underground or if he's been taken out by Fallon. So, we currently have Jack, Mepham, Osman and Jamie missing. And we need to establish what Jamie means by telling you to watch your back. If he is sending a warning, then it sounds like someone out there either wants you as collateral or dead. And right now, nobody around here wants another missing or dead person.

CHAPTER 34

Detective Chief Inspector Fallon is on the move. Just before the motorbike crash.

Albi, thought Fallon, was probably the only person in his circle that he could trust. And in the drugs business, that's a lucky thing to have. Most people had no one to trust. Albi had been given his instructions to go and carry out, and Fallon had no doubt that he would carry them out dutifully and professionally.

Fallon had just spoken to Charlie Mepham. He didn't trust him, but he had got things done in the past. Things that would implicate him if he ever tried to turn against Fallon. Mepham had also given up Terry Osman. Fallon wasn't surprised by this given what he had heard earlier on the tape recording, but he was disappointed. Not necessarily by Osman, but by the fact that Jack had formed a collusive relationship with him. And that collusion might well extend the time it takes to get the money transferred from the Albanians. And that was not acceptable to Fallon.

Twenty-five million pounds worth of drugs were currently being held in a lockup in South London. This was the discounted value to the Albanians. The real value was twice that. The Albanians' greed was proving to be Fallon's liberator. The lock-up had to be impenetrable. He had spent a hundred grand on new steel doors and reinforced walls for added security, all fitted by someone who had gone on a permanent holiday to Benalmadena and had never been heard from since. Drugs that Fallon had skimmed and stockpiled over the years from other drug gangs that he and his team had leaned on, abused, arrested, put in prison and in several cases, terminated. Fallon's reputation was uncompromising. But even he knew that being in the drugs business was not a perpetual occupation. But it had outlasted his occupation as a police officer. As of now, he was formally retired from the service. It was also time to bring his time as a drug lord to a close.

Fallon had sent a text to release Mepham's prize into his bank account. It was only half a million. Not a huge amount in Fallon's world, but it was a huge one in Mepham's. As yet, Mepham wasn't aware the transfer had been made. He would find out the next time he checked his bank account. If indeed he ever got to check it. But as far as Fallon was concerned, it would be a pretty tough conversation for Mepham to have with the force if there was a double cross. Receiving that kind of money as a police officer meant one of three things. Inheritance, lottery or theft. Mepham's parents were both dead, and they left him enough money to just about cover the cost of the funeral. Mepham never did the lottery and was never one to gamble his own money. So, that just left theft. Even if Mepham blabbed, he would still get a decent amount of prison time, most of which would be spent in solitary; all of which would be spent looking over his shoulder. Much as Fallon would break someone's neck for treachery, Mepham's fate, if he did double-cross Fallon, would be a pretty scary one. And Fallon was fine with that. No, he was prepared for it. And his choice was made.

He had left the café through the rear exit. In one of the car park spaces behind the cafe sat a black VW Transit van that had been registered through a now-defunct property company set up by Jack. The MOT, tax and insurance were all above board, and the V5 was registered to an address somewhere in London. He opened the driver's side door and got in. He put on a bright hi-vis jacket. In the tradesman's world, being conspicuous actually made you inconspicuous. People generally didn't give you a second glance. And right now, that was exactly how Fallon wanted to be. He pulled out his phone.

"Everything alright, Guv?"

"All good, Andy. Got your text. So that's Mepham on his way, then?"

"Watched him lock up and head to his car. He checked all the cars on the way. He wasn't looking for a motorbike courier, though, so he didn't see me. He made a couple of calls and then ditched his SIM. Did you ask him to do that? Anyway, thought that was a bit strange, so I waited until it was clear, then went and picked it up just in case. Bright red in colour. It was knackered, though. Other than that, all quiet here. Still want me to keep an eye out?"

"Good work, Andy, thanks. Yeah, I told him to ditch the SIM. Preferably not by the bloody car, though. And yeah, if you could sit tight, but could you do it in the lock-up for me? Saves buggering around when I get there. I won't be long."

"No problem, Guv. See you then."

The phone call ended.

Although it was cold, the sun was shining. Fallon put on a pair of sunglasses, retrieved a black baseball cap from the glove compartment and put it on. Not only was he wanted by rival drug gangs, but he also had to assume that he was now wanted by his ex-employers as well. He started the vehicle, reversed out of the space, and headed out into the traffic to criss-cross his way through London towards Shepherd's Bush. He had been right about Mepham. Ditching the SIM card just proved it. Yet another reason to take him down. He was preparing to jump ship. Just not one headed for Dubai.

The SIM that Mepham had discarded was the new one that Fallon had given him. He needed that SIM to confirm the details for the property in Dubai, as well as the code for the money. Mepham didn't relish the thought of retirement in the Middle East. But that was fine. It meant more money for Fallon, and anyway, Mepham would be picked up sooner or later. But that's not how Fallon did things. He would face the consequences.

Fallon, in the meantime, had three things to get done. The money. The drugs. The handover. And they all relied on one man. Jack Andries.

Chapter 35.

En Route – Fallon's perspective. Still, before the motorbike crash.

Fallon indicated left as he pulled out onto Shepherds Bush Green in West London. He was minutes away from the lock-up. He had sent a text to Andy Patterson, who was waiting for him, to get Jack ready to move.

The car in front of him had slowed down to let a bus out from its stop. Fallon's attention was drawn to his left, to an area outside an Italian restaurant around twenty yards down a side road. An elderly gentleman was remonstrating with a young lad over a white carrier bag full of something. It was unclear whether the lad, dressed in blue jeans and a black hoodie with the hood up, was trying to take the bag from the gentleman or whether the gentleman was trying to retrieve the bag from the hooded youth. However, Fallon wasn't in the slightest bit interested in the struggle being played out in the side street. Other people were watching, wondering if they should intervene or continue to go about their day. What Fallon was interested in was the black Ford transit van parked a further ten yards down the road. He had been involved in enough drug busts over the years to recognise that the van he was looking at was an armed response unit, presumably from the West London team. Given that Fallon was less than four streets away from the lock-up, he doubted very much that it was a coincidence that the van was sitting randomly in a street in Shepherd's Bush. If the team inside were not on operational duty, they would have surely alerted the local beat officers to the fracas that was still happening right in front of them. Bring into play the fact that Mepham had decided to cut himself loose from Fallon, there was no guarantee that he hadn't already talked to someone. It was obvious that the van was here for him, Jack or both. The intel that had been sent to him by text earlier at the café had been good. Whilst most of his team were running scared and haemorrhaging information, there was at least one reliable insider he still had in his pocket. He now had to move quickly. He hit redial on the phone.

"You alright, Guv? Where are you?"

"Listen to me, Andy. We've got a problem. I need you to go and have a quick walk onto the main road. See if there's anything suspicious. Cars or vans that weren't there when you arrived. If there are, keep walking and get out of there. And don't look back. If it's clear, then I need you to get Jack ready by the back door. I'm two minutes away in traffic. Armed response is waiting a few streets back from you. They must be waiting for movement at the lock-up or for further support to come in. And as you're on your bike today, keep the visor down on your helmet, just in case. Now go, have a look. I'm staying on the phone."

"Shit! Got it, Guv. On my way to have a look."

Fallon could hear Patterson open up the roller door at the lock-up. The traffic in front of him was at a standstill, waiting for a badly parked van unloading bags of vegetables to move on. There was plenty of noise from car horns.

The disagreement between the gentleman and the hooded youth had now escalated into a street brawl between several different people who had arrived to watch. Given that most of them were trying to take down the hooded youth, it would appear that a robbery had been averted. However, the violence had escalated, and the hooded youth was on the floor, currently having the living daylights beaten out of him.

The side door to the police van opened, and a single police officer in uniform jumped out and ran over to the brawling good Samaritans. Thankfully, someone in the police van had some scruples or just felt plain guilty for not doing anything about the robbery-cum-assault. He quickly pulled off two individuals from the no-longer-hooded youth. There was a lot of blood, and the lad had taken a real pounding. Blood was pouring from his head, nose and mouth. However, as the police officer continued pulling people back, the youth spotted an opportunity to make his escape. He ran off like his life depended on it, and given the beating he had just taken it probably did. Within seconds, he had cut across the road in front of Fallon and disappeared behind a small, wooded area on the green.

The traffic had started to move again.

Patterson's voice came back over the phone. "All clear, Guv. Cars are empty on the road, and no sign of backup vans that I can see. You on your way?"

"Well done, Andy. Yes, on my way. Get Jack by the back door. Soon as I have him in the van, I'm going to give you the key for the other lock box in there. It's at the far end. There's a hundred grand in fifties in it. It's all yours. See you in two." Fallon didn't need another one of his officers to get cold feet. The money ensured that Patterson didn't run.

Following the road for one hundred yards, Fallon then turned left. He followed the road to the bottom and turned right. Halfway down, he stopped. He reversed the van down to the bottom of a narrow lane and parked at the side of his lock-up. As he did so, the roller door opened upwards, and Patterson emerged.

Fallon jumped from the VW and immediately ran to the back and opened the rear doors. "We need to be quick, Andy. I don't know how long we've got before the cavalry arrives. Is Jack ready?"

"Inside the back door, Guv." Patterson had perched Jack up against the wall by the door. He was still in a state of semi-unconsciousness, although Fallon knew it wouldn't be long before the drugs wore off fully. Fallon took hold of Jack. He slipped his arms under his arms and pulled him up. Jack groaned loudly in his induced slumber. His face was a mess, covered in dried blood, but Fallon was sure it was the injuries you couldn't see that were causing the groaning.

"Andy. Tie his hands together, grab his legs and throw him in the back. We need to get moving quickly.

Hands now tied, they picked up Jack easily. Fallon stepped up backwards into the van, followed by Patterson, and they then unceremoniously dropped him. Jack screamed out in pain. Fallon checked that his hands were secured. They were tight together. It would have to be good enough. Fallon didn't really want him coming around in the van while he was driving to the next location. But given his injuries and the amount of drugs he had been given, Jack should be quieter for a little while longer.

Fallon handed Patterson a small key. They both walked to the far end of the lock-up. Patterson used the key to open the box and retrieved a black holdall. He unzipped it, checked the contents, zipped it back up and nodded at Fallon. They both walked back out into the sunshine.

"Spend it wisely, Andy, and speak to no one. Mepham and Osman have dropped out, but they don't know you're involved, so don't worry about that. I'll send details of some more money when I get Jack into a new place. Good luck."

Fallon jumped back up into the VW, which had been left running while he retrieved Jack. He drove to the top of the small lane. A now helmeted Patterson was walking behind the van. Fallon turned left into the road, the opposite way to which he had arrived. At the end, he turned right and headed back in a loop towards Shepherd's Bush Green. As Fallon came to a stop at the junction to the main road, two speeding black vans turned into the road he was leaving and headed to where he had just come from. Fallon looked the opposite way and drove off into the traffic.

Everything was starting to close in. He wasn't panicking just yet. He had anticipated that this was probably going to happen. Let's face it, he was hardly going to swan off into the sunset, heralded by cheering crowds of well-wishers bidding their farewells towards him. For now, he needed to stick to the plan. And he needed to remain calm. He just hoped that Patterson managed to evade the inbound armed officers and didn't panic.

CHAPTER 36.

The Chelsea Garden Care Home – Vanessa's Office.
"Sorry, am I keeping you from something?" Chief Inspector Teresa Clayton sat staring intently at Vanessa Foxx. Vanessa had glanced at her phone after yet another vibration had indicated a message.

"As you can imagine, I get a lot of messages. I look after quite a number of different properties housing well over a thousand residents. It's not a nine-to-five regime we have here, and I like to keep my finger firmly on the pulse of my business." She knew before the policewoman had even entered her office that she had to be careful. She had probably met her match with this one.

"Well, I'm sure that your dedication to duty is very much appreciated by the families and loved ones of your residential clientele, but I'm here to understand exactly what happened to Krystina Benko, so if you could give me your full attention, I would be very grateful." Teresa Clayton was in no mood to entertain. She needed answers without the accompanying bullshit. She had just missed out on locating Jack Andries; Fallon was now a very wanted but missing person of interest, and Mepham and Osman had seemingly decided to turn informant. The loose ends were piling up, and if she was going to sort this right royal cluster out, then she needed to start tying them off. And Vanessa Foxx was her first loose end.

"Now, if you don't mind, would you like to tell me exactly what you know about the events leading up to the death of Krystina? And please, take your time. The detail is very important, no matter how insignificant you think something might be."

Clayton mellowed her tone, but only slightly. As far as she was concerned, being a police officer gave her the upper hand in this room right now. And she needed to get information.

Vanessa sat upright behind her desk, pulled the chair in closer and placed her hands together in front of her on the polished surface. She had purchased the desk during a recent visit to Hong Kong from an antique dealer and had it shipped back to West London. She felt in control behind her desk.

"We had had a small incident between two residents earlier in the day. Nothing we hadn't dealt with before, but it was a tad messy. I needed to go home and get changed. I was having a late dinner when I received a call from a police officer, who told me there had been an incident at the care home and that I needed to attend as soon as possible. So, I got here within ten minutes and was informed by your Detective Chief Inspector Fallon that our poor, unfortunate Krystina was dead. It was, of course, a huge shock for me. It still is. Krystina was a wonderful member of staff and a fine chef. I believe she was even talking about getting married quite soon. It's just such a shame, really. But I don't understand why you are asking me all of this again? I gave a statement last night to one of the police officers, and he said that that was all they would need from me."

"You say that Krystina was a wonderful member of staff here. How well did you know her? Did you ever meet her boyfriend?"

"Well, she has been working here, er, worked here, for quite a while. I believe she had been working in Burger King before, and she was taken on as a kitchen porter with us. She had moved here from Estonia, I think. Very brave of her to leave her family for somewhere she didn't know. From all accounts, she was a quick learner and soon became one of the chefs. Our culinary standards are extremely high, and she appeared to meet them. The residents liked her, and they loved her food. She'll be a huge loss for us here."

"Yes, of course, a huge loss for you and also her family as well. I believe one of our liaison officers has already been in contact with her father. So, tell me, what was the relationship between Krystina and Gerald Compton? And please, tell me what you know about her boyfriend."

Vanessa exhaled. "I'm not aware of any relationship between the two of them. And I never really knew Krystina's boyfriend. I assume one of your officers has been in contact with him, though."

"We've been trying to get in contact with the boyfriend. We know him quite well, as a matter of fact. He likes to deal drugs and seems to be very proficient in the art of persuasion. But of course, no one deserves to lose a loved one. So, just to be clear, you are positive you never met him?"

Vanessa knew she wasn't being asked a question. She was being given a statement. "I meet a lot of people, Chief Inspector. That doesn't mean I remember everyone."

Clayton stood up from her chair and walked to the back of the room. She gently ran her hand up the classic gold and white wallpaper. Still facing the wall, she said, "We have a statement from one of your staff who swears blind they saw you having dinner in the apartment that Krystina was murdered in. You were having dinner with Krystina and her boyfriend. Quite recently, apparently. And yet you say you haven't met him? Are you sure about that?" Clayton turned to see if there was any physical reaction from Vanessa. There was nothing. Just a cold, stern, and Clayton had to admit, a rather beautiful face looking right back into her own eyes.

"I can't say that I do remember, Chief Inspector. As I said, I meet a lot of people in my job."

"Why would Krystina have been in the apartment? And why do you think she was there with Gerald?"

"Well, it rather sounds to me like you are jumping to conclusions. I have no idea why Krystina and Gerald were there in the apartment. I can't account for all of my staff every moment of the day, now, can I? Gerald, as head of security, would have had access to the apartment. Who knows. They may have had something going on together, they may have just crossed paths. That's for you to find out."

"Yes. Indeed. So, do you think that Gerald was the type of person who was capable of killing someone? And not just killing them. But brutally murdering them. From what I've seen, it was a frenzied and violent attack. And from what I've heard, Gerald was a gentle giant. Whilst waiting to see you, I asked two members of your staff what Gerald was like. They both said, without hesitation, wonderful. He would help anyone. And he would never harm a fly. Someone who, it would appear to me, would not seem capable of committing such a heinous crime. What do you think, Vanessa?"

"I think you are asking a lot of questions that I don't have the answers to. Now, unless I'm being placed under arrest, you will have to excuse me. I have work to do. This kind of crime being committed at a care home creates a huge amount of paperwork and reports. So, please, if you have nothing further to ask me, at least give me enough time to get my solicitor. That way, there will be no hypotheses made around your questions and my answers. Hearsay, I believe you call it, Chief Inspector."

"Very well, Miss Foxx. I understand. Just one thing before I go. Do you like lavender and geranium bath oil? It would appear that Krystina did. It also seems that she had a bath shortly before meeting her brutal termination. If she wasn't meeting with her boyfriend, then who was she meeting? Don't you find that strange, Miss Foxx? I do. Anyway. We'll know more very shortly. Our wonderful scenes of crime team found some DNA in the bath. Appears that it hadn't been cleaned particularly well. I'll be in touch. And just to be safe, maybe worth putting a call in to your solicitor. Oh, sorry, just one more thing. It would seem from our records that this is not the first time that a certain Detective Chief Inspector Fallon has had the pleasure of your company, is it, Miss Foxx? I understand that the two of you have some history together. I can thank one of my colleagues for uncovering that little gem of information. Seems that you know her as well. Inspector LaSalle. Interesting. Anyway, don't forget the solicitor, will you? You never know, you might just need one. Oh, and don't stray too far from here. I'm sure we'll need to talk to you again. Hope you get your reports done."

Chief Inspector Clayton opened the door and walked out into the reception area. She stopped just before she reached the main entrance doors and removed her phone from her pocket. She then took a picture of the security camera placed to her left in the far corner of the reception area. It was pointed towards the entire reception area, including Vanessa's office and the door that led to the scene of the murder. She put the phone back in her pocket and walked out of the care home.

Vanessa had watched Clayton leave the building before checking her phone for the messages that had been arriving. Clayton was holding information back; Vanessa was sure of it. She mentioned Fallon's name. Why the hell would she do that? Unless she knew. And the DNA stuff. Surely a good solicitor would sort that one out. After all, there's no crime in having a bath at work.

The messages on Vanessa's phone were all from Fallon. She read the last one first. It simply said. *Confirmed.* Vanessa read through the other messages. Although Fallon's texts seemed very pragmatic about the situation, Vanessa was starting to panic. *Confirmed* simply meant that Fallon was now exposed. It also meant that Fallon was accelerating the whole exit strategy and had begun his plans for an early retirement. And hopefully not one spent in Belmarsh Prison.

The codeword between Fallon and Vanessa had also been activated. SHE1. Simply meant, Safe House East 1. Fallon had a small apartment block in Whitechapel. Apart from Fallon, only two other people knew about the flat. One was Vanessa, the other was Jack.

And Jack, where the hell was Jack? His phone was dead, and his office was closed. She needed Jack, and she needed him now! Vanessa knew that this was it. The time had come. She now had to put in motion a plan that had been years in the making. But one that was happening too soon. All of her boxes weren't yet ticked. Things weren't in place for her as they should have been.

And she was scared. No, scared was the wrong word. She was terrified.

CHAPTER 37.

The previous evening. Forget Dot's, Jamie needs to watch his own back.

Police Constable James Andries was at home. Home was a small one-bedroomed flat in Ealing that he had bought, with the help of his dad, who had put down the bulk of the deposit. It was a great place for what he needed. Close to work, close to shops, close to bars and pubs, but not too close to his dad.

Jamie had just emerged from the shower. He had been working on an assignment from work for hours, which was proving tricky. He was hoping Dot would be able to help, but she was always chasing her tail doing something somewhere. Despite being a total cock most of the time, his dad tried to be a good dad. But things had been different with him recently. Not that he had become a bad dad per se, but he had changed over the last few months. He had become quieter, worked incessantly and seemed stressed. Jamie had put it down to the fact that things with Dot hadn't been good for quite a while. It was obvious they had all but split up and were waiting for the right time to divorce, but it seemed that his dad was taking it all badly. Jamie kind of sat in the middle of his dad and Dot. As far as he was concerned, Dot was the only person who had come close to getting his dad to settle down, but he was never going to take sides. He liked Dot a lot. And she had helped him so much to settle into the police. But as far as his dad was concerned, right now, something was wrong. He was different.

Jamie's fears were confirmed when he listened to a voicemail his dad had left for him a quarter of an hour ago while he was in the shower. He was scared of something, that much was clear. "Jamie, look. I, er, I need to disappear for a while. Some stuff has happened at work, and it's not particularly good stuff either. I want to say to you not to panic, but that's not what I need to say. I need to say be careful, mate. Listen to me. I need you to do something for me. I need you to go to the house. Go now. Dot is still at the care home; there's some stuff she's trying to sort out by all accounts. But I reckon she'll be home soon. If you don't get this message 'til the morning, then wait until Dot is out and go in then. Oh, and the alarm code. It's 0445. Dot changed it. Go into the study and open the bottom drawer of the filing cabinet. In there, you will find a file called Anna, Boring Stuff. Take the contents of that file and guard them with your life. I know you'll read the stuff in the file, Jamie, and I'm sorry. I really am. Now. If you don't hear from me in the next 48 hours, give the file to Dot and tell her to get it to whoever she needs to get it to. You're the only person I can trust with this. That's why I'm asking you to do it. Thanks, mate. And Jamie – take care."

Jamie had repeatedly called his dad's phone. Every time, he just got the same message. The number was no longer in use. So, where the hell was his dad? And what the hell had he done that was so bad? Why did he not trust Dot to take the file straight to whoever she needed to take it to? Why get him to go and get it? It didn't make sense.

Jamie took his fluorescent police jacket off the back of the front door, picked up his car keys and headed out into the night. It had just gone 11, and the roads were empty, and it only took him about ten minutes to get to Chiswick. He had been given a spare key to the house when his step-grandmother lived there. He used to go and help Dot on the occasions when Grandma became difficult and sometimes violent. He turned into a wide avenue of houses and drove down the entire length of the road. As he passed his dad's house, he slowed. There were no cars on the driveway, and the house was in darkness. He turned the car around and parked on the road just down from the house so that anyone coming from the main road wouldn't pass his car. And generally, that's the way that Dot would drive home.

Jamie got out of the car and pulled on his police coat. If anyone got suspicious, then all they would say is that they saw a police officer in the area. If anyone challenged him, he had his warrant card to shut them up.

He walked along the road, entered onto the gravel driveway and walked up to the front door of the house. The floodlights burst into life, illuminating Jamie's high viz jacket. Ridiculously, he felt like he shouldn't be there. That what he was doing was wrong. He was just going into his dad's house, for crying out loud, something he had done lots of times before. This time definitely felt different, though. He put the key in the lock, turned and pushed the door open. The alarm immediately started its incessant beep-beep-beeping. Jamie entered the code. 0445. The beep-beep-beeping stopped.

As he closed the door behind him, he noticed there was a pile of letters. Curious, he took them out of their cage and thumbed through them, but there was nothing that seemed out of the ordinary. Out of habit, he took the letters, walked into the kitchen and placed them on the table.

He then headed to the study. Entering the room, he turned on the light and followed the instructions that his dad had left him. He opened the bottom drawer of the filing cabinet and thumbed through until he found a file that said Anna - The Boring Stuff, written in black ink on the top right of the file. Nervously, he took it out and opened it.

The first document was a Power of Attorney for his grandma. He placed it on the floor and continued to thumb through the documents. Page after page were printed notes on how to complete a Power of Attorney until he reached the last four pages in the file. They were all headed – FA Holdings. The first page showed rows and rows of numbers, each line ending with what Jamie assumed was a place name and a date.

125CC25HSW16JTO4Harwich010805
100CC10HW2ATO3.2Harwich070905 and so on

There were thirty lines on each page, one hundred and twenty lines in total. They were obviously transactions, and Jamie already had a rough idea of what they were showing. To him, they looked like drug shipments. And not for just a few wraps of crack. Jamie suspected he was looking at weights, locations and the value of shipments. And if his thought process was right, these were huge shipments. But what was his dad doing with this type of information? Surely, he couldn't be involved in any of this. Then again, if he was, and the information was real, no wonder his dad had sounded scared. If this is what he was involved in, he had every right to be.

Jamie finished looking at all the lines of information and then turned the final page over. On the back of the fourth page was an address. Flat 17c Christian Rd, Whitechapel. This must be significant. Was it a dealing address? Jamie didn't know. What he did know was that he would need to go and find out for himself what or who was there. He had a cursory look through the rest of the files in the filing cabinet to see if there was something that stood out to him. He couldn't see anything. Not that he knew what he was looking for.

Jamie suddenly froze. He heard a car drive onto the gravel at the front of the house and watched as the floodlights lit up the lawn outside the study window. Shit, he thought. It must be Dot. His dad had made it clear he didn't want Dot knowing anything at all. Why? Didn't he trust her? Did he want to protect her? Until Jamie knew for sure he had to do what his dad had asked.

He scooped up the paperwork, turned the study light off and ran to the front door. He reset the alarm, winced at the beep-beep-beeping, and stepped back into the open coat-hanging cupboard to the side of the door. It was full of coats but had an alcove at each side, which he could push himself back into. He couldn't be seen unless someone physically did what he did and pushed themselves behind all the coats. He waited. Hiding in his own father's house. And he didn't know why. Not yet anyway.

The door opened, the alarm was switched off, and Dot headed straight for the kitchen. As soon as Jamie heard the fridge door open, he slipped out of the cupboard, opened the front door wide enough so he could squeeze out sideways, and gently pulled the door closed behind him. He jumped over a short box hedge and walked along the grass, avoiding the gravel, back to the road. The kitchen was located to the side of the house, so Jamie felt sure that Dot had not seen him walk back to his car. He had to be careful as the PIR lights were still illuminating half of Chiswick.

He unlocked his car, threw his coat on the back seat, got in and headed east towards Whitechapel. He was sweating, and both his hands were shaking. This was utterly ridiculous, but he had done what his dad had asked him to do. Now all he had to do was figure out why. He leaned across to the glove compartment and pulled out an A5 version of a London atlas. He was now suspicious of everything. He was only going to use his phone for the normal day-to-day stuff. Stuff that wouldn't raise any eyebrows. The fact that his dad had asked him to go to the house and retrieve the file meant only one thing in Jamie's eyes. His dad needed help to dig himself out of whatever hole he was stuck in. As he sat at a set of traffic lights, he sent a text to a colleague. *Hey mate. Give me a shout when you wake in the morning. Need some help with a work assignment.*

Jamie continued his journey east. His phone rang almost a minute later.

"Russ, you alright, mate? Not asleep then?"

Russell Wootton, aka Russell the muscle, was the closest friend that Jamie passed out of the police training school with. Since leaving the school, they had been allocated stations very close to each other in London, and the friendship had continued to be close ever since. Russ was smart. He just also happened to be 6 feet 2 and eighteen stone of pure muscle. Hence his nickname, which was awarded to him during very one-sided self-defence lessons. Russ was a good friend to have around. He was an even better police officer.

"Alright, Jamie. Trust me, I'd be asleep if I was at home. Got called in to work to cover a sickie and just having some grub. That's put me on a double now. Still not finished your assignment, then? Where are you? Sounds like you're in the car."

"I'm still trying to close the assignment. Skip's doing everything he can to catch me out on stuff, but I'm getting there. Yeah, I'm in the car at the mo, just checking something out. Didn't expect you to call me back straight away. Glad you did, though. Could you check an address for me? I was going to do it when I got back to work, but the sooner the better, so I can get this bloody assignment cracked."

"Should be ok, Jamie. Text me the address. I'm just in the restroom. I'll head to the front desk and use their computer. Tess is on tonight so won't be a problem."

"Thanks, Russ. I'll text it through now and give you a shout in the morning."

"It's nearly the bloody morning, Jamie. It's been a long enough shift as it is. And it's not even midnight yet. Speak later."

Jamie pulled the car to the side of the road and texted the address through to Russ. Caution now thrown to the wind. He then continued his journey towards Whitechapel. After another 20 minutes of driving, Jamie slowed the car down. He indicated right as he saw the road sign for Christian Road and turned. Even though the streetlights were illuminated, they were not much more than a dim orange glow, which was making it difficult for him to identify all of the house numbers. He passed several larger older houses that, given their multiple doorbells, had been converted into either rooms or flats. The numbers that he did see ran concurrently, meaning there was no odd or even. The flat he was looking for should be ahead on the left. His phone let out a quiet ping. A text from Russ.

Not much detail mate. 17a,b and c all owned by FA Holdings. Registered in Dubai to another company registered in the Cayman Islands. Dug deeper. Can't find anyone listed as living in any of the properties. Sounds like a tax dodge mate. If you get above 80% you owe me a beer.

Jamie texted Russ back. *Deal mate. Sneaky bloody detail for the assignment. Thanks.*

Twice in the last hour, Jamie had seen the name FA Holdings. This was no coincidence. What was the connection between the property and the paperwork he had taken from his dad's house? He now sat outside the property that made up 17a, b and c Christian Road. There was a light on in what Jamie assumed was the hallway entrance leading to the flats, but the rest of the property was in total darkness. He got out of the car and pulled his coat back on. He opened up a breast pocket and took out a small but powerful Maglite torch. He then walked up the concrete path and looked in through the front left and then right windows. Both windows were covered with wooden blinds, but he could just pick out that the rooms were empty. The layout of the flats looked like a and b were on the ground floor, with c commanding the whole of the top floor. There were three post boxes attached to the wall. Jamie managed to squeeze his fingers in. None of them contained any post. It wasn't the most prestigious of areas, but properties still cost a fortune in this part of London. There were no For Sale or For Rent boards anywhere. The place seemed deserted. There had to be a reason why all three flats were apparently empty.

Jamie turned his attention to a driveway that was to the side of the property. The driveway in turn led to a small car park at the rear. Even though the streetlights on the main road were dim, Jamie could see most of the detail around him. Now that he had moved to the back of the property, it was pitch black, and his eyes took a little time to adjust. Using his torch, Jamie could see that all of the windows had blinds in them, and there appeared to be no sign of life anywhere. He shone the torch in a long arc around the car park. In the far corner, there was a car under a dark cover. He walked over to the rear and pulled the corner of the cover back to reveal a silver Peugeot 307. Jamie took out a pad and pen from his coat and wrote down the registration number. Contemporaneous notes. That's what they taught you in the police.

It was late, and Jamie felt there was nothing more he could do without someone becoming nosey. What he wanted to do was break into the property and have a damn good look around, but what he didn't want was for someone to report a burglary or the local plods to catch him breaking in for no good reason. That would take some explaining to the duty inspector, and as of now, he had no feasible explanation for anything that was going on. He needed access to the police computer, and there was only one person who wouldn't ask too many questions about what he was doing.

CHAPTER 38.

Russ. What friends are for?

Jamie had driven straight over to West London and headed for the police station where Russ was begrudgingly working overtime. Jamie had sent a text to let him know he was on his way and needed access to a computer. And, please, he said, don't ask any questions just yet. Russ had simply replied with a single question mark. "Smart arse," said Jamie out loud.

He parked his car in the car park at the front of the police building, got out, walked up to the front door and pressed the intercom. A female voice enquired who was calling. "PC Jamie Andries here to see PC Russell Wootton."

"Thank God," came the reply. "He's done nothing but drink my bloody coffee for the last hour. Come on through and restore my sanity, Jamie." The door buzzer sounded, and Jamie entered the front of the building. The main desk was situated straight ahead of him.

"You must be Tess. Good to meet you. You do know that Russ doesn't stop talking about you." Jamie grinned childishly as he said it.

"Oh, is that right? Well, for his information, I can assure you that I prefer the smart skinny type, not meatheads like him."

"Sorry, you do realise that I'm right here, don't you?" Russ's muscled frame walked into the front desk area. "And you never complain when I feed you custard tarts, Tess, do you?"

She chuckled. "Well, unlike you, PC Wootton, a custard tart happens to be my guilty pleasure. Now, why don't you bugger off somewhere else so I can get some work done?

Lovely to meet you, Jamie. Now, if *you* want to bring me custard tarts. Well. Just ring my buzzer. Anytime."

"Tess, you are a nightmare. Jamie. Don't listen to a word she says. She's a police officer. It's all lies, mate. Come on through, I've got better coffee than Tess."

"Lovely to meet you, Tess. Next time, I'll bring the tarts."

Jamie followed Russ through a secured door and into a long corridor. They walked to the third door on the left and entered a small, empty office.

"Welcome to the home of serious vehicle crime. You've got until six am, Jamie. You're going to have to use your own login, mine's being used on a drunk driver RTC out back at the moment. I'm not going to ask any questions unless you want me to. If you need me, back towards Tess, turn left at the bottom and straight on to the custody suite. I'll bring a coffee in a bit."

Russ opened the door and disappeared off to deal with his offender.

Jamie looked at his watch. It had gone midnight. He sat down at a desk belonging to a Detective Constable Wilson, hoping he wouldn't object. He logged on to the computer and immediately did a vehicle check on the Peugeot 307. He knew that the request would show up on his search history, and he might have to explain why at some point. Standard procedure. But he had to start trying to piece together what was happening to his dad.

The vehicle check came back showing a valid MOT and insurance in place. The registered keeper showed up as one Anthony Elkins living at an address in Streatham. A marker at the side of the screen showed that he was a serving police officer. Sergeant Anthony Elkins. Shit. Sergeant Anthony Elkins, Fraud and Financial Crime Unit. Shit again. The Tony Elkins, whose boss just happened to be his stepmother. Shit! Jamie didn't believe in coincidence, luck or chance. Should he, though? No. He dealt with facts. And the fact right now was that FA Holdings, whatever that was, was linked to his dad, a whole bunch of narcotics transactions and a serving police officer who just happened to work for Dot. His dad had pointed him in this direction for a reason.

The door opened, and Russ entered with a large mug of coffee. "It's the good stuff. I nicked some of the inspector's coffee. Never trust a cop, eh. Blimey, you okay, mate? You look like you've seen a ghost."

CHAPTER 39.

Russ. What friends are REALLY for?

"Look Jamie. I get what you are saying, but seriously, there has to be a logical answer to all of this. Granted, it sounds like an old episode of *The Bill,* but do you really think your old man is involved in that kind of thing? I mean, think about it, if you've deciphered the numbers correctly, that kind of money is about the same as the GDP of a small country. You would have to money launder on a colossal scale to get rid of that kind of dosh."

"Yeah, yeah, I understand that. But there are still too many coincidences involved in all of this, Russ. And my dad is missing. He's deliberately put me onto the trail, I know he has, and I need to find him. But I have to understand what he's involved in in the first place, to figure out where I need to look. He wants me to find him, Russ. But I need your help, mate. I don't think time is on my side, and I can only be in one place at a time." Jamie explained everything that had happened to Russ. First off, he needed to make sure he wasn't going mad. Russ hadn't laughed him out of the building, which was a good thing. It meant Russ was listening, even if he had doubts about the story.

"Ok, even though I'm coming off close to a double shift, I'll humour you. So, the message from your dad said he was going awol for a bit because work was getting a bit shitty. He sends you to his house to find the paperwork that, you think, now reveals a whole load of drug movements. You go to a house in East London, seemingly connected via one company, FA Holdings, yeah, and there, you find a car belonging to a police sergeant who works for your stepmum.

Now, this particular skip may well have a legitimate reason for having his car there. That could be coincidence mate. The other stuff, gotta say, not sure how to read that. But you are right. First priority is to find your old man. And given the paperwork you now have in your possession, I guess this isn't one for missing persons. Yet. We need to do some stuff under the radar."

"Thanks, Russ, yes, we need to watch our step. I'm going with my gut feeling that Elkins is involved in this somewhere. Just don't know where yet. I'm going to head over to my dad's office to see if I can find anything that may help or give us a clue. Could you see if you could find anything on FA Holdings and do an intel check on Elkins? You know, the normal. And check his personal stuff as well. As much as you can without raising eyebrows."

"I'll have a look, mate. Right, I need to go and check on my esteemed guest in the cells. Give me a shout if you find anything. Oh, and before you go, delete the history on the computer. Wilson tends to get in early, and I will probably forget. Keep in contact, eh. See you later."

"Thanks, Russ. I appreciate this, really do."

"It's what friends are for. Now let's see if we can find your old man."

Jamie, out of curiosity, entered one more name into the computer. Dorothea LaSalle. He wanted to cross-check any detail with Elkins to see if they had worked anywhere together before. For obvious reasons, only limited information was available on individuals who worked in the police, but what filled the screen in front of him just enhanced his curiosity. There was nothing about Elkins, but there was something else. Eight years ago, Dot had been involved in a complaint against another police officer. The name of the individual who filed the complaint in the system was a Superintendent Truss. There were no further details, but even this restricted amount made Jamie inquisitive. The fact that it was recorded meant that it would have had to have been a pretty serious complaint. He put the date of the complaint and Truss's name in the system as a query. Nothing came up for the date, but two weeks later, Superintendent Truss had noted a closure of a complaint. Listed on the complaint were Dot and someone called Patrick Fallon. No ranks or departments were listed. But the nugget for Jamie was that the reference numbers between the two pieces of data were the same. They were connected.

Curious, he entered the details for Patrick Fallon and hit return on the keyboard. Two words flashed up on the screen. Restricted Access. Every file on Fallon was restricted. It didn't even say if he was still a serving police officer. Ok, well, he had found something. Just not sure what, and it didn't appear to be immediately obvious to the current situation that Jamie was dealing with. He deleted the search history on the computer, picked up his cup and headed back into the front office.

Tess was on the phone trying to calm someone who had something to complain about. Jamie waved over, and Tess put her hand over the mouthpiece. "Next time, bring tarts."

Jamie raised his eyebrows in Tess's direction and pressed the green exit button on the wall beside the main door. He pushed the door open and walked out into the early cold. The light would soon start to stretch out in the sky above him. On any other day, he would have probably felt happy. Today, he had work to do, and his current state of mind was a long way from happy. He walked over to his car and smelt bacon. The windscreen had a fine mist of moisture from the early morning air.

Jamie decided to leave the car and pop out on the street beyond the station to an all-night greasy spoon trailer. The delicious smell of bacon wafting into the police car park had done its job brilliantly. It was a ruse that most officers, either departing night shift, arriving on earlies, or anything in between, found irresistible. He hadn't eaten since lunchtime the previous day. He walked out of the police car park and followed his nose to the café.

He ordered a bacon sandwich and a coffee. As he waited for his food, he sent Russ a text. *Have a look for someone called Patrick Fallon. It's a restricted-access name. Just didn't have time to dig deeper. Probably nothing but wouldn't mind seeing what you can find out. Cheers mate.*

A uniformed officer was standing at the counter. The woman behind it was loading a cardboard box full of rolls with various fillings of bacon, eggs and sausages. Given the state of perfection of the officer's uniform, the recipients of the food had sent the sprog over for the task. The new boy. It had been nearly two years since Jamie had been the sprog. The sprog picked up the box and headed off.

Jamie took a step back to move out of his way, but stopped as a piercingly loud police radio burst into life from the new officer's shoulder.

"*Control from Sierra 62.*"

"*Go ahead 62.*"

"*Yes control, that's us all clear from the Chelsea Garden care home. SIO Fallon told us last night to remain on scene until private security had been established. All established now and returning to base.*"

"*Understood 62. There's overtime tonight if you're up for it.*"

"*Thanks, but no thanks control. I'm done in.*"

"*I reckon we all are 62. Thanks anyway. Control out.*"

As the sprog went to walk past him, Jamie put an arm out to slow him down. He then turned one of the knobs on the shoulder-worn radio until it clicked off. "That's a forfeit right there"

"Yeah, I know, cheers, mate."

One of the first things that you learn is never to share your radio messages with anyone who is not authorised to hear them. Turn the radio down and stand back away from anyone who could hear. And even with the noise of frying eggs, bacon and sausages, just about half the street would have heard the radio communication that had just been transmitted. But on this occasion, given the information that had been imparted, Jamie was very thankful for the minor ineptitude of the officer. Very thankful indeed.

"Any sauce with the bacon, love?" said the woman behind the counter to Jamie.

"No, all good, thanks, I'm watching my weight."

"Course you are, darling."

The bacon sandwich, wrapped in a white paper bag, was put, alongside the coffee, on the melamine counter in front of him.

"Have a good one," said Jamie as he took both.

He watched as the sprog hurriedly jogged back with the food for the overnight shift. Life in the police force as a sprog is all about forfeits.

Jamie walked back quickly to his car.

He unwrapped the bacon sandwich and took a large bite. He needed to rethink his next step. He thought he had it planned out about ten minutes ago. That was until the sprog had unwittingly given him a potential new lead. As a result of what he heard, he now believed this was all more than a coincidence. He could now place the mysterious Fallon somewhere. And that somewhere was where he could also place Dot. The care home where his grandma was living. And what the hell happened there to warrant police intervention over their security?

Jamie had no idea if there was any connection at all between the care home and the fact that his dad was missing, but he needed to find out. If nothing else, to eliminate it. But he needed to find out about this Fallon character. And besides, if nothing else, right now, he had a plan of sorts. He would go to his dad's office after he had been to the care home.

CHAPTER 40.

Jamie. Just like adding cornflour. The plot thickens.
Jamie, now nice and warm with a full stomach of bacon roll, was about to start driving towards the Chelsea Garden care home. He was racking his brain as to how best to find out what he needed to find out there. It was too early to go and see his grandma, even though in all likelihood, she would be awake.

He sent Russ another text, aware that he might be pushing his friend, especially as he would be knackered after an impromptu night of overtime.

One more thing mate. It seems there was some kind of incident at my grandma's care home last night. Weirdly the SIO was Fallon. Can you see if there's anything on the system about the offence? Curious eh.

A reply came through almost immediately.

On it now. Careful mate. You know what curiosity did to the cat.

The cat wasn't curious, Russ. It was stupid.

Yeah, exactly J!

Russ had a point.

Jamie needed to be careful. He was almost into a new position in CID and his record so far had been impeccable. Becoming an amateur sleuth whilst being a serving police officer was not tolerated. He put the car into gear and drove out of the car park. He headed due West.

The London traffic was quite heavy, but Jamie was headed out of town. Almost everyone else was headed in, so his journey was easy. It gave him time to think about how he would ask questions at the care home. His phone started to ring. It was perched in the ashtray that he used as a makeshift phone holder. It was Russ. Jamie answered it. "Alright, Russ, found anything out about Fallon?"

"Jamie, Fallon can wait for now. You heading to the care home?"

"Yes, I am, why?"

There was a hesitation before Russ answered.

"Be careful you don't go sticking your size twelves into something you shouldn't, mate. I've found the job sheet from last night. From all accounts, it looks like one of the staff was murdered. An arrest was made. Apparently, the security guard at the care home. Although there's also an all points out on the victim's boyfriend as well. I don't think anyone is going to take too well to a sprog asking questions."

"Wow, I wasn't expecting that. I've no idea if any of this is relevant. I hope to God it isn't, but it's sure as hell strange. I wonder who the victim was and whether I had met them or not. Sorry, mate, just thinking out loud. Dot was there last night. It seems weird that she didn't say anything to Dad. Or me for that matter. I rang her yesterday, and she texted me back later to say she would call me today. A murder isn't exactly something that you wouldn't want to talk about. If nothing else, if it gets out in the press, I would sure as hell want to let people know before it hits the breakfast news."

"Give you this one, Jamie. Weird beyond weird if you ask me?"

"Think I might wait a bit and start with seeing my grandma. Much more plausible. Also need to see if she has been told anything. Might spook her. But then again, knowing her, I doubt it."

"Just tread carefully, mate. Don't go asking too many questions. I'll do some digging into Fallon. See if I can find anything. Let me know how you get on, eh?"

"Will do. Cheers, Russ."

Jamie drove the last ten minutes, his head trying to come to terms with what Russ had just told him. He was taught to always make complicated situations simple. In his own inimitable style, he had concluded that to do this, he always thought about a bowl of vegetable soup. To truly understand anything, you had to deconstruct it. Figure out all the ingredients and what part they play, and then you will understand the end result. Whilst it sounded utterly ridiculous, it had worked so far in his fledgling career.

His dad was still missing. He had a message saying his dad was in trouble. He had four pages of what he believed to be drug shipments, dates and amounts. He had an address connected to FA Holdings, where a potential occupant just happened to be a police officer connected to his stepmum. Now he had a murder where the SIO was also linked to a previous complaint with his stepmum. More than enough ingredients to make a soup, but at the moment, Jamie couldn't work out what type of soup it was going to be.

He pulled into the care home car park. He cursed as he saw a police van parked at the back of the building. Someone was still on scene, with the van parked in a position where most people wouldn't see it. They didn't want to raise any concerns with the residents or their families. They were trying to keep a murder low-key. Good luck with that one.

He took out his phone and had a scroll through the news, national and local. There was no mention of anything to do with a murder at a care home. Either the press hadn't got hold of the story yet, or someone was suppressing the crime. Either way, time would tell which one it was.

Jamie thought about calling Dot. He was intrigued as to why she had not mentioned anything about a murder. After all, if nothing else, his grandma just happened to be one of the residents there. Surely that was reason enough to tell him something. He needed to play it simple. He would tell her that Dad was missing. He would tell her what was left in the voicemail from his dad. Let's see what she says. Given the parlous state of their marriage, she might not actually give a damn about him, who knows? Even though it was still early, the only way he would find out was by calling her. Before he could press the call button, his phone glowed and emitted a quiet ping noise.

Bugger all info on Fallon. Something's not right. It's as though he has been deleted from the police force. Elkins is a weird one too. Got him showing in Fraud for the last 2 years, with a 3 year gap before that.. Either hackers are deleting chunks of the forces systems, or you have found a couple of ghosts. Will be here for a couple more hours and then heading to get some kip. Be a good boy out there.

Jamie sighed. *Thanks Russ. Always a good boy.* This was getting stranger by the hour. He found Dot's number in his phone and was about to press it.

It was still early. And he was shattered. He would be useless without sleep. He just needed an hour or so. He set an alarm on his phone. Grandma would still be asleep, and so would Dot. He couldn't do anything for now. He closed his eyes. A minute later, he was asleep.

CHAPTER 41.

Anna – More cornflower. Inside and outside the care home.
"Don't you dare let that nazi bitch anywhere near me. I swear next time I'll throttle her. You didn't listen to me, and look what happened. Now you'd better believe what I say. Are you listening to me? Is anyone listening to me? And where's my bloody breakfast? You are supposed to be looking after me, not treating me like a prisoner. And WHERE is my bloody telephone?"

The night staff in the memory care wing of the Chelsea Garden care home were handing over to the day team. Today's handover was a long one, given the deadly incident that had occurred overnight.

Most of the residents were being fed in their rooms rather than the restaurant. The staff didn't want the residents asking too many questions. One of the female residents in her nineties already had to be calmed down after spotting a police officer in uniform last night. She nearly collapsed as she tried to run back to her room. Not because she feared the officer, more the fact that she needed to put her teeth back in so that she could flirt with him, the clear intention being that she was going to try to snog him. So, this was a change to the residents' day, and the residents did not like the change. They liked routine. Well, most of them anyway. The staff were still in shock at the death of Krystina, but they were under the strictest of orders to say nothing to the residents or their families. Whilst deaths in a care home were generally good for business, allowing for an increase in fees for new entrants, murders were definitely not good for business. And Vanessa Foxx had made it exceedingly clear to the staff that she would not tolerate a single one of them speaking about what had happened to anyone outside of the care staff. It was, though, inevitable that at some point the news would get out.

Two nurses were currently doing a round of rock, paper, scissors to see who would take breakfast into Anna LaSalle. Ever since she was moved to memory care, she was creating hell about Ingrid being a nazi. She had spent her waking hours having a screaming match with her front door. Even an increased dose of diazepam wasn't shutting her up completely. If she had any more drugs, she would go into a coma.

Rosie lost. She had rock. Her opponent, paper. Just as she was about to take Anna her breakfast, the duty phone at the medical station rang. Rosie walked over and answered it. She listened for no more than six seconds, put the phone down and exclaimed: "There is a god."

"Since when do you believe in God?" said the nurse.

"Since Anna's grandson just turned up to see her. He can feed her breakfast."

There was a buzz at the door. Rosie looked over and saw Jamie looking back at her through the small glass window. He had slept, and he had just finished his phone call with Dot.

She pressed the buzzer at the medical station, and he walked into the corridor. She walked over to meet him, introduced herself and shook his hand.

"How's grandma doing? I heard from Dad that she had an incident yesterday with another resident."

"Yes, you could say that. Hopefully, it's all sorted between them, though your grandmother has been rather vocal about it all. I was just about to take her breakfast in. Would you like to do it?"

Jamie nodded. "Yes, of course, happy too. Is that the breakfast on the trolley?"

Rosie looked visibly relieved. "Yes, it is. She'll complain that she likes her coffee hot, but for obvious reasons, we have to keep it rather cool. Other than that, she normally eats most things. It's all pretty much purified for her now. It's the dementia, unfortunately."

"Got it, thanks, Rosie. By the way, you guys must be in shock from what happened last night. Hope you are all ok. Must have been unnerving having police here."

Rosie looked across at her colleague, who had pretended not to hear what Jamie had just said.

"It's ok, Rosie. Like Anna's daughter, I'm a police officer. Picked up what had happened here from the night shift and thought I'd better come over to see how grandma is doing."

Rosie looked again at her colleague. She was busy being busy, counting out tablets that didn't need to be counted out. "It's a huge shock. I mean, who would want to do that to Krystina? She was lovely. Wouldn't harm a fly. And Gerald, well, oh, I don't know. He's just lovely, and they took him away in handcuffs, apparently. I don't get it. Why would someone want to do that to Krystina? It's shaken everyone up, that's for sure." Rosie was starting to cry.

"I'm so sorry for the loss here, Rosie. I didn't know Krystina, but from what I've heard, everyone says the same thing. She was lovely. Has everyone been spoken to by the police now, do you know?"

"I haven't been spoken to. Miss Foxx said that it wasn't necessary. Most of us don't need to. She said that if the police needed to talk to us, they would probably do it later."

"Makes sense. I'm sure everything is under control. By the way, what's Gerald's surname?"

"It's Compton, Gerald Compton,"

"Ok, great, thanks, Rosie. Look, if there's anything you need, just let me know, ok. I'll put one of my cards on the desk when I leave." Jamie had bluffed the truth out of the staff. But what he had been told didn't make sense. Somehow, he needed to find the connection with Fallon. The more he was hearing about this man, the more things didn't add up.

Rosie had pushed the small food trolley in front of Jamie.

"Room 6 over there. She'll be delighted to see you"

Rosie knocked on the door and opened it about six inches. "Anna, your breakfast is ready. Okay to come in?"

"It's poison, that's what it is. The nazi bitch has poisoned my food. I want my food checked. How many times do I have to tell you? You never listen. Outrageous."

Rosie looked at Jamie, raised her eyebrows and stepped back away from the door. "As I said, she'll be pleased to see you."

Jamie nudged the door fully open and pushed the trolley into the room. "Hi, Grandma. It's me, Jamie. Your grandson. How are you doing? I've got some breakfast for you."

Anna was sitting at the small dining table watching TV. The sound had been turned down. "No need to treat me like a bloody idiot, Jamie. I know who you are. I trust that you have tested my food. When I depart this world, I'll do so on my own terms, and not terms dictated by some bitch down the corridor."

"The food's fine, Grandma. In fact, it's delicious."

"Then I know you haven't tasted it. There's no place on earth that the food they serve here could ever be described as delicious. It's pig slops, that's what it is."

Jamie took the plastic cloche off the large plate to reveal scrambled eggs and the tiniest, soggiest pieces of toast that he had ever seen. Anna was clearly a choke risk, although given her current demeanour, the food might not be the only choke risk for her. "There you go, Grandma. It's fine, look." Jamie took a fork, picked up a very small piece of scrambled egg and put it into his mouth. There was no flavour to the eggs at all. To be fair, her comments about the food weren't that far from the mark.

"Next time you visit, I would like some Coquille Saint-Jacques. The ones from Marks and Spencer. Your inheritance is being wasted on the slop they serve in this place. At least spend my money wisely. Now, how is school going? Have you done your O levels yet?"

"I passed all of my O levels, Grandma. I'm a Police officer now. Don't you remember? We talked about it last time I was here."

"Last time you were here? Yes, yes, of course, I remember now. A Police officer. Yes. Well, then you can make yourself useful and go and arrest that bloody nazi woman Ingrid. She's done nothing but try to kill me ever since I've been in this place. No one believes a word I tell them. Away with the fairies, that's what they think of me, all of them. And all of them useless. You will see. It's either her or me. One of us will die soon, and then you'll believe me. They've even taken my phone away so I can't call the police in an emergency. It's a conspiracy, that's what it is. A bloody conspiracy. Ask that Vanessa woman. She's the one behind it. Along with that nasty Jack person. I keep telling them they can't have it, and they won't have it. Not even over my dead body. I keep telling them."

"Can't have what, Grandma?" Jamie had been in the room for less than three minutes, and he was already exhausted.

"The house, for God's sake, the house. Don't you listen to anything I say?"

"Grandma, Dot, your daughter, sold the house. You moved in with her and my dad, Jack. In their house in Chiswick. Remember?"

Anna went quiet. She was thinking hard. Her brow dropped, and she started to rub her temples with her right hand. "No, no, they can't have sold it. It wasn't theirs to sell. Stephen promised me, he promised me he would never sell it."

Jamie sat down at the table next to his grandma. He put his arm around her and gave her a gentle squeeze. "Grandma, I need to get back to work. Please can you finish off the breakfast for me? I'll come back soon and see you again, I promise. And I'll go to M and S and buy you a lovely meal."

Anna showed no emotion. She simply stared at her plate of scrambled eggs. Jamie got up and walked to the door. He looked at his step-grandma, walked back over to her and gave her a gentle kiss on the cheek. Anna may not be his natural grandmother, but she used to care about him. And that's what he cared about. She gave a damn.

He walked to the door, opened it and closed it gently behind him. He hadn't taken more than two steps when there was a deafening crashing sound from where he had just left.

Rosie jumped up from her seat and ran to the room. She pushed the door open carefully. As she did so, the door pushed a broken plate and scrambled egg across the floor.

Jamie went to move towards the room, and Rosie looked at him and shook her head. "It's all good, I'll take it from here. She'll be fine; I'll take good care of her."

"Thank you, Rosie." Jamie walked over to the nurse's table and placed his card on it. He turned and walked down the corridor towards the door that led through to the main reception. No one saw the tears rolling down his face.

CHAPTER 42.

Jamie. Dad's office.
Jamie brushed his upset to one side. Seeing a woman who used to be so strong, in a position where she now had to rely entirely on other people, was not nice. Chuck in a vile dose of dementia, and it makes it much harder.

But at least Jamie had corroborated the death of a staff member at the care home. It didn't make sense, though. The victim was, by all accounts, a wonderfully nice and friendly person. The accused, equally by all accounts, was just as wonderful and just as nice. It didn't make sense. Not that Jamie had all the details, but from where he saw it, it all seemed rather odd. He needed to find out more about Fallon. As SIO, he would have made the call on the arrest of the suspect, yet apparently, they were also looking for the boyfriend. If that was the case, then the evidence they had on the arrested suspect wasn't watertight. Nope, it didn't sit right from where Jamie was looking.

He drove out of the care home and headed towards his dad's office. Maybe he would find something there. Anything to help offer a clue to where his dad was. He was still no closer to finding him, and not really any closer to gaining any new information. What he had found out had gone into the mixer and been stirred around. There were snippets, but what Jamie really needed was a lead of some kind. Something positive to help him find his dad. He had given Dot some of the story. He didn't want to give her all of it until he knew what had happened in the past between her and Fallon. Jamie trusted Dot. He trusted her a lot. But with Fallon's name now in the mix, he needed to be sure that Dot was on his side. She promised she would help him look into it, but she was heading to a meeting in SW1. You don't get invited there for no reason. She was going to be distracted, and distractions cost time. Time that his dad, most likely, didn't have. No, it was down to Jamie to sort this out. Whatever 'this' was.

He drove slowly in front of the offices of Andries Legal. There was a small enquiry office at the front, with a bigger office behind. The bigger office was favoured by Jack. The smaller front office was beside a staircase that led up to the main office on the first floor. This office was normally occupied by twelve or so staff. Even though it was almost eight in the morning, the premises were dark and empty. Dad's staff were early birds. It was one of his things. Vertical blinds obscured most of the view, but they hadn't been pulled fully closed. He continued for twenty or so yards and turned left into a maintenance road that led to the rear of the building. He turned left again into a large car parking area, half of which was allocated to Andries Legal. There were two cars in the Andries car park. One belonged to his dad, the other he didn't recognise. He parked his car next to his dad's and got out. Jamie tried all the door handles and the boot, but they were all locked. He glanced in through the front windows, but there was nothing visible anywhere. He walked over to the other car, a newish Vauxhall Astra, and looked in through the windows. There was a coat of some kind on the back seat and a pair of women's trainers on the front seat. The only thing in common between the two cars was that they both sported the same window sticker, giving the vehicles the relevant authority to park there. Using his phone, he took a photo of the Astra. So, wherever his dad was, he hadn't driven there; he had been taken there. He walked over to a back door to the property, which had an Andries Legal metal plate screwed to it. The door was made of solid metal and had two separate locks in it. It would take something big and heavy to break it down.

Jamie walked back along the route he had driven and continued to the front of the building. The morning post had already been unceremoniously dumped onto the mat behind the front door via a metal-plated letter box. Jamie peered into the reception area through the large glass window, hampered by the almost closed floor-to-ceiling blinds. Through a small gap, he could just make out that one of the chairs was lying on its back in the corner, and the paperwork on the desk looked like it had been swept away to one side. There was a large pile of disrupted paper on the floor at the end of the desk. It looked like an argument of some kind had taken place. Other than that, perhaps someone was just having a bad day and took out their frustrations on the chair and paperwork. Inevitably, what it probably meant was that something had happened after hours, otherwise one of the staff would have surely cleared up the mess.

The traffic on the pavement and road was busy. Rush hour and school runs combined. Whoever called it rush hour, though, had a sense of humour. The traffic was crawling.

Jamie needed to get inside, but for one thing, he didn't have a key, and secondly, there were far too many people about to even contemplate trying to break in. He stood back in front of the main door to see if he could identify any of the post on the floor. As he looked down, he noticed a dark patch on the pavement. His first thought was that a dog had relieved itself by the door, but the patch had a slight shine to it as though it was wet. But it wasn't wet. He knelt down and pushed his finger into the patch. A small spot of dark red transferred to his finger. He looked closer and saw small specks of red, spattered on the bottom of the door. It was blood. No question about it. But whose blood was it? Again, coincidence? Jamie didn't think so, but he couldn't be sure. It was either another small piece of the jigsaw that Jamie was building, or just a random nosebleed or a drunken fight that had occurred outside the office.

*Russ, can you check a couple of things for me?
Sending you a pic. Can you confirm owner of the car for me.
2. Can you check for keyholder info at my dad's office? Need
an alternative number to my dads. Andries Legal. Thanks,
mate.*

Jamie felt hopeless about having to rely on his friend
for so much information. He decided to walk back around
to his car and wait for a response. He needed to get into the
office and have a look around. Something had happened
there, and he needed to see if it was connected to his dad. As
he walked round the corner into the car park, he spotted a
man in a black coat with a hi-vis waistcoat standing by his car,
writing something on a notepad.

"This your car, sir?" said the man as Jamie
approached.

"Yes, it is. Anything wrong?"

"You're parked in a restricted area with no permit
showing in your car. Don't tell me you didn't see the signs; I
can see at least four from where I'm standing. Twenty quid.
Ten if you pay up in 14 days. Bang to rights as we say in the
business, sir." The car park enforcer hadn't once looked up
from his notepad as he spoke.

"I'm a police officer here on an investigation, mate.
Where were you hiding? Didn't see you earlier. I've been
here no longer than ten minutes, so you must have got here
quickly."

"Luck of the draw, sir, and appreciate the police
officer bit, but I wasn't born yesterday. Given the state of this
heap of junk of a car, no police force would allow one of their
officers anywhere near it. Unless, of course, it was being
towed. So, as I said. Twenty quid, or ten before 14 days."

"My name is PC Jamie Andries. As I just told you, I'm
here on a police investigation."

The enforcer looked up at Jamie and grinned. "Ah,
very good, sir. Wasn't born yesterday, you know. If you're
going to pick a name at random, I suggest you pick one that

isn't on a sign on the door right in front of me. Not very smart for a police officer, are we?"

Jamie took out his warrant card and slapped it on top of the pad that the enforcer held in his hands.

"Ah, apologies. A police officer indeed. The ticket still stands, though. Let your people talk to my people. You know the kind of thing. Any relation to the Andries on the back door sign, then?"

"As it happens, it's my father's business, but I am actually here on a police matter."

The enforcer ripped off the top sheet of his pad and duly handed it to Jamie. He then, slowly, put the pad and pen back into his coat pocket. "Just doing my job, sir. As it would appear you are doing yours. Now, going to pop in and see Sophie. We have an unwritten agreement. I keep the car park clear, and she provides a nice hot cuppa. Look, even she drives a better car than you." He pointed over towards the Vauxhall Astra.

"Sophie, you say. And she works here at Andries Legal? Well, I've just been round to the front, and the office is locked. I couldn't see anyone inside." Jamie's phone pinged.

"Strange. She normally opens up at eight on the dot. Apparently, the boss is a real stickler for timekeeping. Might be on a day off or had one too many last night and left the car here, I guess. Shame, that. Anyway, remember what I said about paying the ticket. Off to find myself a coffee. Have a good day now, won't you?"

Jamie folded the ticket and put it into his pocket. He looked at his phone. A text from Russ. *Call me. Now.*

"Hi, mate. What's up? You found something?"

"Could say that, Jamie. The car details you sent and the secondary keyholder for your dad's business. They are the same person, mate. When I ran the keyholder information, I double-checked the address and did a full search. I bloody well hope it's a coincidence, mate, but the serious crime boys are dealing with a burnt-out car further out west from you. They found a body in the boot with one possible ID. Looks like it's your car owner and keyholder, Sophie Blackburn. And Jamie. It gets worse mate."

"How can it get worse, Russ? That's bad enough as it is."

"Yeah, yeah, I get that. But here's the thing. Sophie Blackburn's address. It's Flat 17c, Christian Road, Whitechapel. The same address you found Tony Elkins' car at. The FA Holdings property."

Jamie finished the call with Russ and dialled Dot's number. No answer. He left her a message. "Dot, watch your back." To make sure she got the message, he sent a text. If Elkins was working for the other side, then he needed to make sure that Dot was being vigilant. His dad was missing. He didn't want the same outcome for Dot. He went back to his car to think about his next move.

His phone pinged. He read the text he assumed was from Dot. *Jamie, its me dad n big trub dont no where iam dont call back hidden this phone from them its DCIfallon hes coming after you and Dot.* Jamie read and re-read the text. It was a quickly written text from a number he didn't recognise. It didn't sound like his dad, but then again, it sounded like it was from someone who was scared. For now, he had to assume it was from his dad. And, if the content of the text was right, he also knew now that Fallon was definitely involved in some way. And apparently, he was coming for him and Dot. He wrestled with his head not to reply. The text was clear. Don't call back.

Jamie needed help. He needed someone inside the force who had access to systems and someone he could trust. He had access to certain systems, as did Russ. But they were both still in their probationary periods. Any digging into systems beyond their current remit meant trouble. Given that his dad, possibly Dot, and now him, were in trouble, he could justify doing some digging, but the hierarchy might not see it the same way. He turned his phone off. One, as a precaution and two, to maintain the battery.

There was only one place left for Jamie to go. He started his car and drove out of the car park.

CHAPTER 43.

Vanessa. You've made your bed. Who are you going to share it with?

Massimo Albricci had been given his instructions. He pulled his hood up over his head and walked in the opposite direction to Fallon. Despite the assurances that Fallon had given him about not being wanted, he still felt on edge. Given his current employment status, it was always sensible to keep your senses heightened. If it wasn't the police trying to get to you, it could be a rival dealer. If it wasn't a rival dealer, it could be a new OCG making a play for your territory. Even though Fallon planned to hand over to the Albanians, Albi didn't trust them. The bigger the discount you give to someone, the more they try to negotiate. Anyone giving any kind of discount in the drug business is showing weakness. And if you show weakness, you will be exploited. And Albi wasn't about to be exploited again. Ever.

He arrived at his cloned Vauxhall combo van. It was basic but vanilla. People didn't take any real notice of it. It even had paint, ladders, rollers, tin pots and old decorator overalls in the back. To all intents and purposes, Albi was just another hard-working tradie out there in London. He had even been left handwritten notes from people wanting a quote for their own decorative requirements. It was never going to happen. He hated the smell of paint.

He criss-crossed his van through south London and headed over Battersea Bridge towards Earl's Court. He was playing this morning's meeting with Fallon over in his head again and again. Fallon didn't seem worried that some of his inner circle had turned on him. Yeah, he was angry, but that just meant more money for those who hadn't turned on him. Fallon had told Albi there would be around six million waiting for him in Dubai. Six million quid. Whilst it was a huge amount of money, was it going to be enough for him to hide away for the rest of his life? He honestly didn't know. But the time to decide was close. Very close. He owed Fallon a lot. Fallon had tried to be a father figure to him, something he had never had, and it felt good. And he knew that. But he also knew that Fallon had used him. Ever since that day, his mother had been brutally murdered, Fallon had used him to do his dirty work. Slowly but surely, extolling his virtues all the time, but slowly and surely lowering Albi into a hole that was getting deeper and deeper and harder and harder to get out of. He was just another tool that Fallon had used to be able to get what he wanted and to further his influence and power in the London drugs market. He was conflicted, but he also felt guilty. He continued driving over Hammersmith Flyover and towards the Hogarth Road.

"Be nice, no confrontation, stick to the story, and you'll be fine." Fallon's last words now secured firmly in his head. He turned the van off the main road and drove towards the sign that heralded the arrival at the Chelsea Garden Care Home. He pulled into the driveway, drove across the gravel car park and pulled up towards the back, out of sight of the main entrance.

He pulled his hood down and looked in the mirror. The dark rings around his eyes, rather than making him look tired, made him look sad. He looked older than his years, that was for sure. He got out of the van and walked into the care home.

Standing by the main desk, talking to the receptionist, was a tall man dressed in a dark blue security outfit. Given that the cap he was wearing was balanced on his ears rather than his head indicated that he was very new to the job.

"Tradesman's entrance round the back, pal. Go past the staff car park to a large door. Ring the bell. Someone will come and see you there."

The security guard was leaning in the direction of the receptionist, clearly irked that he had been disturbed during his discussion.

"I'm here to see Vanessa Foxx." Albi stood tall and imposing in front of the reception desk.

"Is that right, pal? Well, piss off round the back, ring the bell, and I'll get someone to tell Miss Foxx you're here. How does that sound?"

Albi took a slow pace forward. "Well, that doesn't sound very welcoming to me. If I were a tradesman, I would be more than happy to do as you have asked, but, despite my appearance, I can assure you I am not a tradesman. So, as I said before, I'm here to see Vanessa Foxx, and I would be grateful if you could let her know that I'm here to see her. How does that sound?"

The security guard stood upright, realising that he was being belittled in front of his morning pursuit.

The receptionist, clearly feeling the security guard's testosterone kicking in, asked, "Who shall I tell Miss Foxx is here to see her?"

"Tell her I'm here on behalf of Detective Chief Inspector Fallon. Thank you."

The new security guard looked at the receptionist. The receptionist's look in return was clear. Go and do your job, you idiot, and leave me alone.

"I'll let her know you are here." The receptionist dialled a number on the phone in front of her.

Albi nodded his acknowledgement and noticed movement in the office beyond the reception. He knew it was Vanessa's office.

Vanessa's face showed surprise more than anything else. She walked across the reception to Albi. "Any particular reason why Chief Inspector Fallon isn't here in person?"

Albi grinned. Feisty as always. "Good to see you too. He has requested your presence down at the station, Miss Foxx. I'm just carrying out my orders. I would be very grateful if you could accompany me to a meeting with the Chief

Inspector. I've been instructed to drive you there immediately."

"I see." Vanessa was not impressed at all. "And which station exactly are you to escort me to? Just in case. My staff will want to know where to reach me. I'm sure you understand."

"We are going to Scotland Yard, Miss Foxx. Now, if you have nothing further to ask, I must insist that we get going. Traffic is a nightmare today, and I don't want to keep Chief Inspector Fallon waiting any longer than we have to."

Vanessa's mind was in a state of alarm. This was not in the plan. The last message she had from Fallon had shown that he had gone into escape mode. People had found out what he really was. It was all about the exit strategy now. Fallon hadn't told her that Albi would be picking her up. And if she was going to go anywhere, it was to the safe house in East London. Not Scotland Yard. She also had plans with Jack. But Jack had disappeared off the face of the earth, so she had no idea what he would do. And she knew the man standing in front of her. Worse though. She knew what he was capable of.

Albi walked over towards Vanessa so that the reception desk and security guard were behind him. "We should go, Miss Foxx. Now." As Albi spoke, he discreetly lifted the front of his hoodie up to reveal the grip of a black handgun. "If you don't mind. Thank you."

The colour drained out of Vanessa's face. This most certainly wasn't in the plan, which meant only one thing. Fallon saw her as a threat. "Of course, I was in the middle of signing off Lizzie's performance review." She nodded towards the receptionist. "I just need to get it and give it to her. I also need to get my jacket from the office and log out of the computer." She turned and walked back into her office. She leaned over her desk so that Albi couldn't see what she was doing. Within seconds, she had written a single word on a Post-it note. Albi moved to the door and stood watching her. If he walked over to the desk, he would see what she had done. Luckily, she had indeed been finalising performance reviews. She found Lizzie's, opened it to the final page and placed the Post-it note on the paper. She closed it and waved it at Albi. "Got it." She reached for her jacket and ushered Albi out of the office, closing the door behind her.

As they both walked past the reception desk, Vanessa stopped and placed the performance review in front of Lizzie. "I'll be gone for the rest of the day, Lizzie. You can call me on my mobile if you need anything. Just one thing. I need your signature on your performance review, please. Best do it straight away for me. I want to make sure we get it into head office for a year-end bonus. Thanks." She took Albi's arm. "Shall we?"

Lizzie watched as her boss and police officer-ish person, whoever he was, walk out of the building. She had shooed away the new security guard. She didn't want her boss to think she was cavorting during working hours. Which, of course, she wasn't. Strange that Vanessa gave her the review. She normally got one of the supervisors to go through it with her. She skimmed through the performance indicators to the bonus bit and smiled. Enough to put towards a holiday at least. She turned to the last page to sign it and gasped. There was a bright yellow Post-it note with a single word written on it. **KIDNAPPED.**

CHAPTER 44.

Never count your chickens. Just ask Charlie.

Sergeant Charlie Mepham was conflicted. Or should that be Mr Charlie Mepham, most likely erstwhile police officer, was conflicted. He had made the decision that Dubai was going to be just too bloody hot. And quite frankly, if he was going to spend the rest of his life, either on the run, in witness protection or in prison, he would rather be somewhere he could understand the language and enjoy the food. He had committed enough crime over the last ten years to put him behind bars until the day he died, but he also had something that he could bargain with. He had information; a lot of it. And given the state of corruption amongst constabularies, there were senior officers in the force who would walk a mile over hot coals to have access to what Mepham knew.

His first point of contact for information regarding Fallon had been another sergeant who smelt a rat a couple of years ago. Fallon had had a ridiculous idea that the safest way to transport drugs around London was in the back of a police van. And let's face it, who in their right mind is going to hold up a police vehicle? It was all fine until after one of the handovers between Fallon and a drugs boss, when Mepham took the van back to a police station to give it a clean. Mepham always cleaned vehicles during the small hours and checked in advance which police officers were on shift. Unbeknownst to him on the particular night in question, the local K9 officer had decided to appropriate Mepham's van, as his own van had blown a gasket and was out of use. Mepham had been told that K9 was not active as a result of the broken-down vehicle. The K9 officer had other ideas and opened the rear van doors on Mepham's return and allowed his dog to jump in. As the fully hyped-up dog entered the van, it had the equivalent of a canine meltdown. Having entered a trained drug dog's version of the promised land, it took the K9 officer half an hour to get the dog out of the van, which led to the over-curious officer making enquiries as to how the entire vehicle had traces of cocaine in it.

Mepham had managed to talk himself out of the situation by saying that he had only just picked the vehicle up, which had not been used in a number of days. Fallon, luckily, had signed the vehicle out to a garage for repairs, which obviously didn't exist. This line of enquiry led back to a meddlesome sergeant by the name of Elkins. And although Elkins couldn't pin anything on Mepham, he knew that something wasn't right. And he had told Mepham exactly that.

There was another problem with Elkins. One that seemed all too familiar to his peers. He liked money. And he had figured out that in order to extract traces of cocaine from two-thirds of the way up the inside of a police van meant that someone linked to Mepham had access to an obscene amount of drugs. Elkins had also figured that blackmail was the best way to make money without actually handling the drugs. And, of course, he was a police officer. A trusted member of the service who had gone above and beyond more than once. Which meant that he had credibility with senior officers. And that credibility was a major thorn in the side of Mepham as it allowed Elkins access to areas that most officers didn't know existed. As such, this allowed Elkins to give constant reminders to Mepham, requesting ever-increasing demands for money.

It wasn't as though Mepham hadn't thought about breaking every bone in Elkins' body, every day, but Elkins was smart. Very smart. He had used whatever IOUs he had built up throughout his career to establish that Mepham had had money transferred into a bank account bearing his wife's name. This money had then been almost immediately transferred out to an unknown account based somewhere in the Caribbean. The transfer happened almost instantaneously, but Elkins had managed to find enough of a footprint to recognise that the amount was half a million dollars. Ever since then, he had become a resident leech in Mepham's life.

Now, however, Mepham had put himself in a position to pull the leech off and throw it into the fire. The assumption would be that Elkins would never contemplate that Mepham would turn and potentially bury himself in the process. Smart vs stupid. Well, let's see who is smart now.

Mepham was still in possession of a burner phone he had used for various SIM cards that Fallon had given him. Having earlier left Jack in a bad place, he had to move quickly. Fallon would only keep him alive for as long as he needed him, or, if he realised he was being double-crossed about the money. Mepham had been tasked with delivering the drugs to the Albanians after it was confirmed by Jack that the money had been received. But, like almost everyone around him, he also had a reason to keep Jack alive.

Driving back towards the East End, Mepham pulled his car over onto double yellow lines outside one of the many mobile phone repair shops in the area. Most were fronts for some sleazy crime group, but this one wasn't. It was the personal electronics unit for Fallon and his team.

"Alright, Charlie boy? Lost another fight, I see. Belter of a black eye, mate. Anyone tell you; you might want to look at an alternative career? Preferably one that doesn't involve getting your arse whopped. Anyway, what can I do for my favourite police officer?"

"Mike," said Charlie, totally unimpressed with the observations of the shop manager, known as Mickey the mobile. "Treat all of your customers like that, you'll end up playing water polo in the Thames."

"You serious, Charlie, the Thames is full of shit, mate."

"My point exactly, Mike. Now, I need a new SIM and need to borrow your laptop for five minutes. The one that can't be tracked."

"Yeah, there we go. Pillar of society, my arse. Outside of Wormwood Scrubs, the best place to get taught the art of criminality is your lot. Twenty quid for the SIM. Thirty quid for five minutes. Still cheaper than driving up and down King's Cross."

"Well, Mike, at least you can make daylight robbery seem almost legal. Bloody thief."

"Takes one to know one, my esteemed police sergeant. Walk this way if you will, preferably with cash in hand, and I will, of course, oblige." Mike walked through a plastic strip curtain, which revealed a room around a hundred square feet. There was a table facing the left-hand wall as they walked in. Mepham followed him through.

Mepham handed him the burner phone and sat at the laptop indicated to him on the table. Mike leant over Mepham, keyed in the relevant password, and walked back into the shop.

Mepham logged into his offshore bank account. It was split into US dollar and sterling accounts. He checked the dollar account first. One hundred and thirty-five thousand dollars. He then checked the sterling account. Two hundred and fifty-seven thousand pounds. There was no additional five hundred thousand dollars in either account that had been promised by Fallon. Which basically meant one of three things. Fallon was either in custody, he had figured out that his team was shrinking, or he was dead. Whichever way, the money wasn't there, so it helped cement the next step.

Mepham opened his secure email, one he used with Fallon, as well as others tangled up in this mess, along with him. As yet, Jack hadn't sent through confirmation of the transaction with the Albanians. That didn't mean it hadn't been sent. Fallon might have told Jack just to tell him and no one else. Time was now of the essence. The assumption had to be that Fallon knew his closest people were dropping off.

And Mepham knew, above anything else, that he had to stay one step ahead.

"Mike, you got the phone with the new SIM? I need to make a call."

Mike walked back through the plastic curtain into the office. "Yeah, yeah, here you go, Charlie"

Mepham started to turn around in his seat to take the phone. Mike stood just inside the curtain with a 9mm suppressed Glock pointed at the police sergeant. "Fallon asked me to tell you to sleep well and not to take this personally. Chickens come home to roost, mate."

Mobile Mikey then pulled the trigger twice in very quick succession. Both bullets entered Mepham's forehead, the second bullet hole entering slightly lower than the first. Charlie Mepham was already dead by the time he slumped onto the table.

CHAPTER 45.

Fallon's VW Van. Logistics HQ.

Fallon's mobile phone rang. He looked at the number and then answered. "Mikey. How's it going?"

"All done. Going to need at least twenty grand to redecorate the office, though."

"Consider it done, Mikey. As Mepham won't be needing it, I'll stick an extra four hundred and eighty grand on top as well. How about that?"

"Sweet. What do you want me to do with him?"

"Usual, Mikey. Steelworks, mate. He always wanted to be cremated."

"Not a problem at all. I'll get him over there as soon as I hang up. Guess, as you are destroying the evidence around you, we won't be talking anymore after this."

"I guess not. Keep your head down, Mikey."

"You too, nice doing business with you."

Fallon finished the call. He had parked his van in a street not far from the lock-up garage in South London where the drugs were currently being stored. He didn't have a resident's parking permit, but if any parking wardens made their rounds, he had his warrant card to shoo them away.

He had installed a top-of-the-range police scanner in the van, as well as having three different police radios from different stations in the area. They were all misappropriated and had no connection to Fallon. He had an innate skill at being able to hear through the chatter and pick up what he needed to hear. At the moment, it was the lack of chatter that was giving him the most information. There was no news on Jack's disappearance. Or Vanessa's. There was no chatter about the stupid bitch that Jack had been screwing, now disposed of in a burnt-out car. The only slight piece of information that came through was about a smash between a motorcycle and a van in a street just down from the lockup where Jack had been held in West London. A member of the public had reported it and phoned it through. The scanner picked up a brief conversation between a controller and a traffic car to attend the scene. Andy Patterson's phone was dead, so Fallon had to assume that he was the motorcyclist. Then the comms about the accident stopped. There was nothing. Absolutely nothing. On any of the radios or other comms. That meant that, as he knew would eventually happen, separate law enforcement agencies were now dealing with him. Normal people would be worried about this, Fallon not so. He saw it more as a badge of honour. Bring in the big guns to take him down. Well, despite all of that, here he was, cleaning up right under their noses.

He needed to stay focused. Now, more than ever. Decisions of the type that he now faced making didn't happen in most people's lives. Even those who operated in his world would be unsettled by having to determine the fate of so many people. Having already eradicated quite a few enemies, Fallon was still having to make more of these decisions within the next few hours. It was frankly exhausting. And getting just one decision wrong would not hold a particularly beneficial outcome for him.

In his head, the only outcome that must never happen as a result of his peripheral occupational endeavours was being captured by his now previous employer. Being sent to prison would be a mammoth task in itself. Getting past his previous work colleagues without being maimed or killed would be the primary challenge. And if he did indeed make it to prison, there would be large numbers of incumbents waiting for any opportunity to exact retribution for past arrests and subsequent sentences. Did he regret all of the decisions he had made previously? One or two, perhaps. But in general? No. He was too good for the police service. He was smarter than them. And, unlike many others in the police, his sense of duty and service to the public was about one step away from being non-existent as anyone could possibly be. The skill involved in manipulating criminals whilst using a warrant card as a bargaining chip and disciplinary tool was far more exciting. The outcomes were worth a lot more than a police salary. However, he also knew that if it went wrong, the consequences would be monumental. And that, in Fallon's mind, meant failure of any sort was not an option.

Fallon's phone glowed and vibrated. It was Albi. *Safely at the house with your little lady. Bitch has got a temper. What next? Wait for you?*

Fallon sniggered. She certainly had a temper. He liked that. *Put her to sleep for a couple of hours. One more job for you. Need a pick up done and taken back to the flat. Just around the corner from you but he's uniform so be careful.* Fallon sent the text, followed by another with the address for the pickup. He needed to get everyone where he could see them. Too many people had decided they were better than him. And thought that they were smarter. They weren't, and he knew it.

Fallon felt a slight movement in the van. His passenger was groaning. He was awake. Yet again, his mobile phone glowed and vibrated.

Sent you twenty-five for the birthday present. Where's the party?

Eleven words, that's all. Eleven words that were the culmination of years of work. This was it. The Albanians were ready. They had sent over the first half of the money. Now it was time to get Jack to check it was in, show the drugs and wait for the final payment.

Fallon took a deep breath in. "Jack, I know you can hear me. It's time for you to go to work. I won't be happy if you try to screw me, though, and as for the Albanians. Well, if you screw them, they'll make me look like Prince

Charming. I couldn't even begin to imagine what they'll do to you if you try anything foolish. Let's just hope we never find out, eh."

As always, Fallon needed an insurance policy in case Jack didn't play ball. And boy, had Jack given him the biggest one possible.

Fallon reached into the glove compartment and took out an old-style mobile phone. How on earth Jack thought he wouldn't be searched, Fallon would never know. And how could someone with such a brilliant mind also be so stupid? Still, it helped no end. Fallon switched on Jack's phone.

Jamie. Its Fallon. I have Jack. Meet 17c Christian Rd Whitechapel in 1 hour. I have eyes everywhere. If you are not there or you are not alone then Jack dies. Very simple. 1 hour. Alone

If Jack refused to help, then Jamie was Fallon's indemnity. He grinned again inwardly. He was too smart to be a police officer. He started the van and pulled out from the parking space into the one-way road. He headed south. It was only a short drive to his destination.

CHAPTER 46.

Laney.

Jamie pulled into the car park at Dot's office. He threw open his door and ran across the car park to the staff entrance of the police station. He went to swipe his general pass and noticed the out-of-order sticker on the box. Underneath another sticker read, 'press for attention'. Wow, thought Jamie, twenty-first-century policing at its finest. He pressed the buzzer.

"How can I help?"

"PC Andries to see DC Craddock. It's urgent."

"Warrant card up to the camera for me"

Jamie took out his warrant card and held it up to the camera.

The door buzzed, he pushed it open and walked into the reception area.

There were a number of officers in uniform as well as in civilian clothing gathered around the desk where a female sergeant was openly weeping. Jamie couldn't hear what was being said. There was a reinforced glass barrier between him and the other people there.

The assumed voice from the buzzer looked up and pointed Jamie through the internal door leading to where Dot's office was. He nodded his thanks and pushed open the door. He walked along the corridor and knocked on Dot's office door.

A familiar voice sang out, "Come in."

Jamie entered. "Hey, Laney, how are you doing? What's up in reception, looks like someone's died out there."

"Oh, hey, Jamie. Wasn't expecting to see you. Nice surprise, though. Er, yes, as it happens. Someone has died. You remember Andy? Andy Patterson, you know, the desk sergeant. He was killed riding his motorcycle this morning. Can you imagine, just like that. Gone. Weeks from retirement as well. So sad."

"Oh, God, I'm sorry. I didn't know. Normally, word gets out quickly on these things. Did you know him well?"

"Knew him to say hi to most days. Dot knew him better, though. I don't know if anyone has told her yet. She'll be gutted. They used to have lots of chats. Anyway, what are you doing here? Dot isn't here. She is over at HQ doing something secret squirrel. I saw her first thing this morning, and then she hurried off. How's your assignment going? Have you started working in CID yet? You must be very excited about it."

DC Elaine Craddock was probably six or seven years older than Jamie, but the evidence was crystal clear. She had a crush on him. And to be fair, Jamie wasn't exactly putting her off. She was five and a half feet tall, give or take an inch, with short ginger hair and mesmerisingly green eyes.

"It's going ok. I think. That'll be down to what sort of mood the skip is in when he marks it, I guess. But look, Laney, listen. I need your help. And I really need you to trust me. Please just listen to what I am going to say, and I could really, really do with you saying, yeah Jamie, of course, anything you need."

"Ooh, very intriguing. It's already been a strange morning, what with Dot coming in here earlier asking me to do some digging on a chap that was arrested at the nursing home your grandma is in. And arrested for murder, if you please."

"Yeah, I heard about that, weird; anything more on the wires here on that?"

Laney's eyes were fixated upon Jamie. "Well, it wasn't exactly on the wires. I had to make a few calls to find out what happened. But listen to this. The main suspect for the murder, who was the security guard at the care home, apparently only went and committed suicide in the custody suite last night. Can you even begin to imagine sorting the paperwork out on that one? Don't you just love this job? Anyway, now, what is it that's so important I need to swear an oath in blood?"

"Suicide? Wow, the assumption will be that he's the guilty party, but they need to prove it beyond all reasonable doubt now he's dead. I'm sure I'll hear more on this one when I get over to CID. Look, can you find the main fax number for me at HQ reception and then get an urgent message to Dot? I need to send her a fax, but it needs to look like it has come from you. Something that needs signing urgently. Something you're working on that only she would know about. Something that if someone else saw, they wouldn't be suspicious about."

"Oooh, riddles, I like riddles." Laney had this habit of sounding much younger than her years, but Jamie knew there was a devil inside her. And right now, he needed the devil to come out and help him.

"Well, I've been working on a juicy money laundering case. Car showrooms of all things. Not your street corner Arthur Daley types, but very expensive motor car types. Between London and the Middle East, of course. These people adore the cars, just don't like paying the tax on them. I could easily ask Dot for a permissive sign-off on some information out of one of the embassies over there. She did it once before. I've still got the original paperwork, just need to Tippex over the date. Any good for you?"

"My God, Laney, you are a bloody genius, you know that. If you can sort that, I just need to add one line to it."

"Becoming very James Bond all of a sudden, Mr Probationer. Am I allowed to ask any questions, or will you have to kill me if I find out what you are up to?"

"Very funny, Laney. In all seriousness, for now, the less you know, probably the better for all of us. I promise I'll fill you in when I'm done with this. Whatever this is. Is that ok?

"As you request, Mr Bond. As long as when you do eventually tell me, it will be over a very nice, expensive dinner at a restaurant of my choosing. Fair?"

Jamie grinned. "Sounds fair to me, DC Craddock, but let me remind you that I'm not on a detective's salary just yet. Now, can we have a look at that document you mentioned earlier?"

Laney walked over to a wall of filing cabinets and went straight to one of the dark green drawers. She opened it and took out a file that was about two inches thick. She returned to her chair, sat down and started thumbing through the file. "Voila. Here we go." She had kept both the original incoming document as well as the executed one. "Make yourself useful, Jamie. Head left out of the door. Go to the bottom and turn left again. You will see the photocopier there. Use my pass to get the copy, and whilst you are there, I'll have a black coffee with one sugar." She handed the front page of the document with the date on it to Jamie, and he went off to follow Laney's instructions.

Laney, in the meantime, made a call to HQ to establish the best fax number to send an urgent document for the attention of Inspector LaSalle. She asked the receptionist to look out for it. And whilst she was on the phone, she asked for clarification that Dot was actually in the building.

"Yes, I can confirm that Inspector LaSalle is currently here. Is that all?"

"Thank you so much for your help. Just one more thing. Can you confirm who Inspector LaSalle is meeting with, please? She forgot to put it on her calendar, and we have our five-year audit happening today. I need to be able to tell the auditors how long Inspector LaSalle will be otherwise, as I'm sure you are aware, it will cause a bit of a commotion."

The response to Laney's request was a large exhale of breath from the other end of the phone line.

"She is in a confidential meeting all day. The organiser, however, is not restricted. Detective Sergeant Elkins. Now, anything else?"

"No, no, thank you. You have been more than helpful. The fax, though, please remember to look out for it. I'll let Inspector LaSalle know it's on its way."

Laney hung up the phone. Well, she must have got that one wrong. Tony was a sergeant, but certainly not a detective. And how come he was the one at HQ with Dot? She never mentioned anything, and he sure as hell didn't. Detective, she thought. That's her job. Weird. Just to make sure, she typed in Sergeant Elkins' name into the internal police address book. There you go, Detective my arse. Just boring, Sergeant.

The door to the office opened, and Jamie walked in holding the copied paperwork in one hand and balancing two mugs of coffee in the other.

"Spoke to HQ. Dot is there with, get this, Tony, as in Elkins. Hope it's not a meeting about reducing the budget here or something crappy like that."

Jamie put the mugs on the table and handed Laney the copied paperwork. He took out his mobile phone and switched it on. A single text came through from the same number that seemed to belong to Dad. He read the text and remained silent.

"You okay, Jamie? You've gone a tad pale. Drink your coffee. That stuff supercharges your insides."

"Can you get your phone, Laney? I need you to send that text to Dot. I need her to read the fax as soon as possible. Can you fill in the gaps on the paperwork so it looks like it came through today, and then I can add something before it goes?"

"Just so you know, the D in my rank stands for Detective, not dogsbody. Right, given you know absolutely nothing about the content of the paperwork you just copied, would you like me to formulate the text for the boss?"

Jamie raised his eyebrows toward her. "Please. And can you read it out as you write it, if that's okay with you?"

Boss. Big problem. Need your signature on a Possession paper for Dubai right now. Perp's lawyers want to charge us ten grand an hour for false imprisonment. Way outside my expenses brief. Fax coming through to HQ reception in 1 min. Return signature page only. Laney.

"Sounds good, thanks, Laney. Now let's hope that she reads it quickly."

"I think she will. I always sign off with two kisses. Piss-take kind of thing, you know. Hmm, maybe you don't. Oh, Christ, sorry, I keep forgetting she is your stepmum. Anyway, she'll know something's wrong because I haven't put the kisses in the text. Now, what did you want to put on the form? We need to fax it as soon as possible. Can't have Dot running to reception to find nothing there."

"Yeah, of course, can you hand me the signature page? That's the only one I need, but we'll need to fax all the forms across."

"I hope you know what the hell you are doing, Jamie. There's enough secret squirrel shit going on as it is. I really don't want any more to be honest."

"Then close your eyes, Laney. You aren't going to want to see what I am about to write."

Laney passed over the last page of the document. She had already Tippex'd out the date and was waiting for the liquid to dry. She leaned over Jamie's shoulder and watched as he wrote his message to Dot.

When he had finished, she took the document and filled in the date. She then placed it on the office fax machine, entered HQ's number, and hit send. They watched in silence as each page went through until finally, a long beep indicated a successful transmission.

"What you wrote in the fax didn't sound very urgent to me. Fallon? Fallon?" Laney screwed her eyes up, angled her head slightly upwards and put a finger over her lips. "I know that name. That's the person you asked me about earlier, isn't it? Someone of that name was asking after Dot earlier. Andy buzzed through just before he went off shift. That's a bit weird, don't you think? Wow, still can't believe he's gone. So, so sad. Anyway, what's this Fallon character got to do with Elkins and Dot? I assume that Elkins is working for Dot? Isn't he? Or am I missing something? My mum used to say my attitude was more blonde than redhead. But you're not making it easy for me to figure out this riddle, are you? Come on, tell me. So. Who is Fallon, and why does Elkins appear to be working with him now, not Dot? Has he moved teams? If he has, I'll give him a piece of my mind. He can't be doing something like that and not tell me about it."

"Laney."

"Yes, Jamie."

"Can you just shut up for one second? How can I explain when I can't get a word in edgeways? I'm on the clock here and need to be somewhere else. But I need to wait to make sure that Dot has got the message. Now let me explain what is happening. And this goes nowhere else, and I mean nowhere, Laney. Understood? Otherwise, dinner is definitely cancelled."

Laney simply stared at him.

He then spent the next ten minutes explaining most of what he knew about the situation that he now found himself in. Hopefully, he would still get to take Laney out for dinner.

The fax machine rang, stopped, then started to spit out paper. A single page came through. Next to where Jamie had written *Elkins works for Fallon* under the signature box, there was now a tick. It seemed to indicate an acknowledgement. Under where Jamie had written, someone, presumably Dot, had responded. It simply said *Comms compromised.*

"Laney, I need to get going. There's somewhere I need to be. I'm going to send one more text, but this time it's coming from my phone. I know that this is all strange, but this whole situation is as perplexing as it is just bloody crazy. You can't tell anyone else about our conversation. Not until it's sorted. Please trust me on this and help Dot in whatever way you can. Is that okay with you?"

"Well, that's dinner out of the window then. As you have just upped the ante, this deserves at least a spa weekend. Oh, and by the way, that FA Holdings stuff you told me about. Fallon and Andries. Has to be. What is it with this Fallon chap? Got his fingers in a lot of pies by the sound of it. Can't believe you hadn't thought about that one. I'll do some more digging from here. We have access to some terrifying little systems that can find out all sorts of things. Now, send your text. We've got some work to do. Oh, and give me that Russ's bloke number you spoke about, he sounds nice."

Laney smirked at Jamie. She swore she saw a glint of jealousy in his eyes.

Jamie had indeed thought about FA Holdings but refused to believe it would be that simple. But then again, sometimes the harder you look at something, the less you see.

Jamie typed a text into his phone. *Dot, I know where Fallon has stored the drugs. I'm getting Drug Squad involved. Where are you? Dad's still missing, but I think I know where he is. Call me. Urgently. J.* He hit send. Comms compromised, eh? Let's see who comes crawling out of the woodwork now.

CHAPTER 47.

London. And yet again, back at the glass room at the posh police station.

Dot sat silently in the van watching as Elkins sent a stream of texts on his phone. Her whole being felt bruised, and she couldn't let go of seeing Patterson's broken body lying in the road. Less than twenty fours before, she had been bumbling along in her own ridiculously convoluted world. Now, she was surrounded by, allegedly, the best people law enforcement had to offer, yet even she could see they were one step behind in whatever goal they were pursuing. Of course, she knew that the main target was Fallon. Of course, she knew that nobody wanted London flooded with cheap drugs. And it would appear that Jack held the key to the entire OCG. Of course, he did. So, given the resources at their disposal, the fact that they also had an inside source, and quite frankly, the fact that they had the entire police force at their disposal, they should be making it easy to find both Fallon and Jack. Yet they couldn't. They kept missing their target. What was it? Bad luck? Coincidence? Flawed intelligence? Highly unlikely. And that was the point.

"We'll be back at HQ shortly, ma'am." Elkins still had his head down, sending and reading texts. He spoke without looking up at Dot. "How are you feeling? Any bumps and bruises that you would like to have someone look at when we get there?"

"No, thank you, I'm good. Are you any closer to finding out where Jack and Fallon are?"

"Not yet. We're trying to find the link between Patterson and Fallon. The bag of money at the scene contained close to half a million quid. Enough to disappear if you wanted to."

"I saw him this morning when I went to my office. He seemed fine. 10 years he was there." Dot deliberately held back some of the information Patterson gave her about Fallon.

"Yes, of course, he was a duty sergeant at your station, wasn't he? So, nothing else you can think of about him that could help us. Anything at all."

Dot shook her head. "No. It's still bloody raw, to be honest. He was so close to retirement. Why throw it all away?"

"Yes, yes, it is, sorry. I don't know the answer to that question, but that's what we'll find out. Ten years at one station is going some nowadays. Right, that feels like us. You ready, ma'am?"

The van had come to a stop; The driver had jumped out, and the side door opened. Dot stepped out first. "I need to go to the ladies' room. I'll see you upstairs, Elkins."

"It's all good, ma'am; I'll wait for you."

Dot had started walking through the underground car park. "Holding my hand is one thing, Elkins, but you are not here to wipe my arse as well. I need a breather; I need to have a wash, and I need to have a pee. Once I'm done, I'll meet you back at the conference room. And that is an order. Like it or not."

Elkins stared at Dot and nodded. He could look downright nasty when he wanted to. They both got into the lift. Elkins pressed the button for the twentieth floor.

Dot then pressed the button for the ground floor. "There is a perfectly good bathroom on the twentieth floor, ma'am", Elkins said, coldly.

"Then, best you get your body armour on. I need some air, and I need some space. You are nowhere near old enough to understand, but my post-menopausal body is about to explode. So do yourself a favour and give me ten minutes to sort my shit out. Otherwise, I will not be held responsible for my behaviour. She needed ten minutes alone. She felt stifled by Elkins, and she needed to breathe to take stock of exactly what was happening. It felt like there was a new twist around every corner, and she didn't like it. She didn't like not being in control. And right now, her whole world seemed out of control. More importantly, though, she needed to check her phone.

The lift stopped on the ground floor, and Dot walked out without looking behind to see if Elkins followed. The door closed, and she turned. Elkins had continued in the lift. Dot watched as the numbers on the panel at the side of the lift flashed through the different floors. All the way to twenty. Then it stopped.

She headed over to the ladies' toilet. Once she was in, she went straight to the wash basin and filled it with hot water. She looked in the mirror. The face staring back looked old. Despite numerous attempts to keep a head of blonde hair, she could see grey creeping through, pairing brilliantly with the bags that had developed under her eyes and accompanying the lines of red blood vessels that had appeared en masse in her eyeballs. The sink was now full. Dot cupped up handfuls of hot water and threw them across her face. Funny how the simple things can make you feel human again. She repeated this a few times, oblivious to the water that was splashing down her top.

She went over to the hand dryer and attempted to dry her hands, at the same time, performing a limbo to get her top dry as well.

When she was satisfied that her top was dry, she took out her phone and switched it on. She had turned it off earlier, figuring that those smart arses upstairs could only listen to live calls, not voicemails. She still didn't understand why they had insisted on listening in on her calls. They clearly have some serious trust issues. The phone beeped and vibrated as it came to life. A text from Jamie. Butterflies built in her stomach as she read the text. Shit. She assumed that texts could be monitored at all times. Well, if they were, that one would certainly get the eavesdropping brigade choking on their tea. Another text. This time, it was one from Laney. She read it twice. It didn't sound like the way Laney spoke, although the gist of the text related to something that only she would know about. And it didn't have the obligatory Laney kisses. Strange.

Dot went into one of the cubicles and performed the longest wees she had ever done in her life. The copious amounts of coffee had finally burst from her bladder. She left the ladies' and walked over to the main reception.

The receptionist looked up at Dot and simply queried, "Yes?"

"Inspector LaSalle. I believe you have a fax for me?"

The woman turned and picked up a small stack of papers, then smacked them on the glass counter of the reception desk. "Twenty-eight years of service have amounted to nothing more than being a bloody skivvy."

Dot picked up the paperwork and turned away without responding to the peeved long-standing receptionist.

"That'll be a you're welcome, then."

Dot just shook her head. She was skimming through the document that Lany had sent. She got to the last page and turned back to the receptionist.

"Pen, please." Then Dot froze. She read the words below the signature page. She put a tick next to the signature page and wrote 'Comms compromised'. Instinctively, as when someone gets a feeling that you are being stared at, Dot turned. Elkins was walking from the lift towards her.

"Shit, shit," Dot murmured under her breath. "You!" she hissed at the receptionist.

"This page. It needs to be sent back to the number at the top of the page, and it needs to be done now. Right now. If this doesn't go in the next twenty seconds, I swear you won't make it to twenty-nine years of service."

The woman, whose face was starting to turn a shade of red, was about to remonstrate.

"I said NOW. Right now. It's a matter of life or death, and if it isn't sent right now, then it will be death and probably yours. Do I make myself clear?"

Elkins was now no more than twenty feet away. Dot's eyes were fully focused on the woman now sending the fax. It rang several times, and then the single sheet of paper started to slip into the machine.

Dot picked up the remainder of the paperwork and turned to head off Elkins. He looked over Dot's shoulder. The receptionist was trying to say something to Dot, but Dot was ignoring her.

"What was that all about, then?" queried Elkins.

"A problem in Dubai. Laney is trying to stop the hard-working taxpayers of this wonderful country of ours from getting charged a lot of money by an unscrupulous lawyer over there. Needed an urgent signature, that's all." She held up the paperwork in Elkins' direction and walked straight past him towards the lifts. "Are you coming? I need a coffee, and I'm bloody starving." She walked over to the lift and pressed the call button. Doors to her right opened up, and she stepped through them. She turned and called back to Elkins. "You coming or not?"

It was obvious that Elkins was intrigued by her behaviour. He looked back at reception and then walked to the lift and got in with Dot. She pressed the number twenty, and the doors slid closed in front of them. She let out a slow but silent exhale of breath. She couldn't look at Elkins.

"You do know I can just log into the reception fax account and get a copy of what you sent."

"If you've got time to waste, then be my guest and go ahead. You will find a fax to Laney to do with the Dubai money launderers. You would know about the case if you actually spent time doing your job in my team instead of lying to me."

"I'm sure you understand the need for my surreptitious nature, ma'am. And with all due respect, I believe what I'm doing far outweighs chasing down a few swindlers and cheats."

"Well, wouldn't you be the one to know all about those, Detective Sergeant Elkins?"

The lift came to a gut-dropping halt, and the door opened on the twentieth floor. Dot walked out and almost bumped into McKenzie talking on his phone. He put his hand over the mouthpiece. "Ah, you're here. Good. Events are moving quickly. Both of you straight into the conference room." He then started to talk again on the phone.

Dot stopped. "Sir. Sir. SIR, I need a word. Now, please."

Once again, McKenzie placed a hand over the mouthpiece. "In the room, Dot. I need to finish this call. Now go. The landscape has changed. And Elkins, you, too, please." McKenzie then continued to talk on the phone and turned his back on Dot.

"Important, was it, ma'am? Anything I should know about at all?"

Dot ignored Elkins and walked quickly to the end of the corridor and entered the glass conference room yet again.

Commander Truss stood drinking a coffee and looking out at the outstretched landscape of London.

"Sir," Dot acknowledged as she entered.

"Ah, Inspector LaSalle, DS Elkins, good to see you both. Grab a coffee, it's fresh. Just waiting for the Chief Super to finish up and for Chief Inspector Clayton to arrive, and we can crack on. There are a number of developments we need to bring you up to speed on, and of course, we need your debrief as well. Bit close by all accounts."

Elkins returned to the same chair and opened the laptop in front of him. He started typing.

Dot walked around the table and poured herself a coffee. "It's a shame that such a beautiful view can be spoiled when you know just how many rats are running around, don't you think, Commander?"

"I would most likely have concurred with your view when I was younger, Inspector." Truss looked deep in thought as he spoke. "But I think we are slowly winning the war against the rodents out there. Will we ever be free of them? Who knows. You, of course, know the story about the Pied Piper of Hamelin?"

"Yes, I do, sir. He got rid of all the rats in a river from a town in Germany hundreds of years ago. Maybe we need our own Pied Piper to do the same here. Save a lot of expenses."

"Maybe so, Inspector, but the real moral of the story always seems to get forgotten. The mayor of that particular village reneged on payment to the piper, so the piper stole all of the children away as revenge. You see, even many hundreds of years ago, life was all about greed. Subterfuge. Not unlike the world we live in today. So, all the time there's greed, there will always be rats. Our job is to create a tainted equilibrium. Slightly skewed in our favour, if you will. We won't always win, but provided we beat the rats more times than they beat us, then I'll take that. And as long as we make sure the nice townsfolk of our village don't get to see what's really happening in the sewers, then, like me, we all get to see a London that, in general, we like, and we all want to live in."

Dot was listening to the commander as well as watching Clayton leave the lift, and started to walk with McKenzie towards the conference room. Their heads were close and tilted towards each other as they walked. They had news. And it didn't look good in Dot's eyes.

"Afternoon, team." McKenzie was first into the room, followed by Clayton, who gave the door a helping hand to close. Neither of them went to sit down.

Clayton walked straight to the table, placed her hands on it, leaned forward and spoke. "Elkins, what went wrong with the raid to find Andries? You said the information you had from Mepham would be good. Where's Mepham now? Have you spoken to him to find out what went wrong? And when were we going to get the intel on Patterson? Some bloody curve ball that was."

Tony Elkins looked up from his computer screen. "The information from Mepham was solid, ma'am. We were close. Either someone knew we were on the way, or it was just unfortunate that we got there after they decided to move him anyway. Mepham is safe. Spoke to him, and he is working on finding out where the drugs are being stored, although I do believe Inspector LaSalle may well be able to update you on that detail. Sounds like Jamie Andries is poking his nose in trying to find his father."

Dot snorted. "Well, he seems to be doing a better job of it than you are. And yes, Jamie texted me to say that he was getting close to finding out where the drugs were being held. What is crystal clear is that the drugs are going to be handed over soon. We don't have long. But what it does mean is that Jamie, for now, appears to be safe."

"You didn't forward me that text, Elkins." Clayton was staring directly at Elkins.

"There's a lot of chatter happening at the moment, some good, some bad. It takes time to try to figure it out. It would help if Inspector LaSalle wasn't hampering things along the way."

"That's bullshit, Tony, and you know it. You've been caught out, mate. How much is Fallon paying you? How long have you been in his pocket, Tony? Do you think swapping sides is worth it? Greed, nothing else. Pure greed, you total piece of scum."

"Whoa, hold your horses, Inspector." Truss walked as he spoke to Dot. He had moved and now stood by the side of McKenzie. "That's a damn bold statement you are making there, and a theory that should have been passed by either me or McKenzie first. So, what the hell are you talking about?"

"Yes, Inspector LaSalle, what the hell are you talking about? You seem to be the one with more to hide than anyone else in this room. And that's precisely why you're here. Nobody trusts you. You're married to a high target member of an OCG, you shagged the highest target leader of the OCG, and you play the holier than thou goody bloody two shoes running around with your menopausal head up your arse." As he spoke, Elkins stood up to face Dot eye to eye. "You, ma'am, seem to be the real problem here."

Dot was trying her damndest to stay calm as she started to speak. "Commander, Chief Superintendent, Chief Inspector. I have it on very good authority that DS Elkins is actually working directly with Patrick Fallon. And not in a professional capacity. He has gone rogue. Dirty. And very simply, that's why we are always one step behind. He is feeding Fallon and his associates progress reports and conning all of you into believing we are very close to apprehending members of the OCG. And let's face it, Elkins has been party to highly confidential information at pretty much every stage of this investigation."

"Commander, seriously, you can't believe a word that comes out of her mouth. I have no idea what LaSalle is talking about. There's not a single word of what she has said that even makes logical sense. She is the one who has to be hiding something. You yourself said that it was highly likely that she had to be involved." Elkins sat back down, shaking his head in disbelief.

There was a knock at the door. Truss walked over and opened it. "Commander Templeton. Glad you could join us. Come in and take a seat."

"Thanks, happy to stand. So, what's the progress report? Are we closer to shutting these people down yet?"

Truss began the update. "Just running through some differences of opinion at the moment. Quite pertinent to the investigation, though. Wouldn't you agree, Chief Inspector?"

"Yes, sir," Clayton agreed, nodding at Truss.

"Would you care to enlighten us all as to where we think we are currently? Should throw some spanners in the works. It's been a very busy day so far, very busy indeed. Please carry on, Chief Inspector.

"Thank you, sir. Yes, a very busy day indeed. A number of updates, if you will. Inspector LaSalle, let's start with you. Please don't worry about the implications of your accusations earlier. You are indeed correct in your assertions. We've thought for a while that Elkins must be involved with the OCG. Too much information was getting leaked at crucial points of the investigations."

"Oh seriously?" Elkins blurted out. "That's utter rubbish, ma'am. And you know it. You just need a scapegoat to justify to the other top brass why you can't close this one down. I've led you to more suspects in this case than anyone else. And we are closer than ever before in shutting this whole OCG down, once and for all." Elkins was holding his own pretty well. But not well enough.

Clayton remained nonplussed. "Anthony Elkins, I am arresting you in relation to the following offences. That between 1998 and now, you did commit the following. Misconduct in public office, money laundering, tampering with evidence and accessory to murder. And that's just for now. Given the audience in the room, I must ensure I get that procedure correct. Anything you would like to say, Elkins?"

"Accessory to murder. How in the hell did you come up with that one? You haven't got a chance in hell of this standing up in court. And you know it. This is ridiculous." Elkins was in full denial mode.

"It may seem ridiculous to you, Elkins, but we just needed some confirmation, and we got that today. As well as monitoring Inspector LaSalle's comms, we've also been listening to yours. Given your demeanour throughout, we were quite honestly stunned that you didn't think that that would be the case. And your comms held far more interesting and useful information. We've now established that you communicated with Fallon when you left this morning for the rendezvous to find Andries. We've also established that you communicated with Sergeant Mepham at the same time. Let me know at any point if you have trouble remembering the conversations. I would be more than happy to show them to you. It would appear that part of that communication shows Fallon advising you to tell Mepham to obtain a new SIM. Fallon knew Mepham wanted out and had turned informant. You were party to that decision, we believe. Mepham didn't know that you were working for Fallon, did he? He thought he was going to be handed a get-out-of-jail card from you, but he panicked. Mepham was about to run, wasn't he, Elkins? How is this sounding so far?"

Elkins stared at the table, shaking his head. "I want a solicitor. That's the only comment you will get from me."

Clayton acknowledged the comment. "Yes, of course, procedure once again. That will be dealt with formally in a moment. Just so that we are clear here, the accessory to murder may change to conspiracy to murder. As I'm sure you are aware, it carries a longer sentence. We like that. You see, when you told Mepham to get a new SIM, Fallon knew that he would go to his main contact. You know the chap, don't you, Elkins? Mickey the Mobile. Sound familiar? It's where you get the electronic kit sorted, isn't it, Elkins? SIM cards, new phones, and access to private networks on the internet. Commander Templeton's team at Military Intelligence have given us some wonderful intel. What was Mickey's mantra? Ah, yes, of course. No questions asked, for the right price that is. Well, as of now, there'll be plenty of questions being asked, Elkins. So, let me remind you of one particular instruction to Mepham, shall I? Get the new SIM sorted. And do it ASAP. That's what you told him, wasn't it, Elkins? Well, just for your information, while Mepham was in the phone shop, following your instructions, he unfortunately succumbed to two bullets through his head, courtesy of your friend and accomplice Mickey the Mobile. Although we had undercover officers stationed near the premises and saw Mepham enter, we certainly didn't expect that outcome, otherwise we would have intervened. That said, Mepham wasn't the nicest of people around and, quite frankly, was giving honest, hard-working police officers a bad rep. So, I think, given the evidence, it's fair to say that we'll crack on with a conspiracy to murder charge, just so you know. The final piece of the puzzle fell into place when you intercepted Jamie's message to Dot earlier. Your sweaty fingers must have been on fire on your keyboard at this point. We have yet to clarify whether anything in Jamie's text is currently true or not. We are working on that one right now. Problem is, because you have told Fallon, he'll now be hell-bent on either using Jamie to get what he wants from his father, or he might just decide to try to kill him anyway. So, for now, it's just the one conspiracy to murder charge. I hope that it doesn't become two or even three. Commander Truss, would you let those two wonderful officers I can see outside the room in so that they can take care of Elkins for us? Ridiculously, it would appear that not one of us in the room is in possession of a set of handcuffs."

The Chief Inspector walked around the table and pulled Elkins up from his seat. As he stood up, he leaned towards the middle of the table and, before anyone could stop him, picked up a jug of water and emptied the contents onto the laptop he was using. He then began using the jug as a hammer, beating it down on top of the computer. The machine made a fizzing sound and emitted a loud pop. Elkins knew it might not stop the information on the laptop from being found, but it might just make it a bit harder and take a bit longer. Maybe long enough for Fallon to close the deal. Clayton slapped Elkins hard across his cheek and pulled him back from the laptop. The shock of the slap stopped Elkins in his tracks. Commander Truss was now standing next to Clayton and pulled Ekins so hard that he was propelled out of his chair. Truss held Elkins in a vicelike grip. Elkins glared at Clayton.

"Apologies, Clayton, but I forgot to back up the computer. By the time you get into whatever is left of it, London will be swimming in drugs. And just so you know. You lot were far too easy to deceive. I might spend a few years in prison, but by the time the press gets to the bottom of this, your career, along with the other idiots in this room, will be destroyed. Now, where's my solicitor?"

McKenzie, by now, alongside Clayton and Truss, pulled up Elkins by the scruff of his neck and dragged him backwards towards the door. Holding Elkins by one hand and opening the door with the other, he threw Elkins out of the conference room and directly in front of the two police officers who were waiting. "Do me a favour, gentlemen. Rumour has it, he has a USB stick hidden somewhere on or in his person. Make sure you give him a full body and cavity search, won't you? It will get him used to his new surroundings."

They picked Elkins up and placed a pair of handcuffs on him.

Elkins wanted the last word. "Handcuffs? Really? It's you lot that should be slapped in cuffs. Barefaced and deliberate incompetence, the whole lot of you. And make sure you keep an eye on LaSalle. Screwing your top two suspects, and you think she is harmless. Who else are you screwing, La Salle? Who else?"

Truss walked in front of Elkins. "Well, given the number of people you have angered out there amongst both the criminal and law enforcement fraternities, we'll obviously ensure they all know just how helpful you have been throughout this investigation. And then you, too, can look forward to a damn good screwing, followed by quite a bit of reflection in solitary, Mr Elkins. It will be for your own protection, of course. Now, before you go, hand me the mobile phone from your pocket. Preferably without having another tantrum, there's a good chap. Oh, and while you are at it, you can also hand over the pager in your other jacket pocket as well. Thought we didn't know about that one, didn't you?"

Elkins took out the mobile phone and pager. As he did so, they were snatched quickly by one of the recently arrived officers.

"Now, gentlemen, please do me a favour and take this piece of scum away. Thank you."

They all watched as Elkins was led away down the corridor towards the lifts.

Mckenzie shut the door and turned around to face the others. "Everyone ok? Anybody need a break after that? No? Good. And Dot, don't worry, we've known about Elkins for a little while now. We just needed the proof of exactly who he was dealing with. We now know it's Fallon. We couldn't let Elkins carry on for any longer. He had to be close to suspecting that we knew about him, and we need to protect our own out there. He was starting to ask too many awkward questions. But there we go. So, if we are all happy to proceed, I'll hand over to Clayton again for a full update. Clayton?"

"Sir, indeed, thank you."

"No, no, no. Hang on for one bloody moment, will you?" Dot hadn't sat back down again yet. She looked shell-shocked as she spoke. "I, me, I need a break. I need to think. I need to understand what the hell has happened since eight o'clock this morning, and if nothing else, I need another pee. You can't just sweep this stuff under the proverbial bloody carpet. I haven't been party to anything that you've been doing. Nothing. All you have done is use me for your own benefit to uncover the mess you should have figured out long before now. Oh, and let's throw in a good measure of accusational bullshit along the way as well, shall we?" She was pacing the room between the table and the door as she spoke.

McKenzie walked towards her and placed his hands upon her shoulders so that she was forced to stop moving and face him directly. Leaving his hands in place, he started talking in a quiet, almost acquiescing tone. "Dot, you are well aware that, for operational reasons, certain things can't be spoken about. And for those exact reasons, we sometimes need to do things that force someone's hand. We needed to do that with Elkins. Now that's done, what we need to do right now is halt the transaction between Fallon and the

Albanians. So, before we let you out to powder your nose, we need to explain exactly where we are right now with this, and if you think you know anything different to our own thought process, now would be a good time to tell us. Please, just listen to what Chief Inspector Clayton is about to say. I need to make a call to the drug squad and get them to call off the stampede that your stepson has no doubt created for them. We can't have anyone else taking the glory on this one, now, can we?"

McKenzie slowly, but gently, guided Dot onto the nearest seat, then went over to the window and took out his phone to make the call to ruin someone's day within the Drug squad. There was still some water on the seat from Elkins' outburst earlier, but Dot sat down all the same. Commander Templeton had pulled several large sheets of paper from a flipchart frame and wrapped the laptop in them. She carefully moved the laptop to the far end of the table, then continued using the paper, attempting to wipe the water off the table. Given that the flipchart paper had a shiny surface, Templeton was merely moving the water around. There was something almost comical about watching a commander play cleaner. And not a very good cleaner at that.

McKenzie nodded at Clayton. "I need to get tech to come and pick up the laptop. Chief Inspector, carry on."

"Sir." Clayton stood, flattening down the ruffles in her pencil skirt as she did so and pulled a chair next to where Dot sat. She then sat down beside her. It was clear that Dot was about to be the main focus of what was about to be said.

"But first I need to use the toilet."

CHAPTER 48.

Jamie. Careful out there, son.
Jamie had left Laney doing the things she loved to do and, quite frankly, was damn good at doing. And that was uncovering stuff. If people or companies tried to hide things, she could generally find out where and what was being hidden.

He was now on his way to East London to have another look at the house where Elkins' car was. The same address that Fallon had told him to go to. This, according to Fallon, was where he needed to be and where his dad was going to be dropped off. And until, and if Laney could work her magic, at the moment, it was the only lead he had on Fallon and his dad. He was also hoping that the text he sent to Dot would at least grip someone's curiosity out there. It was late afternoon now, and his intention was to stake out the house from a distance and take another look when it was dark. His phone rang. It was the same number as the text from Fallon. He pulled over quickly into a side street, away from the congestion of the main roads.

"Jamie speaking."

"Ah, the prodigal son. Patrick Fallon here, Jamie."

"My father better be alive, Fallon."

"Oh, he's alive, Jamie. Well, for now at least. You might want to keep your phone on, though, he is being a tad uncooperative at the moment, and I need him to concentrate on me."

"I'm not surprised, Fallon. By all accounts, you are a prize bastard. I think I would be the same."

Fallon chuckled. "Well, it's good to hear that my reputation precedes me. Now, listen to me, young man, and listen hard. Your father doesn't deserve to suffer a bullet in the back of his head. I think thirty-odd years inside should be punishment enough for him. Just to be clear, though, for me, a bullet would be a lot cleaner. So, you're going to do something to make sure he doesn't get that bullet. Do you understand? He needs to do what I tell him, and if he doesn't do it, then I will kill him. Make no mistake. However, he does what I ask, then he gets released. Now. You have the address where he'll be dropped off, and it's up to you to decide what you want to do with him. I'll be long gone by the time you figure that one out. Sound fair, Jamie? I think it does."

"Sounds to me like my father has got you by the balls, Fallon. And in all honesty, I don't even know if he'll listen to a word I say anyway. If you need him that much, then you are hardly going to put a bullet in the back of his head, now, are you?"

"Ok. So let me put this a different way to see if he'll listen to you, shall we?"

Jamie could hear Fallon's tone changing. He sounded angry. Jamie needed to be careful not to push him too far.

Fallon continued. "Maybe, just maybe, I can help you decide that what I'm saying is the best thing, which will help your father, and in turn, help me. Win, win, win." Fallon had put the phone down as he spoke to someone in the background. Jamie had to assume Fallon was speaking to his father.

"You're bluffing, Fallon. You need him. Fallon!" Jamie was shouting into the phone.

Fallon was ignoring Jamie. All Jamie could do was listen. "Your son wants me to punch you, Jack. How about that, eh? He doesn't care about you. So, don't blame me for this, eh, Jack. It's all down to your boy." Jamie heard what sounded like a thump followed by a groan.

There was a muffled sound as the phone was picked up again. "Fair to say he didn't like that, Jamie. Now. I can keep hitting him. To be honest, I just need him to speak when the time is right so I can continue to hurt him. Up to you, son."

"You are nothing more than a sick animal, Fallon. You need him alive for whatever reason." Jamie was struggling to keep calm.

"It's not a bluff, Jamie. Your father is ok, for now. So, I suggest you do what I asked you to do earlier and LISTEN TO ME! Go to the address I gave you earlier. Go there and wait. Do nothing. If your father does what he is told, he'll be there. Do I make myself clear?"

"Crystal clear. And when that's done, Fallon, I am going to find you, and I am going to bring you in."

"Of course you are, son, of course you are."

The call went dead. Jamie didn't move. He was thinking the conversation through, and the sound of the punch inflicted on his dad. A text came through, breaking his thoughts. It was the address he was already heading to in Whitechapel. *This is not worth dying for Jamie. But if you don't do as I have asked, you will both be dead.*

Jamie knew that he was keeping him alive for a reason. Not just to keep Jamie from trying to find him. Something else. Something transactional. He knew his father wasn't the fighting type. It had to be the money, and Fallon was worried enough about it that he fell for the text bait that Jamie had laid and now needed Jamie to help persuade his dad to give whatever information was needed. It also confirmed that Elkins and Fallon were working together. His phone beeped yet again.

Ooh just spoken to Russ. He might have to take me out to dinner instead of you. He is coming over to help me do some digging. He sounds better at it than you. FA Holdings is linked to around fifteen other holding companies. But because I'm brilliant, I have found one in London. Hightower Holdings. It owns warehouses Jamie. All of them in South London. Give me an hour to find out where they all are. Laney xx

He replied. *Thanks Laney. He's not your type. He's a meathead. Just spoken to Fallon. He took the bait on the text. He has dad but I don't know how long we've got. Hurry up. J xx*

Jamie sent one more text. *Dot, phone is on. Confirmed Fallon has dad. Call me. J xx*

He put the car into gear and pulled away. He was less than half an hour away from the house in East London. Time enough to get there and have a look around, and hopefully by then, Laney and Russ would come through on the warehouse locations. Jamie wasn't being fooled. He knew his dad wasn't going to be in Whitechapel. But hopefully, the person who wanted him dead would be.

CHAPTER 49.

A couple of hours earlier. Another chicken comes home.
Terry Osman was panicking. Something about this whole situation he was in didn't feel right. No, more than that. Nothing felt right. Mepham wasn't picking up his phone. There was no way Jack would go AWOL when Fallon needed him to facilitate the drug deal with the Albanians. And besides, Jack would have told him if he was getting out. The one thing that Terry and Jack had in common was the increasing loathing that they both felt for Fallon. It just wasn't adding up.

He had decided to go for a walk. To clear his head. To try to think straight. He had walked to the end of his street and headed into what used to be his favourite café, but which had recently been turned into an upmarket arty farty bakery-cum-coffee shop. To be fair, the coffee was ok, if you could understand the different names, and the tea was just about acceptable, but the price was daylight robbery. Still, it was somewhere he could think, and more importantly, it was a place that had a view right down the street that he lived on. He had been a police officer for too long not to recognise when the fan was about to hit by the clichéd brown stuff. Luckily, his wife wasn't due back until later that evening. She was heading off to bingo with her friends after work. At least that made Terry's stomach a little less distressed, and something that he didn't have to deal with straight away. He was struggling to figure out exactly what it was he was trying to figure out.

As he opened up one of the little brown sachets of sugar to empty into his coffee, his eye caught the flash of an orange indicator on a white transit van turning into his street. He watched as it slowed to a crawl, the brake lights illuminating red each time it slowed. Like the occupant or occupants were looking for a specific house. The van came to a stop fifteen feet up the road from the front entrance to Terry's house. It waited for no more than ten seconds and then moved away down the road at a normal speed. Routinely, Terry memorised the licence plate from the vehicle. He didn't recognise it.

Terry looked down and stirred his coffee. He hadn't taken a sip of it since he bought it nearly twenty minutes ago. He scooped what was left of the white creamy milk onto a teaspoon and licked it off. No wonder this place made a profit. They charged twice the regular amount for only half the coffee. He looked up and stared down his street again. The white van had turned left at the bottom end. The driver *was* looking for something. If he was a delivery driver, he would have simply abandoned the vehicle on the road to find the house he had to deliver to and thrown whatever it was he was delivering at the door. It's what they did. This particular van was looking for something. Or someone

Terry decided to spend some more of his hard-earned money on yet another overpriced coffee. He walked up to the counter, leaving his coat draped over the chair behind him. "Any chance of a normal coffee, please, pal? None of that frothy stuff on top."

The young man behind the counter looked up and behind him towards a large board that had just about every conceivable type of coffee imaginable written on it. "Latte, espresso, americano? We don't do filter. Lowers the tone. Take your pick." His nonchalance made Terry want to wipe the smug look from his face.

"Black coffee with some milk on the side."

"An Americano, in other words. Hot or cold with that?"

"Is that a trick question or something? I would like my Americano hot if that isn't too much trouble for you."

A young female couple had entered the café and now stood behind Terry. The young man was far more interested in them than he was in Terry. "Hot or cold. As in for your milk." The young man shook his head and raised his eyes while looking at the two women.

Terry was looking out of the window of the café. The van had returned and was doing exactly the same thing it had done a couple of minutes ago. It had been around the block and turned onto the road where Terry's house was. Again. Terry missed the opportunity to see who was in the van, as it had already turned when he looked. The van slowed parallel to a parking space six houses down the street. Terry's house was eight houses down the street.

"Er, excuse me. Other customers are waiting. Do you want the Americano or not?"

Terry said nothing. He watched as the van reversed and then parked in a space on the same side of the road as his own house. The driver's door opened, and an absolute athlete of a man got out. Tall, sleek, enormous shoulders, young looking and clearly fit. He stopped and looked up and down the street before walking around the van to the passenger side. He opened the door, reached in and pulled, rather than helped, a woman out of the seat. He held the woman by the arm as he pushed the van door shut, then walked around the front of the van. Terry momentarily lost sight of the pair before they emerged again, stepping onto the pavement. His stomach dropped. The man was escorting Terry's wife, holding tightly onto one of her arms, whilst guiding her towards the house. Terry continued to watch as the man led his wife up the path to the front door. She then used her key to open the front door, and they both disappeared inside the house.

"Mate, seriously. It's not that hard, surely? Americano with hot or cold milk?" Terry took a five-pound note out of his pocket and placed it in a jar on the counter labelled tips. "Use that to buy yourself some manners." He walked back to his table, retrieved his coat and headed back towards the door.

He pulled open the door and walked out onto the pavement. As he did so, his phone rang. He pulled it out from his coat pocket and looked at the screen. It was his wife calling. "You alright, love?"

"Mr Osman. My name is Albi. We haven't actually met yet, but we do have a mutual connection. Mr Fallon. He sends his regards. Now, just so that you understand the seriousness of this situation, I have someone else here who also sends their regards. Are you listening to me, Mr Osman?"

"I've heard about you. What do you want?" Terry was walking slowly towards his house.

"A man of few words. I have your wife. I suspected you wouldn't take me seriously if I didn't have something to bargain with, but let's be clear. I don't want your wife, I want you. Straight swap. Nice and simple."

"Nothing is ever simple with Fallon. Where are you?"

"Oh, please. Don't insult my intelligence, Mr Osman. You know full well where I am. Enjoy your coffee, did you? Now, walk to the house. I'll open the door. You will walk in, and I'll let your wife go. No fuss. Do anything different to what I've asked, and your wife will get hurt. Now we don't want that, and we don't need that, do we, Mr Osman? Best get walking if I were you. Mr Fallon is an impatient man."

The call ended. Terry crossed the road and walked fast down the street towards his house. He had no other plan than to get his wife to safety. Life is all about the choices you make. Terry had made some bad ones. Very bad ones. The only bad choice his wife had made was to marry him. Whatever the outcome, she didn't deserve this. She was just happy, looking forward to a retirement knowing that when the phone rang or there was a knock on the door, it wouldn't be some police family liaison officer telling her that her husband was injured, or worse, dead. She had had enough years of waiting for that to happen.

Terry took a deep breath in and turned onto the pathway leading to his front door. He knocked hard on the dark wood and took two full paces back. The door was opened partially. Terry waited for it to fully open. It didn't. He stepped the couple of paces forward and pushed the door open. He could see right through to the kitchen at the end of the entrance hallway. His wife was sitting on one of the kitchen chairs. She was bent over double with her head positioned almost as low as her knees.

He heard Albi speak, "Come in slowly, hands by your side, close the door and walk towards your wife."

Terry did as he was told. As he walked into the kitchen, his wife's captor came into view, holding a suppressed handgun pointed directly at the back of her head. "Good to finally meet you, Mr Osman. Mr Fallon isn't too pleased with you, by all accounts. Just so that your wife would understand why I'm here, I have told her just how corrupt you are, Mr Osman, and how many people you have killed in your alternative line of duty. Isn't that right, Mrs Osman? Been a naughty boy, hasn't he?"

"What do you want? If it's me, then just get it done, but get my wife out of here first. None of this is her fault. She doesn't deserve to be involved in any of this."

At this point, Terry's wife, Angie, tried to move her head up to look at him. Albi didn't hesitate. He slapped the side of her face. Half with his hand, half with the gun. She cried out in pain. Albi raised the gun again to strike her a second time. As he did so, Terry bolted as quickly as he could, lowering his body and ramming himself into his wife. The momentum of Terry, his wife and the chair slammed into Albi, knocking him off balance, and he fell backwards, hitting his head on the edge of the ceramic butler's sink as he did so. He slumped to the floor, bright red blood flowing from the back of his head.

Terry stood up quickly and picked up the gun. He placed it in the waistband of his trousers. He kicked Albi as hard as he could in the ribs. That was for his wife.

He lifted Angie up from the floor, pulled up the overturned chair, and sat her down on it.

"Is it true, Terry? What he said. About you and the drugs and killing people. Is it true? Tell me. If it isn't, then why the hell is this thug in my house? Why, Terry? What have you done?"

"Listen, Angie, I'll explain everything later. You need to go. Now. Go and stay with Emmie. Just until this is sorted out. There are more people like him out there, and if he found you, they can find you as well. You need to go somewhere they won't know about. That's why you need to go to Emmie's." Terry went to one of the kitchen drawers and took out a pad of paper and a pen. He wrote down a name, then the words Warehouse south of Battersea Power Station. Fallon's Drugs.

"Terry, look at me for God's sake. Just like that, Terry? Run away from my own house. Because of what? You? Is it true? What he said? Just bloody tell me, or, so help me God, I'll kill you myself."

"I don't know what he told you, Angie, but, yes, some of it sounds right. I'm sorry. Now you have to listen to me. You need to go. I'll come and get you after this is sorted, and we can figure stuff out then."

"Oh, Terry, you daft bastard. What have you got yourself mixed up with, eh?"

"No time to explain. Just get out of here, Angie. I'll talk to you later. Take this." Terry handed Angie the note. "Phone the nick. Tell them to get hold of Jamie Andries. Anyway they can. Life or death. And then read them the message. Tell them it's all that I know. Make sure he gets it. It's important love. Now. Will you just get the hell out of the house? He walked her to the door, took a long raincoat from a coat hook, handed it to her, opened the door and pushed her out. Before she had time to react, he had already shut the door. She would be safe at Emmie's; she was a good friend from work who was widowed and whose family lived up north. She would be safe, and that's all that mattered to Terry.

He turned around and walked back into the kitchen. Kneeling down, he felt for a pulse on Albi's neck. Still alive. Head wounds tend to bleed heavily to start with and then slow up as long as they aren't gaping. He lifted Albi's head and looked at the wound. It wasn't gaping, and the blood was starting to congeal. He pulled him around into the middle of the kitchen and threw him back down into a prone position on the floor. He then took a jug from one of the cupboards and filled it with cold water. He also flicked the kettle on. If cold water didn't work, then hot water probably would. Albi's eyes were closed, and the blood had slowed. Terry stood over him and poured the cold water from the jug into his nose and mouth. After a few seconds, Albi coughed and spluttered whilst choking on the water. As he tried to sit up, Terry placed his foot in the middle of his chest and pointed the gun straight at him.

"Stay exactly where you are, or my foot will be on your face, not your chest." Terry then aimed another strong kick into Albi's ribs. Albi grunted under his breath. "That's for hitting my wife. You were asleep when I kicked you last time. I just wanted to make sure you felt this one. So, what were you going to do to me? Kill me or take me somewhere to kill me? It's pretty obvious that Fallon is bailing. I'd be careful if I were you, son. I've worked with him for twenty odd years and he's now ditching me. You. Well, you've worked with him for a lot less time. What makes you think he's going to leave you alone?

Albi grinned.

"Glad you find this funny," said Terry.

"It's funny that you can't see your life is over anyway." Replied Albi. "You are done. Fallon's done with you, the Police are done with you, and given the conversation I have just had, even your missus is done with you. Finished. All that effort to end up with nothing."

Albi shuffled on the floor.

"Don't you dare move, you piece of shit. What have you done to Jack? Where is he? I know Fallon's done something with him."

Terry was about to kick Albi again. "No need for more police brutality. My ribs hurt, and I'm trying to get a bit more comfortable. What makes you think I know where he is? I'm just an order taker. Keep my nose clean, do as I'm told and get paid. That's me. Should have taken a leaf out of my book. You might have had a life left. Instead, you've ended with nothing. So, who's the piece of shit now, eh? Doesn't matter if you kill me, you know that. Fallon's going to get you one way or the other. And then he's going to go for your missus. You know that as well, don't you? He won't leave any stone unturned. We both know that. So, I guess you need to think about what you're going to do next. You can take me out, but Fallon will get you and your missus. Or I can take you out, and your missus gets to live to a ripe old age. Not the best choice, I'll grant you, but that's the way I see it. And Jack? Up to Fallon. Not a clue what's happening with him, but I think we both know, he's not coming to help you anytime soon. So? What's it to be?"

The kettle flicked off, and Terry momentarily looked over at it.

In a split second, Albi took hold of a knife he had secreted in his right trouser leg and plunged the three-inch blade into Terry's thigh. Taken by surprise, Terry screamed. As he did so, Albi frantically continued to stab into the thigh and leg as he pulled Terry to the floor. Terry reached for the kettle, pulling the cord with him as he fell heavily onto Albi. The boiling water splashed onto Terry's thigh as well as the side of Albi's face. They both screamed out in unison. As he fell, Terry went to pull the trigger of the gun he still held onto. Even though Albi's scalded flesh was burning, he was one step ahead. He had dropped the knife onto the floor and, with both hands, grabbed hold of the gun, twisted it into Terry's body and pulled the trigger. Again, and again and again.

"That's what you get for not checking for weapons. Albi stood up, walked to the sink and cupped cold water onto the side of his face. The pain was excruciating. He looked down at Terry. No question he was dead. Albi left the kitchen and headed towards the front door. But not before he had kicked Terry as hard as he could in the ribs.

That was for earlier.

CHAPTER 50.

On the way to Whitechapel. A beacon of light. Dusk.

Albi was not in a good mood. The boiling water had penetrated his nostrils and scalded his cheeks. Luckily, he had closed his eyes just in time before the water landed on him. The pain was distracting him as he drove back to the house in Whitechapel, and he couldn't bring himself to look in the rearview mirror. He would wait until later. He had to deal with the bitch from hell first, before getting back over to Battersea. Pain or not, he wasn't missing his payday for anything or anyone.

He picked up his mobile phone and called Fallon.

He answered curtly. "I trust you have him on board and on the way to the flat?"

Albi knew from his voice that Fallon was stressed. "Bastard took me by surprise. I had no choice. I had to take him out, boss. Heading back to the flat now. You still want me to sort out the posh bitch?"

"Hmm. Getting sloppy, eh, Albi? It is what it is. And, Albi, haven't I taught you any manners? Vanessa is a lovely lady. You just need to treat her with a little respect, that's all. Do that, and she'll be putty in your hands. But I'm afraid to say, yes, take care of her. You know what to do. Soon as that's done, head over and meet me at the warehouse. And make sure you're armed. Trust always seems to be an issue with drug dealers. Oh, and one last thing. Jack's son, Jamie, will be waiting at the flats when you get there. Take him upstairs and make him a nice cup of tea, will you? Then leave him there with Vanessa. They can keep each other company. Call me when you're done and on your way."

"Got it, boss." Albi cut the call. Instinctively, he felt for the handgun in the door compartment of the van. He had been thinking long and hard about the direction he wanted to take when this was over. He had grown up in London. He knew it like the back of his hand. It was his manor, his home. But above everything else, he knew how to distribute drugs. Trouble was, Albi was mentally conflicted, and time was nearly up. He had to make a decision. Stick it out where he was with what he knew and build an empire. Or take the money and run to Dubai. One was considerably safer than the other. Huge risk, huge reward versus smaller risk and decent reward.

He was struggling to think straight. His scalded face was distracting him. There were painkillers back at the flat, so he would wait until he got there. If he stopped to buy some, chances are someone would probably faint if they saw his face. And he didn't need to be the centre of any attention. Not now. He was zigzagging through the backstreets to keep as low a profile as he could. Nearly there.

CHAPTER 51.

The house at Whitechapel. A bigger beacon of light. Much bigger.

Jamie had driven slowly, watching carefully, and parked his car a hundred feet up from the building in Whitechapel. His dad was still needed by Fallon to do something. Therefore, as Jamie thought previously, he wouldn't be here. Jamie doubted that Fallon would be true to his word and drop Jack there at all. It was a ploy to get Jack to do what Fallon wanted him to do, as well as keeping Jamie away. He needed to keep his wits about him. This had all the hallmarks of walking into a trap.

Elkins' covered car was still parked at the rear of the property. There were no other cars parked there, but there was a light on inside the building. Not a standard hall light on a timer, rather, a light on in the top-floor flat. Most probably the lounge, given the window's large size. The wooden window blinds on the inside had been pulled tightly closed, and from the time he had been there, he had seen no movement.

Leaving his car parked on the road, Jamie had made the decision that now was the time to try to get into the property and have a look around. Coincidence was out of the window, given that the property was owned by FA Holdings and apparently lived in by someone who worked for his dad. Someone who was now dead. And the fact that Elkins' car was parked there, Jamie now reckoned, gave him the right to enter as he was potentially searching for evidence of criminality. Weak excuse if he was pushed about it, he knew that, but he needed to find something that helped lead him to his dad. And then to Fallon. Because Jamie was sure his dad wasn't coming.

He walked along the opposite pavement to the building he was now staring at. Everything appeared quiet. A couple walking towards him were holding hands and chatting quietly. Jamie nodded politely as they passed, and he crossed the street, walking confidently onto the driveway of the building as though he had every right to be there. He was checking each part of the building, looking for any signs of security. There were three individual white boxes with the name of a security company printed on them. He assumed these were unique to each property and not to the building itself. They could be a problem. He might have to find out for himself. He walked to the rear of the building and instinctively placed his hand on the cover of the car belonging to Elkins. It was stone cold. He walked back towards the main door, which was situated to the side and noticed that there was a light above it. It looked like a security sensor light, so he stayed far enough away in case he was picked up by it. Besides, he could see the door. It looked like a plain Yale lock, but Jamie was no locksmith. It was looking like a window would have to come out. Which one, though, especially as he wasn't sure if the alarms in the flats were all set. And given the top-floor flat had a light on, he needed to tread carefully. He started to head towards the back of the building to check the windows when a van came into view, travelling from the opposite direction and heading back up towards the main road. The offside indicators were flashing. The houses on either side of the flats didn't have any driveways, and there were no available parking spaces on this side of the road. The van was turning into the building he was now standing beside. And Jamie had to move out of sight. Quickly.

He walked quickly from the side of the building around to the back. There were low flower beds in front of wooden fence panels edging along the perimeter of the car park, which afforded no cover for him. The only choice he had was to reach Elkins' car and use it for protection. When he turned the corner of the building, he ran as fast as he could before the occupant or occupants of the van had a chance to spot him. He saw the beam of yellowish light from the headlamps moving closer and threw himself down behind the car just as the van pulled around the corner. Jamie was lying in a prone position by one of the rear tyres and watched as the van turned into a parking space two away from where he lay.

Jamie couldn't yet see who or how many occupants were in the van. The engine was turned off, and the lights extinguished. He could hear the muffled voice of a man having a conversation. He couldn't hear any replies, so he knew that the driver was on his phone. The van door opened. It now sounded like the occupant was having a conversation with himself, not on the phone.

"Just don't get why I had to come back and do it. I could have sorted this out earlier. The boss is losing the plot. And where the fuck is the son? Nowhere. I'm done with this. Time for the party to begin."

As he jumped out of the vehicle, the man grunted, as though in pain. Jamie held his breath. He watched as the man in a dark hoodie walked to the back of the van. He opened the door and retrieved what looked like a water bottle and a large black plastic toolbox. The man, either in pain or just angry about something, was cursing under his breath the whole time. He shut the van door and walked towards the main door to the building, looking all around him as he walked. As he disappeared out of view, the security light illuminated, letting Jamie know that the man was now close to the front door. Jamie was hesitant. If he tried to follow, the noise from the gravel might just give him away. He heard the rattling of keys and seconds later, the dull thud of a door closing.

Jamie pulled himself from behind the car and squatted so that his head was just below the vehicle's roof. He ran across to the rear of the van and gently tried the door handle.

It was locked. He moved to the front of the van, obscuring the line of sight from the building and the road. He looked through the windscreen and could just make out decorating equipment in the rear of the van. A red light flashed on the top of the dashboard, indicating that the van was probably alarmed, so Jamie moved back to the cover of the car.

A light came on in what looked like a hallway on the top floor of the building, followed shortly by another in the flat where one light was already on. Jamie still didn't know if the man was alone up there or if there was anyone else in the flat. Was his father up there? He didn't know, but he seriously doubted it. He felt his mobile phone vibrate in his pocket. He half-pulled it from his pocket so he could see the screen, trying to hide the glow that it created. It was the police station where he was currently working with CID ringing him. He left it. Some thirty seconds later, the phone vibrated again. This time, a voicemail. Jamie had been watching the top-floor flat the entire time. For the first time, he saw movement. Another light had been switched on. Not as bright as a main light, more likely a table lamp. There was a blind that was very slightly open in the smaller window he was watching, so he assumed the person was in a bedroom. The movement looked like it was the same man that Jamie had seen go into the building. Tall with a dark top on. Jamie was racking his brains as to his next move. Unlike every police movie out there, he was no master locksmith, so the only way to gain entry would be to break a window. That would create some noise, and what if there was an alarm inside? That would certainly alert the man in the top-floor flat. And Jamie also had to factor in that the man in the top-floor flat may have every reason to be there. He might actually live there and has just had a bad day at work, given his earlier grumbling. Jamie was clutching at straws. He didn't actually know what to do. Yet again, his phone vibrated. He took it from his pocket and glanced at the screen. *Listen to your voicemail.* He moved round to the rear of the car he was using as cover and squatted low down. He unlocked the phone and immediately pressed the voicemail icon. It was Russ. "Jamie, Laney has just taken a call from your nick. They have been trying to get hold of you. Apparently, they've taken an anonymous call from a woman who said something about drugs being at a warehouse near Battersea Power Station and that the message was for you and you alone. Hazard a guess here, mate, but if the drugs are there, then so is Fallon and hopefully so is your old man. I'm going to try to get hold of Dot to let her know. If the peeps at your nick think that you are involved in drugs, they will be all over you like a rash. Going to head over there myself in a bit, mate. Call me when you get this message."

Well, at least Jamie now had his answer. It would appear that he didn't need to be where he was. His instinct about his dad had been right all along. He needed to be on his way to Battersea. He looked up again at the flat but couldn't see any movement. He stood up from his squatting position and flinched as the muscles in his legs were pushed straight again, and started to walk back across the car park, keeping an eye on the window

A sensor light switched on behind the main entrance door. Someone was on their way out of the building. 'Shit,' he thought, and he froze. He couldn't go forward. He would be spotted by the person as they exited the front door. He had no choice. Jamie turned and ran as hard and fast as he could back to the car he had just come from. He didn't once look back. Reaching the car, he slid down below the level of the window and held his breath. All he could hear was his chest beating hard. Slowly, he lifted his head higher.

The same man he had seen earlier came into view. Jamie had missed him by seconds. The man was walking back towards his van, but stopped about twenty feet short. He turned, checked all around him and then looked up towards the top-floor flat. Turning back around again, he headed towards the van. As he got into the driver's seat, the interior light came on, illuminating the front of the van. Jamie could see what looked like red sunburn on the man's face. As he started the van, the light went out.

The man reversed round in a half loop, stopped and then drove slowly past the front of the building before bringing the van to a stop again. Jamie moved. The front of the van was out of view, so Jamie knew he couldn't be seen. He walked quickly to the back of the building, which he could use as cover. He moved his head slowly around the corner of the building as the whole of the van came into view. It had stopped just short of the main road. Jamie was about to move towards the main door to get a better view of the van to see which way it would head. The van remained stationary, though, so Jamie didn't move. For at least two minutes.

The man stepped out and headed to the rear of the van. He paused, stared straight at Jamie and took something from his pocket. Jamie turned to take cover once more. If the man was armed, Jamie didn't want to be the target. He stood and listened. He couldn't hear any movement on the gravel, so Jamie took a risk and slowly poked his head around the corner of the building. The hooded man hadn't moved. He had taken a pack of chewing gum from his pocket and was placing a piece into his mouth. Once again, the man looked at Jamie. This time, he smiled. Then there was a blinding white flash, followed by a muffled explosion. Jamie hit the floor and covered his head as glass, brick and plastic showered down on top of him. Luckily, it was only small stuff. The larger debris had missed him. After ten seconds or so, he stood up and brushed himself down. He looked across to where the hooded man had smiled at him. The man was gone. And so was the van.

CHAPTER 52.

Vanessa at 7c. Lunch, dinner & cooking on gas. A couple of hours earlier.

Patrick Fallon had seemingly lost the plot. Instead of paying people off when things went wrong, as he used to do, he had garnered a predilection for killing them instead. All the while that this was happening away from Vanessa's world, she could just about cope with it. The moment it happened on her own home turf, well, that's when things got really scary.

She had heard Fallon talk about Albi, but until today, she had never met him. Fallon had used words and phrases such as protégée, the son he never had, a real talent and the one that worried her most. Heir to Fallon's world. If Fallon ran a legitimate business, such as an accountancy practice, or a solicitor's or even a baker's, that would have been sweet, treasured, all the words one would associate with real pride. Not the heir to an empire whose sole purpose was to make as much money as possible, where killing people was part and parcel of most negotiations.

And this had never been Vanessa's plan when she met Fallon. That was for sure. When she saw Albi walk into Chelsea Garden, Vanessa knew that a choice had been made by Fallon about how he saw his future with her. And she was pretty certain that she wasn't included in it.

Vanessa could only hope the message she had left would at least ensure the police were called. But they didn't know where she was. And she was scared. Albi had made it clear to Vanessa that if she didn't do as she was told, he would have no hesitation in putting a bullet in her. She did not doubt that Albi would carry out his threat. No one messed with Patrick Fallon, and she knew that.

Albi had helped her into the passenger seat of his van and remained silent for the forty-five minutes, or so it took to get to the flat in Whitechapel, which was the supposed safe house that Fallon had told her about. She didn't understand why she was no longer in favour with him. She thought that she would be rewarded for her loyalty in passing people to Jack. It was easy enough to do, and this should have been her payday.

"Walk normally, or a bullet goes into your spine." That's what Albi had told her when they walked to the main door at the flats in Whitechapel. Hardly the words of someone who should have been an ally and was getting ready for a new life in the future.

They had gone up in the lift and entered the front door of the flat on the top floor. All the while, Albi held her arm tightly as he manoeuvred her to where he wanted. They walked into the hallway. Looking ahead, Vanessa could see that the flat was almost bare. She saw a single table and chair in the lounge area and nothing in the kitchen area beyond that. Albi stopped Vanessa and pushed open the first door on the left. He shoved her forward again, and they both entered a bedroom. There was a single, metal-framed bed with no mattress, as well as a small table with a drawer in it with a lamp sitting on top.

He pushed Vanessa towards the bed but told her to sit on the floor. She breathed a huge sigh of relief. She had thought that she was about to be raped. "Don't kid yourself. That's not my thing." Albi spoke as though he had anticipated Vanessa's thoughts. He walked over to the small table and opened the drawer. He took out a roll of black gaffer tape, pulled off a single ten-inch strip and placed it across her mouth. Albi went back to the table and this time took out a handful of cable ties. He pulled Vanessa up into a position where her back was straight up against the bed. He took her hands, pushed them behind her back and tied them together with a cable tie. He pulled the tie tight. Then he placed a cable tie around her neck and pulled it through the metal bars of the bed. He slipped the tie through the ratchet and pulled slowly. He was watching her as he did so. He pulled until her eyes told him it was tight enough. She wasn't going to choke, but she wasn't going to move either. And Vanessa didn't move. She could already feel the ties cutting into her hands and neck, but at least, for now, she was still alive.

Albi checked all the ties and then, seemingly satisfied, left the room. Vanessa didn't hear but rather felt him leave the flat. There was a small pull of air as the door shut. Her mind was in a complete mess. She couldn't think straight. If she was going to die, why not now? Get it over and done with. Or perhaps it was Fallon who was going to kill her instead. No doubt he would enjoy that. She assumed that whoever it was, they were keeping her alive for a reason. But for now, she needed to get herself calm and stay in a position that didn't choke her to death. Her hands were starting to buzz. That sensation you get when blood is restricted. Pins and needles.

She thought back to when she first met Fallon. She had just taken on Chelsea Garden Care Home. She also looked after other care homes for a wealthy board of directors, hell-bent on making as much money from the elderly as they could. Given that the facilities were good, the chefs were good, and the staff weren't too badly paid, the board had figured that they would have happy residents. And to be fair, if you make residents happy, they don't want to leave, and therefore, they pay more money to stay there anyway. An ever-increasing cycle of money. And the board of directors liked money. So did Vanessa, through her bonuses from resident retention. This, however, led to other issues. The board always wanted costs to be cut. That meant paying less for things like security and the stuff behind the scenes that people didn't see. And that's what brought Vanessa and Fallon together. Residents who knew no better, through no fault of their own or in other words, those with dementia, liked to go walkabout. One 86-year-old male escapee caused a huge upset to a local uber-wealthy family whose property shared the same access road to the care home. He was caught standing on the bonnet of a recently acquired Lamborghini Gallardo, masturbating while singing *Nessun Dorma*. And singing it brilliantly by all accounts. The CCTV was pure gold, and said gentleman became quite the celebrity with his fifteen minutes of fame. Clearly, his mental and physical cognitive functions were in full working order for that part of the day. The patriarch of the family had called his lawyer first and the police second. Hence, the visit by Fallon to the Chelsea Garden. This wasn't the first time it had happened. But it was the first time that they had met. The police, having been called in numerous times to repatriate geriatric absconders, called in the big gun to sort it out - aka Patrick Fallon.

On one of his visits to yet another senior Houdini performance, Jack Andries happened to be there advising a resident on their legal matters, something that he had a monopoly on, along with just about every other high-net-worth care homes in London, helped ably by Vanessa connecting his people to her people. It was here that Jack met Fallon and, somewhat surprisingly to Vanessa, given that Jack and Fallon were total chalk and cheese, the two hit it off immediately. Almost as if they already knew each other. Vanessa and Jack had initiated a habit of using empty care home rooms for sex. Or as Vanessa called it, lunch. And she had already made up her mind. She was going to start having Fallon for dinner.

Vanessa was grinding every bit of concentration her body had just to keep still. The cable ties were cutting and hurting. Her neck had started to chafe from the rubbing tie, her hands were now numb, and she was feeling lightheaded from the restricted amount of oxygen reaching her lungs. Her mind was foggy. How much longer would she have to wait? The answer came from the sound of a vehicle travelling on gravel. It sounded like the van earlier. It stopped, and so did the engine. She heard what sounded like a van door closing. Shortly after, she heard footsteps on the gravel.

Not long afterwards, the front door to the flat opened. Vanessa's nerves were starting to shred. The front door closed as she heard footsteps, presumably Albi, walking past the room she was in and heading into the all-in-one lounge, kitchen, and dining area. Everything went quiet. A minute or two later, she heard what sounded like tools being sorted through in a toolbox. Metal on metal. Soon after, she heard banging. Again, metal on metal. Like something was being repaired or deliberately broken. He was also grunting. She then heard the sound of what she thought was some form of tape being pulled and torn. She thought it was the same tape that had been used across her mouth. Next, she heard something being wound up. Like an old alarm clock. Or a timer you used in the kitchen for cooking, followed by a ticking noise. Vanessa's body was tense. She was trying to figure out what was happening on the other side of the door. She didn't want to move a muscle in case she missed something, and she wanted to be ready for when her door opened. Not that she could do much, but she was incensed at what was happening to her.

The footsteps walked slowly on the floor outside the door to the room she was in. The steps were measured. Was he looking for something, checking for something, she wasn't sure which. It then went quiet, she thought for around a couple of minutes until the footsteps started again. Heading towards the bedroom. Towards her. Vanessa braced. The footsteps stopped for a few seconds before starting again, but this time, they were heading away from the door. Away from her. Once again, she felt the now familiar pull of air as the front door opened and then a click as it closed again. She wasn't sure whether to be relieved or not. Obviously, it was not her time. Not yet, anyway. She relaxed slightly but didn't move. She was listening hard. She heard what sounded like a van starting. Then she heard a vehicle driving on the gravel. It sounded like it was leaving.

Then she smelt it. Her eyes grew large. A subtle sulphury smell, almost like rotten eggs. Infusing the air around her. Creeping into her nostrils and into her throat. She was struggling to breathe as it was. Now, the smell seemed to claw at her, causing her to swallow more. She went straight into panic mode. The cable tie cut deeper into her neck with each move she made to try to free herself and breathe easier. She looked at the window to see if it was even remotely possible to reach and, as if by some absolute miracle, smash the glass to get rid of the gas that was now permeating into the room and getting stronger. That was just stupid. She couldn't move, and she knew it. Wishful thinking. She forced herself to relax. Slower breathing. Less tension in her arms behind her and less tension in her legs. Her backside was numb. Although the room was carpeted, it was a thin material. Not much better than a hard floor. After a few minutes, the tension had subsided slightly, but she was more aware of the smell of gas. How long did she have before she was overwhelmed? Would she just fall asleep and never wake up? In the scheme of things, there were worse ways to die. Weren't there? But she didn't want to die. Not yet. Not now. But she couldn't see a way out. She was trying to count time in her head. How long had it been since Albi, if that's who it was, had left? Five minutes? Ten minutes? Shit. No idea. She heard a click. What was that? Was there still someone outside? Then an alarm sounded, followed by a bright orange flash under the door. She felt a thud hit her body, followed by the noise of a thunderclap. Her eardrums felt like they had exploded, and the air was being sucked out of her body through her nostrils. Then she felt the heat. This wasn't the way she wanted to die.

CHAPTER 53.

Jamie. Choices, choices.

A cacophony of car alarms started to pierce the air around Jamie. An explosion had burst out of the building. From where Jamie now stood, he could see that half of the top of the building was now ablaze. His phone rang. Withheld number.

"You won't have a very long career if you keep disobeying senior officers now, will you, Jamie? Anyway, sounds like Albi's done a good job by all accounts. Knows gas and electricity pretty well, as it happens. Now, you know me, son. I don't tend to piss about, so best you stop listening and get your arse into the building. I'm not in the habit of blitzing one of my own buildings unless I have a damn good reason. And the reason is about to become barbecued inside. So do your duty like a good little officer and go save someone. Never know, you might even get a commendation." The phone clicked off.

Fallon wanted Jamie dead; he knew that. Albi missed him earlier. Was this Fallon's way of trying to kill him again? Get him into the building, and God knows what else could happen. Was Fallon right, though? He wouldn't destroy a building without good reason. There must be an explanation for this. Or was he just stalling for time? Earlier, Fallon needed his dad alive. Even trying to use him as bait to get him to do whatever it was that needed to be done. Has Fallon changed his mind? Has his dad done what was needed to do and is now surplus to requirements? He must have something to hide in there.

There was a further, smaller explosion from the top floor, and the flames were now spreading into the flat below. Residents of the houses opposite the burning apartment block had come out into the street to get a closer look at the inferno. Some were on their phones, hopefully calling the emergency services.

He wouldn't be able to live with himself if there was someone in the building. He ran over towards the building. Moving quickly, he got to the main entrance door. The fire was most prominent on the road side of the building. It had yet to take hold fully at the rear, despite the explosion having blown out the windows. One large piece of debris had fallen straight onto Elkins' car, right where he had been hiding only moments ago. If Fallon had wanted him dead so badly, he would have got Albi to do it. Instead, Albi saw him and left him there. He was doing something in the building; He had another reason to be there. Something or someone. They had something or someone to hide. And Jamie needed to know what that was.

Chapter 54.

London – The glass room at the posh police station. For the last time. Hopefully.

Dot was in a state of total incredulity. Surrounding her were people who seemed alien to her. These same people were also trespassers in her world. They were squatting in her psyche, asking questions about her own life that she didn't have the answers to. She was listening but struggling to hear. She was acknowledging, but felt the acknowledgements were coming from someone other than her. Outside of the panoramic window that she stared, London's humanity had gone through an entire day of purpose, work, holiday or whatever else it was they had decided to do that day and were now wending their way back to wherever they needed to be. But right now, above all else, she was doing everything she could so as not to show the others in the room that she was, indeed, in a state of incredulity.

"So, to recap then." Chief Inspector Clayton had led the party for the last few hours. There had been interruption after interruption throughout, and with each interruption, the plot had either thinned or thickened. Some would call this situation fluid. Dot called it chaotic. The conference room had become more an operational command centre, and brows had become more furrowed as the minutes passed. Flip charts now covered one wall, while a large map of South London covered the other. The large screen on the wall showed direct links to armed units as well as to the head of the drug squad. All of them now awaited commands from the glass room at the posh police station.

"We have conflicting information as to exactly where the drugs are currently. What we do know is that they are somewhere in a small area south of Battersea Power Station. We have an undercover team searching all probable locations, but there are thirty to forty warehouses, and God knows how many lockups. We have to assume that this will take time unless we get lucky. I think we're all agreed that until we are sure of the exact site, we can't progress any overt teams to the area without fear of losing the drugs, Fallon and the Albanians. Unless, of course, we lock down the entire area, but that would be too messy and, dare I say it, an expensive situation. We don't want a gun battle on our hands. Correct?" Clayton looked around the room and received positive acknowledgements from all but Dot.

"So, if he hasn't already, Jack becomes collateral damage, correct?" Dot spoke whilst still staring out of the window.

"Dot, we've been through this before. We will do all we can to ensure that Jack is found, but right now, as you know, he appears to be a part of the OCG and a very significant part at that, working directly with Fallon. We aren't going to take any chances. We would rather someone go down than disappear. You know that." Clayton had made it clear. Jack was on the other side.

"Fine. Well, at least that saves me the cost of a solicitor for the divorce. What about Jamie? We need to stop him from walking into something he's not expecting. They don't teach this kind of scenario at training school."

"Jamie is a different problem for us right now. We need to stop him from creating a total cluster. He doesn't know what he has got himself into."

A mobile phone rang in the room. "Truss." The Commander turned his back on the rest of the occupants of the room as he took the call. "Ok, but what's that got to do with this operation?"

There was silence as Truss listened to the person on the other end.

"Ah, I see. The Chelsea Garden care home you say. And this happened when exactly?"

More silence.

"And you have only thought about contacting us now? Fine, it's ok."

Truss listened for another minute or so, with small grunts of acknowledgement throughout the call. "Thanks for the update, Superintendent. Keep me up to speed if you find her." Truss faced Dot.

"Dot. Chelsea Garden. That's where your mother is, right?"

Truss was faced with a stunned silence.

"Dot, did you hear me? Is that where your mother's living?"

"Yes. Yes, it is. But what the hell has this got to do with my mother?"

Truss exhaled through his nose. "Funny how everything seems to come back with your handprints all over them, Dot? Do you know Vanessa Foxx?"

Dot stood up from her seat and walked over to where Truss stood near the window.

"Is my mother ok? And yes, I do know Vanessa. She is in charge of the care home. A right snotty cow. Why? What the hell is happening here, Commander?"

"I'm not exactly sure what's happening, Dot, but earlier today, Vanessa Foxx was kidnapped from the care home. I assume your mother is ok. I'm actually more concerned that we now have a kidnapping on our hands. The CCTV at the care home wasn't working, but one of the staff arriving in their car captured Vanessa Foxx being forcibly taken to a vehicle and driven off. We believe the kidnapper to be Massimo Albricci, a well-known associate of Patrick Fallon. Care to give me any explanation for this that would likely make sense, Dot? Notwithstanding the fact that we have yet another individual who is now missing at the behest of Patrick Fallon."

Dot was silent. She walked back over to the table, returned to her seat and stared straight ahead. "Fallon was the investigating officer for the murder of one of the staff there a couple of nights ago. The main suspect was found hanged in a custody cell. The duty sergeant was one of Fallon's people, by all accounts. I don't know. Maybe she found something out. Maybe she saw something. It has to be a coincidence that my mother is there. It can't be anything else." Dot was rubbing her eyes as she finished talking.

Rubbing eyes was clearly infectious. Truss was doing the same. "I don't believe in coincidences. And certainly not where Fallon is concerned. This bastard seems to have a hold in a lot of places."

There was a knock at the door. McKenzie opened it. Facing him was a man wearing a suit with no tie. He had CID written all over him. He handed a note to McKenzie and waited while it was read.

"If this is correct, you'd better get someone over there sharpish. Let me know the minute you have some information."

The man in the suit nodded at McKenzie's request, turned and walked quickly back towards the lift.

McKenzie shut the door. "Apologies, Commander, carry on."

"Thanks, Mac." Commander Truss took his typical shoulders back, hands behind back stance. "I think we have enough information to make some better-informed decisions now, Dot. It's probably best that we get you home. Thanks for all your help, but we'll take things from here. Clayton. Would you be good enough and do the honours? Make sure she gets back safe and sound. Thank you. And thank you, Inspector LaSalle, for everything you have contributed. That will be all."

Dot was about to speak, but before she could say anything, Truss held up his hand towards her. "I said that will be all. Now, go home. We'll be in touch when we think it's safe enough for you to return to your normal duties. Until then, sit tight. And that's an order, Inspector."

Dot stood and turned toward the door. As she left, she turned back and faced Commander Truss. "I have absolutely nothing to do with this. Fallon raped me. I'll never forgive the man. And I'll struggle to forgive you for covering it up. For the good of the force. That's what you said. For crying out loud. Listen to yourselves. Maybe I should've finished Fallon off when he raped me, but I thought that I might get justice from my employer for what he did to me. Well, if you had done your bloody job and arrested and charged him when the rape happened, a lot more people would be alive today. And you had the bloody audacity to call me out for being involved in helping Fallon. Shame on you. Shame on all of you." She turned, opened the door and left the room, Clayton following directly behind.

McKenzie watched as Clayton hurriedly tried to catch up with Dot. "Have to say, she's got a point, Nick. We've put her through the wringer. But, for the purposes of here and now, I think that we've got everything we need from her. The note I had earlier was in connection with an explosion that's just happened over in Whitechapel. It appears that the building that's been blown up is connected to Fallon. He wouldn't do it without a reason. Unless, of course, someone with a grudge has blown it up. I'll send a team over to find out as much as they can."

"Don't worry, Mac. I have someone I can send over," said Truss "And in the meantime, we need to get this bloody location nailed down before we lose the drugs and Fallon. With a bit of luck, we can catch the Albanians red-handed as well. That would be the only result deemed sufficient.

CHAPTER 55.

Dot. Respect. Finally.

"Teresa. Is it okay that I call you that?" There was a definite air of sarcasm in the question. Dot and DCI Clayton watched the lift doors shut after they entered on the twentieth floor of Police HQ.

"Press minus 2 Dot. We need to head to the car park."

"Indeed, we do, Teresa. Don't mind if I call you that, do you? Kind of had enough of hierarchical bullshit for one day. Yes, of course, minus 2. That's where my car is."

"Your car will be staying where it is, Dot. I'm under strict instructions to drive you home and make sure you stay there. And I prefer Terri. But only my friends call me that."

"Ok, no problem. Teresa, it is then. And with all due respect, Teresa, there's no way that my car will remain here. And I'll not be going home first. I'll be going to see my mother at the care home, if it's all the same to you."

"Well, Dot, given I'm the senior officer here, with instructions from a commander, you will do as you are bloody well told."

"And if I don't, ma'am?" Dot sarcastically wiped back to Clayton.

"You will be suspended and reported for refusing a direct order from a senior officer. And, as you know, that will be gross misconduct."

The lift came to a slowing measured stop in the bowels of police HQ, and the doors opened straight out to the car park. Dot strode out of the lift and headed to where she had left her car. She was digging into her handbag to retrieve the keys when Clayton spoke. "Detective LaSalle, take one more step and I will -"

"And you will what, ma'am? What will you do? Because believe you me, there's nothing more you can do. I've been walked all over for the last God knows how many hours by you and your superiors, who, quite frankly, haven't given one single damn about the shit you lot have put me through. If I were a threat, you would have never let me go. Therefore, as I do not appear to be a threat, I'm going to get into my car and try to rescue whatever dignity I have left. And in the first instance, that means I'll go to see my mother to make sure that she hasn't been affected by the murder and kidnapping that has taken place right under her nose. A murder and kidnapping that would never have happened if you had arrested Fallon right after he raped me. Now. As I know that you can't possibly have a set of handcuffs hidden somewhere in that tightly strained skirt of yours, and senior officer or not, I'll be disobeying your order. And if you had one iota of compassion in your body, you would understand." Dot continued walking, waiting for a stinging retort. It came.

"LaSalle, I suggest you stop right there."

Dot slowed. She let out a heavy sigh. Without looking back, she said, "Or what, DCI Clayton? What exactly are you going to do?"

"I'm going to show you where your car is. You are walking in the wrong direction."

Dot stopped and slowly turned around to face the DCI. The woman lifted her arm and pointed to her right. "Thank you, ma'am." Dot's voice had quietened to almost a whisper.

"You are welcome, LaSalle. And next time, call me Terri. Good luck with your Mum." With that, Terri Clayton headed towards the lift and pressed the button.

Dot watched as the doors opened and Clayton stepped in. She turned and pressed the button inside. Just as the doors closed, Clayton nodded an acknowledgement to

Dot. Dot knew that Clayton would be reprimanded for not fulfilling her orders, but there was a newfound understanding between the two of them now. And to Dot. Well, that counted for something

CHAPTER 56.

Doing the right thing.

Jamie started to feel the heat from the fire on the top floor of the residential building that housed Flats 7a, 7b and 7c. He had shouted to some of the bystanders to call the fire brigade. They all acknowledged that this had been done and that they would be on scene in the next ten minutes or so.

Given it would take them four or five minutes to investigate the scene after they arrived and get their hoses going, that would probably be too long. Jamie ran round to the back of the building, where the fire was not nearly as ferocious, but it wasn't going to take long before it was. The explosion had taken out some of the windows in the top-floor flat as well as one in the flat below. Jamie's guess was that it was gas. And as it appeared to be deliberate, the man he had seen earlier had probably opened the gas main.

He ran to the double-glazed front door, took a deep breath in and threw himself at it with all his might. The impact forced his breath out, and he simply bounced off. Two men, either in their late teens or early twenties, ran over to Jamie to offer their help. Between the three of them kicking, pushing and shoving, the main door eventually gave way. Air was sucked in through the gap and into the building. Jamie didn't have much training on fires, but what he did know was that oxygen was the fire's best friend, and any additional fuel wasn't going to make this easier.

He thanked the two men and told them to stay back, but to inform the fire brigade that he was in there, as he suspected that someone was in the building. With that, he entered through the gap where the door had been, looked around, saw the stairs to his right and he headed into the stairwell. Other than a single dull emergency light emitting about half a candlepower, it was dark. There was no light switch, which probably meant that it was activated by movement. But it wasn't activating. He ran up to the next floor, where the smell of smoke was far more acrid.

He opened the door to the first floor and could see flames under the front door to the flat in front of him. It wouldn't be long before the fire from the rest of the ground floor put a barrier in the way of his exit. He ran back into the stairwell and headed up to the top floor. His heart was pounding, and he could now feel the heat from the fire on his face. He reached the door at the top and opened it a fraction. The metal handle was hot to the touch. Immediately, the smoke poured through the gap. It was even more acrid here and instantly stung his eyes. He wished he had some water to wash his eyes out. He couldn't see because of the smoke. The flames must be raging in the flat and had probably burnt directly through the floor into the area below. The fire doors, though, had so far seemed to have served their purpose.

He pulled the stairway door open enough to squeeze through. He could hear the crackling and creaking of the building, which was becoming louder. The sweat was dripping into his eyes from the heat, making it even harder to see. He needed to get in and out of the top floor as quickly as possible. Now on the landing outside the top-floor flat, he tried to open the door. It was locked. He took a couple of steps back and ran full tilt, shoulder down, straight at the door. The top of his body connected right in the centre of the door, and it burst off the frame and back into the flat, propelling him right into the burning property. The flames were everywhere. The densest part seemed to be ahead of him in a large room. He stood up and moved towards the room. The main part was inaccessible. The heat was too intense. Jamie opened a door to his left, expecting to see an empty room. Once again, the fire door had done its job. The room was full of smoke being pulled through a hole where a window had been, but there was no fire. He took a few steps into the room. Seeing nothing, he went to turn around and, as he did so, kicked something soft on the floor. He reached down and felt flesh. Someone's leg. And the leg jumped. Whoever it was, they were alive. Jamie knew he didn't have long. He was struggling to breathe now, but he turned and shut the door behind him. Quickly, he moved to the hole in the wall and took some big, deep breaths. The air was delicious. He went back to the person. He found the head and lots of hair. It was a woman. His hands went lower. They caught on something. Shit, it felt like a cable tie. Around her neck, of all places. He carried on feeling the body and felt her arms behind her back, again tied by more plastic cables. He placed his hands on her face and felt the tape covering her mouth. He pulled it sharply, apologising for the pain it would cause.

"Oh, thank God. I thought I was gone there. Thank you. Thank you.

"Don't thank me just yet," said Jamie. "We need to get these ties off you first, and I don't have anything to cut through them."

The woman was struggling for breath, coughing out more than she was breathing in.

Jamie stood and went to the window once more. The oxygen helped, but it was feeding the fire next door. And the door was now on fire. He could see blue lights bouncing off the smoke outside.

Turning to the woman, he said, "Let's just hope that's the fire brigade out there, eh?"

Remembering something, Jamie put his hands into his pocket and took out his car keys. Worth a try.

"I'm going to use my keys to try to get the ties off. I'm going to do your hands first."

The woman moved her body towards Jamie as much as she could without strangling herself. He grabbed the tie and felt where it went through the little ratchet used for tightening. He managed to get the end of his key into the small gap and tried to prise the tie open. He tried at least half a dozen times. It wasn't working. All it did was create pain where the tie had bitten into the woman's wrist. He had no chance of getting the one off her neck.

"Listen, I need to go and get help. I need something to cut the ties. I'll be as quick as I can, I promise."

The woman started to cry. And cough. She was starting to choke in the smoke, and so was Jamie. He needed to get out.

Standing up, he started to retrace his steps into the corridor. The flames were much stronger now. He was torn about leaving the woman, but he had to go. It was the only chance she, no, they had. He bowed his head and ran out of the flat. He found the stairwell and felt every step he trod on, so he didn't fall. As Jamie was about to open the bottom fire door, it burst open in front of him. He was met by a fully clad fireman wearing full breathing apparatus. He screamed directions for where the woman was and told him about the ties. A hand reached out from behind the fireman, grabbed hold of Jamie and pulled him through the door. The other fireman headed up the stairs towards the fire.

In less than 10 seconds, Jamie was breathing clean air again, which made him cough up smoke.

The firefighter who guided Jamie out of the building was now getting a dressing down from a white helmeted colleague. "Wow," thought Jamie. "That's some thanks for what he just did." Jamie was being ushered away from the building, but felt that he had to wait to see if the fireman got to the woman in time. He was moving slowly backwards away from the building, watching as more than a dozen firefighters aimed hoses towards the building. After what seemed an eternity, the woman emerged in the arms of a firefighter who took her straight to a waiting ambulance and its crew.

A female paramedic was approaching Jamie, armed with a foil sheet and a rucksack.

"Bloody lucky if you ask me. He's getting bollocked for coming in to get you. If the commander had his way, you would be toast by now. Luckily, one of the public saw you go in, and those two boys took it upon themselves to be heroes. Mind you, they didn't realise there was someone else in there with you. Unlike you, though, sweetheart, she looks like she is in a bad way. Now, let's see about you, shall we?"

Jamie was staring at the building, contemplating the inevitable had the firefighters not intervened. "I need to thank them. They really did save my life. Probably not the smartest decision I've ever made, but that's what I've been taught. It's my job."

"What's your job? You a fireman or something? Now that would be ironic if you ask me."

"I'm not asking you." Jamie was getting annoyed at the paramedic's opinions. "And I'm a police officer, not a fireman."

"Well, that makes you even more stupid in my book. Thought you lot were smarter than that. My sister's one of you. And she has got not one, but two degrees. And she is certainly smarter than you. Anyway, let's see if you were worth saving, shall we?"

Jamie's annoyance just increased with the verbal castigation he was receiving from a person who was supposed to be there to help him.

"Look, I'm fine. Just cold and wet, that's all. Where's your sister based?"

"She's over in West London. Works in some secret squirrel shit department. Doesn't really talk about her job. Never stops talking about the blokes she meets, though."

"What's her name? I might know her. I can then tell her what an opinionated pain in the arse you are."

"Oh, very funny. You wouldn't know her. She's way out of your league. Her name's Elaine. Elaine Craddock."

"Bloody hell. And she's your sister? Elaine? Laney?"

The paramedic looked as shocked as Jamie did. "As I said. Far too good for you, sunshine. Now, are you hurting anywhere, other than your thick head of course?"

As Jamie was about to counter the retort, he saw two men approaching him from the road. From experience, he knew they were police. He just didn't know which branch. He felt in his left trouser pocket. Empty. Then his right trouser pocket. Empty also. Shit. His car key was missing. He must have left it in the room. So was his phone. It must have fallen out somewhere in the building. Jamie turned his back on the police officers, facing the paramedic again, as they drew closer.

"Look, I don't know what your name is, but I need you to do me a favour. Phone Laney and tell her to come here. Tell her it's Jamie, and I have no car or phone, and I need to get to my dad. Tell these guys that are heading our way that I have concussion. Please, can you do that?" Jamie was trying hard not to appear too desperate.

"Sounds like you are in some kind of trouble to me, and you don't want to talk to the police. Where's your I.D.?"

"It's in my phone case. I lost it in the fire."

Laney's sister threw her head back and guffawed loudly. "Ha! Of course, you did. Mind you, not everyone would do what you did and get that woman out. Jamie, you said. Jamie who?"

"Andries. Jamie Andries. Please. Just call Laney. It's important. Please".

"Sir, do you mind if we have a word with you? A few questions to run through. Nothing to worry about, just routine stuff, you know how it is."

The two officers had arrived and nudged themselves in between Jamie and the paramedic. The one who spoke showed no expression at all towards Jamie and very briefly flashed a warrant card.

"Inspector Prosser, before you ask. Now, can you tell me what you are doing here, at this address?"

"I'm a police officer. Jamie Andries," said Jamie, trying to stall so he could think what he was going to say.

"Please just answer the question for me. Why are you here?"

"I thought that someone was in the building when it exploded. I went to have a look and decided to go in. Simple as that."

Both police officers were quiet for a moment. The paramedic had stepped back away from the three men and was now talking quietly into her phone.

"I see." The policeman sighed and looked back towards the building. He turned back around and was now staring directly at Jamie. There are those police officers who have been in the force for a long time and have a face that exudes evidence of their experience. Pain, sadness, tiredness and toughness. This officer was one of those. Hard as nails and bored as hell at having to question some little upstart about what he was doing somewhere he clearly shouldn't be. He already had the answers to the questions he was asking, and Jamie knew it. Jamie, though, was still trying to figure out how best to avoid the answers. For now, at least.

"Sorry, gents, but I need to transfer my patient into the ambulance. He is suffering from concussion and smoke inhalation. The questions will have to wait for now."

The paramedic slid between the two officers, grabbed hold of Jamie's arm and pulled him around to face where her ambulance was parked. Her partner was in the driving seat of the vehicle, having helped the other ambulance crew deal with the woman who had been extricated after Jamie.

Inspector Prosser put his arm out and blocked the departure of the paramedic and Jamie. "Well, he looks OK to me," he said. "Maybe PC Andries would prefer we move to a nice warm police station to continue our questions. What do you think, PC Andries?"

The paramedic pushed Prosser's arm out of the way, steadfast and with an unsettling look of anger in her eyes. "Well, quite frankly, I don't give a shit what PC Andries thinks, Inspector. Now, unless you have seven years of training as a paramedic under your belt and can identify a concussion along with severe smoke inhalation, then I suggest you get back into your cage, I mean car, and wait for him there. Until then, he is under my care, and I, for one, am not releasing him until I am completely satisfied that he is okay to be released. And if you want to complain about that, then I'll take him to hospital, and you can carry on the conversation with the doctors there."

Jamie nodded in gratification. And as if prompted by an unseen force, he started to cough, holding his head as he did so. The paramedic glared at Jamie. If she hadn't, she would surely have laughed out loud.

"Firey little bitch aren't you. Fair enough," said Prosser. He nodded to his silent partner to walk back towards where their car was parked, but stopped himself and stared straight at the paramedic. "Hmm, well, we'll see, won't we? Best you use your seven years and get him patched up sharpish. We'll be waiting in the car for him." The two officers walked slowly away.

Jamie knew that something wasn't right. How did they know he was a PC? He hadn't told them that.

The paramedic flicked her head in the direction of the ambulance. "Lucky for you, Laney came up trumps. Said you are a total dick, with which I wholeheartedly agreed, but she is on her way. I need to keep you away from Inspector Grump over there until she gets here. Being a lot smarter than you, Laney will figure out what needs to be done. Now. Look like someone who has concussion, which in your case shouldn't be too difficult, and head towards the ambulance over there. Oh, and the coughing thing? Don't!"

"Thank you," Jamie said, looking as relieved as he felt.

"Just doing my job, that's all. Eliza, by the way. My name. It's Eliza. Right. Hold on to my arm and let's get you into the ambulance. As it happens, I do actually think you are suffering from smoke inhalation, so let's see what some oxygen does for you, shall we?"

Jamie took Eliza's arm, walked the short distance to the back of the ambulance, and they both disappeared into the vehicle through the one open door. The door was then pulled shut from the inside.

The two police officers had returned to their car, which they had left parked on the grass frontage to the side of the entrance of the now half-smouldering, half-burning building.

"What do you reckon, guv?" The silent one was no longer silent.

"Not sure," replied a pensive Prosser. "Elkins said that the Andries boy had heard from his old man, but he's not sure what was said. Fallon told me that Jamie should have been here when Albi arrived to take care of the woman, but Albi reckoned that there was no sign of him. Dunno. Maybe Jamie was waiting for Albi, who knows? The chances are, though, if he was here when the building blew, we would have to assume that he saw Albi. And if that's the case, then there's a possibility that Albi can be identified here at the scene. And that's something Fallon doesn't want to happen. That means as soon as the boy is done and leaves the ambulance, he's coming with us. Then we can reunite father and son. Permanently. Which also means we get our payday. Now. Pass me a wine gum and keep your eyes glued to the back of that ambulance."

CHAPTER 57.

On the way to payback. Hopefully.

Dot wasn't naïve. There was a reason that Clayton knew where her car was. As of right now, Dot knew her car was being tracked. In fairness, she would have done the same, but at least she was out of that bloody room. She felt like she had been subjected to a tidal wave of verbal abuse, delivered in a way which was meant to justify the pathetic actions of her employer. The crazy thing was that she still didn't know how this game with Fallon was to be played out. Despite having been in the company of, allegedly, London's finest crime fighters for an entire day, they had given very little away about their plans. But for Dot, they had given away enough. She knew that Fallon was somewhere in the Battersea area, and it was likely that Jack was there as well. She knew that Jamie was trying to find Jack and that the Albanians were taking over the drug business that Fallon was relinquishing. Jack was of no real consequence to Dot anymore. He had made his own smutty bed and was very clearly in a whole heap of trouble as a result of his chosen bedfellows. No, Dot was more concerned about the impact this could have on Jamie. The problem now was how she could deal with Fallon without facing the wrath of McKenzie, Truss and anyone else in HQ who would love to throw her under the bus.

It was dark as Dot drove out of police HQ. She called Jamie's mobile phone. It went straight to voicemail. She left a message saying simply that she was free to talk and to call her back urgently. She turned onto Victoria Street and headed towards Battersea. She had no real plan in her head other than to make sure Fallon failed in his endeavours, and

Jack came through this alive. If indeed he was still alive. She drove past Victoria railway station, pulled into a small side street and turned the engine off. Flipping the bonnet lever, she got out of the car. Pulling up the bonnet, she only had the yellow glow of a streetlight to see by. Having attended a course last year on brand-new car tracking technology, she knew where the best nooks and crannies were for hiding these devices. She checked the battery tray. No device there. She got down onto her knees, reached under the front of the car and ran her hand inside the entire length of the lipped metal bumper. Bingo. She gave a small six-inch square black box a strong yank, and it came away from its magnetic housing. Triumphantly, Dot walked along to a gold-lettered Westminster litter bin and dropped the device into it. She closed the bonnet and got back into her car. Her hands were covered in dirt, but she allowed herself a small triumphant smile. She felt a pang of guilt for Clayton, though. If the top brass didn't get what they wanted as a result of Dot screwing up their plans, then Clayton would be in deep trouble for letting her free. But of course, Clayton knew that. And besides, they were probably tracking her phone anyway. Not sure who 'they' were, now that Elkins was out of the picture, but no doubt someone sat in a darkened room adorned with headphones, feeding any potentially important information into the operations room.

Dot got back into her car and set off again. She made two right turns before taking a left back onto Vauxhall Bridge Road. She headed over the bridge across a dark River Thames, its coal-coloured surface twinkling from the lights of office buildings and flats. She followed the road onto the one-way system around Vauxhall Station. Most of London's outbound evening traffic seemed to be heading the same way as her. She continued along Nine Elms Road towards Battersea, an old stomping ground, and an area she knew well.

Dot had a good enough knowledge to find her way around Battersea. When she was in CID, there had been a series of violent crime incidents linked to one person in Battersea, which meant she spent time holed up watching and waiting in different insalubrious establishments. A lot of that time was spent learning the area around where the perpetrator could disappear in and out of. She remembered the areas south and east of the famous Battersea Dog's home that accommodated a large number of different-sized warehouse facilities as well as rows of lock-up garages. It was a haven for anyone wanting to hide stuff that they didn't want found. Unlike the television series and films advocating the brilliant apprehensions by tough-talking police officers of all of the criminal nasty bastards, not every crime gets solved, and not every criminal is awarded their just desserts. And in the case of Dot's sick suspect, this was exactly the outcome. No one was ever arrested, and her failure rate increased yet again. No doubt the perpetrator would resurrect themselves in later years through an allocation of cold cases, and, with any luck, become another police officer's promotion. If ever there was to be an honest recruitment campaign for the police, it should say, it's more bad than good! Or perhaps Dot was more jaded than most from her career so far. But what it did do was give her a damn good knowledge of where things could get hidden in Battersea.

She turned into a side street in Nine Elms and decided to leave her car and have a look around the area. Having a hunch is a very real thing, based on years of experience, not about how to be a police officer, but how to be a criminal who can outsmart a police officer. One simple phrase that had been hammered into Dot's head also led her on a path of slow mental destruction. Learn to think like a criminal, LaSalle. Do that. The cases get closed, and the criminals get put behind bars. Dot knew she wasn't the only one who had to remember the fine line between good and bad. Several police officers had fallen on the wrong side of honesty and integrity. Officers that Dot knew and held in high esteem. But ultimately, they ended up on the wrong side of a prison cell door, something that Dot was never going to do. She did believe in honesty and integrity, even if her superiors had done all they could to push her across to the other side.

Anyway, first, she needed to look a little less conspicuous. She had dressed for HQ and, right now, stood out like a sore thumb. Opening the boot of her car, Dot took out a week-old running kit that smelt worse than a custody cell on a Monday morning. She sat back in her car and butt-danced her way into a pair of dark blue joggers. She then pulled on an old fleece-lined hoodie she had been given at a conference a few years ago. She swapped her sensible work shoes for a pair of not-so-sweet-smelling Reebok running shoes, and then finally, she took out an old New York Yankees baseball cap. Given she had never been to New York, she had probably found it in a gym somewhere. She packed her changed clothes into the kit bag and threw it back into the boot. Commander Truss said earlier that there were undercover teams in the area. If there was one thing a police officer could normally identify, it was another police officer, especially undercover ones. At least Dot now looked like she was a bit more becoming of her surroundings. Or so she hoped anyway. In the distance, she could see the Thames, with plenty of well-intentioned fitness fanatics working off their anger from the day. Dot knew she looked kind of similar to them, only older and, in her opinion, more saggy-arsed. In her own mind, she thought that anyone watching her attempting to jog would have an "Oh bless her" look rather than a "phwoar". The former meant, hopefully, eyes wouldn't stay on her for long. And that suited her nicely.

Dot started a slow jog in the opposite direction from the river and headed down an avenue of sixties-style, four and five-floor flats. They all had walkways along the front of each floor, so it made it difficult for surveillance from these flats unless someone had gained entry into one of the ground-floor properties. This made it more likely that any undercover teams were either on foot or in vehicles, usually vans that were made to look like traders. And this was tricky for Dot if she had to pass them. They could have eyes on her from the front, back and in between, which could prove a problem.

When she was last in this street, there was a small lane toward the bottom end, which was used as a cut-through to one of the small trading estates. This was her first hunch. The area was perfect. Away from the large industrious warehouses with flood lights, modern security systems and guards. Dot couldn't imagine that Fallon would take those kinds of risks. He would want something inconspicuous. Here, there were around twenty small, ageing, warehouses and garage lockups used for everything from storage to car repairs. All still standing because they probably contained asbestos, and the owners didn't want to pay huge prices to get them demolished and disposed of properly. Dot couldn't imagine that Fallon would use anywhere large. He would want smaller, maybe more than one lockup or warehouse that had more than one access, giving an escape route at all times. Split the drugs up to give himself some protection and leverage. The newer, larger warehouses were around half a mile away as the crow flies from where she currently was. Beyond that, several more estates were harbouring the new influx of storage companies that seemed to be blighting most areas of London. These newer trading estates had more open spaces and were generally built with a single route in and out. Fallon would have done his homework on this, and equally so should have the police. But as of yet, she had seen no one who looked like either friend or foe.

Running on the main streets in the dark was ok. There was enough street lighting to see ahead and behind. It was after seven o'clock in the evening, and she knew that the trading estates would be quiet. And dark. Dot usually ran with headphones, listening to anything that would give inspiration to continue to take the next step. So, jogging without them exacerbated the noise from her breathing. In her head, she sounded like a cross between a steam engine and a pervert breathing down a phone. She slowed as she came to the cut-through. It was just as she remembered and was genuinely grateful for the respite. Christ, she was unfit. She was in no doubt that anyone watching her would feel nothing but pity for her.

Dot was bent over slightly, with her hands resting on her knees as she took in some breaths. This also gave her the advantage that she could look behind her from where she had just run, as well as look ahead. She couldn't see anything to make her suspicious. There were two vans parked on the road ahead, both facing her, so she could see that the seats were empty. She took a look to her left, down the tarmacked, unlit path toward the small trading estate and shivered slightly. Was it just her getting cold, or something else? She hadn't felt like this since her days in CID. She stood upright, took another look around her and started to jog down the darkened path.

CHAPTER 58.

It's about to get real.

"Well, I wasn't expecting to see that, Jack. Looks like your missus has decided to get herself on a bit of a keep-fit drive. Got to say, she isn't looking too bad. Did I ever tell you about the time we had a little fling? Gotta spiky temper on her that's for sure. But then again, I guess you already know that."

Fallon sat in the driving seat of his van, having reversed down a small entrance to a block of flats. He was far enough back to be covered by darkness, but close enough to the road to see directly down to the dark cut-through that led to the lockups where his drugs were being stored. But he was getting twitchy. And for good reason. The Albanian's assumed the entire drug haul was being held a mile or so away. Well, the packages were there. The top row of the pallet contained cocaine. The rest? Just chalk and lime. Hence why he was twitchy. He made sure that, to see him inside the van, someone would have to walk pretty close by. Something Dot hadn't done. And hopefully something anyone from Albania wouldn't do either.

Jack couldn't verbally reply to Fallon. His mouth was taped up. But from the grunts and the movement behind him, Fallon knew that Jack could hear every word he was saying, and given the beating that Jack had taken from Fallon, he was holding up pretty well.

"Well, it appears we have what some would call an irritating problem, Jack. But here's the thing. For me, it could actually be a bit of a blessing. Not that I believe in God, you understand. I don't. Let's face it, I am beyond all reasonable help, eh, Jack. Now, I'm going to need you to behave for a few minutes. Because if you don't, not only will I kill your precious Jamie, I'll also make sure that I do the same to your wife. And the good news is, Jack? I'll let you watch. In fifteen minutes, if you have done your job properly, we'll have the access codes from the bank to confirm all the money is in. So, not long to wait. You'd better start remembering those decryption sequences, sunshine. If that money isn't transferred across to my accounts straight away, then you and your entire family will cease to exist. That's what happens when you double-cross your partner, Jack. Consequences. Now, be a good chap, and stay still for me, will you? I'll be back in a jiff."

Fallon jumped out of the van and gently pushed the door shut. He didn't want noise. He locked the van. The alarm had been disabled. If it hadn't, any movement from within would have set the orange indicator lights off along with an intermittent screeching blare. He had fifteen minutes. He stood in the shadows watching Dot. He was angry. She was a real inconvenience and one that he wasn't expecting. He watched her as she slowly jogged to the end of the cut-through and stopped. Fallon never made mistakes. His life depended on that. But he was becoming distracted. He had started making several. He hadn't counted on Dot remembering where he had assaulted her. It was years ago for God's sake. But here she was. And she seemed to be outsmarting him. The other police idiots were patrolling the streets a mile away in Battersea. Fallon had been dropping false hints for days as to the location of the drugs, and until now, his strategy appeared to be working. There was no way the Albanians would come anywhere near if they saw London's finest in attendance. But then again, Fallon had to hope that the undercover teams were bloody good at doing their jobs. It was always a risk that the Albanians and the police would come together before Fallon needed them to. But now, only Fallon and Albi knew where the drugs were located. There was no one else left that he felt close enough to trust. But Albi had failed to do what he was told with Jamie, so he was now also one of the reasons that the police and whatever other agencies were all scuttling about empty warehouses less than a mile away, looking for drugs and Albanians. Fallon had sent him to wait as covertly as he could in his van and to cover as lookout for both him and the Albanians. Fallon knew full well that Albi would stick out like a sore thumb. "Sit tight and wait for my call, Albi. If it all kicks off beforehand, get yourself out of there, stay low for a while and then get to Dubai. I'll see you there." Of course, they were lies. Necessary lies that enabled Fallon to do what he needed to do. He needed to be in total control. And the last thing he wanted when the job was done was any hangers-on. As it was, he had to pull in Prosser to clear up the mess that Albi had left behind at the flat. And Prosser was costing Fallon a lot of money. Not that that worried him. He would have more than enough money at the end of this. But Jamie had become a threat. Not in the physical sense. But a threat to the operation. A threat to the outcome. Somehow, Jamie was, so far, able to figure out things quicker than the so-called experts. Therefore, he needed to be taken out before he made things worse. And Prosser would do just that. All this talk about killing Jamie and Dot in front of Jack was helping his cause. He needed Jack to sort the transfer codes out. The biggest mistake he had made was not allowing himself control of the final transaction. But Jack was the smart one and understood the encryption process. Despite that, Fallon had it all nicely figured out. He was in complete control. Well, that was until Dot turned up. Fallon took out his phone and dialled a number. Speaking quietly, he said, "I'm in position. Time for you to move." He listened as the person on the other end spoke. Fallon continued. "Well as long as they don't get cold feet, it will be fine. That's why they got the discount. As soon as this is done, I never want to see you or speak to you again. Clear? Good." Fallon cut the call. Thirteen minutes left.

CHAPTER 59.

Déjà vu.
Dot had slowed her jog down to a walk. She was coming to the end of the cut-through and could now see most of the lockups in front of her. Why was it that all the older-style industrial estates had almost no street lighting? The place looked like a cross between a scene from *The Sweeney* and *Batman.* And it gave her the creeps. Dot was doing everything in her power to eradicate the memories of the last time she had been here. Even though it was years ago, it still felt like yesterday. That sort of pain may well leave the body over time, but it still haunts the soul. Even though it was still only mid-way through the evening, it felt like midnight. Similar to the night Fallon assaulted her in his car. That night, they had just finished a sweep of the area where yet another woman had been raped. Fallon needed to go to a lockup that he had purchased after his wife had walked out on him. He said that the lockup was full of his furniture. Dot had since questioned in her mind if the Battersea rapist and Fallon were one and the same. The problem was, though, given her disciplinary after she punched Fallon in the eye, she knew that any investigation against him would be seen as pure revenge. But maybe one day soon, she would ask more questions. There was a darkness that sat over the estate in front of her, hiding the hum of surrounding traffic and dampening the glow of suburbia just a few feet away. She counted twelve roller doors on either side of the estate. Some had signs outside, and some didn't. She looked as closely as she could to see if there were outside CCTV cameras installed on the buildings, but couldn't see any. That, of course, didn't mean that there

weren't any. If someone had something to hide or legitimate goods worth money, then there would be cameras and alarms inside the units. If someone was hiding tens of millions of pounds of drugs, then Dot had to assume there would be some serious security in place. And, right now, that was probably Dot's only real hope of finding something. She couldn't exactly break into all of the units. And she didn't want back up here. She wanted to find Jack. God, wouldn't it have been a thing if Jack had given this much of a shit about her? No, if she found something and called it in, then Fallon would be gone. Jack would be gone. The Albanians would be gone. And she would have the entire weight of police HQ dropped onto her shoulders. Again.

She moved out of the shadow of the cut-through and started to walk towards the left-hand side of the estate when her phone vibrated. She jumped. She had slid the phone into the side of her knickers and under the elasticated waist of her joggers. The vibration went through her body, and she was annoyed at how startled she was. She stopped and looked all around her. A three hundred and sixty-degree turn. She saw a man walk across the other end of the cut-through, but nothing else. Being jumpy was not good. She turned her back to the estate and took out her phone. Thankfully, she had dimmed the back light. She opened up her text messages. There was one from Laney.

"Am on route to pick up Jamie. He has lost his phone. Dick! Where are you? xx"

Dot felt a sense of relief that Jamie was ok. He had obviously set up an alliance with Laney, which, to be fair, was no bad thing. She fancied him rotten, and in Dot's opinion, he could do a lot worse. She was also bloody good at finding stuff that people didn't want found. And that's exactly what Dot needed right now. She sent Laney the address to the road where her car was parked and told her to call as soon as she arrived. The phone vibrated once again. Two kisses from Laney. Dot somehow felt a little bit bolder.

She turned around and walked quickly into the darkness across to the first building. Looking across the entire estate, she continued to look for any sign of CCTV or infrared lights that might give unknown eyes a heads up that she was there. Although she couldn't be completely sure, she still couldn't see any. The units were all pretty much the same in design: glass door, large glass-fronted window with a roller door next to an entrance door. The only difference seemed to be the units at the end, where they also had another door at the side of the building. The glass window in the first unit had been covered with black protective film and was adorned with a banner of a courier company. Probably not a very good one, or just being used as a front for another business. In Dot's experience, most courier companies operated from early morning to late at night and this one wasn't. Dot cursed the fact that she had left her small Maglite torch in the car. It would have made a big difference. Silly mistake. She thought about going back to retrieve it, but continued walking along the row of buildings. There was another not-so-good courier company, a storage company where two of the units had been knocked through and then a tyre business. So far, Dot hadn't seen anything out of the ordinary or anything that raised her suspicions, other than the spurious courier companies. But, she thought, that was exactly the point and precisely why she was looking here.

Somewhere behind the lockups, a dog barked. It was a big dog. The bark was deep and guttural. Hopefully, it wasn't a guard dog. And if it was, even more hopefully, it would be tied up securely to something solid. Every noise echoed around the estate. The late evening air had cooled and was crawling its way into Dot's bones. The hoodie was thin, and she wasn't moving quickly enough to keep warm in her jogging kit. She was looking across at the units opposite as well as the ones she was walking in front of. It seemed fruitless. There was nothing to see other than locked or shuttered doors. She was now at the opposite end of the estate from where she entered. She could see the headlights of the cars driving on the road beyond the entrance. Her nerves were up again. Her stomach was tight. Every time a car went past, she half expected it to turn in and light her up on high beam. She looked back at the cut-through to the road where she had parked her car. Nothing there. She ran over the large tarmac area and across to the units opposite. All she could hear was her own heartbeat thumping in her ears. This was ridiculous, she thought. She had been in far worse places than this in her career. And besides, no one knew that she was here. Check this side of the units, get back to the car, and wait for Jamie and Laney. That was the plan in her head.

As she approached Unit Number 13, she saw a small silver reflective sticker on the side of the unit. She wouldn't have noticed it if it hadn't been for a security light that had flicked on in a property beyond the estate and was reflecting at the exact angle where she now stood. The sticker had an arrow pointing to the back of the unit. Dot looked closer. Underneath was another non-reflective sticker with 13A handwritten on it in black marker pen. Now she was really annoyed that she didn't have her Maglite torch with her. The arrow pointed into the darkness between the unit and a fence. It must have been for 13A. The fence had succumbed to a slowly encroaching mass of thick bramble bushes. This created a natural but darkened corridor. There had been some traffic to the unit recently. Where the tarmac ran out, it met mud. And in the mud, Dot could just make out large tyre tracks as well as footprints. The hairs on the back of Dot's neck prickled just a little bit, forcing her inner vigilance to push up a gear.

She walked gingerly towards the mud following the arrow and then stopped abruptly. She took out her phone and typed a text to Laney. *Cut through near car into Ind Est. Starting unit 13A In case I'm not at car. Bring a torch. x.* She hit send. Rule 3 of policing ahead of one, saving life and two, protecting property. Number 3. Well and truly cover one's arse.

Dot continued along the side of the unit marked number 13, the darkness quickly swathing her body with every step. Her trainers were ill-equipped for the mud. There hadn't been much rain recently, but the weight of whatever vehicles were here previously had created a slippery surface. As her eyes adjusted to the lack of light, Dot could just make out that the front unit had been extended to the rear by around twenty feet or so. She could now also see a roller door on the side of number 13A. Not as wide as the main one at the front of the unit, but about three times the size of a normal front door.

Dot steadied herself using the wall as she continued past the roller door and towards the rear. She walked around the corner to the back of the unit. A sliver of light shone from a street lamp beyond the overgrown hedge that bordered the trading estate to what lay beyond. There was no visible entry to the rear of the unit. Dot had to admit that the chances of this particular unit being linked to Fallon were, at best, marginal, and at worst, wishful thinking. She held onto the corner of the building as she turned back up towards the tarmac and relative safety from slipping in the mud. Then she froze. In her way stood a familiar large man framed within a dark silhouette.

"You and your family are turning out to be a real source of irritation for me, Inspector LaSalle." Dot was about to reply, but couldn't breathe, and her legs were seemingly glued to the ground. She stared, powerless, as the shadowed figure lunged at her. The next thing Dot felt was an excruciating explosion of pain erupting inside her head. Then her whole world went dark.

CHAPTER 60.

The penny drops.
"Well, it's pretty obvious that someone out there doesn't like you. Just as well Laney knows you. She's a brilliant judge of character, and luckily enough for you, that's good enough for me. Now, stick this mask on for a few minutes and get some clean air into your lungs."

Eliza, the paramedic, had been correct. Jamie had swallowed in a fair bit of burning building smoke, and although he wasn't struggling for breath, he could feel the effects it was having on his body. Most noticeably he was a bit dizzy from the lack of clean air. That, however, was now being addressed, and as soon as Jamie placed the oxygen mask over his mouth, the queasy, nauseous feeling that accompanied his light-headedness started to dissipate.

Eliza had taken Jamie's coat off and was now rolling up a sleeve so that she could fit a blood pressure cuff on his arm. She simultaneously put an oxygen monitor on his right index finger. Jamie looked from where he sat on the mobile bed and was about to speak.

"Sshh. I ask the questions for now. Wouldn't do to have you faint on me, would it?"

Jamie concentrated on breathing in the clean air.

"Your BP's a bit high, and your oxygen levels are a bit low, but other than having a smoker's cough for a few weeks, you should survive. I would say, given the state of the building you came out of, you have got off lightly. Very lucky, Mr Policeman. Might want to buy a lottery ticket as your luck is in. And I will, of course, demand a ten per cent fee for keeping you alive if you win so much as a tenner." As Eliza was monitoring Jamie's blood pressure and heart rate, she reached into one of the breast pockets of her uniform and took out her mobile phone. No sound was emitted, but as Eliza showed it to Jamie, it was illuminated with the word SIS. "Hey, sis. You on your way?"

Jamie couldn't hear the reply as the cuff on his arm started to inflate again to take the next blood pressure reading.

"Yeah, he's alive. Sounds like he's smoked forty cigarettes a day for years, but other than that, he's good to go. See what you mean as well. Not bad at all. Yeah, of course. Hang on a sec." Eliza passed the phone over to Jamie. "Wants to talk to you, Mr Policeman."

Jamie took off his oxygen mask, placed the phone to his ear and spoke. "Hey, Laney. Small world, eh? How you doing? What's happening? It appears that I am being stalked by a two-pipper and his goon. It doesn't smell right to me at all."

"Very small world, Jamie. Never told you about Eliza as she's the pretty one. Anyway, it's all a bit weird out there, to be honest. Dot has texted me the location where she is. Russ is on his way to me. Should be here anytime now, and then we need to get over to Dot. She's somewhere in Battersea. I checked the comms on who has been sent to your building fire. Uniform should be there, but no mention of an Inspector. That's a bit weird on its own, but I also gather that Chief Super McKenzie is also on his way. There must be something else going on with this situation, Jamie."

"There is. There's a lot more going on. Listen, I need your help to get away from the guys that are here and come with you to Battersea to find Dot. My dad is also over there somewhere, and he is being held against his will, so we need to get there fast. I can fill you in on what I know when I see you, and thanks for getting hold of Russ. He's a good guy. Now. Listen. If you come into Christian Road from the top end, three sixty before you get to the flats. Can't miss them. They are still smoking. Once you have turned round, wait up near the junction. I just need to figure out how to get away from the two pipper and his mate without being seen, and I'll meet you there. What do you reckon your ETA to here would be?"

"Rush hour is calming down, so I reckon I can get there in about 20 minutes or so. Just be careful, eh."

"Of course. And Laney. Thanks. See you in a bit." Jamie returned the phone to Eliza, who went to speak but realised that Laney had already ended the call.

"All sounds very cloak and dagger to me, Mr Policeman. Me? Much prefer patients to criminals. They don't tend to try to hurt you as much. Well, other than a Saturday evening in Leytonstone that is."

"Trouble is, Eliza, some of the criminals also have a valid warrant card. And that's exactly the problem I have right now. I need to get out of here to meet Laney without those two in the car seeing me. And I don't want to get you into any trouble either."

Eliza leaned over and removed the cuff and oxygen monitor. "Shouldn't be a problem at all. Let's give it ten minutes and then get your jacket on and get ready to peg it. This is all very exciting." Eliza had the same devilish look in her eyes that he had sometimes seen in Laney. Jamie briefly remembered the conversation with Laney about Russ which sparked a quick flash of jealousy. He would make sure it was him who took her out to dinner and not Russ. "Give me a minute. Just going to pop out and give our two friends an update. Don't want them knocking on the back door, spoiling our plans now, do we? "Right, lie down. I'm going to put the mask on you. Need to make it look real when I open the door. Jamie lay back on the bed and let Eliza put the mask on. When she had, she opened the back door, jumped out and ran over to the other officers. The driver opened his window. Whatever Eliza was saying, it appeared to work. She did plenty of finger pointing. At them and at the ambulance. Moments later, she jogged back, stepped up into the ambulance and closed the doors. "All done. Bought a bit more time for you. They are very grumpy, those two."

"Wow, thanks Eliza. So, what are you thinking? It's a bit awkward as the back doors are facing directly towards the car with Prosser in. I'm not sure I could outrun their car with these lungs right now."

"And you're supposed to be the one with the brains. Ha!"

Eliza banged on the panel separating the front cab of the ambulance from the back of the vehicle. "Tdog, need a favour mate. When I shout, need you to do a long slow one eighty, head out of here with blues and twos going, turn left onto the road and make a beeline for the Royal. Fast as you can when we hit the road. Might get us a bollocking and you'll have the police on your tail, but I promise it's for a good cause, mate. You up for that?"

There came a slightly muffled reply from Tdog. "Sounds good to me, Eliza. Need some refs anyway and the canteen at the Royal does good grub. Even better when it's you buying. Just give me a shout when you want me to head."

Eliza smiled and turned back to face Jamie. "As soon as I give Tdog the shout, I want you at the back door. When we hit the top of the turn, open the door, jump out, head over the picket fence to next door and onto the road. We'll turn the opposite way out of here when we leave, and hopefully, your two colleagues will follow us all the way to the hospital. And don't worry. When we stop, we'll say you got out of your own accord, and we had to go on a shout. What's the worst that can happen? A bollocking? Whatever. Sound good, Mr Policeman?"

Jamie was surprised. "And you would do that? For me?"

Eliza chuckled. "Not for you, Mr Policeman, for Laney. Well, maybe a bit for you."

"Eliza, you're a star. Thanks. And Tdog, say thanks to him as well. Yes, that should work. It will take those two by surprise, hopefully. If they believe I'm still in here, they should stay on your tail. Genius." Jamie pulled his coat on.

"His name is Tarquin, by the way. Tdog sounds better as far as he is concerned. Especially in these parts of town.

Fifteen minutes of pretending to play the sick patient was just about long enough to keep Prosser at bay. Jamie was nervous that any longer and their bluff would be called.

Eliza nodded at Jamie.

"Ok, here we go. Be good to see you again, preferably with Laney. Right. You ready?"

Jamie nodded.

Eliza banged twice on the metal panel behind the cab. "Let's go, Tdog. I'm starving." She went to the back of the vehicle, pulled the catch on the door and ushered Jamie close.

The diesel engine of the ambulance increased its revs and pulled off into a long arc of the car park. As soon as the vehicle reached the top of the arc, Eliza pushed open the rear door and shouted at Jamie to jump. Without hesitation, Jamie leapt out of the vehicle and headed straight for a small fence that marked the boundary of the next-door property. Tdog had swung close to the fence. Jamie didn't need to take more than ten paces, and he was straight over it. He turned and watched as the ambulance, now with its rear doors closed, blue lights flashing and sirens screeching into the night air, raced past the two bewildered police officers in their car and turn left on the road. The occupants of the car jumped into action. They did a very tight wheel spin manoeuvre, sending the gravel stones in the car park in every different direction. By this time, they were a good fifteen seconds behind the ambulance that supposedly held their target. They exited the car park, their tyres screeching as they hit the tarmac on the road. They hadn't seen Jamie get out. Eliza was a bloody genius. Jamie just hoped that they wouldn't get into too much trouble when the two officers eventually caught up with them.

Jamie turned and ran towards the road where he would meet Laney. His lungs felt like they were bursting with every elongated step he took. He suddenly felt guilty for not asking Eliza about the woman he had helped in the burning building. Her lungs would be in a darn worse state than his. Fallon wanted them both dead. He hadn't succeeded, and that's why Prosser and his sidekick had been sent. He wanted the woman dead for whatever insane reason. And at first, he wanted Jamie dead; then alive, and now dead again. He needed to figure out why. This was all getting very complicated, but, for now, he had to focus on getting to his dad and Dot. Get that done, and the rest would no doubt start to become clearer. One thing was for sure. Right now, there were quite a few bent coppers running around London.

He continued fast walking along the road until he saw the junction he had spoken to Laney about. He waited for about ten minutes and then watched as a car drove slowly towards him, manoeuvred into a parking space on the opposite side of the road and did a perfect three-point turn. The headlights flashed twice. Jamie walked up to the car. The front passenger door opened, and he got in. Laney smiled at him. And it felt good. As he sat in the seat, Russ, who was squashed in the backseat, gave him a hard pat on the back. He shut the door; Laney put the car into gear and pulled out onto the road.

"Sounds like you've been a busy boy by all accounts, PC Andries." Laney was watching the traffic straight ahead as she spoke.

"You never told me your sister was a stunner. Super smart as well. I owe her big time. Good to see you, Laney."

"Now, you listen to me, you lecherous child. My sister is off limits. Period. And as I'm the only one in this car who knows where we are going, heading towards whatever it is that I have bugger all knowledge of, I urge you to turn your attention to the job at hand. Clear?" Not once had Laney looked at Jamie.

"Crystal, Detective Constable."

Laney half smiled.

"Good to see you in one piece, mate. I listened to the wires about that fire. It sounded pretty nasty to me." Russ sounded genuinely relieved.

"Fallon wanted that building and its entire contents gone; that's for sure. I saw the guy who did it as well. Weird thing was, though. The guy saw me, but he still drove away. Almost like he was doing me a favour. So I guess Fallon wanted me dead. He told me to go there. I can only assume the guy I saw was there to take me out. And when he didn't, some bloke called Prosser was sent to either pick me up or finish the job. Not sure which. Hopefully, we can find Dot, and from there we'll know what the hell is actually going on."

Laney saw Jamie's eyes narrow slightly. She could see how close he had been to not making it. She wanted to give him a huge hug. She was already looking forward to her weekend away.

CHAPTER 61.

All that glitters sometimes, just sometimes, isn't gold.

"Ma'am, we've run over six hundred cars through PNC in the last two hours, and other than the usual no tax or insurance, there's nothing in the immediate vicinity that gives us any cause for concern. We have five separate teams, all in covert locations, as well as another ten individual officers scouring the streets for anything suspicious. Which, of course, there is, but just not the suspicious we're looking for. We've eyeballed every warehouse we can find, along with anywhere else that can potentially hide a couple of tons of cocaine, and I have to say we're struggling. Gold Command is going to need to justify the overtime on this one, and I, for one, don't want to be in the firing line for that. What's the next move, ma'am? If, indeed, there is one?"

Chief Inspector Clayton had changed out of her office attire into her police uniform. She was sitting in a windowless room in police HQ, surrounded by monitors showing various live feeds to potential hiding areas for a couple of tons of drugs. Situated around her were eight other officers, conducting various roles of information gathering and interpreting, all of which should be good enough to find what would be, potentially, the largest ever drugs haul made by a UK police force. But right now, that wasn't happening, and she was feeling the strain. She was also watching an image on a separate screen. A small red spot showing a location in Nine Elms. And another red spot showing a location in Westminster. It would appear that Dot's car had split into two. Clayton had had her team install two trackers in the car. She had a choice to make. Given the intel and where a whole bunch of expensive over-timers were currently placed, Clayton assumed that Dot was in Nine Elms.

"Hold tight and keep the same pattern, Claire. Intel didn't give an exact time, just a date, so for now we sit tight and watch." Clayton's voice belied the strain. She spoke calmly and clearly. Even though McKenzie had up and left to go to the building fire in Whitechapel and Commander Truss was, apparently, in with other top brass justifying the cost of the operation, Clayton's exterior was calm. In fact, it should have been screaming. Gold Command should be conducted by a Gold Commander, not a bloody Chief Inspector. She was feeling exposed, and she didn't like it.

"Hotel Bravo One Seven over." The hushed tone of a sergeant in a mobile unit holed up in a trader's van came through on one of the many radio sets in the room.

"Hotel Bravo One Seven, go ahead over."

Clayton looked over at the communications desk, the operator's face one of total concentration.

"Urgent PNC on vehicle W24 YLS, black Mercedes panel van. Three Eastern European looking IC1 males in the front seats, one of them looked like he was talking over his shoulder, so possible additional occupants in the rear. Quick as, please, they had eyes all over. Foxtrot unit will take over surveillance, over."

Immediately, two operators were typing ridiculously quickly on their keyboards. Foxtrot unit was a foot patrol. She checked on the screen in front of her. He was the far side of Battersea. Over towards the power station. Right on the edge of the current investigative area. Further away than the intel had told them. And the opposite end of Battersea to where Dot was currently located. Who had the better intel here?

One of the operators looked over at Clayton and waved her over. The operator pointed at the third line on the screen. The address line for the vehicle. It was registered at the same address that McKenzie was en route to in

Whitechapel. The one that had been firebombed with at least one serious casualty.

"Gold Commander to Hotel Bravo One Seven."

"Go ahead, Gold."

"Proceed with caution. Repeat, proceed with caution. This would appear to be a target vehicle for us. Eyes on at all times. Move another Foxtrot to give cover. And do not, I repeat, do not lose this vehicle. Over."

Clayton's demeanour had changed. The strain was gone. The nerves were in. Like a lot of police officers, she did not believe in coincidence. She believed in facts and experience. And right now, both seemed on her side. She knew that McKenzie would be listening and pick up the relevance of the radio conversation.

"Roger that, Gold. Understood. Hotel Bravo One Seven out."

She then texted Superintendent Truss. Maybe this information would help alleviate any pressure he was receiving about the cost of the operation. And, of course, prove that she was capable of holding the fort. Just as she finished texting, the radio burst into life.

"Foxtrot Alpha One Gold."

"Go ahead, Foxtrot Alpha One."

"Three more vehicles, two Mercedes vans and one Mercedes Box van, all parked up just south of Battersea Park tube station. All vehicles containing eastern European looking IC1 males. Now being joined by the initial vehicle. If I had to hazard a guess, they look like they're waiting for a go signal. Over."

"Gold Foxtrot Alpha One, we don't guess, do we? Keep under observation. Position the teams so that if the vehicles exit the area and split, we can cover all of them. Send through vehicle IDs when you have them. For all we know, they may be going to a birthday party. Do not approach. Repeat, do not approach. Over."

"Roger that, Gold."

Clayton was starting to get nervous. Again. There were possible decisions about to be made which were way above her pay grade. If it all kicked off, she wanted corroboration of any decision. Where the hell was McKenzie? He was supposed to be Gold Commander. She reached for her mobile and dialled his number.

"McKenzie."

"Sir, it's Clayton. We have a situation. We believe the Albanians are getting ready for the takeover. And this is way above my security level, sir. Where are you?"

"Clayton, stop flapping, will you? You are perfectly capable of dealing with this. I'm operating remotely and have full control if required. I'm dealing with a concurrent situation as we speak. Can't be sure that Commander Truss will be with you at any point. He's tied up. In the meantime, Commander Templeton is on the way to hold your hand. That should be sufficient for any investigation if this all goes to shit. Do you understand?"

"Yes, sir, completely. My main concern is that we have not seen Fallon at all. Either he is already with the drugs or eyeballed one of our teams out there. I will assume both as a potential strategy, but should I proceed as is and wait for further movement, Sir?"

McKenzie sighed down the phone. "There you see. You already have a plan. I'll get Templeton down there with you right away. She may well be Military Intelligence, but she has been Gold with us for quite a few previous operations. Now, get back to it. I need to deal with my end of things."

"Well," thought Clayton. "That's about as clear as an arctic snowstorm." The door behind Clayton opened, and Commander Templeton strode over to where Clayton stood. Wow, that was quick. McKenzie was one step ahead. Guess that's why he is Chief Super, thought Dot.

"I gather you need a number two, Chief Inspector. So, update me and then tell me your thinking. Under no circumstances can we have our lovely citizens awash with Colombian sherbert now, can we? Oh, and I believe we have a dirty cop to take down as well. Have you thought about taking your Superintendent exams at all, Clayton?"

Clayton breathed a tangible sigh of relief. Superintendent. Really? She had enough crap to deal with as a Chief Inspector." She started to quickly update the Superintendent and outline her thoughts. Nerves were gone. This was now all encompassing. This was her job.

CHAPTER 62.

Payback. At last. Or is it?
Fallon was about to cross the road in front of him when a car turned slowly off the main carriageway. Instinctively, he stepped back onto the kerb and retreated quickly behind the parked cars. The car was driving slowly towards him. Something didn't feel right. The fact that Dot was close by meant he had to be alert. Did she know something that he didn't? Of course she did. She was here. Fallon quickly returned to his van, opened the door and got in. He watched intently at the road. He could see the illumination of the car's headlights cast onto the black tarmac ahead, but the car itself didn't go any further down the road. The movement of the lights in front of him suggested the driver had reversed and parked. The lights then went out.

Fallon switched on the police radio scanner that Mikey the Mobile had expertly acquired and fitted into the van. He turned the large black knob slowly, ignoring the obvious local beat chat. He kept doing this for a few seconds. There was nothing else of note that he could hear. Nothing to give him any idea as to what was happening close by. That was until he heard the word, Gold. That meant an operation was underway. And when he heard the words Eastern European IC1s in black Mercedes vans, he knew full well that they were talking about his operation. He looked at the clock on the dashboard of the van. The red illuminated numbers told him he had two minutes to wait until he could get the codes to release his money. Yet again, Fallon was annoyed that he had given so much control to Jack. Jack had set the timing of the call for the transfer of money. Something he should have done. It was all getting far too tight for time. Too many people out there were intent on spoiling the ending. The Albanians, of course, were already there. He'd agreed to send the warehouse details once the money was secure. He had already given them a down payment of fifty kilos of top-quality cocaine as a gesture of goodwill and intent. He needed to keep them where they were until everything was ready. Mind you, if he knew the undercover teams as well as he thought he did, they would stay put until they actually had something to go at. And although a few Albanians wandering around Battersea were suspicious, it was not Gold Command suspicious. Yet. But if his Eastern European customers so much as sniffed an undercover police officer, they would disappear along with the money and his fifty kilos of drugs. Fallon needed to stay calm. He reached over behind himself and prodded Jack in the ribs. Jack grunted. Acknowledgement that he was still alive. That was good enough for Fallon. For now, at least. He briefly refocused his sight on the road ahead. Nobody had walked across in front of him. And nobody else had walked into the cut-through that led to the lockups. His lockups. But where the hell was Dot, and what was she up to?

"Okey dokey, Jack my boy, it's time to go to work." Fallon reached into the glove box and took out a pad and pen. He shut the box with his left leg and, turning in his seat, squeezed through the gap between the seats into the back of the van. He leaned over Jack and pulled him up into a sitting position, pushing his back against the side panel, so he was supporting himself. With a slight grin, Fallon took hold of one end of the duct tape that was firmly in place across Jack's lower face and mouth and pulled the strip off in one brutal swipe. Jack grunted and grimaced in pain. Fallon took his phone and dialled a number starting +41, the international code for Switzerland. After a few seconds, there was a distinctive long intermittent beep. After the third beep, the call was answered. Fallon held the phone to Jack's ear. "Do it right, Jack. Dot and Jamie are counting on it." He showed Jack the pen and pad. Jack shook his head.

An English educated foreign voice on the phone spoke. "Arsenal one, Tirana one."

Jack replied, "1966 was a good year for England."

The educated voice responded. "Indeed, it was."

The voice continued, this time with a series of numbers. "One, six, six, six."

Jack was silent for a moment. Fallon clenched his fist and pulled it back, ready to punch. Jack held up his good hand to Fallon.

"One, seven, three, one," came Jack's reply.

"One, six, zero, eight," came an immediate response.

Again, Jack was silent for what seemed an eternity to Fallon. "One, six, seven, four" came his second reply.

Fallon placed his hand over the receiver and glared at Jack. "This better work, Jack, otherwise I swear I will unleash hell on your family."

Jack met Fallon's stare. Even though he was in pain, his concentration and determination were evident.

The educated voice from Switzerland continued. "One, three, four, three."

Jack inhaled deeply and then slowly exhaled. "One, four, zero, zero," came his emphatic reply.

"Thank you," said the voice from Switzerland. "That concludes the encryption process." And then the line went dead.

"Phone your bank, Fallon. The money should be in the three linked accounts."

Fallon reached into a plastic bag and took out the roll of duct tape. He pulled off a strip and secured it across Jack's mouth once again. Taking the phone back, he dialled another Swiss number and waited for someone to answer. A voice at the other end stated, "Account number, please."

Fallon reeled off a string of numbers.

The voice requested a passcode.

Fallon responded with an eight-digit number. The years of birth of his deceased parents. He listened for a few more moments, smiled and whispered, "Yes, that will be all for now. Thank you," and rang off. "Thirty million dollars, courtesy of the Albanians, Jack. The Albanians have paid. Just like we planned. Ten million of that could have been yours. Instead, well, look at you. At least Jamie and Dot will be relieved that you gave the right codes. Right, time to move." With that, Fallon shuffled into the front of the vehicle, sent a text, and slowly drove towards the road ahead.

The text contained an address and postcode. The Albanians were in the game. They now knew where the drugs were being kept.

Jack grinned under the tight strip of duct tape across his mouth. Encryption codes. Fallon was just too thick to work them out. Always had been. English authors. Very simple. Dates of birth and dates of death. Defoe, Milton and Shakespeare. Jack had once asked Fallon what, if anything, he enjoyed reading. Suffice it to say, it was never any of the greats.

Fallon touched the brakes a little too sharply. The van stopped. He instinctively sat back in his seat and lowered his head. "Shit, shit, shit."

As he looked left along the road, towards the river, he saw Jamie with two other people. One very large male and one female. They were all walking, slowly, along the pavement, deep in discussion. Walking towards him. Twenty feet away. Fallon had only met Jamie once, at his dad's office. And his dad had simply told him that they were business associates. Fallon had made his excuses and left, not wanting to open up on any police conversation. But it was clear that, given the intensity of the stare that Jamie now met Fallon's eyes with, he hadn't forgotten the meeting.

Fallon sat up in his seat, wheel spun the van out of the drive and onto the road. He turned right, heading in the opposite direction to Jamie and Co. He knew he was heading the wrong way. He was heading straight towards the Albanians and half of London's police force.

He checked his rearview mirror as the van increased its speed. He watched as Jamie grew smaller. He was speaking on his mobile phone, no doubt releasing information about the whereabouts of London's most wanted police officer. Fallon also knew that the Albanians had access to the most up-to-date police scanning and radio equipment. He knew because he had provided it to them. A trust sweetener as part of the drug deal. As Fallon checked his mirror for a second time, he became aware of something dark, moving quickly towards him from an adjacent road. He only had a small window to react and attempt to stop the van. But the window closed almost immediately. He had seen the black Mercedes van too late. With no headlights on the Merc and distracted by Jamie and Co behind him, Fallon had no time to stop. The Mercedes collided with an explosion of grinding metal and sparks, caving in Fallon's door and throwing him across the front seats of his van. His body, held firmly by his seatbelt, forced his head to whiplash from left to right, which then struck the edge of the door, rendering him instantly unconscious. Almost immediately, blood started to pour from his face. The shattered glass from the destroyed window sprayed him with blistering velocity, lacerating the entire right side of his head and ripping his ear to shreds. And if and when Fallon eventually emerged from his state of unconsciousness, he would realise that his right eye had been rendered useless.

CHAPTER 63.

Here, there or anywhere?
Jack Andries was clearly evil in a previous life. Granted, he had made a few enemies in this one, and certainly vexed quite a few people, Fallon included, but ... this was getting ridiculous. First, his business had sailed nicely down the river without him, followed by people he cared about being murdered by an utterly barking, bent police officer. Out of hand was an understatement. Jack's life was a total cluster. And for what? Swindling a few geriatrics out of money that would most likely have gone to some dog or cat homes.

Now, he found himself thrown across the back of his own personal prison van, adding more pain to the agony he already felt from the lunatic beating the living daylights out of him. Who the hell does that? When someone like Fallon asks you to do something, unless you are wired like a psychopath, you say yes. And Jack was always going to say yes. His money was at stake. But because Fallon had insisted on acting like a Mexican drug lord high on his own drugs, Jack had looked for a way out. He had no choice. Jack knew that Fallon had got to a place where he was never going to survive any outcome. Fallon was beyond evil.

Whatever had struck the side of the van that Jack was in did him at least one favour. The cable tie that held Jack's hands together had caught on a piece of sharp bodywork that had burst inwards on impact. Despite being completely disoriented, he was sharp enough to understand that this could be a way out. Fallon had taken a battering in the front of the van, the amount of blood certainly testament to a nasty injury.

Jack pulled hard on the cable and started to pull back and forth along the bent metal. After five or six pulls, it snapped, freeing his hands. He immediately pulled the duct tape from his mouth. Just as he was about to stand up, he heard foreign voices. Eastern European voices. Shouting. Not loudly but emphatically. Jack lay down and pulled himself behind the frame of the front seats. He could see through a small hole in the side of the van caused by the collision and watched the vehicle that struck them move backwards away from the van. He continued to watch as four men moved quickly towards where he now lay. They all carried weapons slung over their shoulders. The shouting got louder as they approached, and then Jack jumped out of his skin as a volley of gunshots was dispensed from at least one of the weapons, if not two. He couldn't see which one or what they were firing at. He was lying as much out of sight as he could. They were short, sharp bursts. At least four of five. And then they stopped. There was no return fire, so whoever the bullets were intended for was probably unarmed. The voices grew closer, so Jack didn't move. He jumped again as the sound of scraping metal resonated around the van and someone tried to open the driver's door. It was stuck firm. Fallon still hadn't moved. Another man came to help, and they grunted hard together until the door was open enough for them to unceremoniously drag Fallon out and onto the street. The men moved away quickly, and within a matter of seconds, Jack heard vehicles wheel spinning their way from the scene. The Eastern Europeans knew their target. And thankfully, it didn't appear to be Jack. How could it? No one knew where he was, and in some cases, people probably expected to find him in another burned out car somewhere. Within a few very short minutes, his entire outlook for the future changed direction. And right now, he had one moment to decide which direction to head.

He slowly stood up, his body silently groaning in defiance at his movement. He looked out of the front of the vehicle. A small crowd of people had started to walk towards the van. He could see the trepidation on their faces. The locals may well have been used to a few gunshots going off now and again, but certainly not submachine guns. He climbed over into the passenger seat. Fallon's mobile phone was still in the cup holder of the centre console. Jack took it and put it into his pocket. He opened the door as much as he could. The van had come to a halt at an angle and was partially wedged against a parked car. He pulled the handle and pushed the door. It swung open, and he almost fell out. Several people were staring at him. Not surprising, given the way he looked. He looked a mess. He certainly felt a mess. He knew he had to move quickly. The police would be here soon. His only thought was to get somewhere away from where he was so that he could think about what his next step was going to be. He had been given an unexpected new lease of life. And he was going to take it. One of the approaching men asked him if he was ok. The voice sounded as though it was being spoken through cloth. It sounded muffled. Jack didn't respond. He walked straight ahead, ignoring pleas from passers-by to stop and get treatment. Fallon's last act had been his most foolish. He had allowed Jack to hear an account number and passcode. He must have already known that Jack was as good as dead. Whilst he may not have the violent capabilities of his former business partner, he did have one very useful skill. A photographic memory. Ideal for amending Powers of Attorney and complex trust documents, but even better for retaining numbers that would allow him access to huge sums of money. It was the least he was owed. Small reparation for what Fallon had done to him. But where to go? He couldn't stay here in London. Not without lengthy jail time. Not Dubai. Just too damn hot, so not there. Anywhere, then. Anywhere away from here or there. He turned off the main road and headed away from Battersea. Away from the police. Away from the Albanians. Away from Fallon. But the hardest of all. Away from his son. Away from Jamie.

When he was far enough away from the van and the people that were gathered there, Jack stepped into a covered bus shelter and pulled out Fallon's phone from his pocket. He hit the last number redial. After a brief pause followed by two long ringing tones, a Swiss voice answered. "Account number."

Fallon had made a huge mistake. He should have killed Jack when he had the chance. That was a thirty-million-dollar mistake for him, for which Jack now took full advantage. He just wished he could have seen Fallon's face when he found out.

Jack pulled up the collar of his shirt with his good hand. He felt cold. His head was pounding, and his bones were hurting. He was still wearing the same suit trousers, and shirt he had worn to the office. He noticed one of his cufflinks was missing. That angered him. They had been a birthday gift from Jamie. Fallon had taken his jacket off when he was being beaten earlier in the day. The clothes he was left wearing were unfit for the evening chill. His hand was throbbing, undoubtedly requiring medical attention, but he was alive. And he was rich. Very rich. He smiled. A bittersweet grimacing smile. He lowered his head and walked briskly into the anonymity of the dark South London street ahead.

CHAPTER 64

Who doesn't love a large wing mirror?
"That's him. In the van. That's Fallon." Jamie had already started to run as soon as he recognised the man responsible for the kidnapping of his father. Russ followed suit, his large frame hampering his arms as they swung almost horizontally to his body. If he met someone as he ran, his windmilling arms would render them immediately unconscious.

Laney, on the other hand, held back. She had no idea what Jamie and Russ were heading into, and it made far more sense to keep a safe distance until she saw what was going to happen. And boy, did she make the right decision.

As Jamie passed the halfwayish mark to the van driven by Fallon, there was an almighty crashing noise, and the pursued van was pushed across the road by a black Mercedes van, colliding into a parked vehicle. The crash reduced Jamie and Russ to a slower run, which was just as well, as a couple of demented mafia-looking replicas unleashed merry hell with an automatic weapon each. They fired in the general direction of anyone who looked like a threat. And at this particular moment, that threat was Jamie and Russ.

Not wishing to be statistics, first Jamie and then Russ, ducked quickly between the front and rear of two parked cars. No mean feat for Russ, as the mere process of stopping quickly was an art form in itself. He saw Jamie duck down quickly in front of him and he followed suit, changing direction slightly, but not stopping quickly enough. Russ's large, muscled frame landed on top of Jamie like a battering ram, flattening him to the floor. Every ounce of air in Jamie's body was slammed out, leaving him gasping for breath.

Breath that was already depleted from inhaling an entire bonfire night's worth of smoke earlier.

Laney heard a bullet whistle past her right ear and instinctively ducked. Ridiculously, she had moved her head behind the wing mirror of a small white delivery van as though that would extend her total protection from further bullets. Her body, from the neck down, was completely exposed to the incoming ballistic barrage. But she obviously had a woman's instinct, pure ingenuity or just downright unbelievable luck. The next bullet struck the wing mirror, shattering the glass and outer case into a million pieces. The bullet ricocheted away from her, and she stood unharmed on the pavement. Not a scratch on her. She continued to stand, not moving an inch. As if she thought that she was currently invisible or just immortal.

Her dream-like status was broken when Russ screamed at her to take cover. Which she did, unceremoniously throwing herself between the small van and the car parked in front of it. She could see Jamie pinned under Russ through the gaps below the vehicles ahead of her. She decided not to move until they gave her the all-clear. She much preferred spreadsheets to bullets.

Jamie arched his back, trying to force Russ off his prone body. Russ rolled off rather than stood up. Wise move given that he would have made a target even for someone standing half a mile away.

"Can you see anything, Russ? I can't see a damned thing from down here. Given all the communications have been about Eastern European IC1s a mile away, how the hell did our boys miss this one? We need to get to the van. We need to find Fallon. We need to see if my dad is in the van." Jamie struggled with each word. His diaphragm had had enough.

"Whoa, slow down, Jamie. What we need to do is not get bloody shot. Once it's clear, then we can have a look at what's out there. And not before. Laney! Laney! Can you hear me? Are you ok?"

Jamie immediately felt a pang of guilt. Too busy trying to figure out what was happening ahead of him, he had forgotten that Laney was back behind them.

"Nice to know one of you gives a damn," came the response. "You said nothing about guns and bullets. Heading over to meet Dot, that's what I said. She's having a look around a warehouse or two. Don't forget the torch, she said. Where was the, you better stick a bulletproof vest on for good measure just in case, hey? Where was that? This. This is the reason I stay in the bloody office and let idiots like you become target practice for drug dealers."

"She's pissed, Jamie. Guess she has every right to be. I can hear sirens. And if I can hear them, so can those nutters up ahead. Forgive me for not playing the hero, but I don't think my baton is any match for an Uzi. I'm going to have a look to see if the coast is clear."

Jamie subconsciously helped Russ move forward towards the road to get a better vantage point. Russ sidled forward and sideways until he lay almost flat on the tarmac with a view up to where the black VW van had rested after being side-swiped. He watched for about thirty seconds.

"The driver's door is open, Jamie. I can't see the guys with the Uzis. And a few people have started to move up to the van from the other way. I don't reckon they would do that if it wasn't clear. I'm going to stand up and head up there."

Russ slowly pulled his frame off the tarmac, brushed himself down and started to walk slowly up the road. "All clear, Jamie. Laney, good to go, mate."

Jamie swore he could feel every rib move back into place as he shuffled forward and stood up. He tried to take a deep inhale of air. He got about halfway and ended up coughing. He could still taste the smoke from his lungs. By the time he stood up, Russ and Laney were already heading towards the crash scene. Jamie looked beyond the smashed VW. Two women had caught his attention. They were pointing and shouting at something that he couldn't see. Had one or more of the men left on foot? Maybe it was Fallon. His attention swung back to the van. Russ had reached it. He shouted back towards Jamie. "It's empty. There's a lot of blood in the front, though."

Laney was already in attention-to-detail mode. She had walked beyond the van and was pulling the bystanders in towards her. Showing her warrant card and speaking in a firm tone, she was making sure that any potential witnesses were staying put until more officers turned up.

Jamie arrived at the van and walked to the passenger side door. It was already open. Not wanting to disturb any evidence, he craned his bruised body across the front seat and looked into the rear. He could see what looked like blood on the floor. It was difficult to tell, though. The floor was black, but he could make out jelly-like smears. He also saw discarded pieces of duct tape. Then he saw a cufflink. A solid silver one with a single diamond placed in the centre. His dad had been in here. Jamie had given him the cufflinks for his last birthday.

Russ tapped Jamie on the back. "We need to move, mate. Otherwise, we are going to get stuck here with a whole load of awkward questions being asked by ranks far higher than ours. And we need to find Dot."

Laney came running back towards them. "I'm going to stay here. Need to preserve the scene and keep the witnesses from pegging it. You two need to go and find Dot. The cut through is back up the road on the right. And here, take this with you." She took a small black torch from her waistband and gave it to Russ. "Right," she continued. "Look for number 13A. I've texted her to say we are here and phoned her as well. Her phone is switched off. I just hope her battery is dead and not her. Ooh, that didn't sound good, did it? One of the women I spoke to said that she saw a man run from the van and head down one of the side streets further up the road. She says the driver was dragged from the van and taken off by the men with the weapons. Now go. Go and find Dot.

CHAPTER 65.

What is it with fire?

Russ turned away from Laney and started to jog back up the road towards the cut-through.

"Russ, hang on, mate. My lungs are shot. I can't run."

"Well, at least walk quickly, or I'm going to have to leave you behind." Russ reduced his speed.

Jamie jogged slowly alongside Russ up to the dark passageway where Laney had guided them. They both looked down into the blackness where the warehouses were.

"Ok, let's do this. Given how much you have smoked in the last couple of hours, I'll take the lead." Russ started to walk.

"Not funny, Russ. And move to the side. I can't see a bloody thing past you."

Russ kept the torch switched off. If there was anyone else ahead, he didn't want to give their presence away. Not yet anyway. Mind you, with Jamie's rasping breath sounding like a seventy-year-old who had smoked since they were ten, it was going to be hard to keep quiet.

"We need to find number 13A as quickly as we can, Russ. It's been quite a while since Dot texted Laney the location. My dad was in that van at some point. I found one of his cufflinks in the back. There was a lot of blood, mate. A lot."

"I know it's tough, but we need to concentrate on what we know right now. And that's to get Dot. There are more police in this square mile than at a Spurs-Arsenal game. If anyone can find your dad, they can. So, let's just find Dot and figure it out from there, eh."

"Yeah, yeah, you're right. Let's get this done."

Russ, followed by Jamie, emerged into the old-style industrial estate. They both shivered. Russ held up his hand to stop Jamie. Whispering, he told him to stay behind. They both walked over to the left-hand side of the estate and found the number of the first unit. No 12. They continued walking and found the number on the next unit. No. 11. Concurrent numbers. That meant that 13A had to be on the other side. But which end? They walked quickly across the open tarmac to the units opposite. Jamie pointed to the number above the entrance door. No. 24. Russ pointed down the row of units, indicating the very end on the right-hand side. That's where Nos 13 and 13A should be.

As they started heading along the line of units, Jamie grabbed Russ's arm and pulled him down into a crouching position. It would seem that they weren't the only ones looking for No. 13A. A small light could be seen pointing away from them. They were too far away, and it was too dark at the opposite end to see who was holding the torch. But they knew whoever the torchbearer was, he or she was tall. Very tall. So that conclusively eliminated Dot. Even if she did have a torch, Laney had specifically been asked to bring one so the presumption was that the flashlight the two rookie police officers could now see didn't belong to her. And Dot wasn't six and a half feet tall.

Russ pulled Jamie in close as they knelt against Unit No. 23, their eyes glued to the moving light ahead. "Dot must have known something that everyone else didn't. Why else would she be here, Jamie?"

"I don't know, Russ. She's been holed up all day with top brass at HQ. Maybe she found something out there. I don't know. Maybe it's just a security guard having a wander. My gut feeling is we get as close as we can to have a look. That unit was the last known location for her. I don't know about you, but if I had something to hide, this place would be perfect."

"Agreed. That light has disappeared. I reckon it's down the side of the unit. Let's go slow. If anything kicks off, I go in first. I want to stand a chance of getting out of here."

"Ah, cheers, mate. Nice to know I inspire so much confidence. Ok, slowly goes it, eh."

Russ nodded his agreement and stood. Jamie let Russ move off and followed a few feet behind. They had taken less than half a dozen steps when the first of three transit vans came screeching into the trading estate. One van after the other, they headed straight for the end unit and looped around in an arc. Luckily, they looped in the opposite direction to where Russ and Jamie had crouched down. One by one, the transit vans reversed to the end unit and stopped a few feet away. Perfectly synchronised, the back doors of the vans opened, and three men jumped out from each van. That was thirteen men in total, including the one holding the torch and the three drivers.

"Shit, Jamie, it's the Jamaican crew. And three vans in sync. That can only mean trouble. We're way outnumbered. We need to call this in, mate."

"Call what in, Russ? Three vans with men turn up at a trading estate in South London. Happens every day around here. Until we know what they're doing, we can't call anything in. We don't know what they're up to. Yet. Look. They don't know we're here. The speed they came in at, they're either here to pick up or drop off or both, that's for sure. And they look like they want gone pretty sharpish. Let's see what it is they're so excited about in the unit. I think we both know the answer already, but until we can confirm it, HQ is just going to laugh at two rookies making idiots of themselves. And we need to find Dot. I don't fancy upsetting this lot until we have to. Ok?"

Russ nodded in agreement, watching what was happening ahead of him.

The men had formed a chain and were moving cardboard boxes between each other and into vans. Russ counted twelve boxes into each van. The entire operation took less than two minutes. Even from this distance, he could see there was nothing to identify what was in the boxes. They had a shine to them, which probably meant they were well sealed with tape.

Jamie was inwardly questioning whether or not the boxes could actually contain drugs. It was a huge haul if they did. Thirty-six boxes in total. And the way they were passed between the men showed they had some weight to them. He was trying to do a quick calculation in his head. He knew the rough street price for cocaine in London. It was talked about a lot recently because demand was currently outstripping supply. Around about fifty-eight grand for a kilo of cocaine. Even if each box weighed ten kilos, that's five hundred and eighty thousand a box. Sterling. Thirty-six boxes could be worth nearly twenty-one million. And the way each box was being handled, they looked heavier than ten kilos. But that's only if they did indeed contain cocaine. His mind was spinning. The vans were getting ready to leave. The tall man with the torch was talking to one of the men from the first van. They then stopped talking. They were waiting for something or someone.

"You're right, Russ. We need to call this in. And now." Jamie had turned to lean in close to Russ. They were both still crouching low to the ground. "If it's cocaine in those boxes, there's enough there to flood the entire country. If I'm wrong, I'll take the rap on this. I reckon we're in enough trouble already, so one more rollicking won't make a lot of difference."

The two rookie police officers kept their heads close together as they spoke. Russ took out his mobile phone and shielded the light from the small screen. He looked around to see if there was any movement from the vans. There was. They had been spotted.

"Get ready to run, Jamie. We've got company on the way. You go; I'll hold them off for as long as I can."

Jamie looked over Russ's shoulder. Three men were heading towards them. It may have been dark, but Jamie knew what the outline of a man holding an automatic weapon looked like.

"You can't take them on your own, Russ." Jamie was watching them advance.

"Probably not, but I can do some damage. If you stay, that only means that both of us get taken down. So, sort your cough out and run. Now. NOW!"

Russ stood and used his body as a shield as Jamie started to run. He ran as quickly as he could, heading back towards the cut-through. His lungs were burning, and his heart was pounding, but he didn't look back.

CHAPTER 66.

Gold starts to glitter.

"Hotel Bravo One Seven, Gold."

Even though the chatter on the radio was constant, DCI Clayton still jumped at the incoming request. "Go ahead, Hotel Bravo One Seven."

"All target vehicles are now moving. We have one heading West, one heading South, and two heading East, citybound. Each vehicle travelling within speed limits. Looks like a stand-down, Gold. Awaiting orders. Over."

Clayton looked across at Commander Templeton, who in turn stared at a screen showing where all the officers involved in the operation were currently located.

Templeton spoke without looking up. "It's either a stand down or they've clocked our units. Either way, it sounds like whatever the deal was, it's now off. We still need eyes on those vehicles, but we don't have enough mobile units in place to cover. Call the foxtrots back in and tell Hotel Bravo One Seven to split and follow two of the target vehicles. Their choice which ones. And continue to report. We should have had more mobile units in place."

Clayton immediately forwarded the message to the team in situ. "Ma'am, I'm concerned about the call we took earlier from DC Craddock. She was wholly credible with the information and handling of the shooting incident in Nine Elms. The perpetrators there sounded identical to our own targets, so we missed something. Something important. Our units were a mile away. And perps don't generally let loose with automatic fire in a built-up area without good reason. Plus, we haven't got time to wait for the results from Scenes of Crime team. We need to find the shooters now. Otherwise, they will disappear for good."

"Fair enough, so what are you thinking?"

Clayton walked over to an enlarged map of the area they were operating within in Battersea. "Here's where we were watching the Albanians." Clayton was pointing to the area southwest of Battersea Power Station. "But here is where a conflict of some kind has taken place." She pointed about a foot to the right of the Battersea Power Station. "This is the area where shots had been fired. Less than a mile away. Craddock's given us the location where she believes Inspector LaSalle is. Why she is there, we don't know. This location also coincides with the tracker we put on LaSalle's car. It's only a few hundred yards from where our team is now dealing with multiple shots fired. This can't be a coincidence, ma'am. There must be a reason that LaSalle is there. I think there would be merit in at least sending another armed unit to the location to have a look. Two are en route as it is. Let's divert one to LaSalle's last known location. And if there's nothing to see, then at least they can double back up with the other units."

Templeton was looking at her phone. Clayton was getting annoyed. "If nothing else, it would at least clear up any ambiguity about the last known whereabouts of LaSalle.

Templeton looked up. "You are, of course, working on the assumption that she is one of us still, and not one of them. Never make assumptions. Assumptions are different from gut feelings. If you make one wrong assumption, all the previous correct ones will count for nothing. Assumptions are part of a rational process. Gut feelings are not. They are pure intuition. Remember that. Get hold of Foxtrot Alpha One. There are four in that team. The map shows two entry points into the area where LaSalle is allegedly reported to be. Send two to enter here, and two here. Let's see what they find."

Templeton had been pointing at the cut-through and the entrance to the industrial unit. She wanted it sealed. She turned away, walked to the very back of the command centre and took a call on her phone. She didn't look pleased.

Clayton confirmed the instructions with the operators in the command centre and hit the communicate button. "Foxtrot Alpha One, Gold Command. Urgent. Over." Clayton had never assumed LaSalle was working on the other side. The trackers had been placed on LaSalle's car more for protection than anything else. So, protecting her was what Clayton needed to do. Her gut feeling told her that LaSalle was in trouble. And that LaSalle was one of the good ones.

"Guv. Gotta call over here for you. Patched through from CID. PC Jamie Andries. Something about Jamaican Yardies and Inspector LaSalle. Sounds urgent."

Clayton smiled. She knew she was right. "Jamie, DI Clayton. Heard a lot about you. So, what have you got?"

CHAPTER 67.

Friends.

"What the hell do you mean you left him? We need to go and help him. Jamie, how could you do that?"

"Laney, I had no choice. If I'd stayed, we would have both been taken down. Russ stayed so that I could get out and get help. And help is now on the way. Listen, I had no choice, ok. Russ is a big boy. He can look after himself."

Laney was almost in tears. "Not against a frigging machine gun, he can't."

"Laney, listen to me. Other than the shots they fired at me when I ran, I haven't heard a single gunshot come from the direction of the industrial estate. The unit that we were heading to is on this side. There's a row of houses about thirty feet behind the units. I want to get into one of the gardens and get to the units from the back. But I need to move quickly." Jamie was in no doubt about his plan.

"Then I can help you. I need to come with you." Laney was already looking for the road that provided access to the Industrial Estate from their gardens.

"No, Laney. You need to stay here. You need to guide armed response to the cut-through. Tell them the unit is the furthest away from them and diagonally in the corner. Around a dozen or so Yardies were there when I left. I told this to Gold Command. As far as I know, the situation hasn't changed. They'll be here soon. But I need to get to Russ and Dot. I can't wait, Laney. Understand?"

She nodded. "You go. I'll guide the others when they arrive. Good luck, Jamie. And – Jamie? Get your arse back here safely, eh?"

Jamie was already walking towards a road up ahead on the left-hand side. As he turned into the road of mostly Victorian semi-detached houses, he looked to see if the units were visible behind the gardens. He couldn't see any. He kept walking, trying to work out mentally how far he had to go to reach No. 13 and 13A. He walked past ten houses and stopped. He could hear shouting in the distance. It was coming from the direction of the units.

He reached a side gate with a 'Beware of the Dog' sign screwed to it. He pulled up the latch, but the door didn't move. He took a step back and kicked it hard, and it gave way. Almost immediately, he heard barking. Thankfully, the bark was more falsetto than bass. He ran past the back door and into a long, narrowish garden. He glimpsed a small white dog going apoplectic in the kitchen. Jamie had seen bigger rats. He headed to the bottom of the garden. It had been maintained nicely. Reaching a seven-foot-high larch lap fence, he took one leap and pulled himself up to the top. The fence wobbled under his weight. He could now see the units. And he estimated he was about two-thirds of the way down towards No. 13 and 13A. He was faced with a huge amount of bramble between him and the units, but he threw himself over anyway, landing on his back. Immediately, he felt a thousand thorns holding him. As he moved, his legs pushed through the bramble, and he found himself wading against the sharp spikes, his trousers being torn and his skin thoroughly pricked.

The voices were closer now. He threw himself forward and clawed his way through the brambles until he reached a narrow strip behind what he believed to be Unit 15. He could feel droplets of blood on his legs, being pressed through the material of his trousers.

He stumbled along behind the units, concentrating on keeping his balance through the endless undergrowth. He was now behind Unit 13. Unit 13A stuck out further. He crept slowly around it to the very end. He could feel a warmth. He realised that the back metal wall of the unit was slightly warm to the touch. Something must be burning inside the unit. He could hear voices, not close, but close enough. That's when the gunfire started. Automatic fire mixed with single pops. Handguns. Jamie assumed that the armed response unit must have arrived. He pushed his body as close to the unit as he could and gingerly stuck his head around the corner. He could see the car park straight ahead.

Four men were behind one of the vans he had seen earlier. Either the other two vans were elsewhere on the industrial estate, or they had left. All four men were pinned behind the van, taking turns to shoot at the police who were positioned at the entrance to the estate. Jamie could hear bullets fizzing past his position. He needed to be careful here. He didn't want to end up being shot, especially by his own side. He could see a small roller door ahead of him. He got down on his knees and crawled over to it. He reckoned he was now considered fair game for target practice. He reached the door and pulled the roller up from the bottom. It moved a little. He gripped the bottom of the door and pushed up as hard as he could. It moved again. He stood up and pulled upwards as hard as he could. Someone had smashed the track halfway up the door, making it hard for the roller to move. He got it to about a quarter open. Jamie lay flat on the floor and rolled himself under the door. The fire was coming from the back end of the unit. A pallet of something that was covered was alight. Someone had thrown a lit piece of cloth underneath. The smoke was starting to build. This was a déjà vu moment he didn't relish. Jamie could see Russ and Dot to his right. Russ saw Jamie immediately."

"Jamie, over here. Quickly. Dot's unconscious. We haven't got long. There are a couple of gas canisters behind the pallet."

Jamie went straight over to Russ. "Are you ok, mate? Christ, Dot's face is a mess. She is, er, alive, isn't she?"

"Dot's ok. Taken a punch, judging by the look of her face. I'm ok. A broken nose, but I took out three of their men. We are secured to this ruddy great pole. The bastard that tied me here took out some cable from a toolbox behind me. He left it there deliberately to piss me off."

"Gotcha."

The gunfire was still in full flow outside. Several bullets had collided with the unit, sounding like firecrackers being let off. The smoke in the unit was starting to get thicker and more acrid.

Jamie jumped three or four steps behind Russ and grabbed hold of the toolbox. He could taste the smoke, and it was starting to make him gag. He pulled the toolbox and grabbed a screwdriver and a pair of pliers.

"Reaching Russ and Dot, Jamie reached behind them. He felt for the cable. Electrical cable. He used the pliers to cut through the one holding Russ, moved away immediately and grabbed the cable securing Dot to the pole. Jamie cut straight through, releasing Dot's arms, which flopped to the floor. Something in the lit pallet started to hiss.

Russ said. "Get the door, Jamie. I've got Dot."

Jamie moved back to the door and tried to pull it up further to allow Russ's large frame to get through. The hissing was getting louder. "Russ, we need to move quicker. One of those canisters you saw is about to blow." "I know, mate, I can hear it." Russ had half lifted and half dragged Dot to the door. He dropped her as close as he could, and they both pushed her through the gap into the open. Russ grabbed Jamie and forcibly pushed him under the door, then, following close behind, squeezed himself through into the fresh air. The air now being pulled into his lungs was bliss. A bullet ricocheted off the side of the unit, inches from where Russ lay. He stood and, lifting Dot in one swift movement, ran around to the back of the unit for cover. He turned to shout at Jamie, who was lying on the mud floor.

"Jamie. Jamie. Get your arse over here. We need cover. Jamie. Can you hear me? Jamie!"

There was no movement. Russ took half a dozen long strides to where his friend lay, slipped his hands under his armpits and dragged him swiftly to safety. He let go. As he pulled his hands away, he could see that his right one was covered in blood. Jamie had been shot and was losing blood quickly. He must have hit his head when he was shot, knocking him unconscious. Russ looked back towards the van. He could see three bodies close to the van, not moving. He could also see one man had moved to the side of the van. He was constantly switching his angle of fire from the front to the back of the van. He was being shot at from two different directions. And struggling. If he continued, it was evident he would share the same fate as his fellow associates. It was just a matter of time, or more precisely, bullets.

Russ moved over to Dot. Her face was a mass of blood and bruises. Her eyes were barely visible under the surrounding swollen flesh, and her nose had been broken, with congealed blood creating a mask-like image across her face. But she was still breathing, albeit more snorting the air in and out. Russ's immediate concern now was Jamie. He was in a bad way. And from the blood stains on his shirt, the bullet had pierced his chest and exited through his lower shoulder.

Another bullet fizzed into the bramble, ending up thudding into something solid in a garden beyond.

Russ had to move. But where? He sidled over to Jamie and went to pick him up. As he did so, the first of the heated gas canisters inside the unit exploded. A muffled boom filled the air. Then there was a flame closely followed by a rushing heatwave being forced through the partially open door to the unit. One minute earlier, and they would have all been badly injured, if not dead. Moments later, a second canister exploded. They would definitely be dead.

The one remaining assailant, shooting at the police, turned as the explosion destroyed the unit behind him. Taken off guard for one compromised second, he had exposed enough of his body for an armed officer to take the shot. The officer didn't miss.

CHAPTER 68.

A couple of weeks later. That bloody glass room at the posh police station. Are we there yet?
The assembled individuals in the glass conference room on the twentieth floor of HQ looked like a veritable who's who of police hierarchy yet again. Alongside them sat what looked like the walking wounded from an 1880s Wild West bar room brawl and shootout.

"Thank you for coming this morning. I know some of you have had a challenging last few days, but suffice it to say, I'm delighted to have you all in the room, alive and well."

Chief Superintendent McKenzie spoke with his back to the large panoramic window, facing the rest of the room, with everyone seated around the conference table. Long white vertical blinds in the window had been narrowed, diffusing the sunlight that cascaded over the London skyline. McKenzie was dressed in full uniformed display regalia, complete with an entire row of commendation ribbons, his cap polished and placed on the coffee table. "Apologies for the outfit, I'm off to see the Home Secretary after this meeting, along with the press pack. So, I will be as brief as I can. I know you all have far more important things to be doing.

"In 1998, I was asked to set up a branch of the police service called CIB 3. To the uneducated, a complaints bureau. To those in the know, an Anti-Corruption unit with extraordinary powers. Some would say CIB 3 had too much power. As a result of what the politicians and some top brass were saying, my job role changed from the original description. My job became that of one to find the corrupt inside of anti-corruption. Ghosts of the ghost squad, as it were."

Every face in the room watched intently as the Chief Superintendent spoke.

"Each one of you, either knowingly or unknowingly, became part of one of the largest, if not *the* largest, anti-corruption cases in the history of this police force. The complexity was at a different level; everyone should be proud of the way you each dealt with your journey throughout. For that, I thank you."

"Thank us? For what exactly? Being pawns in your bloody game of human chess? I'm sorry, sir, but I don't buy this. I, we, have been used the whole time." Dot struggled to form her words properly. Her mouth was still swollen where she had received a few stitches, and her nose and eyes were a brilliant hue of deep purple. Her attacker had certainly done a decent amount of damage to her face. Enough to scare children. "And why the hell didn't you warn us, sir?" Dot continued. She could feel herself getting angrier with each word. "My outstanding career now carries an assault by a police commander as well as sexual assault by a police inspector. Exemplary? I don't think so. A travesty? Bloody right. Sir."

"You know I understand your anger, Dot, but we had no idea you would stumble upon Commander Truss at that Industrial Unit." McKenzie looked genuinely concerned with a furrowed right eyebrow creating deep lines on his forehead. "Truss had levels of access to places a criminal could only dream of, which gave him great value amongst the criminal fraternity. Although we had our suspicions about him, we only found out how fully involved he was when one of Fallon's men double-crossed him. One Massimo Albricci. Jamie, you know him. He was sent to kill you at the property in Whitechapel. That's when I found out for sure that Truss was involved with Fallon. Actually, more than involved, they appeared to be partners. Albricci suspected that Fallon was going to have him killed, so when he found out about Truss,

Albricci offered him a way to take overall control, which is how he ended up working with Truss to double-cross Fallon with the drugs and the money. A double, double cross if you will. While we've managed to detain the now ex-Commander Truss, Albricci has gone to ground. We believe he is working at the top level with the Yardie gangs in South London. And we also believe they are now in control of tens of millions of dollars of cocaine. They currently own the market. For that, we as a force have failed in our duty to the citizens of this great city. We failed to stop the flood of drugs."

Jamie shuffled in his seat. His right arm was being held in a cotton sling. The rogue bullet that had struck him at Unit 13A missed everything vital between his right breast and just below his shoulder blade. He was a very lucky boy. But that wasn't to say it wasn't painful. It was. Very painful. "Sir, forgive me for asking here, but you are speaking about the Jamaican Yardies. Weren't you looking for the Albanians? And CIB 3, by the way, sir. Heard the rumours about you lot. Scary!"

"Indeed, but as you can see, some of us are also human. Yes, you are correct, Jamie. All of our intelligence, all of our undercover operations teams, they all pointed to a deal being done between Fallon's group and the Albanian OCG. We knew that Fallon had been involved in small-time drug dealing for a while. He was using drugs that his team stole through legitimate operational methods and paying other officers off with enough money to keep their silence and loyalty. What we didn't know until recently was just how much drugs he had gathered and his means of laundering the proceeds. And, again, it wasn't until recently that we discovered the additional access he had to large amounts of cash through Jack Andries' business. We thought the figures were in the low millions. Maybe two or three. What we have subsequently discovered is that the drugs alone were worth well over thirty million. And that doesn't take account of the properties and other laundered cash. Quite possibly an additional thirty million. Big stakes lure in big people. Just ask Truss and Fallon. The property they had burnt down in Whitechapel had planning permission for twenty-four apartments. Value, somewhere around six million. By destroying it the way they did, Fallon must have known it would eventually be linked back to him. But DC Craddock had already found the link between the building, Fallon and Jack Andries, working this out ahead of an entire team of our so-called experts. It was brilliant work by her. Fallon was prepared to sacrifice six million just to cover his tracks. So overall, this was big money."

Russ shook his head in disbelief. "They don't tell you this at Police Training School."

"Indeed, Russ. If they did, we would probably need a few more classrooms. Thirty million is a big salary. A big enough carrot to turn officers rogue, that's for sure." McKenzie blew air through his nose at his own joke. He continued. "Ok, so for your benefit, I'll run through the timeline of what we know. If there's anything that you think you can add that would be helpful to the inquiry, please let me know." McKenzie walked to the coffee table and filled a glass with water. He took a sip and studied the glass.

"Dot, you have to forgive what I'm going to say, but it may give you a bit of comfort in trying to understand some of the rationale behind our actions. Same for you, Jamie. As you know, we are still searching for Jack Andries. We believe that he is either in or on his way to Dubai. There's plenty of CCTV around up to Dover, but then the sightings stop. We believe Dubai because that's where most of the property and money leads to. But that's down to others to deal with. Andries, by all accounts, had a legitimate business, mostly dealing with older clients. These clients, generally wealthy women with no or little family, tended to be where the bulk of his business came from. The legitimate part of his business, though, was struggling. To any layman, they would say he should diversify. And diversify he did. Just not legally. And, on a monumental scale. Over two years, we believe his business was responsible for the theft in the region of eight million pounds. Yes, Dot."

Dot stood and walked to the coffee machine, where she poured some black sludge into a cup. The dregs. She took a sip, barely realising what she was drinking. "For the last few months, Jack complained that his business was struggling. He was about to make some of the staff redundant. He was angrier than normal, to put it bluntly. A right bastard. If he were so rich, why would he let his business suffer like that?"

"Simply put, Dot, Fallon had taken control of what he was doing. You can see why we had to act cautiously with both you and Jamie. But this gets worse." McKenzie took another sip of water and carried on talking. "It was common knowledge Andries was having affairs with his staff." McKenzie looked at Dot. She was staring down at the table while picking at the stitches in her lip. "We believe one member of staff in particular was asking a lot of questions about his other work. We assume he shared some of the details of his illicit sideline with her about Fallon, even letting her use one of Fallon's properties for free. He had a meeting with his accountant, who suggested that she, along with a few others, be made redundant. We have to assume that she made some kind of threat to Andries or Fallon about what she knew, which is how we believe she ended up in the boot of a burnt-out car. The ultimate redundancy package, by all accounts. I suspect, though, it wasn't just to shut her up, but no doubt to send a message to Jack. Dot, you know that we were tracking your phone, don't you?"

"Until I met Elkins, I had no idea. Mind you, until Elkins, I didn't even know the man I was married to appeared to be screwing everyone in his firm. I even thought that someone had broken into my house the other week, but nothing was taken. That's what paranoia does to you. A window into the life of a woman living in alternative parallels."

"Bugger."

Everyone looked at Jamie.

"God, I'm sorry, Dot, that was me. Dad sent me there to check out some stuff. He was scared. He knew he was in big trouble, but I don't think he wanted to drag me into any of it. I wasn't exactly going to walk away. I'm sorry, Dot. I just thought if you knew I was doing something for Dad, you would be angry with me."

"Jamie, it's fine. At least I now know I wasn't going mad. Anyway, I assume my phone was being tracked because of Jack. To find out if I knew anything. To find out if I was involved."

McKenzie put his head to one side. "That became secondary to the investigation, Dot. The initial reason was Krystina Benko. During our investigation into Fallon, you received two missed calls from her. Hours later, she wound up murdered in the Chelsea Garden care home. As you know, Fallon was SIO, deliberately taking the case. He knew the premises from previous dealings. He knew the crime would get reported because he committed it, and then, with the help of other corrupt officers, he framed Gerald Compton for the murder. Poor old Gerald paid the ultimate price for nothing other than being in the wrong place at the wrong time. Anyway, we were trying to rack our brains as to the relationship between you and Krystina. Our assumptions are crude, but we think the right ones. She knew you were a police officer because she knew your mother very well. We think she was trying to reach out to you. And Fallon found out."

"Bloody hell, I think I remember. I checked the missed calls on my phone and then found out she was one of the chefs. I was going to call her back, but I got sidetracked." Dot let out a long, slow sigh. "Seems to be the story of my life. Why, why didn't I phone her back? I could have saved her life."

"You can't blame yourself, Dot. Her life was already over when she made the calls to you. How well did you know Vanessa Foxx?"

"Vanessa Foxx? Me?" said Dot, looking at the Chief Superintendent in surprise.

"Yes, Dot, the Regional Director at the Care Home. Ironically, the one your mother is resident at."

"Yes, of course, I knew her. I knew her because she was in charge of the care home. I certainly didn't like her, though, and I think the feeling was mutual. Mum's spending a fortune in that place and I always got the impression that, well, that she just sees Mum as a commodity. Nothing more. Rubbed me the wrong way. Why are you asking?"

"Well, there's no other way of saying this other than just saying it, Dot. Jack was having an affair with Vanessa. And so was Fallon."

Dot looked like she was about to explode. Which indeed she was, but then she looked at Jamie. He was staring intently at the hand that wasn't in the sling. Dot nodded to McKenzie to continue.

"We believe Andries was doing it for the sex, but for Fallon, we think it was to keep her under control. You see, she was key in finding new clients for the firm. As Regional Director, she insisted on being introduced to all the new entrants coming into some of London's most exclusive care homes. She vetted these individuals, so she knew if they had no immediate family. She was the first line of the sales pitch. She could ask all sorts of questions without raising any suspicion. She then handed them over to Jack Andries to become their legal and financial representative, which gave him the ability to move assets, property and money into trusts. Trusts that he alone controlled. And when they passed away, which they inevitably did, very possibly using enhanced methods, the money was quickly transferred into Fallon's network of offshore accounts to buy more and more drugs, thus creating a huge stockpile for his exit strategy. Over the last couple of years, we believe that around thirty individuals have had their lives cut short as a result of Vanessa, Andries and Fallon. That in itself has opened up one hell of an investigation."

"Enhanced methods," said Dot. "You mean killing them?"

"Yes, we think so. But that's for a whole other department to deal with."

The room was silent. McKenzie took a moment to fill his glass with water.

DCI Clayton picked up the internal phone and asked for more coffee to be brought in.

Dot listened, dumbstruck. Her tone had softened, almost to a whisper, as she spoke. "I had no idea. I knew there was a reason I didn't like that bitch. Christ almighty, no wonder you lot didn't trust me. I honestly had no idea. Have you got Vanessa in custody?"

McKenzie continued. "Well, we have someone resembling her under arrest in intensive care. Fallon wanted rid of her and tried to blow her up. As you know, Jamie put his own life at risk and helped rescue a woman from the building in Whitechapel. That woman has been confirmed as Vanessa. She'll require extensive surgery for the burns she received, which gives us time to work out just how many charges she is going to face. Right, coffee anyone?"

The door to the conference room opened, and one tray of coffee and one tray of biscuits were placed on the coffee table.

"Help yourselves," announced Clayton. "And feel free to have a quick comfort break if you need to."

Other than Dot filling up her cup full of coffee, nobody else moved from the table. McKenzie grabbed two handfuls of biscuits and scattered them across the table.

"The force's finest culinary minds have chosen these for you, so you may as well tuck in. As you all have bladders of steel, do you have any questions for the room or any insights that we may have missed? Don't be shy, none of us is speaking under oath. Yet." He opened a packet of custard creams and placed an entire square biscuit into his mouth.

"Sir?"

McKenzie put his finger in the air. A silent, holding gesture whilst he swallowed the remnants of his custard cream.

"Ah, yes, Russ. Another potential in the room for a commendation. Go ahead."

"I think I get why we're here. Laney, Jamie, Inspector LaSalle and me. We seem to be pretty key to figuring some stuff out, I get that. But this isn't over, is it? I know that you've been working on this in CIB 3. Which, by the way ... Wow. Utter respect, sir. But as far as we've been told, we don't know where Fallon has gone and, well, we still don't know what has happened to Jamie's dad. Every time you speak, it seems like someone else has died, and, well, I don't know how to say this, but massive amounts of drugs seem to have flooded the market. Every night this week on TV, they're reporting on another drug-related shooting. This isn't a good outcome for the force, surely, sir?"

"I take your point, Russ, and from an outsider's perspective, I grant you it looks rather bleak. Throughout the course of this investigation, we've lost good men. Some were corrupt, some weren't. The thing is, we found out about it and irrespective of who was doing what to whom, a serious message has hit this force like a shockwave. We'll find those who see themselves as above the law that they are there to uphold. Fallon was good once. But he became greedy. The same for Sergeant Mepham, Sergeant Osman, and Sergeant Patterson. They all paid the ultimate price. Not just for them, but for their families as well. Elkins' life destroyed. Commander Truss, for crying out loud. A bloody Commander. And lord knows how many other people have been pulled into this. But we'll find them. We are currently drawing up a charge sheet for Patrick Fallon, which includes multiple murders, accessory to murders, extortion and money laundering. And that's just for starters. The reason we are doing this is to act as a deterrent. A deterrent to those police officers who may feel tempted to cross lines in their careers. The irony here, though, is that we believe that Fallon is probably dead by now. According to several witnesses to the crash and shootings that happened at the location of Fallon's van, a man fitting Fallon's description was dragged out of the van by the shooters, thrown into a different vehicle and driven off. These were the Albanians. And it would seem that they were themselves double-crossed. Russ, the reason that the drugs are out there on the streets is quite simple. We were all duped. And quite frankly, if Dot hadn't uncovered the other warehouse, we would all be none the wiser. Anyone need a break before I finish off? No? Ok, I'll crack on."

All you could hear in the room was the faint noise of London traffic, twenty floors below. Everyone was listening intently to McKenzie.

"So, then. We know that Commander Truss was at the warehouse that Dot went to that night. We know because Dot saw him, and he did some pretty nasty damage to her. His intention, though, was to do something far worse. And indeed, he would have succeeded had it not been for the bravery of some of you in this room. But what was Truss doing there in the first place? Every piece of intelligence we had pointed us to an area over a mile away where the Albanians were. The Albanians were there; we had them under surveillance. So, here comes the double cross that fooled us all. The only person other than Fallon who knew the location of the drugs was Albricci. We now know that Albricci was working with Truss. We also know that Albricci felt threatened by Fallon. Enough so that Albricci used his connections within the Yardie gangs to set up a meeting. A meeting where he and Truss made a deal to sell Fallon's drugs to them. And from what we can establish, the double cross worked."

"Ooh, this is so exciting, sir." Laney sat bolt upright and clapped her hands. "So, in essence, what you are saying then is that one great big load of cocaine was sold to two different drug gangs. One dealing with Fallon and one dealing with Truss."

"Exactly that, Elaine. Jamie and Russ had stumbled upon the Yardies picking up the drugs. As soon as Jamie's message with his location was received at Gold Command, we shifted resources. By the time our teams engaged, most of the drugs had gone, but we took down a number of the gang and still a substantial amount of cocaine."

Dot let out a loud chuckle. "So, just to back up what Laney said and to confirm my understanding. The Albanians paid Fallon money for drugs they never received, and the Yardies paid money to Truss for drugs they did receive?"

"Spot on, Inspector. Sixty million quid in cash for thirty million in drugs. We suspect that even if Fallon repaid the money to the Albanians, they would still kill him. That's why they abducted him. They smelt a rat. As for two potential winners in this. One is Massimo Albricci. With Truss gone, he would be in control of the money paid by the Yardies. A very rich man indeed. And secondly, we have to assume that Andries would also have access to the money that the Albanians paid. He was in control of the financial logistics. Fallon didn't understand that side of the business. If he did, he would have got rid of Andries long ago. And I would bet my bottom dollar that he made suitable alternative arrangements for his own access to the funds, given that he was scared for his life. I'm sure he would have orchestrated his own route out. He was a smart man. Just remember, though, there's a lot of conjecture in what I've said, but for now, it's the best we have.

Dot let out another sarcastic chuckle. "Who says crime doesn't pay, Chief Superintendent? I reckon your department is going to be busy for a long time yet. Now, if there isn't anything else, can I be excused, please? I need to figure out how to divorce a criminal on the run, and quite frankly, I'm exhausted, Sir."

"Yes, yes, of course, Dot. We'll let you know of any developments that may affect you directly. And thank you for everything you have done. You have paid a price for which we are, of course, very grateful. Anyone else have any burning issues they wish to discuss, I'll hang around for another biscuit to answer anything I can."

Dot stood and headed to the door. She had had enough. She needed to get out of the room. All of a sudden, it felt claustrophobic. It seemed to be squeezing the air out of her body. Her head was a mess. She had so much she wanted to say about her treatment, but now wasn't the time or place to bring it all up. Again.

"Jamie, why don't you come round to the house later? I owe you a pizza."

Jamie nodded. "Will do, Dot. Make it three pizzas. Russ is driving Laney and me, so she'll be there as well. See you later."

Dot left the room, followed by muffled goodbyes. As she walked into the corridor, a voice forced her to stop.

"Dorothea, appreciate that you have had a pig of a day, but I need to talk to you. This is something that can't wait."

Dot turned and faced Commander Templeton. "What the hell can I possibly know or have that Military Intelligence would want, Commander? If I need to speak to anyone, it's my solicitor about getting a payout from the police service."

Dot's phone vibrated in her hand. She glanced at the number. She saw that she had previous missed calls from the same number. Her phone had been on silent in her bag the whole morning. "One moment, Commander, I really have to take this call." Dot was relieved that the phone had rung, as it gave her a reprieve from yet more questions that she probably didn't know the answers to. "LaSalle speaking."

"Er, hello, Dot. It's Evie here. From the Chelsea Garden."

Dot cut Evie short. "Yes, yes, I know where you're from. Hello, Evie, is everything ok? Has my mother been upsetting anyone again?" Dot's nerves were shot. She was exhausted.

"Er, no, it's not that, it's just that, well, it is about your mother. You see, she was taken ill earlier this morning, and well, I'm afraid, I umm, I have to, I am so, so sorry to have to tell you. But your mother passed away a few minutes ago. I am so, so sorry, Dot."

"Evie, this can't be right. She was fine when I last saw her. You must be wrong. You must be."

"Dot, I was there with her. I held her hand. We did try to call you. She asked for you. I am so, so sorry. She was a wonderful lady, she really was."

The phone slipped from Dot's hand and fell to the floor with a thump. She leaned back against the glass partition of the corridor, eased herself to the carpeted walkway and burst into tears. Not loud tears. Just quiet sobbing tears. She buried her head in her folded arms as she rocked herself backwards and forwards, trying, but failing, to soothe a pain that hurt more than anything she had ever felt in her entire life.

CHAPTER 69.

A few weeks later. To love and family.

"Thank you for coming, Dorothea. I'm the one who spoke to you on the phone. Bartholomew, Bartholomew Mapplebeck, but please, call me Bartie. I'm the lucky owner of this little solicitors' business. Bought it from Stephen when he retired, you know. He built it from nothing to become one of the largest practices in England. Anyway, enough of that. I'm so sorry for the loss of your mother, Dorothea. Our world has been left bereft by her passing. She was an astonishing woman. A client of ours for some fifty years, you know. Please, take a seat. Tea? I'll be taking an Earl Grey. Always been a Darjeeling man myself, but hellish on the guts these past few years. What would you like? Good God, you have a striking similarity to your mother. Stephen will be with us shortly. Do you know that he hasn't been to this office for over five years? The last time he was here was to see your mother. She was a very special client of ours, Dorothea. Very special indeed."

She nodded, but was already exhausted just listening to Bartie's breakneck speed approach to conversation.

Dot had arrived at Bartholomew Mapplebeck Solicitors Ltd in Bell Yard, London, less than two weeks after the death of her mother. Despite still having things to sort, Bartie had made it clear. She was required at the office. And certainly not the little business, as he had just told her.

After going straight to the care home following the call from Evie, Dot eventually returned home to find a courier waiting for her. The helmeted biker had given her an envelope with strict instructions to call the telephone number contained inside straight away. He was only permitted to leave once she had spoken to the author of the letter, and not before. Dot called the number and was instructed to present herself at the address of the solicitors at ten o'clock on this one particular day, two weeks later, and here she now stood. Curious as she was about the meeting, she had had an enormous to-do list to get through with her mother, work, surgery to straighten her nose and spending time with Jamie.

Curiosity raised its head again after the call from Bartie. Even though it had been during one of her many outbursts, Dot's mother had indeed been correct with the name and location of her solicitor, and it certainly wasn't Jack. She wasn't as mad as people thought she was. But why had she kept this from Dot? Why wasn't she told about Sir Stephen before?

To be honest, Dot wasn't sure she could have handled it at the time. She was a mess. The last few weeks had taken their toll on her. Patrick Fallon, Commander Truss, Jack missing, even Vanessa, and then, the worst of all, the death of her mother. She felt like she was walking through quicksand in a thick fog. Slow and blind. And now this. She was in the outer chamber of an office that looked like it was out of a Dickens novel, completely at odds with the modern décor of the main offices she had walked through from the reception. She guessed that some clients were still old school with old-school money. Or they were just old-school owners.

"Dorothea, tea? Or perhaps some coffee for you?"

Dot shook herself back into the moment at Bartie's verbal nudge. "Apologies, some water will be fine, thank you. And please. Call me Dot. Everyone else does."

"As you wish, Dot. I think they are ready for us now. Shall we go through?"

Bartie politely marshalled Dot behind himself and walked towards a huge carved wooden door.

"They," thought Dot. "How come they and not him? Who else is in there?"

Bartie turned a large brass doorknob, and the door opened silently inwards.

Dot followed him into the room as he introduced her entrance.

"Dorothea LaSalle for you. Prefers to be known as Dot."

Dot stopped in her tracks. "You? Again? What the hell are you doing here?"

"Come on in, Dot and take a seat. I'll explain everything to you. It's probably the least that you deserve. Stephen, by the way. Stephen Hargreaves. At your service."

A tall, tanned man, Dot guessing somewhere in his mid to late eighties, dressed immaculately in a dark grey suit with a pristine white shirt, open at the collar, held his hand out towards her.

Dot took his hand and shook it. It was firm but strangely comforting. "Pleased to meet you. I hope you are going to explain what she is doing here." Dot was pointing to a woman standing in one corner of the room. The first person Dot had laid eyes on when the door was opened.

"I will, in due course. For now, though, please. Take a seat."

Dot looked around the room. It wasn't an office. It was more of a conference room. Mixed with antique and modern furniture, with classic and contemporary art on the walls. Alongside a decanter of whiskey sat a coffee machine. It was as though the owners didn't want to let go of the past.

The conference room table was low but large, oval and made of rosewood. It had room for probably a dozen chairs around it, but today there were only three, all of which had been placed at the far end of the table from the door.

Bartie placed a jug of water and three glasses on the table. "If you need anything, Stephen, you know where I am. Lovely to finally meet you, Dot."

Stephen nodded as Bartie took a step backwards, pulled the door, and disappeared. He ushered the two women into a seat each and then sat down between them.

"His father used to be a butler, you know. He runs a fifty million a year business here, yet he still makes you feel like the most important person in the room. How could I not sell to him? Anyway, Dot. Thank you for coming at such a particularly sad time. You asked why we are not alone. Well, if you will, Commander, please."

"Hello again, Dot." Commander Joanne Templeton was dressed in smart civvies. A black trouser suit that would have been perfect either at an up-market undertaker or a stock market trading floor in the city. She looked different. She wore her hair down. Long grey hair that reached beyond her shoulders. The demeanour between Sir Stephen and the commander was such that they clearly knew each other, so it was no coincidence that she was here.

"Apologies for the ambush, Dot. I would have caught you at HQ, but you had more important things to deal with at the time."

"Ambush is the perfect word. For a start, I've no idea why I'm here, but I'm sure you are going to tell me, Commander. I doubt that it's early retirement with a vast golden handshake for the shit that's been thrown at me by the police, though. I know, because I have only just started that process with HR, so please, enlighten me if you will."

Templeton shot Sir Stephen a glance with an "I told you so" kind of look. Sir Stephen nodded back in Dot's direction. The nod was clear. Just tell her the truth.

"Dot, your mother worked for the government." Dot wasn't sure if the opening statement was supposed to be a huge reveal. It sounded like it. But it wasn't. Well, not to Dot.

"Yes, I know. Actuarial stuff. Pension stuff. I know. She used to call it complicated but boring. A bit like my life." Dot was more annoyed than anything at the comment. Of course, she bloody knew what her mother did.

Templeton continued. "Not quite, Dot. She was one of the earliest and youngest recruits into Military Intelligence at the start of the Second World War. One of the smartest, bravest women we had. And trust me, we had quite a few.

She was a spy, Dot. And more than just spy. She became a double agent halfway through the war. The Germans thought she was working for them, but she was one of ours. She helped hundreds of spies, agents and resistance fighters get to the safety of England and beyond. One of the best we had. Even after the war, she continued to work for us. In fact, she never really stopped." Templeton sat back in her chair. Silent. Waiting for a reaction.

Dot stared at the table. In another life, she would have marvelled at the intricate inlay of the burnished wood table. But not today. Questions were shooting around her brain, but there were so many that she didn't know where to start. She gulped water from her crystal tumbler

"Stephen. Your wife. Karenza. She was my mother's sister. Correct?

"Yes, your mother and my wife were indeed sisters. You have been doing some homework, I see."

Templeton interjected. "That homework was the first reason I needed to speak to you, Dot. We picked up some comms from you. Unauthorised checking of telephone numbers on the police national computer. Ordinarily, a gross misconduct offence, but given our circumstances, easily overlooked. Can you remember requesting information on a particular telephone number a few weeks ago One that is restricted?"

"Yes, I can. It blanked me, though. Couldn't understand why it came up as a restricted file. I queried it and remembered at the time that I might get a call about it. Why? Is that why you are here? Did I hit a nerve somewhere at Mission Control? Must have been a bloody big nerve if it required the presence of a commander to deal with."

Templeton looked across at Stephen. "That's ok, Dot, we just needed to know it was you who was looking. You are aware that the vast majority of what we are discussing is covered by the Official Secrets Act, aren't you? Other than the personal family details that Stephen is about to discuss

410

with you, under no circumstances are you to speak to anyone else about this conversation. And that is an order, Dot."

Dot chuckled under her breath. "I think I've lost count of the number of times I've been threatened by that over the last few weeks. So, let me tell you what I know, and then you can fill in the gaps. With all due respect, I still have a funeral to arrange."

Stephen leant across to Dot and took one of her hands in his. "It's important you listen. There are responsibilities that have passed to you now that your mother is no longer with us, Dot."

"Why doesn't that surprise me? Look, as far as I know, I'm an only child, so I assume I get the money unless she had a penchant for cats, dogs or rabbit charities. I'm not worried about the money; I have enough of my own anyway. The house was sold, so that's gone, and as her Power of Attorney, I wasn't aware of anything else that she had. There, that's me."

"A nutshell indeed, Dot." Stephen rubbed his eyes. He was a handsome man, but his tired and bloodshot eyes gave a glimpse into the soul of a clearly troubled one. "Apologies, a very early start for me this morning. I'll try to be as succinct and precise as you have been to us. You will, though, have to accept that your life is about change in some areas, and we'll help with any transition that comes with that. Your mother and my wife came from wealthy stock, Dot. They were part of a family that held a rich history in both London and Cornwall. Your ancestors played a huge part in the evolution of mining in Cornwall over a long period. This came with enormous responsibilities, along with untold wealth, but with it there also came condemnation and hate from the people they employed and lived amongst. It was a brutal industry to be part of. Your great—great-grandfather saw this and decided to put some things right. He felt compelled to give back to those who gave to him. The work was hard, and quite a few of his employee's lost their lives as a result. Those people who had rented properties from your family were given the houses for free under a peppercorn rent tenancy. Part of the tenancy terms was that these houses could only be sold to other locals at rates set by an independent council. He changed what he could, where he could. Villages became communities, land was given to farm, and boats were paid for to fish. What money he retained, he invested. And he did well. Very well indeed. He built property here in London and in Cornwall. Trereen, the house I live in now, inherited by your aunt, was one of many that he built. Various properties were sold to fund income over the years, but one other in Cornwall remained. And on the passing of your mother, Bay View House, also in Cornwall, now becomes yours, Dot. But don't get too excited just yet, as I'll explain. Your mother was also left a legacy from your grandfather. At the time, it wasn't huge in the grand scheme of things, but your mother was never allowed to touch a penny of it. The money was put into trust for you, Dot. A trust that I act upon on your behalf. The trust invested the money, and as of this morning, the fund stood at a few pennies over three million pounds. As soon as I heard about your mother's passing, I took it upon myself to move the money into cash to preserve the value for you. I hope that was ok. The trust fund is, of course, outside of probate." Stephen sat back in his chair to allow what he had just said to sink in.

"Three? Three million pounds? Christ almighty, I don't need any more money. There's still well over a million in Mum's current account. And I haven't even thought about her jewellery yet. And what about this place in Cornwall? What type of house is it? That'll go straight on the market for starters."

"We understand how difficult this must be for you, Dot. If I may, I will let Joanne, Commander Templeton, explain some more of the detail for you. I can't promise it will make things much clearer, but it will give you some perspective to start with. And then we can deal with the details of your mother's last will and testament. Rest assured, for now, you are indeed the sole beneficiary. But thanks to your husband, you nearly weren't."

"Three million is an awful lot of perspective if you ask me." Dot was unwittingly picking the last remnants of the scab on her lip. Her nail turned red. Her top lip was bleeding. "Hang on, what do you mean I nearly wasn't? God no. He didn't? Surely? He did, didn't he? He tried to change the bloody will. What an utter bastard. How did you know?"

"It was your mother, Dot. She told us. She knew Jack was trying to get the money, but she also knew he was involved in something else. We overrode the will he had her sign, and I alerted Joanne here, who passed the information on. She may have had dementia, Dot, but she still had some wits about her."

Dot just sat and stared at the table.

"Dot, if I may. Let me try to give you some background as to why I'm here. That may take your mind off the financials for a few minutes. And please, call me Joanne."

"Fire away, Joanne, I'm all ears. Let's face it, I doubt there are too many more surprises you can throw in my direction."

Joanne and Stephen both winced as they caught each other's eye.

"Ok, so you now know that your mother worked in Military Intelligence. Let's fill in some of the details for you, shall we? She first came to the attention of the services through her love of the German language. She studied it at a private girls' school and excelled in both written and oral aspects of the language. As war became more certain, the headmaster at the school had been instructed to keep an eye out for any outstanding talent, more for code-breaking potential than anything else. Still, he was so impressed with your mother that he let the military know about her. Pretty soon afterwards, a German woman was sent to the school to help your mother with the internal dialects and understand the various foibles of the language. Your mother, at the time, was told that she was to help translate intercepted German messages. As this progressed, she was pushed towards helping resistance fighters and agents with their accents. One thing led to another, and before she knew it, she became an agent, specialising in the movement of other agents and liaising with the local resistance. Of course, if she were ever stopped, her German was so good that she was never doubted. This led to her becoming a double agent, training German agents to speak the Queen's English, the entire time feeding falsehoods to the enemy while passing delicate information back to London. Wholly ironic but entirely brilliant all the same." Joanne held her breath for a few seconds to see if Dot wanted to say anything. Dot remained silent.

"Ok, at the time, one of the houses that your grandfather owned was on an estate in Cornwall. The land was measured in square miles rather than hectares. During the war, the military searched for large buildings to house seriously ill soldiers and to help with rehabilitation, as far away from the general public as possible. After all, it wasn't good publicity to show the dark side of the war. And Cornwall fitted the criteria. The location, however, was also deemed a perfect training base for new spies, and from 1940 to 1944, the estate grew into a safe house as well as a hospital. A transit point, if you will, for spies, resistance forces, double agents, basically anyone that London needed to get in and out of Europe. And all the time, there was a hospital there, no one grew suspicious of the other events taking place at the estate. A ferry route was established from Newlyn in south Cornwall to Cherbourg, disguised using French fishing vessels. The Germans, at the time, were preoccupied with the Channel Islands, and traffic further up the Channel towards Dover, making it easier and safer to travel for our people. So, therein lies your history lesson. But here's where it gets personal."

"I can't wait." Dot felt that this sounded like someone else's history, not hers.

"The house, Bay View House, that is, that's where your mother met your father. They spent time working together on a couple of missions. Not sure what the missions were, that's classified, even at my level; however, we know they took their leave time together early in 1945." Joanne paused again. And she deliberately held her pause.

"Ah, I get it. 1945. The year I was born. This is weird."

"Weird it may be, Dot, but this is your history." Joanne poured a glass of water, took one sip, and continued.

"Your mother's pregnancy caused a few problems for the powers that be at the time. They lost one of their best agents for a few months, which they weren't too happy about, even though the war was coming to an end. Spies still had plenty to keep them busy. Even mentioned abortion, which, as you can imagine, your mother didn't appreciate. She was pushed straight back out into the field as soon as she was able, but then your parents needed someone to look after you once you were born."

"Abortion? Wow. So, who did look after me, then?" Dot was caressing her nose, which still sported gentle shades of blue, pink and purple.

Stephen interjected. "It was my Karenza, Dot. My wife. Bay View, that's actually where I first met her. She helped with the nursing requirements for the soldiers. I was a captain in charge of operations at the house. Mind you, we didn't start seeing each other properly until after the war. Not the done thing, you understand, but it was love at first sight. Well, from my point of view at least." Stephen smiled at the thought.

Dot put her finger in the air. "You said not the done thing, Stephen. But my parents met there, and I was obviously conceived there. Surely that certainly can't have been the right thing to do?"

"Ah, I can see why you are a detective, Dot. Yes, you are correct. It wasn't the right thing. And your grandfather most certainly didn't approve either. But your mother was a firebrand. Stubborn and bloody-minded. Generally, she got what she wanted. You of all people would have seen that in her. But. And it's a big but, Dot. Here comes the real crux of contention. You see, not only were you born out of wedlock, Dot, but your father was a serving German soldier. Albeit a brilliant double agent, he was still a German soldier. He held the rank of Captain." Stephen allowed time for his words to sink in.

"That would have rattled a lot of cages. Especially back then. She was a one then by the sound of it. So, what happened to him? Where did he end up? My mother said very little about him. I've seen a few pictures of him. She said they were taken when they got married. One of the photos was with her in her bedroom. But every time I asked about him, she always said to me that she would tell me one day. When the time was right. Well, she never had the chance, but I would say now is probably a damn good time for you to tell me what you know about him. Wouldn't you agree?"

Stephen stood up from his chair and walked over to where the decanter was placed on a side table. He picked it up, took the lid off and took a long sniff of the contents. He replaced the lid and put the decanter back in its place. He returned to his seat. "Every night before bed, Karenza would pour us both a small dram of that whiskey. And every night we made a toast to ourselves. For love and for family. I haven't taken a drop since she passed away. For some, a memory is held in the smell of a particular perfume. For me? The smell of a damn fine single malt. Your mother and father were deeply in love, Dot. That much was obvious. They both eloped to London and married, despite the objections from your grandfather, who was incandescent with rage over the whole thing. Sadly, though and in truth, I don't know what happened to your father. No one does. God knows, we tried over the years. All I know is that after what would have been his final mission, heading back to France, he disappeared. Over the years, people have said lots of different things, all sorts of sightings and theories, good and bad, but I suspect the real truth is that he was killed. In your grandfather's eyes, that was a good thing. He never forgave your mother for marrying one of the enemy. Cast a shadow, as it were. A few years after the war ended, all that remained at Bay View House were a few wounded soldiers. Mentally destroyed. Unfortunately, one of these poor, disturbed souls decided to end his life by igniting petrol that he had poured over himself. The resultant fire destroyed the entire house, turning it to rubble and taking several patients with it. Your grandfather saw it fitting that he would leave the ruins of what was left of Bay View House to your mother, whilst leaving Trereen to Karenza. It was as symbolic as it was financial. He believed that Trereen held the real value and would continue through the generations. Bay View House was nothing more than a broken memory. Your mother never returned home. She continued working with Military Intelligence, moving to London. And as you know, she never remarried. She had lost both love and family."

Dot sat still. Tears welled up in her eyes, forcing small droplets to trickle down both cheeks.

"My grandmother, in France, said that my grandfather worked in the resistance and was a brilliant man. I assume they wanted to hide the real truth from me then."

Stephen rubbed his eyes again. "It was your mother who wanted to hide the pain from you, Dot. And that wasn't your grandmother that you stayed with in France. It was your great aunt. She was fuming at your grandfather. She blamed him for splitting the family apart. Her husband was a French politician who was murdered by extremists. They had no children, and she insisted on having you there for the holidays. I assume she felt she was trying to do something right. Look, I know this is a huge amount of information, Dot, and I'm sure that you'll have questions. Give yourself some time to think, and we can talk again soon. We have a tedious amount of paperwork to get through, but I certainly don't intend to put you through that today."

Stephen stood again and walked to the sideboard with the whiskey decanter on it. He opened one of the doors and took out three glasses. He picked up the decanter, pulled out the glass stopper, and poured a small amount of the dark amber liquid into each glass. He gave a glass each to Dot and Joanne and picked up the last one himself. He took a long, hard sniff from the glass and then raised it in the air and held it there.

"A toast, if I may. To Anna and Karenza. To love and family. Welcome to the family, Dot."

CHAPTER 70.

A lot of dropped pennies.
Dot left the offices of Bartholomew Mapplebeck Solicitors and walked into the lunchtime London sunshine. Her head felt numb. Her body felt exhausted. Her face, which people still stared at, thanks to Truss's right hook, throbbed. Putting one foot in front of the other seemed to take a monumental effort. She was hungry. The water and whiskey she had consumed ran into an empty stomach and left her feeling nauseous. She contemplated lunch somewhere, but that would require colossal exertion.

She walked to St Paul's tube station. The next fifty minutes seemed to only exist in a foggy alter ego, changing tubes at Notting Hill Gate onto the District line to Chiswick Park. From there, she walked back to the house and eventually collapsed onto the large leather sofa in the lounge. There, she burst into tears. Tears which continued for an hour.

When eventually the tears stopped, she went upstairs, stripped off her clothes and spent fifteen minutes standing under a hot shower. Feeling a little more human, she put a dressing gown on and did a classic student kitchen raid and ended up demolishing three slices of bread containing cheese, onion and chutney. She was ravenous. And it tasted incredible.

She left the plate on the side in the kitchen and headed to the study. Sitting down, she grabbed a piece of paper. She needed a list. There was too much going on, and her head was full. She started to write.

1. Mum. Funeral. Undertaker. Church. People she knew. Shit. How many people did she know?
2. Burial. Easy. The chapel at Trereen. Stephen insisted. Said her father would be furious. Good!
3. The money. Lots of it.
4. The money. Lots of it. Enough to retire early? Hell yes.
5. Retire where?
6. And do what?
7. Sell Chiswick? Can I? Jack still on the deeds. Double check with Stephen.
8. Where is Jack?
9. Sod Jack.
10. What about Jamie?
11. Buy him a flat. Tell him it was part of the will. Her mother would have approved. Or give him the house?
12. Questions. Still questions about Mum. Different list? One big question. German, spies, Nazis.
    Ingrid? Who is she?

The tears tried to start again, but she held firm and pulled them back. She realised that she was missing her mother and had been given no time to let her death sink in. It had taken weeks to sort the funeral out. Death is a busy business by all accounts. But anyway, there would be time for tears later. Right now, there were things to do, jobs to arrange and some of the finer detail that needed some answers. But first, she needed to talk to Joanne Templeton again. And right now.

She dialled the number for HQ. It was answered almost immediately.

"Commander Templeton, please. It's Inspector LaSalle." She waited as the call was put on hold to a dreadful tinny musical ping of *Greensleeves*.

"Commander Templeton's office, how can I help?"

"I need to speak to Joanne, please, it's urgent." Dot sounded annoyed. She had hoped to get put straight through to the Commander.

"I'm afraid the Commander is tied up in meetings all day. I can take a message if you like." The voice was calm and clear. But matter of fact.

"Yes, please. Ask her to call me. It's urgent. My number is ..."

"We have your number, Inspector. I'll pass the message on." The phone went dead.

Dot picked at her scab. "Rude cow," she thought. She dialled again. This time to the Chelsea Garden care home. "Yes, hi. Can you put me through to Evie, please, it's Dot LaSalle."

No tinny music for hold music. This one was pure classical.

"Hello, Miss LaSalle, it's Evie here. How can I help? Is everything ok?"

"Hi, Evie. Please call me Dot. Yes, thank you, as good as everything can be given the circumstances. I'll pop in in the next couple of days to pick up the rest of Mum's stuff, if that's ok. Sorry it's taken so long, there has been so much to sort out. Listen, I'm just curious about something. Do you remember that lady that Mum had a bit of a spat with, you know, the German lady, Ingrid I think?"

"Yes, I do. Ingrid Moreau. What about her?"

"Well, I just wanted to check she was ok, you know, after Mum's passing. Has she got any family who comes in to make sure she's ok? It must be tough on your residents when people pass away. I know that Ingrid and Mum didn't see eye to eye, but I don't know, I just wanted to check she was ok, that's all."

"It's funny you should ask. Obviously, Vanessa used to deal with this sort of thing, but I never once saw anyone come in to see Ingrid. That was, until a couple of weeks ago. Just after your mother passed away, actually. A lady came in with all sorts of documents. She said she was Ingrid's daughter. She had ID and Power of Attorney documents, that sort of stuff. Said that she had heard about the mistreatment of her mother by another resident and was taking her home. The paperwork all seemed fine. There was a three month get out clause on the contract, but she paid it straight away. In cash. Cash, for crying out loud. Had to go down the bloody bank to pay it in. Sorry, didn't mean to swear. Anyway, that was it. An hour later, she was gone. Room cleared out and everything."

"Oh, wow, ok. Um, did she leave a forwarding address at all, Evie? Would be nice to send a bunch of flowers and a card. You know. To say sorry for what Mum did."

"No, she didn't. She said that she was staying in a rented house but intended to move again shortly. Judging by her accent, probably somewhere in the West Country. She was going to let me know when they moved. Not that she needs to. Everything was in order and paid up, so there's nothing more we need here."

Dot was silent for a moment. "Ok, thanks, Evie. And once again, thanks for everything you did for Mum. I'll be down in a couple of days or so. Take care." Dot ended the call. Yes, it seemed strange that Ingrid was taken out of the home, but certainly justifiable, given her experience with a crappy nappy. "For Pete's sake. I don't know. I'm either clutching at straws, stark raving mad or just looking for something that isn't there."

The doorbell rang, making her jump, even though she knew who had arrived. Her nerves were still raw. She opened the door to be greeted by Jamie, his right arm still in a sling, and Laney, smiling. Dot wasn't expecting Laney. They carried coffee and several small white bags. "Doughnuts! And the best coffee in Chiswick."

Dot chuckled. "And Laney as well. A bonus"

"Ah, yes, my wonderful driver."

"Carer more like. Hi Dot, good to see you."

Laney stepped forward and gave Dot a long, warm hug. It was just what she needed.

"Thanks for coming, Jamie. Come on in, both of you. We've got quite a lot of stuff to go through."

CHAPTER 71.

Two weeks later. Trereen House. AKA The nice house.

"It was a beautiful service. Mum would have loved it. I can't thank you enough, Stephen. You have been such a help organising all of this."

"It's my pleasure, Dot. It really is the least I could do. I've lost count of the number of requests from people who wanted to attend. Not only was she an incredible woman, your mother, but it would also appear that she was a very popular one too."

"It's strange, though, Stephen. She seemed to have so few friends around her. I guess her last few years have taken a toll on all of us. No point visiting someone when they have no idea who you are."

"Oh, I hear you with that one, Dot. Come, let's get a drink."

He took Dot's arm as they walked along the gravel path from the small family chapel, towards the house.

The house was beautiful. Large, but not consuming. Covered in the grey, light brown and dark reddish brown colours of Cornish stone and roofed in traditional grey slate. The gardens covered over a hundred acres, including a small lake and gatehouse, occupied by Mr and Mrs Johns, who, between them, held the positions of gardener, chef, cleaner and housekeeper.

The path led to the rear of the house, to a terraced garden with half a dozen tables, covered in white cloth. Mrs Johns was busy pouring teas, coffees and champagne, depending on the mood of the guests. There were a couple of dozen guests here, but Mrs Johns had a panic that supposed there was at least five times that number.

Dot picked up a coffee and followed Stephen across the garden and into the ballroom. "It's a stunning house, Stephen, you must be proud of it."

"Ah, yes, of course I am, but a house will only ever be a home when you share it with the ones you love. Alas, my love is no longer here, so I have to prepare it well for the next generation."

"Yes, your boys, they are both lovely. A credit. I just wish I could have met them a long time ago. Answer me a question, Stephen. If you can, that is."

"If I can, then I will. Fire away, Dot."

"Was my mum in danger before she died?"

Stephen remained quiet for quite a few seconds. "Hmm. Follow me, let me show you something."

Dot left her coffee on a table and followed him through a pair of huge double doors. He turned into a corridor and walked to the third room on the right. He fumbled in his pocket, took out a key, put it into the lock and turned it. He then pushed open the door and ushered her in.

The room looked like a cross between a small library and an office. The view across the garden was breathtaking. Stephen walked over to an old wooden set of drawers, bent down and pulled open the bottom one. He reached in and took out four square boxes. He turned and walked to a large oak desk, covered in the scars of hundreds of years of use and placed the boxes on it.

He opened the first box. It contained folded pieces of paper. Taking two out, he unfolded them and placed them in front of Dot. She bent down slightly and started to read.

Anna LaSalle. Dec 12 1940 Bravery beyond duty.

She read through the first note. A dispatch from the war. Stephen continued to open them. One by one. Bravery. Captured. Escaped. The plaudits went on and on. There were over thirty pieces of paper. Small in size but mighty and humbling in content. Dot felt tears in her eyes.

Stephen then opened two more boxes. Each one contained medals. Bravery, Distinction. Service Medals. He then pushed the final box towards Dot.

"Open it. This belongs to you now, Dot." She picked up the box and took off the lid. The first thing she noticed was a purple ribbon. She lifted it and folded underneath she saw a medal. She read the words 'For Valour'.

"Is this what I think it is, Stephen? Dot's eyes never left the medal.

"Indeed, Dot. Your mother was awarded the Victoria Cross. And you don't win one of those without making enemies. Especially in her line of work."

CHAPTER 72.

Later that afternoon. Bay View House. AKA The horrible house.

Dot drove out of Trereen House feeling she had said more goodbyes than hellos. Strange really, given she was in the process of meeting new people that, until the death of her mother, she didn't even know existed. She felt sad. Sad that her mother couldn't talk to her about her life, and sad that she would never see or speak to her mother again. Granted, there were still a lot of unanswered questions, but unravelling the life of someone like her mother was going to take time. And time was something she was going to have lots of soon.

Chief Superintendent McKenzie had agreed that Dot could retire a year early. She was a late starter in the police. All of the youngsters who joined in their teens were well and truly retired by the age of fifty. In comparison, Dot was an absolute dinosaur. Well past the proverbial sell-by date. Along with the early retirement, there would also be a no-liability payoff from the police service. Taxpayers' money for being sexually assaulted and smacked in the mouth. Crazy. It should have been paid by Fallon and Truss. Truss, though, was still on remand awaiting trial. Hiding from the hordes of criminality that had been taken into her Majesty's pleasure, all now wishing to pay him a personal visit. It was going to be a long stay for Truss. And as for Fallon. Well, no one knew. Or certainly, no one was saying anything. Hopefully, fish food in the Thames, but he was a slippery bugger.

Jack was still being a pain in the backside, even though he had vanished without a trace. The house in Chiswick was still in both names, so Dot couldn't sell it until he was found dead or alive or had disappeared for at least seven years. If Bay View house was indeed derelict, she had a choice to make. Rebuild or sell. Whatever, she wasn't going to live in Chiswick anymore. Dot suggested to Jamie that he and Laney live there, and they would only have the bills to pay as the mortgage would be cleared. He was delighted with the idea. Not sure which bit delighted him more, though. Living in the house or living with Laney. Or both. They made a great couple, and it was a huge helping hand for them. Living in Chiswick wasn't cheap. Dot spent the next few minutes of the drive contemplating life without the police. She worried about losing a sense of identity. Being a police officer gave you that. She worried about how she would fill her days. She could write a book about her mother. She could write a book about the last year of her life. There's no greater fiction than fact. That had been borne out in front of her, that was for sure.

Half an hour later, she was driving down yet another tree-covered lane, only just wider than her Kia SUV. She slowed as she read her instructions. She was looking for a lane on the right-hand side straddled by two tall stone pillars. It all sounded very grand.

There, ahead, she saw the turning. Indicating, she pulled into the driveway and continued down for nearly half a mile. The car was bumping and grinding its way through part gravel, part mud but mostly holes. Surrounding her were trees – lots and lots of trees. Trees she didn't even know the names of. Eventually, she spotted blue sky ahead and slowly made her way out into the sunshine. Ahead of her were fields. Some had remnants of daffodils in, most were overgrown. All were surrounded by Cornish stone hedges in various stages of disrepair. The lane veered to the left, and there in front of Dot stood the remnants of Bay View House. Most of the outer walls still stood, as did a few of the inner walls. The rest was derelict, bereft of all identity of what had stood before. The road went from mud to stone. In front of the entire house had once been fine stone to bestow the grandeur of the property. Dot stopped the car and got out. She stood still. She closed her eyes and listened. She then drew in a large breath of air. Everything smelled wonderful, and the air was the cleanest that she had ever tasted. She could even taste the salt from the Celtic Sea whose waves, apparently, struck the rocks not far beyond where she now stood. The sheer size and scale made her feel small and insignificant. But she wasn't small and insignificant. She was the new owner of all that surrounded her. And despite being terrified at the prospect of owning the derelict property, she immediately knew that this was where she would spend the rest of her life. Her grandfather had gifted it to her mother as a reminder of his eternal disappointment. Now, Dot was going to make it into something her mother would have loved. The house they all deserved.

.

CHAPTER 73.

March. Two Thousand & Three. Cornwall, England.

Dot shook herself out of her thoughts. London was in the past now. Even in the short time she had lived in Cornwall, she felt her entire body and mind go through a process she wasn't used to. Relaxation. This wasn't something she had been familiar with for a long time. There was a scarily huge amount of rebuilding to do at the house, and even though Dot was daunted by what lay ahead, it still didn't carry the same millstone as caseloads in the police did. Dot had no doubts that it would take quite a while for her to adjust, not just to the lifestyle here, but the pace of life. But she was giving it a damn good go.

"Jean, could I get one more pot of tea, please? The croissant is delicious, by the way." Dot lied.

"Don't need to flatter me, as long as you pay me. I've just washed the floor by the door. Come and get your tea from the counter."

Dot smiled. In London, if someone spoke to you that way in a café, they would get a mouthful of abuse in return. Here, well, it was here. It was just accepted. Dot stood up and walked to the counter to collect her pot of tea. She made sure she didn't step on the newly mopped floor by the door. The rain had stopped, but there were still rivulets of water tumbling down the street outside. As Dot picked up the pot of tea, she saw a letter by the side of the till.

"Is that your surname, Jean?" she asked, pointing at the white envelope.

"Yeah, it is, as a matter of fact. Why you asking?"

"Definitely your surname?"

"Well, no one else owns the café, just me. That's my name. Jean Moreau. Why you asking?"

Dot picked up the pot and took it back to her table. She was silent.

"You alright there", shouted Jean across the café. "You look like you have seen a ghost."

Dot stared at her open laptop. Her phone, which was on the table next to the computer, started to vibrate. An incoming call. She picked it up and answered. "Hello, Dot LaSalle."

There was quiet crackling. Dot thought she heard a breath. "Look, if you want to play silly bu ..." She was cut short.

"Dorothea? Dorothea LaSalle?" The querying voice was deep and measured with a hint of an accent. Almost purposely slow in its tempo. "Hello, Dorothea. My name is Erich. Erich Schmid. I am your father."

Other titles by BLKDOG Publishing for your consideration:

Britannia: The Wall
By Richard Denham & M. J. Trow

THE END OF ROMAN BRITAIN BEGINS.

The story opens in 367 AD. Four soldiers - Justinus, Paternus, Leocadius and Vitalis - are out hunting for food supplies at an outpost of Hadrian's Wall, when the Wall comes under attack.

The four find their fort destroyed, their comrades killed, and Paternus is unable to find his wife and son. As they run south to Eboracum, they realize that this is no ordinary border raid. Ranged against the Romans at the edge of the world are four different peoples, and they have banded together under a mysterious leader who wears a silver mask and uses the name Valentinus - man of Valentia, the turbulent area north of the Wall.

Faced with questions they are hard-pressed to answer, Leocadius blurts out a story that makes the men Heroes of the Wall. Their lives change not only when Valentinus begins his lethal sweep across Britannia but as soon as Leo's lie is out in the world, growing and changing as it goes.

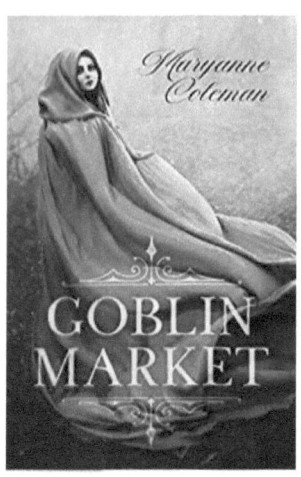

Goblin Market
By Maryanne Coleman

Have you ever wondered what happened to the faeries you used to believe in? They lived at the bottom of the garden and left rings in the grass and sparkling glamour in the air to remind you where they were. But that was then – now you might find them in places you might not think to look. They might be stacking shelves, delivering milk or weighing babies at the clinic. Open your eyes and keep your wits about you and you might see them.

But no one is looking any more and that is hard for a Faerie Queen to bear and Titania has had enough. When Titania stamps her foot, everyone in Faerieland jumps; publicity is what they need. Television, magazines. But that sort of thing is much more the remit of the bad boys of the Unseelie Court, the ones who weave a new kind of magic; the World Wide Web. Here is Puck re-learning how to fly; Leanne the agent who really is a vampire; Oberon's Boys playing cards behind the wainscoting; Black Annis, the bag-lady from Hainault, all gathered in a Restoration comedy that is strictly twenty-first century.

Fade
By Bethan White

There is nothing extraordinary about Chris Rowan. Each day he wakes to the same faces, has the same breakfast, the same commute, the same sort of homes he tries to rent out to unsuspecting tenants.

There is nothing extraordinary about Chris Rowan. That is apart from the black dog that haunts his nightmares and an unexpected encounter with a long forgotten demon from his past. A nudge that will send Chris on his own downward spiral, from which there may be no escape.

There is nothing extraordinary about Chris Rowan...

www.blkdogpublishing.com